VATHEK AND OTHER STORIES

VATHEK
AND OTHER STORIES

A William Beckford Reader

Edited with an Introduction by

MALCOLM JACK

LONDON
WILLIAM PICKERING
1993

Published by Pickering & Chatto (Publishers) Limited

17 Pall Mall, London SW1Y 5NB

© Pickering & Chatto (Publishers) Limited 1993

Introduction and notes © Malcolm Jack 1993

British Library Cataloguing in Publication Data

Beckford, William

Vathek and Other Stories – A William Beckford
Reader

I. Title II. Jack, Malcolm

823.6 [F]

ISBN 1–85196–049–X

Typeset by Waveney Typesetters
Norwich

Printed and bound in Great Britain by
Redwood Books
Trowbridge

CONTENTS

PREFACE

To collect an anthology of a notable prose writer is not an easy task but, in the case of William Beckford, it is certainly a pleasurable one. He wrote widely and well; there is an excellence of language and a high-spiritedness of style which continue to make his work worth reading. Convinced of Beckford's literary quality, my selection has aimed to represent some of Beckford's finest writing and to introduce readers to characteristically Beckfordian moods and flourishes.

Beckford has always had his admirers. Critics of considerable discernment, such as Sacheverell Sitwell and Rose Macaulay, long ago recognised the stylishness of his prose. Fittingly for a writer who produced fine work in English and in French (and displayed considerable ability in a number of other languages), recognition of his genius has been evident across the channel as well: Mallarmé's suave introduction to *Vathek* is a powerful *tour de force*. In this century, the French scholar André Parreaux made significant contributions to Beckford studies. A host of English and North American scholars and critics – especially Guy Chapman and Boyd Alexander but also Brian Fothergill, Roger Lonsdale, Robert Gemmett and Kenneth Graham – have added to our appreciation of Beckford as an intriguing man and as a great man of letters. Beckford's papers have now been admirably arranged and catalogued by T. D. Rogers at the Bodleian Library, Oxford.

I acknowledge my debt to all these Beckfordians but I should particularly thank Professor Kenneth Graham whose kindness, help and encouragement before and during the preparation of this reader have been invaluable. Many other people have helped me in different ways. I should like to record my gratitude to Professor João Flor for his scholarly advice on detailed aspects of Portuguese literature, to Dr Roland Meyer for expert translation of Latin passages, to John Wright for ensuring my reading of Italian was not too fanciful and to fellow Beckfordians, including Sidney Blackmore and Jon and Pat Millington for their kindness. Other friends who helped me, sometimes merely by calm audience, were Robert Borsje, Laurent Chatel and Andrew Lister.

Finally I should express the gratitude of all Beckfordians to the publishers, Pickering and Chatto, for relaunching Beckford to a new generation of readers. To those, I hope, vast throngs this book is dedicated.

M.J.

INTRODUCTION

1. LIFE OF WILLIAM BECKFORD
(1760–1844)

William Beckford's social pedigree was not nearly as pure as he would have liked the world to believe nor in his paternal heredity can we obviously trace the qualities of the artist or writer. The Beckfords, who came from Jamaica, were men of action: they planted estates, ruled over native people and played a prominent part in the public life of the colony. The family's substantial wealth arose from its ownership of sugar plantations and slaves.[1] Deriving riches from one area could have its inconveniences as Beckford himself was to discover later in life. Among his colonial ancestors were governors and speakers of the Assembly at Kingston who, over many generations, had been involved in the sometimes rumbustious politics of the island.

Beckford's father, always known as the Alderman, had been sent to England for his education. He entered political life through City interests, being elected several times Lord Mayor of London. The Alderman, a wealthy Whig merchant allied to Wilkes and the radicals, enjoyed a stormy and colourful career in the House of Commons where he presented the ear of Captain Jenkins to a bemused House. He was also a great populist and his radical politics reached its apogee when, as 'Grand Remonstrancer', he presented a petition to the King complaining of corruption in Parliament. Although a somewhat intimidating figure, involved in the fracas of radical politics, the Alderman greatly influenced Beckford and appears as a character in at least one of his literary fragments.[2]

William's mother was Maria Hamilton, granddaughter of the Earl of Abercorn whose ancestry was undoubtedly more illustrious than the parvenu Beckfords. Through his mother's family, Beckford traced connections with the royal houses of both England and Scotland. While he undoubtedly inherited something of his mother's snobbishness about social status, other more important characteristics may have been transmitted through his maternal genes, for despite their aristocratic connections, the Hamiltons boasted artists and writers among their ranks. In the seventeenth century one such Hamilton, Anthony, known as the Count, had spent much time in France where he perfected his command of the language to such a degree that

---

[1] On the question of Beckford's wealth, see Malcolm Jack 'How Wealthy was England's Wealthiest Son?' *Beckford Tower Trust Newsletter* (Spring, 1987) p. 4.
[2] See Alexander, *E.W.S.*, p. 66 ff and Fothergill, p. 59.

he wrote several literary works in French. His elegant and polished books were in the family library; they certainly influenced Beckford in the composition of *Vathek*, his great Arabian tale.[1] Another Hamilton who made an impression on William was Charles, his uncle, who had cultivated a 'Claudian' landscaped garden at Painshill in Surrey.[2] In later years at Monserrate in Portugal and at Fonthill itself, Beckford followed his uncle by making important contributions to the development of the picturesque in landscape gardening.

While artistic currents of this sort were yet to stir in the young heir of Fonthill, a more traditional career was being planned for him. The Alderman's political connections, which stretched to the mighty Chatham, together with the immense family wealth, held out the prospect of a glittering career in politics for his son. In preparation for this future, William was brought up at the Alderman's country seat, a grand neo-classical mansion, ostentatiously called Splendens, at Fonthill in Wiltshire. Splendens was meant as the model of an important gentleman's country seat. It contained a fine collection of paintings, a well-stocked library and interesting, exotic salons in the oriental style. All of these amenities appealed to William and influenced his taste considerably.

Beckford's early education was conventional enough. He was put into the hands of a dour Scots tutor, Robert Drysdale from whom he learnt basic Greek and Latin. To this was added some philosophy, smatterings of history and such literature as it was thought a gentleman should know. For social accomplishment, he was taught music and drawing. His tutor soon found that his pupil was well above average in intelligence and had a precocious talent for subjects that might have been thought periphery, such as languages, music and art. Before long Beckford's interests ventured into even more exotic areas – he became fascinated by eastern fables and stories after finding a copy of *Arabian Nights* in the Alderman's library.[3]

This interest may have puzzled Drysdale and would have displeased Beckford's parents but it was very much encouraged by someone else who came to teach the young heir drawing, namely Alexander Cozens, himself an artist of considerable talent.[4] Cozens' influence on Beckford was immense and it arose from a combination of his strong personality and dashing background. Cozens had had a colourful upbringing. His father had been shipbuilder to the Czar of Russia, and on that account, in a much favoured position at the imperial court. Alexander, named after an admiral of the Russian fleet, was brought up in the glittering and exotic surroundings of the court at St

---

[1] Beckford acknowledged his debt to his forbear, hoping to meet the count in heaven. See Lonsdale, p. xxvi.

[2] For a description of Painshill, see C. Thacker, *The History of Gardens* (London, 1979), pp. 194–7.

[3] First translated into French by A. Galland in 1704. An English version appeared in 1708. See *below*, p. xvii ff.

[4] Alexander Cozens (c.1717–86). His son, John Robert (1752–97) also an artist, accompanied Beckford on his Grand Tour in 1782.

Petersburg. He made much of this background and it proved highly glamorous to his young ward.

Cozens was a man of wide culture as well as being an artist of distinction. Not only did he teach Beckford to draw, but he cultivated his student's nascent artistic sensibility, encouraging him in the very subjects which others wanted to prevent him from exploring any further. Cozens instilled in Beckford a lifelong love of painting and visual objects; he also pointed his protégé in the direction of Eastern culture and religion, subjects with which he himself had first become acquainted in Russia. Under the influence of the Persian (for so Beckford nicknamed his master) adolescent William began to study Arabic and Persian so that he could delve more deeply into Eastern religions and mythologies. Under Cozens' tutelage, he also began to develop an interest in more sinister subjects such as satanism and the occult. There is a suggestion that his relationship with Cozens may have been homosexual, although there is no direct evidence to prove it.[1]

Cozens' influence on Beckford was no doubt stronger than it might have been because, from the age of ten, Beckford had become fatherless. Although the Alderman must always have seemed a slightly distant figure, rushing to and fro from London to Wiltshire, his sudden death, in 1770, was an immense blow to the sensitive boy. Thereafter Beckford was left in the hands of his mother, the 'Begum' (a Persian lady of high rank), as he called her, and his guardians, mostly political associates of his father including Chatham[2] and Lord Thurlow, the Lord Chancellor.[3] The Begum comes over as a severe, Calvinistic woman whose evangelicalism mixed oddly with her snobbish awareness of the Hamiltons' illustrious ancestry. While ties between mother and son were to prove strong and enduring, to the young, high-spirited William she seemed a formidable figure of authority against whom he felt the urge to rebel.

The Begum and Beckford's guardians took one decision of considerable significance when they decided not to send him to school. Instead of being thrown into the rough and tumble of an English public school such as Westminster, where his father had been sent, Beckford remained in solitude at Fonthill with only the company of tutors and servants instead of boys of his own age.[4] In this isolated and rather grand setting, he began to indulge his innate proclivity to day dream and fantazise. His surroundings – whether the exotic, oriental chambers of Splendens or the shady, idyllic glades of Fonthill – provided just the surroundings needed to feed his imagination. Soon he was pouring out his ideas on paper, sometimes, as in the case of his *Long Story* (*The Vision*) his tales were redolent of mystery and fantasy; at other times, as

---

[1] See Fothergill, p. 43.
[2] Chatham, 1st Earl of, William Pitt the Elder (1708–78) whose son, William Pitt The Younger (1759–1806) was Beckford's childhood friend, later turned enemy. See *below*, p. xxv ff. and pp. 187–9.
[3] Thurlow, Edward, 1st Baron, (1731–1806).
[4] See Fothergill, p. 37.

in the case of *Biographical Memoirs*, they were more light-hearted and fun-poking.

In 1777, at the age of seventeen, Beckford had his first experience of foreign travel, something that was to be a regular and important part of his life until middle-age. He went to Geneva, accompanied by John Lettice, the Cambridge tutor who had replaced the less polished Robert Drysdale. In that city, of which the Begum may have approved because of its connections with Calvin, he was lodged with some Hamilton cousins who turned out to be well connected to the prominent artistic and intellectual community. Beckford met Jean Huber a polymath and dilettante who dabbled in many arts and sciences. Through him an audience was arranged with the ageing Voltaire, an admirer of the Alderman for his radical reputation and 'Count' Hamilton for his literary style. The young traveller wrote enthusiastically to Cozens about his new social life which included mixing with the Necker family, whose daughter later became the celebrated writer, Madame de Stael.[1] He also visited the monastery at the Grande Chartreuse, and, following in the footsteps of Horace Walpole and the poet Thomas Gray, fell into a frenzy of passion for the old, cloistered building and the wild, mountainous setting in which it was placed.

From Switzerland the party made for Italy, a country that had seized hold of Beckford's imagination ever since his early reading of the classics; Cozens too had added to his enthusiasm for ancient art and architecture. In Naples he stayed with one of the greatest contemporary collectors and connoisseurs of classical culture, his cousin Sir William Hamilton, the British envoy.[2] At the Hamilton villa Beckford not only enjoyed Sir William's rare collection but also formed a close friendship with Lady [Catherine] Hamilton, his wife, who was a warmer and more approachable character than the remote Begum. The two spent much time alone while Sir William rode to hounds with his grand, courtly friends. Lady Hamilton counselled Beckford against indulging in homosexual relationships as it seemed he had done in Venice, prescient in sensing that this aspect of his character might ruin him socially.

Back in London and away from her moderating influence, Beckford plunged madly into an amorous tangle which involved an affair with Louisa Beckford, wife of his cousin Peter, and an infatuated liaison with William Courtenay, an aristocratic youth of thirteen whom he had met through family connections some years earlier.[3]. At the end of the year, now in his majority, Beckford staged a spectacular party in the old Egyptian Hall at Splendens in which leading castrati were invited to sing and for which Philippe de Loutherbourg designed unusual scenery with bizarre, 'necromantic' lighting effects.[4] This party was to have a dramatic effect on Beckford's

---

[1] Anne-Louise-Germaine Necker (1766–1817). A leading French pre-Romantic writer.

[2] Sir William Hamilton (1760–1803). His second wife was Emma, who became mistress of Lord Nelson. She accompanied both of them on their visit to Fonthill in 1800.

[3] Peter was author of *Thoughts on Hunting* (1781). Louisa died in Florence in 1791.

[4] Philippe Jacques de Loutherbourg, R.A. (1740–1812).

literary career for he claimed many years later that it inspired him to write his *Arabian* tale, *Vathek*, which he began in the new year of 1782.[1]

To break him out of what they regarded as a highly undesirable cycle, the Begum and his guardians decided to send Beckford abroad once more. In the company of the loyal Lettice, he once again traced a route through the Low Countries to Italy, arriving at the Hamiltons' in summer. The visit was not to be a happy one. While Beckford was staying with his cousin, Lady Hamilton died leaving him bereft of one of his best friends and probably his wisest counsellor. In a dejected state he returned to England where he sublimated some of his anguish in the writing of *Dreams*, an intimate account of his journeys on the Continent. His family were not impressed by its lackadaisical tone and on their advice, he suppressed the small edition that had already been printed by the publisher, J. Johnson.[2] Nevertheless the book was an impressive first effort in a genre that he never abandoned for the rest of his writing life.

Two months after his return to England, in May 1783, Beckford married Lady Margaret Gordon, daughter of the Earl of Aboyne. It seemed to his mother and family that the spell had been broken, that his delinquent years had ended at last. They were greatly relieved. Not only was Lady Margaret of acceptable aristocratic pedigree (something that always weighed heavily with the Begum), but she was pretty, sensible and determined, all the qualities that the Hamiltons would wish for in a mistress of Fonthill. The next year was one of peace. Louisa and Courtenay seemed to be banished; the newly wedded couple went to Switzerland which had so inspired Beckford on his earlier visit. They were warmly received in the local community. When they returned to England in March 1784, Beckford took his seat in the House of Commons as the Member for Wells. All seemed set for the public career that his parents had always hoped he would follow.

It was not to be: it seemed that the doomed character of Caliph Vathek had been transposed into the life of its creator. On a visit to the Courtenays at Powderham Castle in September of the same year, Beckford was accused of having been seen by the family tutor *in flagrante delicto* with William Courtenay, now aged sixteen. Had the matter been kept within the family, it would probably have done little harm. As it was, Lord Loughborough,[3] head of the Powderham household and political enemy of Beckford's guardians, Chatham and Lord Chancellor Thurlow, made it his business to see that the 'story' gained wide publicity in the London press. Loughborough's political motives may have been reinforced by a strong dislike of the effete and languid character of Beckford; at any rate he succeeded in creating what has subsequently been called the 'Powderham scandal' which certainly cost Beckford

---

[1] For Beckford's account of its importance, see Alexander, *E.W.S.*, pp. 80–1.
[2] For a discussion of why Beckford suppressed the book and how many copies survived, see Gemmett, *Dreams*, p. 25 ff.
[3] Alexander Wedderburn (1733–1805) 1st Lord, later Earl of Rosslyn had married Charlotte Courtenay, William Courtenay's aunt.

his peerage and had a profound effect on the course of his life. Against his better judgement, Beckford followed family advice to go abroad. With his young wife and infant daughter, he made for Switzerland in the summer of 1785.

His troubles, however, were not ended. The following year, 1786, proved to be the worst of his life. In May, after a difficult childbirth, his second daughter, Susan Euphemia was born. Two weeks later Lady Margaret died. The death of his wife, with whom he was deeply in love and who had remained calmly loyal throughout the traumatic period following the Powderham scandal, was a bitter blow. It left him in complete isolation, away from home and no longer supported by the stable relationship that had made all his difficulties bearable. However, this was not the end of his misfortunes: at the end of the year, and explicitly against his wishes, the Reverend Samuel Henley published an English version of *Vathek* in London, suggesting that it was little more than the translation of an Arabic original. Beckford was obliged to respond with a French edition, scrambled together quickly and published at Lausanne in December.[1]

These catastrophic happenings might well have broken the spirit of the most resolute man. In two short years Beckford saw his social aspirations shattered, his beloved wife dead, and his major literary work produced in a form of which he did not approve. England had indeed become his Eblis; to escape the curse that seemed to hang over him he travelled abroad for the most part of the next twelve years. He visited Savoy and Switzerland, rattling around the countryside in his *dormeuse* with a retinue of servants and hangers-on, but it was in Paris that he lingered for months at a time. There he could indulge his collector's appetite, finding that the uncertainty of life in revolutionary France encouraged people to sell cheaply. He collected paintings, *objets d'art* and rare books which he had shipped back to Fonthill, staying until the very last possible moment in 1793 when war had been declared against England. However, of all his travels, it was his sojourns in Portugal, lasting almost four years, that were the richest in terms of personal experience and the development of his artistic talents.

Although Beckford arrived in Lisbon in 1787 whilst still mourning the death of his wife, his ambition to re-establish himself in English society motivated him to make the most of his newly acquired connections at the Portuguese court. He thought that gaining recognition by a foreign sovereign would repair some of the damage done by the Powderham scandal and help to begin the process of rehabilitation at home. He therefore set about the business of getting presented to the Queen, Maria I, finding a well-placed and doughty supporter in the person of Dom Diogo, Fifth Marquis of Marialva, Master of the Queen's Horse, who had befriended him soon after his arrival.[2] The presentation was firmly opposed by the British envoy, the Hon.

---

[1] For an account of the tangled story of the text's history, see Lonsdale, pp. xxxiii–xxv.
[2] D. Diogo de Marialva, 5th Marquis (1739–1803).

Robert Walpole,[1] whose participation was deemed essential by the Portuguese Crown. It is not clear why Walpole took such an intransigent line. It may be that, as in the case of Lord Loughborough, he conceived a dislike of Beckford's character which, outwardly, showed traces of arrogance and condescension. He was also probably envious of Beckford's wealth.[2] Rumblings of the affair are felt in Beckford's private diary, the *Journal*, which he kept throughout the summer and which was not intended for publication.

Not all of Beckford's time in Lisbon was so frustrating. He plunged with enthusiasm into the heady social life of the Marialvas and their aristocratic set, attending endless series of lunches, dinners, and excursions to the theatre. He also made a great deal of the church life of Lisbon, enjoying the pageantry and feigned piousness of a decadent, exuberant Catholicism, as well as the fine music that was part of it. If he were not present at some formal evening engagement, he would be at the opera or listening to music at the Patriarchal Seminary or in one of the many Lisbon churches.[3] These social occasions, often glittering and impressive, and in which Beckford is seen cavorting with the highest members of Portuguese society, are amusingly portrayed in the *Sketches*, a work which he did write for publication but which only saw the light of day in 1834.

The visit of 1787 was to prove significant in other ways as well. Beckford's attention was first focused on Dom Pedro de Marialva, the Marquis' fifteen-year-old son, but soon he was infatuated with another youth, Gregorio Franchi, a young seminarian at the Patriarchal School whose dashing good looks, vivacious personality and musical talent were an intoxicating mix he found impossible to resist. Beckford's relationship with Franchi was to prove lasting; indeed their friendship, with its homosexual aspect, was the most intimate of his entire life. The excitement of these amorous encounters provides a racy undercurrent to the *Journal*.

A less emotionally charged tone is found in the one surviving account of his 1794 visit to Portugal when he took time off to make his excursion to the monasteries of Alcobaça and Batalha. On this visit Beckford was at last presented, albeit to the Prince Regent who reigned in place of his deranged mother. But time had taken its toll: by now the English visitor was altogether a more mature, even cynical cosmopolitan. Much though he loved Arcadian Sintra and though, as we know from correspondence between him and Marialva, a Portuguese title was on offer,[4] he had lost the urge to take up

---

[1] Hon. Robert Walpole (1736–1810) was nephew of the great Walpole, cousin of Horace. His tenure of the embassy at Lisbon lasted from 1772 to 1800.

[2] Andrew Lister has suggested that the enmity between Walpole and Beckford may have been a continuation of the disdain with which Horace Walpole regarded Beckford's father, the Alderman.

[3] For an interesting account of music in Portugal at this time, see M. Carlos de Brito, 'A Musica em Portugal no tempo de William Beckford', *William Beckford & Portugal*, Catalogue of an Exhibition at the Palace of Queluz (Lisbon, 1987), pp. 51–61.

[4] See Beckford/Marialva correspondence, MS. Beckford c.24, *Beckford Papers* Bodleian Library, Oxford.

what would have been a comfortable as well as a courtly life. When forced to a decision, he could not exile himself from the Fonthill that he still loved. Indeed both the Gothic buildings he saw and the landscaping that he did in Portugal made Beckford keen to return home to start new schemes for building and redesigning the grounds of his estate.[1] Nevertheless, the *Recollections*, which he did not publish until his old age, is a very spirited work, full of *joie de vivre* and of zest. Later Beckford came to see it as a last expression of a youthful sense of fun at a carefree, happy time of his life.

In the last years of the century, Beckford still harboured political ambitions, either to act as a mediator between England and France or to be English Ambassador to Portugal. However, his advances were disdainfully dismissed by Pitt, now at the pinnacle of his career and an implacable enemy of a man he regarded as effete and outcast. Beckford took his revenge with his pen – the mildly critical tone of *Modern Novel Writing* turns to overt hostility in *Azemia* where Pitt is satirized as a trickster who has led his people into a condition not much above slavery. Lashing out furiously at Pitt may have done something to assuage the inner pain and depression at what seemed his total rejection by the highest ranks of English society.[2]

When Beckford left Portugal in 1798, for the last time, he was barely forty. From then on his life took a curious and rather lonely course. While he continued to write, particularly maintaining a vast correspondence and annotating the numerous books from his library that he read, his real energy was increasingly directed toward collecting pictures and *objets d'art*, as well as books. He also gave full vent to what he recognised as a mania – building. For twenty years he devoted himself to the construction and decoration of Fonthill Abbey, a massive neo-Gothic building that replaced his childhood home of Splendens. The rooms of Fonthill were filled with valuable furniture and objects, its walls were hung with fine paintings, the library was stocked with old manuscripts and rare collector's pieces. For two decades Beckford was absorbed in amassing a vast empire of treasures. By 1822 he faced acute financial problems which resulted from his extravagance and a serious loss of revenue as the price of sugar from his badly managed Jamaican estates declined. Fonthill had to be sold, together with many items of furniture, books and precious objects gathered over the years. Beckford retired to Lansdown Crescent in Bath, where he continued to collect and even to build, if on a more modest scale.

Although he became a familiar figure on horseback around the Bath countryside, his existence became more and more solitary, even reclusive. He continued to read avidly and to annotate his books. In the 1830s he enjoyed a literary revival when he published his 'Portuguese' works. But his literary talent was now parasitic on earlier experience; only in the lamenting tones of his vast correspondence do we get any feeling of the desperation that haunted

---

[1] See Malcolm Jack, *William Beckford: An English Fidalgo* (New York, 1994).
[2] See *below* pp. xxv ff.

him.[1] His energy went into collecting, landscaping and improving his house, as well as furnishing his tower overlooking the city. As his hopes and dreams faded into a sometimes bitter nostalgia, leaving him emotionally desiccated, it seemed that the muse too had all but deserted him.

2. ORIENTAL TALES

We have seen that from his earliest years that Beckford loved books and spent hours browsing in the Alderman's ample library at Splendens. Inspired by exotic and chivalrous tales and accounts of voyages to distant places, he began to create an imaginative world of heroes and demons, castles, towers and caves with labyrinthine passages leading to the centre of the earth. These images, swirling in his mind, were soon to be set down in writing. While some of his imaginings were of mediaeval knights in armour and the mysterious, early history of England, he was also encouraged by his contact with Cozens and his love of the *Arabian Nights* to try his own hand at the oriental tale. We shall see that in Beckford's hands it took a distinct and unusual twist and his emotional plots were, in the way of most young writers' outpourings, distinctly autobiographical in tone.

Beckford was already writing stories in his teens – by his seventeenth year he had produced a number of short works, including *L'Esplendente*, an eastern tale of which only a fragment survives.[2] The hero of this tale is a young Mohammedan boy who is punished by his father for drawing figures in the human form, something proscribed by his religion. The drawings are torn to pieces by his angry parent and scattered to the winds while the youth, distraught by the destruction of his creative work, turns away in grief. However, grief is not the only passion that he experiences. He feels guilty at having raised his father's wrath but angry too because he cannot understand what sin he has committed or why his parent's reaction is so violent. Like young William pursuing his reading of eastern lore, the hero of the story is genuinely perplexed and hurt by his parent's hostility to his favourite and, in his eyes, innocent pursuit. His instinct to rebel, hitherto dormant, is brought to the fore.

The oriental theme of *L'Esplendente* is echoed in another story which Beckford wrote before he was eighteen. He called it the *Long Story* but when it was finally published in 1930, Guy Chapman entitled it *The Vision* and it forms the first extract of our selection of texts. *The Vision* describes the adventures of a young hero, who, driven by an irrepressible curiosity,[3] leaves his family and friends to make a lonely journey through bleak mountainous terrain on a cloudless, moonlit night. He finds himself exposed to frightening

---

[1] Boyd Alexander made a selection of letters from these years in his *Life At Fonthill* (London, 1957).

[2] See Ms.Beckford d.11, *Beckford Papers*, Bodleian Library, Oxford.

[3] Curiosity is also the 'ruling passion' of Vathek, see *below* p. 30.

dangers on all sides – the path he has to take over cliffs passes above ravines and precipitous drops. The landscape is dauntingly lunar; a melancholy air hangs over his mission, the purpose of which is unclear. On the darkened plateau that he is obliged to cross alone, reptilian creatures slink and squirm and all manner of unidentifiable figures lurk in the shadows. Through these nastinesses the hero has to crawl until he finds himself at the entrance of a great cave where he sees two shadowy figures, one the sage-like Moisasour, clutching a rod of gold; the other the emerald-eyed Nouronihar, an Indian princess of exquisite mien. Undaunted by his experiences, our hero enters a Faustian pact with the two spirits: he agrees to endure further suffering and certain unspecified rites of initiation in return for a taste of true knowledge and a glimpse of an ideal existence unknown to any other European. The next stage of the adventure unfolds.

The images that follow, now describing the hero's progress in the underground labyrinth of Dantesque-like circles, are surreal and dreamlike. Led by two luminous spirits, Malich and Terminga, the young adventurer descends into subterranean passages that open up a world of grottos, underground lakes and caverns with crystal stalagmites and stalactites, exotic vegetation and scenery. He beholds frightful scenes in which weird, deformed figures crush the skulls of human beings and wear out a mournful existence in dank, murky chambers. Surviving further ordeals of fire and water, he is at last judged to have triumphed over all adversity and is rewarded by being admitted to the secret pleasure gardens of the Brahmin Moisasour and the wise and beautiful Nouronihar, there to enjoy the sensual luxuries of an earthly paradise where sybaritic living is mingled with strict observance of religious rituals.[1]

The Vision is certainly the product of a young pen. Nevertheless, despite its direct, unrelenting and highly serious tone, it shows considerable sophistication in story telling and reveals a prose style in which nuance and rhythm are superbly handled. The young author is particularly clever at maintaining suspense which he achieves by withholding information that puzzles the reader, for example about the exact purpose of William's journey. Instead of pondering on the hero's reason for leaving his family and friends, the reader is projected into the opening scene with minimal preparation, heightening his sense of the immediacy of the hero's plight. Although the plot is simple, even stark, it has its own momentum; there is no time to linger or dally by the way. These literary ploys maximize the drama of the situation and enable Beckford to sweep his reader along from one image to another, never losing control of the swift pace of his narrative. For all its naivety – written in the first person, a 'William' ejaculates onto the page when the hero is accused of an unknown crime – *The Vision* is a skilful exercise in story telling and it shows Beckford's concern with the theme of the damnation, whether the impious seeker of knowledge is a Wiltshire gentleman or a caliph.

---

[1] Boyd Alexander suggested that another fragment may have been meant as a sequel to the *Long Story*, Alexander, *E.W.S.*, p. 66 ff. The fragment he refers to is to be read in MS. Beckford c.48, *Beckford Papers*, Bodleian Library, Oxford.

The oriental 'wrapper' in which Beckford presented his first 'long' story, was much in vogue throughout the eighteenth century. In France the oriental tale had always served the satirical purpose of mocking society and its institutions and debunking all that was held precious by the political elite whilst in England it was more distinctly part of the crusade to reform morals that permeated Augustan literature and journalism.[1] In 1721 Montesquieu had adopted an eastern motif in his *Lettres Persanes*, using his exotic foreigners to criticize French society. His intention was to be polemical as well as to make observations about the human passions in the heterodox tradition of *moraliste* writing. Only incidentally was he concerned with the louche details of life in a Persian harem. His use of the oriental motif was echoed in Voltaire whose eastern tales, such as *Mahomet* (1742) and *Zadig* (1748), achieved wide popularity.

Meanwhile the oriental figure was becoming familiar to English readers through his appearance in issues of the immensely successful *Tatler* and *Spectator* of Addison and Steele. Here the purpose was strict moralizing: if foreigners could be used to show up weaknesses in English society, they were also a means of trumpeting its advantages. The benefits of 'polite' living, of which the periodical essayists were so convinced, could be emphasized by being contrasted to the far less comfortable existence of the subjects of despotic, Eastern rulers. Committed to these civilized, English benefits, yet plagued by inner doubts, Dr Johnson was later to set his lament on the illusion of human happiness in distant Abyssinia, though the baneful message of *Rasselas* (1759) applies to men everywhere. A similar ambiguity sounds in the exchanges between the Chinese visitor and his English hosts in his friend, Oliver Goldsmith's *Citizen of the World* (1762) where the comparison of customs and manners is undertaken with a delicate sense of irony and good humour. Sometimes the use of oriental imagery is blatantly secondary to another theme: in John Hawkesworth's *Almoran and Hamet* (1761) it is blended into a romantic plot; in Walpole's *Castle of Otranto* (1764) it is added as mere spice. Rarely did the interest of English writers in Eastern culture run very deep.

In Beckford's hands the oriental tale, backed by a more thorough knowledge of Eastern languages and literature than had been possessed by the majority of his predecessors, (which he dextrously reminds us of by commenting on the fairness of spoken Persian in *The Vision*), was being used in a different, more subversive way.[2] We begin to realize that through the rich texture of oriental imagery, more accurately observed in its detail than hitherto, Beckford was in fact exploring deeply emotional themes and was

[1] See M. Conant, *The Oriental Tale in England in the Eighteenth Century* (New York, 1966) and J. Butt & G. Carnall *The Mid-Eighteenth Century, Oxford History of English Literature*, 13 Vols. (Oxford, 1979), 8: 35–7 & 491–4.

[2] On this subject see F. M. Mahmoud, 'Beckford, Vathek and the Oriental Tale' in *William Beckford of Fonthill, 1760–1844. Bicentenary Essays*, ed. F. M. Mahmoud (Cairo, 1960) and K. W. Graham 'Beckford's Adaptation of the Oriental Tale in Vathek,' *Enlightenment Essays*, 5, no. 1, (1974), pp. 24–33.

casting into dramatic form his feeling of rebellion against the adult world of respectability and convention. We shall see that this same technique, of importing a new, Romantic sensibility into an established literary form, appears in his travel writing where we often feel the spiritual and aesthetic superimposed upon the detailed, physical landscapes or scenes that he might be describing. Subliminal wanderings in the realm of mystery and imagination, graphically set out with visual immediacy in *The Vision*, are the beginning of his Romantic quest for the unattainable.

Much has been made of the influence of the Christmas party held at Fonthill in 1781 on his next and greatest venture into the eastern tale, *Vathek*, reproduced in full in this book. Many years later, Beckford told Cyrus Redding that the circumstances of the party, held in the dead of winter of 1781 in the extraordinary Egyptian Hall at Splendens, suffused by the special 'necromantic' lighting created by de Loutherbourg, when the young people were on their own away from the critical eyes of their elders, had had a great impact on his imagination and had inspired him with the idea of Eblis or Hell as it appears in *Vathek*.[1] It may be that he was exaggerating its effects just as he exaggerated when he claimed that writing *Vathek* had only taken him a few days when we know he was working on it throughout the spring of 1782.[2]

In fact *Vathek* shows every sign of a well-crafted work that is most unlikely to have sprung from anyone's pen for the first time in its full-blown form. It consists of a complex amalgam, the prototype of which we have seen in the *Long Story*, of well-observed oriental customs (now supported by learned notes) and an atmospheric creation of vivid, exotic scenes. As critics have noted, elements of the comic and burlesque are used at crucial points to provide a paradoxical undertone to moments of high drama. The very character of Vathek is a mixture of a real, historical person, Caliph al Wathik Bi'llah, a ninth century potentate, and the personality of a cruel and sadistic tyrant, Ike Mulai Ismail, a much later Emperor of Morocco.[3] Careful about his facts, especially in the detail of oriental habits and dress, Beckford nevertheless uses considerable artistic licence to tell his story and shows no hesitation in moulding whatever material he has to hand to the purpose of a powerful drama, at times parodying its own seriousness.

Like *The Vision*, *Vathek* is the story of a journey, this time Caliph Vathek's journey to the halls of Eblis or Hell, spurred on, as in the earlier tale, by an unquenchable thirst to discover, a curiosity that is determinant of the protagonist's behaviour. But there is a marked change in tone from the earlier tale, a development that exhibits a maturity in literary style and sophistication. Although we are still presented with a series of dream-like visions, they are now handled in a confident, even detached manner. The sense of naivety that hung over the earlier work has vanished; instead there is a polish and

---

[1] See *above*, p. xii.
[2] Redding, I:243.
[3] For a description of this monster see Alexander, *E.W.S.*, pp. 87–8.

finesse which is the hallmark of a mature artist. Symbolic of this change is a shift from first person to third person narration: Beckford is now able to distance himself from his own created work and to employ a sardonic humour in mocking what formerly he had presented with such high seriousness.

The complex imagery of *Vathek*, its richness of mood and its lushness of detail have led to many interpretations of the text. The most obvious has been to emphasize the autobiographical character of the work.[1] Carathis is an obvious Begum, Nouronihar an orientalized Louisa and, of course, the Caliph a projection of Beckford himself. Others, abandoning this approach, with its simplistic psychoanalytic undertones, have looked to more intellectual influences. *Vathek* has been described as an exposition of Burkean principles of sublimity and beauty, itself derivative from the sensationalist psychology of Locke whom Beckford studied as a child. Links have been made with the physics of electricity and the biology of vegetables beloved of Erasmus Darwin. When the genre of the oriental tale is the main conceptual reference, there have been suggestions that Beckford's contribution, though apparently concluding with a moral about the need for humility, is not a moralizing tale in the spirit of Voltaire or Dr Johnson. Some have ascribed this deviance to Gothic elements which led Beckford to a perverse enjoyment of black arts and crafts, even more strongly exposed in the *Episodes*, later intended to be part of *Vathek*, and whose subjects – homosexuality, incest and necrophilia – took him to the world of the wholly heterodox and bizarre. The Gothic tale involves the inversion of moral values and even of reason itself: the hero's journey is made through a frightening, dark universe with demonic forces ready to destroy him at every turn. In its landscape are towers, caverns and grottos, as well as fearful abysses into which a hero may tumble at any moment.[2]

Vathek remains a puzzling work. Crafted into a polished whole, its internal dichotomies are inescapable: reverence is mixed with humour, elegance with vulgarity; the oriental with the occidental; damnation with a sense that Vathek's quest was not entirely irrational; detachment with a decadent feeling that the unnatural and the strange have an allure and perfume of their own.[3] The brilliance of its prose, its caustic wit and brittle, wistful comment on life suggest the *moraliste* writings of France. It is significant that Beckford chose to write *Vathek* in French: we feel the sophisticated ghost of Count Hamilton, smiling over its artfulness. Even so, *Vathek* is not easily ascribed to one literary genre. It is an idiosyncratic mixture of an oriental tale of

---

[1] Boyd Alexander states categorically that *Vathek* is autobiographical. See Alexander, *E.W.S.*, p. 92. Fothergill, although somewhat more cautious, tends to this interpretation also, see Fothergill, p. 131 ff.

[2] Some of these interpretations are to be found in *Vathek & The Escape from Time*, ed. K. W. Graham (New York, 1990).

[3] A phrase from the Portuguese writer, Fernando Pessoa, *The Unnatural and the Strange* (1906).

detailed imagery (identified with Persian sufism by one critic[1]), one whose plot and tempo is strictly regulated. While the author is steeped in English and French moralizing literature, he appears to have no moral conviction of his own. We can find in *Vathek* characteristics of the Gothic novel, yet its taut form, its very miniaturism make it recognisably an eighteenth-century tale. Like Beckford himself, dressed as an eighteenth-century gentleman in Victorian England, *Vathek* displays the influence of different period styles. Its power is in the dazzling virtuosity with which its unique and florid eclecticism is put before its reader.

3. THE SATIRIC MODE

If *Vathek* shows distinct touches of humour in its ironic treatment of the Caliph's fate and its bathetic contrast between drama and absurdity, Beckford's other early writings are more fully in the humorous or parodying mode. As much as young William tended to dreamy and romantic wistfulness, he also had a high-spirited and mischievous side which attracted him to jests and jokes, albeit of a literary sort. Even so his satirical forays are seldom unalloyed: we find the darker tones of what is more distinctly Gothic in his most mordant prose. Indeed, his sense of mischief was linked to his feeling of rebelliousness, his artistic frustration at being prevented from exploring themes in art and literature of which his elders did not approve. Making fun of life and laughing at its upsets was a way of protecting his private hidden world from invasion by unwelcome grown-ups.

Beckford wrote his *Biographical Memoirs*, from which we have selected extracts, before his seventeenth year, although there is some evidence that one of the stories, Watersouchy, was added at a later date.[2] There are two versions about the origin of this fun-poking, satirical set of essays on imaginary artists. The first comes from Cyrus Redding, Beckford's friend and first biographer who, unfortunately, has never been known for his reliability. According to Redding, Beckford used to overhear an old housekeeper at Splendens, telling visitors who had come to see the Alderman's famous collection of paintings, an improbable jumble of stories and anecdotes about the artists who had painted them. From these ramblings, the witty young master of the house composed his *Biographical Memoirs*.[3] The other version of the story comes from H. V. Lansdown, who also knew Beckford in his Bath days and who claims that Beckford told him that the caretaker, embarrassed by persistent questions that she could not answer, asked the teenage

---

[1] D. Varma, 'Beckford's Treasures Rediscovered; The Mystic Glow of Persian Sufism in Vathek' in *Vathek & The Escape from Time*, ed. K. W. Graham (New York, 1990), pp. 97–111.

[2] See Gemmett, *Memoirs*, p. 18.

[3] C. Redding, 'Recollections of the Author of Vathek', the *New Monthly Magazine*, LXXI June 1844, 151–2.

boy to write down something that she could read out to the visitors about the artists whose works they so much admired. Beckford produced his *Biographical Memoirs* as a response and, if this account is true, must have derived a great deal of amusement from hearing them read out to the unsuspecting and gullible visitors.[1]

Whichever story is true, part of the inspiration for the *Biographical Memoirs* is a high-spirited sense of fun and a determination, on the part of William, to mock all that is held serious by his elders. The tone is set in the very first story – Aldrovandus Magnus is an 'illustrious' artist, especially venerated because of the 'superior glow of his varnish' and his amazing knowledge of demi-tints which surpassed that of all his predecessors. While Beckford was anxious to show off his familiarity with the technical terms (which he had no doubt learnt from Cozens), it soon becomes apparent that he is ridiculing Aldrovandus for putting such importance on technique. The heavy, provincial society of the Low Countries, which Beckford would parody in his first travel writing, *Dreams*, was the perfect setting to indulge in the old sport of *épater le bourgeois*. This parody is done with many amusing asides and flourishes. While abstract youth is lightly censured for inconstancy and a fondness for roving, the heavy figure of middle-aged respectability is lampooned for a love of money and honour and a thirst for praise, however sycophantic. Aldrovandus' master, Himmelinck, is killed eating a pike; when his paramour, Ann Spindlemans is compared to a bottle of dressing, it is more for her sharp than her oily flavour; when he himself is honoured, it is with the absurd order of the Ram. At the height of his powers and success, attended by his disciples, Andrew Guelph and Og of Basan, Aldrovandus dies when he has news that the warehouse, crammed full of his own pictures, has been destroyed.

The next story which we have extracted is that of Sucrewasser of Vienna who is linked to the disciples of Aldrovandus by a chance meeting. While the old master himself never set foot in Italy, with its 'ancient grandeur so interesting to a picturesque eye', his disciples travelled far, taken by the cascades, caverns and grottos of the delightful Tyrol and impressed by the urbane cosmopolitanism of Venice which Beckford himself found so alluring. There they met Sucrewasser, an accomplished artist of the Arcadian style, one who had had his training in the classical masters but whose pale imitations of nymphs not nimble enough, of cupids too everyday and furies veering to the lean, only managed to banalize the grand classical themes. Trapped by the need to pander to the dubious taste of his clients, Sucrewasser had given up all attempt at vigour or quality, resorting instead to secondrate, sugary reproduction.

The last two characters in our group fare a little better. Blunderbussiana has the Beckfordian virtue of coming from a colourful background: his father was a Croatian bandit living in caves hollowed out of the lofty summits of

---

[1] H. V. Lansdown, *Recollections of the Late William Beckford of Fonthill, Wilts and Lansdown, Bath* (Bath, 1893), p. 35.

Dalmatia. Picked out on account of his precocious talent, Blunderbussiana makes the most of his childhood experience, filling his pictures with scenes of lofty mountains, gloomy caves and perfecting a *sgraffito* or greyish melancholy tint which he learnt from the Italians. He is only lampooned for adhering strictly to anatomical forms in figure painting, a style that bored the vivacious Beckford.

Finally Watersouchy (an old Dutch word for boiled fish) represents artists of still life, particularly prolific in the Flemish school whose 'academy' was the table where, in Beckford's eyes, unworthy, lifeless objects were made the subject of art. Like his celebrated master, the real life Dutch painter Gerard Dou, Watersouchy had spent many years perfecting his technique, spending hours at laborious tasks such as copying point lace and other intricate patterns. By this application he came to acquire a complete control of the brush and an ability to produce paintings exhibiting the kind of ultra-realism that Beckford found tedious and uninspiring. The collar of a lap dog or the head of a dead fish did not seem an edifying subject of painting to the young master of Fonthill. Concentrating on minutiae left artists like Watersouchy incapable of appreciating, let alone expressing, the heroic.

Biographical Memoirs is a *jeu d'esprit* which should not be judged too seriously as a work of art criticism. It was written, after all, at a very tender age and although we can read a serious, adolescently portentous purpose in it – to refine the artistic sensibility of the English collecting classes – only at a loss can its facetiousness be put aside. That is not to say that the work fails to portray those characteristically complicated Beckfordian hallmarks of emotional paradox, swiftly changing mood and sinister undertone, but these elements have not yet been synthesized into a mature literary style.[1] Underlying Beckford's writing is a technical grasp of his subject – just as in his Oriental tales he applied an unrivalled scholarship – and his judgement about painting is radical and impressive. But he is still searching for that fine blend of the real and the fantastic that would give *Vathek* and his travel writing their unique stylishness.

The sardonic tone of the *Biographical Memoirs* never entirely left Beckford: it can be found in the savage humour of *Vathek*, in the ironic observations of the travel diarist or in the pithy asides that embellish his correspondence. Just as we find his dreamy romanticism becoming wistful and airy, this sharper, more malign[2] side comes to the fore and we are treated to a taunting remark about men or manners in the style of the French *moraliste* writers who followed Montaigne.[3] Beckford is seldom in one mood for long but in the novels that he wrote in the 1790s, his satirical stance is most marked.

[1] Philip Ward says he may be alone in preferring *Biographical Memoirs* to Beckford's travel writing. See P. Ward 'Introduction' to *Biographical Memoirs* (New York, 1977), p. 1 (pages unnumbered).

[2] Benjamin Disraeli met Beckford, whose work he admired, in 1834 describing him as 'very bitter and malin'. See Fothergill, p. 350.

[3] Michel de Montaigne (1533–92), essayist who observed the prejudices and manners of his contemporaries with a stoical eye.

Although it may be doubted that Beckford intended to refer to an ideal when he was exposing society,[1] there are two principal strands to his satirical attack in *Modern Novel Writing* – one that is a broad caricature of social manners; the other a distinctly political thrust, directed against his enemy, William Pitt. The plot of *Modern Novel Writing* is more of a pastiche than an attempt to tell a story; by tackling his subject in this way, Beckford also intends to make fun of the sentimental novel of the moment, the kind of sugary romance that his half sister, Elisabeth Hervey, specialized in writing.

Beckford's work tells of the amorous life of Arabella Bloomville, a conventional chocolate box heroine who is languishing after Henry Lambert, a soldier who is on duty abroad. A series of somewhat unconnected and scarcely credible episodes is hung on this thin thread. Characters come and go led on by misunderstandings, confusion and their own lack of grip on reality. Ludicrous, mawkish scenes add to the fun: when the Countess of Fairfax 'rediscovers' her daughter (none other than Arabella), the celebrations to mark the event include a party in which the servants and tradesmen are arranged in alphabetical order. In between the disjointed sequences, Beckford provides pen portraits of famous characters, like Mrs Piozzi, or he shows up the foibles of high society, whose members are obsessed with making money and gaining social recognition. Sometimes the action descends to mere slapstick; for once Beckford seems to allow himself to indulge in a touch of vulgarity, albeit of a restrained sort.

A second thread in the narrative was his altogether more overt and caustic attack on Pitt, his erstwhile childhood companion, whose intransigence prevented Beckford from becoming socially re-established and from gaining the peerage after which he still hankered.[2] In the course of conducting the war against France, Pitt had resorted to somewhat draconian measures, one of which, the Traitorous Correspondence Act, affected Beckford directly. By the terms of the act, anyone still in contact with the enemy could be liable to be regarded as a traitor; it certainly meant that staying on French soil was out of the question and its passing precipitated Beckford's return to England in 1793. In the somewhat relaxed conditions of the eighteenth century when it was not unknown for nationals to travel through countries with which their governments were at war, this was a fairly severe measure. Even more restrictive of personal liberty was the suspension of Habeas Corpus, something that Englishmen always regarded as an inviolable right. While Beckford did not really share the radical politics of his father, indeed he went as far as to describe himself as an autocrat,[3] these illiberal measures made Pitt an easier target for attack.

Beckford opened fire on the *British Critic*, a journal which, purporting to be a defender of public morality, was in fact an organ of government propaganda. It was rumoured that the *British Critic* was funded out of secret

---

[1] B. Willey, *The Eighteenth-Century Background* (London, 1962), p. 99.
[2] See *above*, p. xiii ff.
[3] See Oliver, p. 209.

service money. Certainly its support for Pitt was wholehearted and its praise for his policy fulsome. As our extract shows, Beckford attacked the journal rather than Pitt himself, but when he came to write *Azemia*, his tone became more personal probably because by that time it was clear that his offers of acting as a mediator in the war or as an ambassador to Portugal had been brusquely rebuffed. In the 'Ode Panegyrical and Lyrical', Pitt is portrayed as a monster whose policy is to pursue war at any cost with a resultant scale of misery and squalor unknown to Englishmen before. The verses are set to the tune of a ditty; after cataloguing one crime or another, each ends with a sarcastic refrain to praise or honour Mr Pitt.

Although we may find the tone of satire and parody more venomous in *Azemia*, the whole book is not written in that mood. To show the way in which Beckford jumped from one mode of expression to another, his tale 'Another Bluebeard' which purports to be a 'history' well known in Lincolnshire, is included in the extracts. This 'history' turns out to be a horror story in the full-blown manner of Mrs Radcliffe,[1] with a frightening and grim setting, cloistered rooms in turrets, dark passages and secret stairways, horrendous murders leaving bloodstains that cannot be wiped out. The tale is told seriously and although it ends well, with the heroine's escape, both she and the reader are numbed, in true catharsis, by the harrowing train of events that has unfolded in the plot. Beckford shows himself master of all the arts and stratagems of the horror story: creating a gloom-ridden atmosphere, capable of maintaining suspense by keeping his reader guessing as to what will happen next, dashing his hopes each time it seems that the heroine is about to escape her imprisonment and torture. A feeling of claustrophobia and of sinister, unforeseeable mischief hangs over the reader throughout the telling of the tale. There is all the control of pace and tempo that we have already seen developed in his oriental tales; the movement and dash that sweeps the reader along one locale to another.

4. TRAVEL DIARIES

In the first part of his life, Beckford was an extensive traveller, albeit one who embarked on journeys with an entourage and certain cumbersome artefacts – his bed, his books, and his pictures – which he deemed necessary to make life comfortable wherever he went. We have seen that he loved Switzerland and Italy for quite different reasons, while Paris and Lisbon also had their rival attractions for him. But from his earliest days, Beckford became a journeyer of a different sort; he began those fantastic escapes and daydreams that were intimately connected with his deepest feelings and with the artistic temperament that already showed in his adolescence. Wandering about the idyllic dales and lakes of Fonthill, Beckford allowed his imagination to

---

[1] Mrs Ann Radcliffe (1764–1823), one of the leading exponent of the Gothic novel, published five novels between 1789 and 1797.

transport him into exotic realms far removed from the confines of his father's considerable estate: he peopled the woods and hills of Wiltshire with imaginary inhabitants who had the colourful characteristics of his favourite oriental figures. Blending the real and the imaginary became part of his artistic style and we find it already apparent in *Dreams*, his earliest travel writing which forms our first extract of that genre.

In a startlingly direct address to his reader, Beckford announces, in the opening lines of *Dreams*, that he will describe his travels through a mist that hovers before his eyes, mockingly differentiating himself from previous travel writers who kept to a mundane realism. His new style develops the mixture of descriptive accuracy with superimposed mood, whether of awe, fear or even humorous detachment, that we have found in his oriental tales. But now he adds a greater tone of intimacy, a confessional note that reminds us of Rousseau and which, as in Rousseau's hands, he uses to draw the reader closer to the experience of the author.[1] When he feels impelled to more fanciful story-telling, he feels no inhibition in doing that too.

A tone of dreaminess is set even before Beckford leaves English shores for the Continent. We find him vainly searching for solitariness among the crowds of pilgrims at Canterbury. He tells us that he already misses the seclusion of the native hills of his beloved Wiltshire which, nevertheless, he seems to be able to conjure up effortlessly. This manner of interrupting the travelogue with a dream sequence is repeated at various points on the journey through northern Europe; sometimes his romancing is brought on by physical stimuli such as a landscape bathed in moonlight, or a fine, noble vista. We soon begin to recognise these interruptions as a technique to heighten contrasts and to stimulate his reader's expectation of what might await him when he is transported to regions southward where myth and fancy have ever had a freer reign. In the meantime, Beckford also wants to amuse. He does so by satirizing the plodding, commonsensical way of life of the Flemish, the first Continentals he encounters. With their neat, clean abodes and friendly habits, they seem by his cynical lights, to lead vacuous, stupid existences. The scenes of flat lands with great horizons, canals with windmills and a hazy winter light are described in a way that is meant to conjure, in the reader's mind, images of Flemish paintings. The lives of the inhabitants of the Low Countries are made out to be as flat as the landscape: the smoke-filled taverns and the vile Flemish dialect provide a dreary backcloth for men whose oysterish look and flabby complexion attest to an aquatic descent! Beckford realizes only too well that these outlandish remarks will put him in the same xenophobic category as Tobias Smollett whose carps and grumbles against the French and Italians had made him notorious.[2]

---

[1] Jean-Jacques Rousseau (1712–78). His directness is apparent in his earliest work and attracted the notice of critics; however his *Confessions*, where the address to the reader is most intimate, was published posthumously. Beckford certainly read and admired Rousseau's writings on nature. See Fothergill, p. 161.

[2] See T. G. Smollett, *Travels Through France and Italy* (1766).

When we are transported southwards, to Italy, a richer, more majestic tone is apparent. Here Beckford takes the picturesque more seriously, carefully showing off classical ruins (and his knowledge) against a background that can be primevally rude and even savage. Everywhere the colour, shapes and architectural splendours of classical, sylvan settings dazzle and impress the reader, bringing images of Claudian landscapes to his mind. At times Beckford's story-telling bent gets the better of him; in Letter XXIII, we are entertained to a chilling if somewhat incongruous Gothic tale in the middle of the travelogue.

Travel literature had, of course, had a considerable vogue throughout the eighteenth century although its forms had varied greatly. Early accounts of tours in Britain, like Defoe's *A Tour Through the Whole Island of Great Britain*, 1724–26, concentrated on giving a detailed description of the cities and towns of the country, together with information about the manners and modes of living of its inhabitants. In contrast to this somewhat provincial approach, there had also been a more expansive, tradition of travel writing that treated of all parts of the globe and may be traced back as far as Samuel Purchas's exotic accounts of the East at the beginning of the seventeenth century.[1] Inheriting the mediaeval explorers' tales (with which Beckford was already familiar as a boy) these writers cast their net wide and added another dimension to the genre, tracing the origin and nature of primitive societies so that they could better heap praise on their own 'polite' European estate or, if that was their bent, hark back to the innocence of some idyllic existence for ever out of reach.

When British travellers took to the Continent on the Grand Tour, it was often in search of the physical remnants of that classical civilization with which they had been imbued and which they unquestioningly accepted as the source of their own culture. So in 1729, Conyers Middleton, preparing to write a life of Cicero, went to Rome to soak up the atmosphere and reported back, enthusiastically, that being able to stroll about the Forum and gain an impression of the place, redoubled his appreciation of Cicero's eloquence. As the century went on, this kind of travel writing became infused with a more personal tone, revealing the character of the writer whether it was splenetic as in the case of Smollet, intrepid as in the case of Piozzi[2] or simply frantic as Boswell was among his Corsicans.[3] On the whole, though, these diary-like accounts dwelt upon men and manners, skipping lightly over details of landscape or locale.

By the 1760s the kind of travel writing which we call the picturesque had made its appearance. It entailed paying attention to scenery and vista of place as well as, and in some cases rather than, the customs and manners of men.

---

[1] Samuel Purchas (?1577–1626) whose accounts of voyages cover territory as far flung as the North-West passage and Africa, as well as the Far East.

[2] H. L. Piozzi, *Observations and Reflections made in the Course of a Journey through France, Italy and Germany* (1789).

[3] J. Boswell, *An Account of Corsica* (1768) to which he appended his *Journal of A Tour to Corsica*.

Arthur Young's *Six Week Tour Through the Southern Counties of England and Wales*, 1768, is an enthusiastic outpouring of this sort, celebrating the grandeur of nature and viewing her scenes with the artist's eye. Landscape painters, especially Poussin, Claude and Salvatore Rosa provided models of how to look at natural settings in an idealized, even dramatic way. When this approach was used in a continental setting, such as in Patrick Brydone's *Tour Through Sicily and Malta*, 1773, elements of the sublime and of wild dominate. Etna is shown billowing forth its molten lava into the snowy fields below. In a similar spirit William Coxe evokes the majesty of the Alps in his Swiss sketches showing an admiration for the great irregularities of nature rather than her symmetries. Although he has time to discuss the constitution and manners of the Swiss, it is the evocative description of the mountains, echoing the earlier trip of Thomas Gray and Horace Walpole to the Grande Chartreuse, which is the work's richest vein.[1]

These allusions to the grandeur of Continental landscape are reflected in Beckford and indeed he appended to *Dreams* a description of his own visit to the Grande Chartreuse in 1778. However, his mood as an early travel writer is most akin to that of his contemporary, William Gilpin, when that most English author describes the beauties of the Lakes and Westmoreland.[2] Gilpin suggests that mists and fogs, far from obscuring a view, may enhance its beauty and inspire the observer with an aesthetic vision that is more complete than anything derived from an 'unclouded' and therefore banal sighting. The picturesque calls for a blend of visual landscape and imaginative insight which will lead to artistic expression. If Brydone and Coxe stood apart from the scenes they describe, Gilpin immerses himself in his, finding an individual perspective uplifting. His approach is most similar to that we have seen announced so portentously by the young author of *Dreams*.

Four years after *Dreams*, Beckford was busy on another piece of travel writing, this time a private diary that he kept during his visit to Portugal in 1787. The *Journal*, not written for publication though perhaps intended to be enjoyed by a chosen coterie, shares certain characteristics of *Dreams*: it is directly addressed to a reader, this time the diarist's ambiguous 'you'; and it is laced with stories, anecdotes and references that will amuse and entertain that member of the *cognoscenti*. We find in the *Journal* too the confessional tone already familiar in *Dreams*: it is addressed to an equal and confidant whom the author trusts and respects. The diarist tells the story of his stay in Portugal during the long, hot summer of 1787. While there are detailed and vivid descriptions of courtly life in the decadent, Catholic society of late eighteenth-century Lisbon, there is also a sub-plot in which the writer's emotional anxieties, frustrations and passions are shared with the reader. Not only is the agonizingly slow saga of the attempt to get Beckford presented

---

[1] Their visit took place in 1739; two years later Gray wrote his famous *Alcaic Ode* in the album of the monastery. See E. Gosse, *Gray* (London, 1930), p. 31.

[2] W. Gilpin, *Observations on the Mountains and Lakes of Cumberland and Westmoreland* (1786).

to the Queen of Portugal set out with all its twists and turns, but other much more dangerous subjects are candidly set forth. We discover that the young men of Lisbon, with their dashing good looks, emotional directness and languid femininity delighted Beckford. This degree of candour about his emotional life only recurs in his later correspondence with Gregorio Franchi.[1]

The same events of the summer of 1787, judiciously edited for publication, receive different treatment in the *Sketches*, which appeared many years later in 1834. While the *Journal*'s prose are at times vibrant, at times subdued, reflecting the author's moods and enthusiasms, there is a more consistent polish to the suave presentation of the events of that summer in the *Sketches*, addressed, at it was, to a middle class public of the 1830s. Here the tone is extrovert: stories are rounded off with a smoothness that is lacking in the *Journal*; nothing is allowed to spoil the cosmopolitan and polished impression that the snobbish Beckford, posing as the *Grand Seigneur*, wanted to give his bourgeois reader. The grandeur and decadence of life in the *ancien régime* is played up. All the great, noble families of Portugal make their appearance; church dignitaries, theologians and court celebrities jostle with one another to find a space in the glamorous web of the story. Beckford is seen everywhere, cavorting in high society and attending as an impish observer, the gaudy spectacle of an outwardly pious and extravagantly Catholic society. Editing out all unpleasantness does not make the *Sketches* bland; its elegant prose has captivated critics as discerning as André Parreaux while others, such as Boyd Alexander have preferred the *Journal* with its 'little touches... trifling details' skilfully and more humorously presented.[2]

The last of Beckford's travel works represented in our collection is, in some senses, his finest and must rate highly in his work as a whole. The *Recollections*, written half a century after *Dreams*, once again combines what we now recognize as his Romantic leanings, his need to tarry and sometimes to explore the by-ways, with a mature control of *métier* expressed in a fine tautness of prose. From its first pages Beckford sets a jaunty tone: the opening scene is a clever evocation of Portuguese history and exploration in a tableau of the Tagus estuary, crammed with ships from all nations, which forms the backcloth for the departure of Beckford and his friends, laden with domestic and culinary impedimenta, on their leisurely journey through the Portuguese countryside to visit the great mediaeval monasteries at Alcobaça and Batalha.

The excursion soon assumes that jocular and self-mocking air so familiar to the reader of Beckfordian tales. We are treated to many amusing anecdotes and scenes, to the quarrelsomeness of his travelling companions, the greed of the monks and abbots, the honest virtue of the peasants and the delectable

---

[1] See Boyd Alexander, *Life at Fonthill* (London, 1957).

[2] Boyd Alexander, 'Dry Bones' an Unpublished Manuscript in which the *Journal* and *Sketches* are compared and contrasted. *MSS. Eng. lett. c.687–95 etc.*, Bodleian Library, Oxford.

nubility of the novices that he cannot help noticing in the cloisters. Among these spicy and amusing episodes are the more serious artistic themes: the Portuguese countryside is described with the observant eye of the artist, delighted by the exotic fauna and flora, by sights of cane, bamboo, and enormous bulrushes under a vivid, azure sky. Much lushness there is too in the orchards of plum, pear and apricot and the gardens of thyme and camomile where Beckford wandered alone, having abandoned his travelling companions to their gastronomic treats or the slumbers that inevitably followed their excesses. Taken out into the morning freshness or shown the scarred battle-field of Aljubarrota,[1] the reader of the *Recollections* is never left unentertained. Moments of peace come as well — whether they are in the exquisite Gothic chapel at Batalha or before the finely carved regal tomb at Alcobaça — and then the traveller at last finds some respite from the demands of the trail.

5. CONCLUSION

Pausing along the way, distracted by the sight of a picturesque vista or the threatening gloom of a cavernous entrance, or simply stopped by the beauty of wild flowers, Beckford's protagonist is always observant and always ready to convert what he sees into art. He is guided by a genius much skilled in giving detailed descriptions of locales but adding to them an imaginative flavour that distinguishes the writing from the banal travel accounts written by most of Beckford's contemporaries. Beckford's own journeying spirit, taking him along wayside, sometimes languorous paths, is not always easy to capture by representative passages from his work because we need an expanse of text to follow him at his own pace; to savour the digressions as much as the talent that enabled him to tell a story concisely or bring a drama to a climactic conclusion.

Nevertheless, our selection has trailed Beckford from his early literary production to his last — from the fresh, inspired mood of *The Vision* with its stark, gripping story and surreal description, its tone of threatening horror and foreboding to the lush, effervescence of the *Recollections*, with its sparkling, lyrical prose. We have seen that Beckford's literary moods varied greatly: that while he could lose himself in fantasy or whimsicality, there is always a firm control of *métier*, an innate mastery of story-telling, even in the course of descriptive narrative. Sometimes he is taken by the need to be humorous and poke fun: in the *Biographical Memoirs* we find him at his most bantering, by the time of *Azemia* at his most jaded and cynical. But wherever his moods direct him, his writer's talent finds the right words, the rhythm of prose, taut or languid, the richness of language to embellish the narrative or to flush out its images, a sharpness of tone to complement the sharpness of eye that he undoubtedly had.

---

[1] The battle of Aljubarrota in 1385 secured Portuguese independence from Castile for two hundred years.

Beckford's literary reputation has been assessed by modern critics too narrowly on *Vathek*. Writing in a lachrymose vein, J. W. Oliver, one of the earliest modern Beckford scholars, disturbed by Beckford's heterodoxy, said in 1932:

> One wishes that he had written oftener as he does in those letters[1] of thi..gs and people of his everyday experience and made fewer excursions into the ecstatic and fantastic. We might then have lost *Vathek* (and English literature, despite the undoubted power of that remarkable book, is rich enough to stand such a loss), but we should have gained a body of contribution to social satire and clearly etched pictures of life and manners which would have given Beckford a place among our authors much higher and more secure than the not very high and rather detached eminence which critics have conceded to his eccentric genius.[2]

This is a curious comment from one who was familiar with *Dreams* or the *Sketches*, though he may not have read the *Journal* in its then exclusively manuscript form. For in those works, as we have seen, can be found the 'clearly etched pictures of life' which Oliver seems to have overlooked. Indeed throughout his travel writing and even in the novels, Beckford provides a ceaseless flow of daily images, as well as more flamboyant and picturesque flourishes. If occasionally he is carried away by his own exuberance, it is usually short-lived and his fine sense of balanced prose disciplines any tendency to excess. Two writers of discernment disassociated themselves from Oliver's view. Sacheverell Sitwell, rated Beckford's Portuguese works, the *Sketches* and the *Recollections*, as 'an infinitely greater achievement' than *Vathek*. Sitwell, himself a writer of grace and elegance, finds a rich literary talent in those neglected works.[3] Rose Macaulay, writing in 1946, was equally enthusiastic. She distinguishes Beckford's accounts of Portugal from anything else that had been written by previous English visitors, talking of his 'supple and easy prose' and adding, almost enviously, that 'to write like Beckford is a rare gift'.[4]

Across the channel, Beckford's writing has always been sympathetically interpreted just as in his actual life he was well received on the Continent, even at the times when he was ostracized at home. In a lively and forceful preface to the 1876 edition of *Vathek*, no less prominent a figure than Stéphane Mallarmé enthused over the masterly architecture and the aesthetic fineness of the *Conte Arabe* but he also made his reader aware of Beckford's other works – his novels, his satire (showing that French penchant for sniffing out the political) and his travel writing. His praise of Beckford is warm and his high opinion was shared by his fellow academician, Prosper Mérimée. At the time when Oliver was expressing his grudging opinion of Beckford's literary status, the French scholar André Parreaux began a lifetime's work on Beckford, bringing a sensitivity and insight to his subject little

---

[1] Oliver is referring to the letters that Beckford wrote to Louisa in 1784.
[2] J. W. Oliver, *The Life of William Beckford* (London, 1932), p. 160.
[3] S. Sitwell, *Beckford and Beckfordism* (London, 1930), p. 21.
[4] R. Macaulay, *They Went to Portugal* (London, 1985), p. 108.

matched in England. Parreaux, fascinated by the man, also realized the versatility of his literary achievement. While he understood Boyd Alexander's complaint that the *Sketches* lacked some of the livelier, vivid detail of the *Journal*, Parreaux admired the unity of tone and atmosphere that Beckford managed to create in that work; as to the *Recollections*, which he translated and edited himself, he was delighted with its fluid, subtle style.[1]

From the time of Oliver and Parreaux onward, attention tended to focus either on *Vathek* and its place in the tradition of the Gothic novel or on biography, so fascinating and absorbing is Beckford's life. Two English scholars made important contributions to Beckford studies – Guy Chapman worked on many aspects of Beckford's life and letters; and Boyd Alexander, who for years was keeper of the Beckford archive among the Hamilton papers, published both the *Journal* and later correspondence, an eighteenth-century art form in which Beckford was much skilled. They were followed by several generations of writers and critics who took up particular aspects of Beckford's many-sidedness: H. A. N. Brockman was interested in Beckford's architectural ventures; James Lees Milne in his collecting mania and art connoisseurship; while Brian Fothergill produced an elegant and readable new biography.

Meanwhile, in North America, Robert Gemmett produced scholarly editions of both *Biographical Memoirs* and *Dreams*. Kenneth Graham, whose text of *Vathek* has been used in this collection, focused attention on aspects of Beckford's literary awareness. Recent French effort has been concentrated on publishing texts of which the series edited by Didier Girard is the most notable. These early stories, mostly written in French may lead to a reassessment of the literary value of Beckford's juvenilia.[2] Articles, reviews and commentaries on Beckford have continued to appear in books, learned journals, catalogues and newssheets.[3] Several international seminars, one at Lisbon in 1987 and another at Bristol in 1991 were devoted to Beckfordian themes.

Clearly the time for reassessment of Beckford's literary worth has arrived. The selections from this volume, which necessarily have had to exclude important works such as his *Episodes to Vathek*, his lively and voluminous correspondence or some of his brilliant early tales, show the range and quality of his literary production. They show too how Beckford was always experimenting, changing from one genre to another, mixing story-telling with satire, burlesque with horror, travel description with fantasy, dream sequences with detailed observations of men and manners and all this with that 'curious felicity' which Dr Johnson observed is to be found in the best of writers and poets.[4]

---

[1] André Parreaux, ed. *William Beckford Excursion à Alcobaça et Batalha* (Lisbon, 1956).

[2] A volume from the collection, *Suites des Contes Arabes* (Paris, 1992), includes hitherto unpublished stories. Also see D. Girard 'Beckford's Juvenilia?', *Beckford Tower Trust Newsletter* (Spring 1992), p. 2.

[3] A collection of Beckford's poetry has also been gathered by D. Varma in *The Transient Gleam A Bouquet of Beckford's Poesy* (Cheshire, 1991).

[4] Samuel Johnson, *Lives of the Poets*, 2 Vols (Oxford, 1952), 2:345.

A NOTE ON EDITORIAL POLICY

With the exception of the text of *Vathek*, which is produced in full, it has not been the intention in this reader to produce definitive texts for the extracts from the other eight works of Beckford represented in the collection. However, some attempt has been made to achieve consistency and to present versions that Beckford himself approved. To facilitate the modern reader, the long 'S', the connected 'c' and 't' have been edited out; some punctuation has been added where the sense has required it and capitalization has been standardized. Original spelling has been retained.

Two of the works represented in this anthology were not published until the twentieth century. In the case of the first of these, *The Long Story*, Professor Guy Chapman's edition of 1930 (which he took from the manuscript and entitled *The Vision*) has been used with slight adjustment to meet the requirements mentioned in the first paragraph of this note. In the second case, that of the *Journal* of 1787, the original manuscript[1] has been used since Boyd Alexander, in preparing his edition of 1955, made various alterations and modernizations to the text.

Two further selections from Chapman have been used. The first is for the *Sketches*, where he chose the second edition of 1834, overseen by Beckford. The second is for the *Recollections* where he used the only edition during Beckford's lifetime, that of 1835. In the case of the four other works, the only edition published in Beckford's lifetime has been used. In all six cases, a text which Beckford approved and which least offends modern bibliographical practice has been chosen[2]. That leaves *Vathek*, which has always been Beckford's best known work, unaccounted for.

The history of the text of *Vathek*, as Roger Lonsdale succinctly shows in his introduction, is exceedingly complex.[3] Beckford first wrote the work in French. While an English edition was being prepared under his supervision, it was published without his authority (in fact specifically against his instructions) in 1786 by Samuel Henley while Beckford was on the Continent. In response, Beckford rushed out a French version at Lausanne in the following year, 1787, and late in the same year, a new edition, revised by Beckford, appeared in Paris. A further French edition appeared in 1815. Meanwhile, as Kenneth Graham has pointed out, the English version of the text followed a

---

[1] Manuscript d.5, *Beckford Papers*, Bodleian Library, Oxford. The extract, fols 73–90 is published by kind permission of the Bodleian Library.

[2] See Sir Walter Greg, 'The Rationale of Copy-Text' *Studies in Bibliography* III (1950–1), 21. The most important principle, applied to printed works, distinguishes variants intended by the author (substantives) from those that appear in the text as a result of printers' errors or changes made by anyone other than the author (accidentals).

[3] Lonsdale, pp. xxxiii–xxxv.

course of its own.[1] In 1809 Henley's edition was reissued. In 1816 the so-called third edition was published. Five more editions appeared in Beckford's lifetime: in 1823, 1832, 1834 (two versions) and in 1836; meanwhile in America three versions were published, one in 1816 and two in 1834.

The text used here was established by Kenneth Graham in 1971 as part of his doctoral thesis in the University of London.[2] In producing that definitive edition, Kenneth Graham began with the 1816 (revised) edition; then he examined the variants in all the editions in Beckford's lifetime which we have cited. Where ambiguity persisted, he consulted French editions. By a systematic and thorough implementation of modern bibliographical practice, he arrived at his definitive text. The full critical and explanatory apparatus attached to that edition has not been reproduced here but it may be consulted by scholars in the thesis itself. I should like to record my warm appreciation to Professor Graham for allowing his text to be used in this reader.

Notes to the texts have been kept to a minimum. Where Beckford himself made notes these are included and his authorship is identified. In the case of *Vathek* they are put at the end because of their bulkiness and because they have always been regarded as part of the text.

1992   M.J.

---

[1] Kenneth W. Graham, *William Beckford's Vathek. A Critical Edition.* 2 Vols, Unpublished PhD thesis (London, 1971), 2:404.

[2] *Ibid.*

ABBREVIATIONS OF BECKFORD'S WORKS

Azemia	*Azemia, A Descriptive or Sentimental Novel.*
Biographical Memoirs	*Biographical Memoirs of Extraordinary Painters.*
Dreams	*Dreams, Waking Thoughts and Incidents.*
Journal	*The Journal of William Beckford in Portugal and Spain, 1787–88.*
Modern Novel Writing	*Modern Novel Writing or the Elegant Enthusiast.*
Recollections	*Recollections of an Excursion to the Monasteries of Alcobaça and Batalha.*
Sketches	*Italy, with Sketches of Spain and Portugal.*
The Vision	*The Long Story.*
Vathek	*Vathek, An Arabian Tale.*

ABBREVIATIONS OF SECONDARY WORKS CITED IN NOTES AND REFERENCES

Alexander, *E.W.S.*	*England's Wealthiest Son*, by Boyd Alexander (London, 1962).
Alexander, *Intro*	*Introduction to Recollections of An Excursion to the Monasteries of Alcobaça and Batalha*, ed. by Boyd Alexander (Sussex, 1972).
Fothergill	*Beckford of Fonthill*, by Brian Fothergill (London, 1979).
Gemmett, *Dreams*	Introduction to *Dreams, Waking Thoughts & Incidents*, ed. by Robert Gemmett (Cranbury, New Jersey), 1969.
Gemmett, *Memoirs*	Introduction to *Biographical Memoirs of Extraordinary Painters*, ed. by Robert Gemmett (Cranbury, New Jersey, 1971).
Lonsdale	Introduction to *Vathek*, ed. by Roger Lonsdale (Oxford, 1983).
Oliver	*The Life of William Beckford* by J. W. Oliver (London, 1932).
Redding	*Memoirs of William Beckford of Fonthill* by Cyrus Redding, 2 Vols (London, 1859).

CHRONOLOGY OF WILLIAM BECKFORD

1760 (29th September) Born at Fonthill, Wiltshire or in Soho Square, London
1768 Robert Drysdale appointed his tutor
1770 (June) Death of his father
1772 John Lettice became his tutor
1773 Alexander Cozens appointed his drawing master
1775 Began writing exotic tales
1777 (Summer) Sent to Geneva (with Lettice), wrote *The Long Story* (*The Vision*) and *Hylas*
1778 Visited the Grande Chartreuse
Brought back to England by his mother
1779 Travelled around England, visiting cathedrals and houses including Powderham Castle where he met William Courtenay, aged 11
1780 *Biographical Memoirs* published (June) After witnessing Gordon Riots in London, left on Grand Tour of Low Countries, France & Italy with Lettice
Stayed with Hamiltons in Naples
1781 (April) Returned to England and began writing travel account
(September) Coming-of-age party at Fonthill
(December) Christmas Party with de Loutherbourg's effects, inspiring him to begin an Arabian tale
1782 (January to March) wrote *Vathek* in London while his affair with Louisa Beckford developed
Set out for Germany and Italy, returning to England in November after the death of Lady Hamilton in Naples
1783 Suppressed *Dreams* under family pressure
(May) Married Lady Margaret Gordon
Left England for honeymoon in Paris & Switzerland
1784 (March) Returned to England, became M.P. for Wells
(September) Powderham scandal
Campaign against him in the London press
1785 Correspondence with Henley about *Vathek*
(April) Birth of daughter, Maria Margaret Elizabeth
(July) Left for Switzerland with family on advice of his mother, aunts and guardians
1786 (May) Birth of second daughter, Susan Euphemia (later Duchess of Hamilton)
Death of Lady Margaret eight days after that birth
(June) *Vathek* published in English by Henley without permission
1787 (January) Returned to England from France
(March) Sailed to Lisbon, met the Marialvas

(June) Paris edition of *Vathek* published

(December) Left Lisbon for Madrid

1788 (June) Left Madrid for Paris

1789 In Paris for storming of Bastille (October) Returned to England

1790 (October) Returned to Paris, collecting objets d'art

1791 Published *Popular Tales of the Germans* (translation)

Stayed in Paris

1792 Travelled in Savoy and Paris

1793 France declared war on England

Traitorous Correspondence Act

Hidden in Chardin's bookshop (May) Returned to Fonthill with a plan for a new house

(November) Departed for Lisbon

1794 During his residence in Lisbon, made an excursion to the monasteries of Alcobaça and Batalha

Resident in Monserrate, Sintra

1796 (June) Returned to England

Publication of *Modern Novel Writing*

1797 Publication of *Azemia*

Offer to act as mediator between British Government and France rejected by Pitt

1798 (July) Death of his mother

(October) Departed for Lisbon

Resident in Monserrate, Sintra

1799 (July) Returned to England

Story of *Al Raoui* published

Beginning of construction of Fonthill Abbey (by James Wyatt)

1800 Visit of Sir William, Lady (Emma) Hamilton and Lord Nelson to Fonthill

1801 Resident in Paris, France & Savoy, collecting furniture and antiques

1807 Moved into Fonthill Abbey, supervising and adding to construction

1810 Marriage of Susan Euphemia to Marquess of Douglas, later Duke of Hamilton

1811 Elopement of Maria Margaret Elizabeth with Colonel James Orde

1814 Visited Paris

1819 Visited Paris

1822 Sale of Fonthill and part of his collection through Phillips to John Farquhar for £300,000

Moved to Lansdown Crescent, Bath

1825 Main tower of Fonthill Abbey collapsed

1827 Beckford's tower built at Bath

1829 Began *Liber Veritatis*

1834 Publication of *Sketches*

1835 Publication of *Recollections*

1844 (2nd May) Died at Bath

THE VISION

From *The Long Story*, 1777 published as '*The Vision*' by Guy Chapman, London, 1930

THE VISION

MANUSCRIPT OF A ROMANCE

I happened accidentally to open my casement: the moon shone bright in the clear sky illuminating the mountains. I stole away silently from the gay circle of company and passing swiftly the garden of flowers, the orange trees and the grove betwixt the house and the rocks set my feet to some steps cut in their solid sides. Luckily I had mounted the hundred steps which lead to the first flat crag of the mountain before a dark grey cloud fleeting from the north veiled the moon and obscured the light which conducted me. What could I do! the steps were too steep, too precarious, too irregular, to descend in darkness; besides, tho' darkness may prevail for a moment light will soon return; I must not despair; so folding my arms I sat patiently on a stone which time had smoothed with moss.

Wayward fortune! how many at this instant curse thy power, how many deprecate thy rage by patience and resignation! Of that number heaven grant I may be such was my short prayer. A long series of thoughts crowded on my mind. I recollected past events. I prophesied future. I rejected my prophesies. I thought all a dream; the next moment every thing seemed real. I cast my eyes on a glow worm which glimmered by. 'Ah,' cried I, 'we are all reptiles and the most distinguished of us but glow worms.'

I had almost forgot myself and my situation when the moon emerged from her concealment shewing the leafy woods and the rocks beneath, my mind was travelling in another world of fancy and I forgot that I came to view the lake by the azure moonlight. Rousing from my trance, and calling my strength to my assistance, I clambered the steeps, now grasping the stump of an antiquated oak, now helping myself along by the uncertain fragments of the mountains. 'Surely my time is not yet come, surely I am reserved to fall from the precipices of the Andes or the more probable precipices of ambition,' exclaimed my vanity, when I attained a summit from whence I looked down on the dreadful rock I had surmounted, a rock that in truth I believe was never before trod, 'or else I should have fallen from on high an instant ago and been dashed against the points or mangled by the hawthorns,' those hawthorns I had so often admired, plants to which I had addressed a volume of nonsensical apostrophes to whom I have often sung in the plaintive simple Scotch measures,

> In April when primroses paint the green ground
> And summer approaching rejoices the year
> The yellow haired laddie would often times go
> To wilds and deep Glens where the Hawthorn trees grow.

I was much embarrassed how to[1] get down again but I considered that I was now to think how I should get up to my point; for the lake rose not yet upon my sight. Again I paced along a rugged goat path, hanging over a shaggy pointed promontory jutting forwards over the forests, dark shades enveloping their beauties, and the moon but rarely discovering its glimmer amongst the leaves. Now I found my path finish its course and where think you did it lead to? Not to a summit from whence an extensive landscape was to be surveyed nor to a forest of Pines, the natural production of a mountain, but to a gloomy dell skirted with huge masses of rock troubled by winds that howled desolation, and torrents that flowed in narrow encumbered channels sending forth a discordant hollow murmur. When I cast my heavy eyes upwards, no chearful object appeared to relieve them, no tree was rooted in the crevices, no shrub diversified the shaggy promontories around, nothing was seen but rocks and water; all served to abstract it from the more chearful scenes of nature and to stamp it with a cast of sublime singularity. 'Tis true the moon gleamed the faint light which discovered this scene of melancholy grandeur; but then her orb was retired from the small portion of the concave azure discernible above my head and the scanty opening that the rocks admitted off was canopied with clouds. The glances of that glorious planet gave the rough pinnacles of stone strange fantastic appearances; sometimes they assumed the air of gigantic idols, sometimes obelisks and pyramids[2] of mysterious shape and uncouth sculpture seemed to stand confessed[3] around. The awful majesty of the place bowed me down and I crept along the cold flat surface of the stone, fearfully approaching the torrent brink, casting one glance and then retired shivering to the nooks of the precipices. As I crawled in one of these panics along, not venturing a look beyond my stony track, my eye caught a spot where the moonlight shone most strongly, on which I thought was impressed the stain of blood. 'Ah, 'tis too true, it must be this horrible valley is the temple of some accursed superstition. Here the evil spirit brooding over man instigates some foul compact. These grim idols, these mystic pyramids, this blood, the soul of some wanderer spilt as a sacrifice to fiends too plainly indicate what ceremonies are here acted. Here resort, before an hour past, haggard wretches abandoned by the mercy of heaven, a miserable few shrinking from mankind and burying themselves in this gloom to work mischief and pour destruction on those who ages past may have offended them. Revenge, the baneful passion, is their soul and for which they blot their names from the Book of Life[4] and sacrifice an eternity of happiness. Hark! was not that their yell amongst the mountain peaks on high? No; it was but the wind thro' that time worn crevice; but it was enough to chill my heart. And art thou so sunk, William![5] art thou reduced to the level of such

[1] Confused as to.
[2] A main room in 'Splendens', Beckford's childhood home, was the Egyptian Hall.
[3] Manifested.
[4] The list of those who will inherit eternal life.
[5] Beckford suddenly addresses himself.

as these? Is thy conscience troubled, is thy reason fled, fearest thou the harmless gust of air that makes mock melody amongst the cliffs? Arise then from thy abject posture cast away thy feverish fancies and resume the attitude of man.' I arose! the warm blood flowed again round my heart and my limbs required their accustomed motion. I sternly viewed the pinnacles of rock and saw they were but pinnacles. I looked down on the red stain and it was but the tint of nature. The resemblence of idols, the imaginary purpose of the place, the fears of the torrent had rolled far away and left a sublime landscape rendered placid by the moon. Now I ventured to the farther end of the valley divested of all its terrors and ascending from chink to chink and from one projecting fragment to another set a foot on the healthy brow of the mountain top whilst the other was suspended over the space below. The dangers I had surmounted emboldened me and I gazed at the lake, smooth as a mirror, the range of hills, mountains and peaks projecting seemingly into the waters and casting long tracks of shadow which obscured the cultivated plains, the cities and the villages. How shall I paint the clear azure deep of air, the brilliant silver clouds tempered by modest grey hovering round that orb, that world, that habitation of unknown beings, steering its majestic course along these azure plains of sky, moving by the wonderful impulse of him who fixed it in its sphere, marked out its track and bid it equally diffuse its light to the Hemispheres.[1] Observe! how that peak brightens at its approach, see how its snows imitate the celestial lustre. The long range of Alpine mountains catch the beams, they glisten, they array their summits with the same vesture. All earth seems proud to wear the livery of the moon. The lake receives the glory, becomes a new heaven and displays another orb whose light floats amongst the waters and quivers brilliantly on the waves. I turned my eyes from these glories finding the attraction of the moon too powerful and sat myself peaceably down on the smooth verdure of the thyme which carpeted the brow. At this very moment yon planet may be the object of thy admiration. Yes, tho' so far distant, we may both regard this same object. With what pleasure then did I dwell upon its sight. Yet a little while and the cares of this vile earth will rob me of these serene enjoyments. A few years the projects of ambition, the sordid schemes of interest and all the occupations of the world must seclude from such meditations. No, I will resist them, I will repulse their influence if they rob me of the meridian sunshine, if I must waste those hours in cabinets and councils, if the evening must be sacrificed to debates and to watchful consultations, still they shall not rob me of the midnight moon. Then shall we walk and gather plants by her light and her soothing influence shall calm my soul. Poor mortal! Take thy fill of these pleasures to day; for to morrow thou wilt die. Sighing this sentiment, I got up and viewed the lovely situation in which I now stood. I had now attained the steep peak of the mountain; it was a solid rock perpendicular, sharp pointed and without a blade of vegetation. Time had made no impression on this mass nor were its

---

[1] Beckford echoes the argument from design, a favoured theological explanation throughout the eighteenth century.

sides imprinted with the least mark of his power; there were no crevices, no nooks by whose assistance I could climb; every part was solid and unworn. Nature had formed it inaccessible and I was contented to let it remain above me. Level with its base on the opposite side of a horrid cleft torn probably by an earthquake, was another mountain, its rocks almost concealed by noble sweeps of wood, the growth of a century flourishing in the height of their perfection. The tall fir, the spreading oak, the round headed beach, the walnut, the juniper, the elegant birch whose slender white stems were silver-ed by the beams of the moon, formed a beautiful prospect contrasted to the barren peak near which I stood. I could not help desiring to approach so inviting a scene and warily looked round and round and about and here and there for a place or a path, however dangerous, which might lead me to these bowers. No sooner did I approach the gloomy gulph than I retreated, no sooner did I look down the precipices than I despaired gaining the wished for shore. At last after anxiously pacing backwards and forwards the mountain brow, I spied a very narrow ridge about ten yards down formed of the same rock which lined the sides of the cliffs and joining the side I stood on to the opposite bowers like a bridge. But how shall I descend the steep cliff to gain this bridge? I will, I must. So embracing a huge stone and putting my feet on the tough branches of an ancient juniper I slid down and rested luckily on a spot overgrown with soft moss. What a variety of flowers, of shrubs, of plants has nature placed in these crevices, apparently without soil, her accustomed instrument of vegetation. Art would never have dared to have planted them on so barren a foundation. Surely I smell the perfume of the rose, of the pink, of the honeysuckle. See these; they grow their trunks and stems twisted together and hanging over the steeps in fantastic garlands. Figure to yourself this narrow ridge a dangerous gulph on each side, grim, dark, horrible, itself spangled with flowers many of them unknown to me and sending forth a new smell. See me wantonly treading under foot what, if transported to England, would become the pride of our gardens. Take your eyes off this beautiful spot and let them range along a frightful perspective of steeps, of crags, of impending mountains just admitting the moonlight to shew my path and discover the flowers. But I must own I could not enjoy this delicious vegetation untainted by disagreeable sensations, the ridge was so narrow, that the least false step might have precipitated me to destruction, the very herbs and flowers I trod on, tho' all fair, might give away and put a period to my worldly existence.

Behold then in my countenance a strange mixture of pleasure and pain; haste, mark on your tablets that uncertain character. See how cautiously I measure my steps and poise my body; see how I keep my eyes fixed on the shore and am almost ignorant[1] of the scene on each side. Now behold me leap exultingly on a grassy bank and fix my feet in the soil. Well, give me joy. I have surmounted obstacles that at the first glance, my third even, looked actually unsurmountable. I shiver at the danger I have past in a greater degree

_____

[1] More in the sense of disregarding than not knowing.

than at the moment I was engaged in them; 'tis well, or I should have been no more. I lay a few moments on the bank, a gentle breeze fanned the groves, the Gumcistus[1] which sprouted out of the verdure on my side dropped its flowers over me. How sweet the pleasure of ease after labour; how agreeable the sensation of surmounting completely any obstacle. Whilst I lay indulging in this manner amongst the vast wilds and uninterrupted solitudes, a thought intruded unwillingly upon me of the good people I had left at home. What will they think become of me? Their imagination will form wild beasts to eat me up, robbers to murder me, rocks (as indeed was not improbable) to give way and roll me from their summits mangled at their feet. Alas! it is in vain to repent. I shall fulfil their fears were I to return and measure back my dangerous uncertain way before the morning. Heavens! how shall I descend the steeps, climb the precipices by this fallacious light. The ardour, the enthusiasm which has helped me on will no longer assist me in getting down. There is nothing tempting to return to a house which my vagaries[2] have troubled. All these considerations must be banished for the present from my mind and I will seek comfort as I intended in these shades till the morning. Thus you see how imperfect is our happiness. In the midst of the gratification of my most romantic[3] pleasures, these mean sorrows stole in and troubled my enjoyment. Rising from the bank and shaking off the flowers, I plunged into the thickets and let the cool leaves of the beech tree slap my flushed face. After continually stumbling over antiquated stumps and fallen trees, that some violence had laid low, I penetrated (the ground still rising) into the dark, dark, retired recess of the forest and leaning against the trunk of an aged towering pine exclaimed, 'Where am I? By what strange impulse am I driven? For what end am I come here? Why do I fly like a miscreant from my home and bury myself deeper and deeper in this gloom. What a horrid darkness just visible envelops this wood and fits it for shocking actions. It was to such a solitude, to such a dreary waste that Cain fled, reeking from the murder of his brother, and what murder have I committed, what crime have I perpetrated that I should conceal myself like him from everything human? A sort of madness has hurried me here and I strive in vain to reason with myself. I am not at this instant reasonable.'

Whilst I was saying those passionate words my eye fixed itself on something that bore the semblance of a pool, fed by the snow which melts from the mountains. Into this abyss will I plunge; I will extinguish the flame of life, I will start into eternity; my curiosity shall be satisfied, I will know if.... As I was moving to my destruction something held me back. I trembled; a cold chill froze my blood, my hair softened with a frigid sweat, my soul was shrivelled. I thought my good angel interposed. I heard his instinct speak in me. 'If mercy has preserved thee from crimes must thou form them thyself?

---

[1] A plant or rather shrub with large thin white, red and yellow flowers which the least wind shakes off, common in English gardens. [Beckford's note]

[2] Wanderings.

[3] Of wild scenery.

wilt thou work thy own ruin?' I awoke as from a trance and found myself riveted to the torn branch of the pine against which I still leaned tho' my imagination had aped motion so strangely that I could scarce distinguish the shadow from the reality. With a violent effort that extricated me from my momentary imprisonment, I disentangled my torn garment and pursued my way amongst the forest almost in total darkness. A faint glimmer amongst the leaves declared[1] that I was near an opening and suddenly I emerged to a little knowl covered with smooth verdure and encompassed by the forest on every side, except where a huge rock bulged forth of a bulk, a size, an immensity which exceeded all the others I had passed. Below I could distinguish the aweful mouth of a cavern which seemed to contain the thickest darkness. Its ponderous jaws were hung in fearful suspense and every moment menaced a dreadful fall. From under one of the crags gushed forth clear water tumbling and rolling its course down unseen steeps, till it was heard no more. Another stream of a more moderate kind trickled and oozed from the porous stone and made itself a channel along the valley bordered by a stately species of lilies and flag[2] flowers waving with the gale. Yet another stream flowed out of the cavern mouth black tho' clear impregnated with mineral gold. These three mysterious rivers filled my mind with wonder. The sky was free from storms, unclouded and serene; no vapours except a few and those light, fleeting round the peaked summit of a monstrous rock where no herb or plant or flower ventured to grow. Below, their growth was luxuriant, cherished by an heated soil and their flowers gigantic and rampant, their odour powerful, breathing vivid spirit into the animal frame.

> ———It was now the hour!
> The holy hour, when to the cloudless height
> Of yon starred concave climbs the full orb'd Moon.

A soft delusion like a descending dew stole on my senses and I sunk down on the grass, the scene still distinct before my eyes, my mind in a delirium. Sounds seemed to proceed from the cavern, long protracted sounds wafted over the dark bubbling river, swelling peals of distant harmony. Soon I thought the notes of some silver toned instrument accompanied by an angelic voice stole into the porches of my ear filling me full of rapture. Now a full accord, now a majestic pause; now wildly warbling notes dying away amidst the recesses of the caverns. Silence prevailed for a moment. Then a distant murmur in the woods, on the cliffs, on the vapours, on the waters, melody as faint as a departing mist floated in the Æther[3] ascending higher and higher till but a vibration remained on my ear. An universal calm succeeded for many moments till it was broken by a faint whisper issuing from the cave. My soul was all attention, every sense on their utmost stretch: the sound increased till I could distinguish something like the human voice modulating in two different tones, one deep and faltering, the other clear, smooth and delightful

---

[1] Showed [me].
[2] A larger species of the Iris than I ever saw. [Beckford's note]
[3] An element filling space, conceived of as a purer form of fire or water.

as the voice I had heard before. My eye had not been much longer fixed on the cavern, before it could distinguish two stately forms emerging from the dark gloom and advancing like phantoms stood silently before the entrance. The tallest wore the figure of a majestic sage, his hoary hair bound by a golden fillet inscribed with unknown characters, his beard waving over an ample robe of deep azure of the colour of the meridian sky and concealing his feet and arms with its folds: one hand grasped a taper rod of gold, the other held a woman who had an imperial mien, a sublime port and a spirit in her opal eyes, a fire which I dare not describe. A mazy vesture of muslin encircled her limbs, proportioned with the most polished finish of delicacy: she had neither gold nor silver nor jewels, her hair was indeed braided with a row of pearls, but its luxuriance almost concealed them. I knew not what to think, nor how to fear. I would willingly have retired, but I know not what chained me to the ground. I dreaded the glance of these beings (whatever they were) and yet I loved them. The looks of the sage encouraged me, the woman had turned aside her opal eyes[1] and I lay patiently on the turf, waiting the issue of this apparition.

'Now is the time' (said the deep voice I had before heard) 'and now the hour to consult nature. In silence she discloses her wonders, her mineral powers and the juices of her plants. These herbs have now an influence on every animal, hidden from the generality of even the most careful observers. The philosopher[2] who after the researches of many, many long years, vainly imagines the volume of nature extended before him is deceived, unless by toil, by more than European perseverance, by fasting and by meek resignation he wins the Ætherial spirit[3] to befriend him. Then like my sacred tribe he may cast his eye into the very bowels of a mountain, more huge than these, spy out the lurking ore, the glistening diamond, the mineral fraught with powerful influence on the human frame and the concealed source of mighty rivers. The compact soil, the flinty rock, the layer of binding chalk, fathoms of sand and all the barriers in which nature has studded her choicest productions, are all laid open and explored by him alone. What a glorious supremacy does this knowledge give, my emerald-eyed Nouronihar[4] and thou shalt partake it with me. Thou shalt not remain in vulgar ignorance unworthy of the Godlike race of which thou springest.'

'You, who can read in inmost soul,' answered Nouronihar, 'can see it bend in acknowledgements before your instructions. You, kind director of my youth, have cheered my lonely path when straying in the subterraneous caverns of the globe. By your assistance have I been supported, by your councils have I sustained the horrors I was decreed to view and prevented despair from gnawing my vitals when . . .'

---

[1] Her eyes were of no determinate colour; sometimes blue, then hazel, then emerald, then black, &c. . . . [Beckford's note]
[2] one who searches for knowledge about the causes of things.
[3] Spirits dwelling in the upper regions of space.
[4] Beckford was to use the name again in *Vathek*, see *below* p. 62.

Nouronihar could not continue, she cast her humid eyes on the ground and then on the sage who spoke again.

'The midnight hour will shortly pass away. Therefore let us seize the moment and cull the herb on which the moon shines brightest. It is a plant, which in gross foul material hands might prove the instrument of unlawful power. The evil ones know this and snatch it with their fangs, then commit the prize to their votaries and behold them rise to the summit of ambition, work magical infatuation and cruel delusions, – delusions that mislead, embezzle the noble faculties of the soul and degrade the man to the vile brute or reptile, fill him with destructive passions and hurry him to situations in which he will implore the protection of the instigating fiend and become subject to his power. Such is the influence of the herb, when given into the power of malignity; but when it is pointed out to those bred in our Schools of virtue,[1] like balm it cools the acrid spirit, the tumultuous desire and the turbulent lust of lawless rapine. It is this herb which enlarges and expands the faculties of reason and guides the mind towards the source of all perfection, towards that ALL WISE before whom my sacred tribe fall and at whose mention their inmost soul glows with sensations of love, of gratitude, of awe, too fervent for their mortal frame. In such raptures have I seen them retire to the summit of Gehabil,[2] and glorious was the monument of their dissolution. Often have I stood when the clouds would divide and stream with tracks of vivid pure light shot from the mansions of their happiness. Often have I returned and edified the synod of our sages with their parting hour.'

As the Bramin[3] spoke, his every action was full of inspiration. The elegant Nouronihar, leaning against the rock, had concealed her face within her folding arms. She was awed, she was penetrated with the sublime instructions of the sage and remained entranced till his voice called her to gather the mysterious herb.

'Hasten, Nouronihar,' cried the Bramin, 'whilst the moonbeam points out thy way. Occasion is near at hand when the balm shall be required.'

... A dread without a cause, a sudden tremor had taken possession of my nerves, the conversation I had heard was so unusual, so aweful, so mysterious that I could form no judgment. The music that had sounded in the spheres, the deportment of the Bramin, who at this moment seated on a monstrous blueish stone was poring attentively over the dark river, had a solemn cast that affected me more than I can express.

Nouronihar had obeyed the command of her instructor, she was kneeling on the herbage brightened by the moon and prying carefully for the plant she was directed to cull. Whilst thus employed I had time to examine her features. Never did my eyes behold so majestic an assemblage, her complexion a clear brown was animated with sentiment and vivacity, glowing with health. Her attitude discovered the harmony of her proportions, her beautiful

---

[1] The groves of the Bramins. [Beckford's note]
[2] A mountain in the interior of India. [Beckford's note]
[3] Member of the highest or priestly caste among the Hindus.

bosom was in a very visible palpitation when she gathered the wished for herb replete with such qualities. She arose and with a motion graceful as the wave of the palm tree was regaining the cavern when the herb dropped from between her taper fingers. As she turned to take it up a gleam of light shone full upon the turf where I lay and discovered me to her sight. Hastily snatching up the herb she flew swiftly to the Bramin and exclaimed; 'Father! look! behold that mortal within the verge of this hallowed valley, surely he must be one of the accursed or never could he have dared intrude on this spot and at this holy hour. Speak, Father ... he cannot be mortal or how should those tremendous precipices, these gulphs, these natural horrors that encircle our abode been surmounted. Have you not often told me that none of those that tread the plains of that unknown country I have viewed from the pinnacle of our mountain, could enter here? Have you not calmed my inquietudes by repeated assurances of our security? And now some evil one or some Firengui[1] has violated our retreat and polluted this vale by his profane presence. Who dares affirm the purity of our celestial protectors will not take umbrage at this sacriledge and never revisit us more?'

The Bramin with a smile of complacency that seemed to bode no revengeful intent, answered; 'This is no evil one nor could he have passed the gulphs that encompass our residence had he the mind of a Firengui. His soul has not been yet torn with the avaricious thirst of riches, the malignity and the ferocity of those nations amongst whom he was born; no; had he such passions, he could not have possessed that equal temperature without which the narrow ridge is inaccessible. We will pardon his innocent intrusion; but as his ear has caught the music in the spheres[2] and the harmony with which we invoke the spirits of Æther, he must sustain a reverse purification or venture back ignorant and unbenefited by our converse.'

I had now but one method of proceeding and that my curiosity urged with the greater vivacity, (to return along the forests, encounter the horrid darkness that would shortly prevail and traverse the precipices was rejected as impracticable with safety). Summoning all my resolution, I ventured towards the Bramin and Nouronihar who were seated on the margin of the black river and when I approached, the character of wisdom so strongly expressed on the aged visage of the seer, his garb and the uncouthness of his whole appearance struck me with such awe that I fell to the ground. He raised me up and with an affable benignity bade me be of good cheer. 'No doubt,' continued he, 'the sounds you heard and to which mortals are so unaccustomed, have thrilled your heart; perhaps our foreign habits, our conversation and the appearance of the cave we live in, may have occasioned the sensations that seem to overpower you; but let the gaze of wonder give way to the calmness of attention. Mark me, do you find yourself sufficiently bold to perform some ceremonies? Nay, start not! be assured they are no evil tendency;

[1] An European. [Beckford's note]
[2] The harmonious sound supposed to be produced by the motion of moon, sun, planets and stars.

on the contrary leading to instructions that may then and only then be given. They must be the consequence of a discipline which in truth you will find severe; but if, young man, your soul is desirous of expanding itself, if the acquisition of more than worldly knowledge be alluring, I will answer you will prefer a momentary pain to lasting enjoyments; but still if human frailty, wavering doubts, and the cases of thy mortal body triumph over the pure delights of the mind, speak, use no disguise and I will discover to you a path which will conduct you in security to your world below and there grovel like the herd that are universally spread over its surface. Never shall you behold us more and should you uncautiously disclose what you have hitherto seen, depend, you will never be credited, you will be despised as a raving dreamer and despised with the contempt of those whose sorry imaginations could never rise to even what you have as yet beheld. Now behold your alternative.'

A piercing look from Nouronihar, a look that at once encouraged my enterprize and despised me if I feared it, proved determinative. I fired at the idea of being held dastardly in such eyes and exclaimed with some violence: 'Lead me to the trial; whatever the task I am ready to execute it.'

'Young man,' answered the Bramin, 'this sudden compliance must not be the result of passionate vehemence nor of wanton curiosity. If from the bottom of your heart you can declare a sincere desire of being initiated into the sacred mysteries of the Shastah[1] that fountain of knowledge, your request shall be granted; you shall enter our abode and I will unfold a scene which never before has been displayed to European sight. A story shall be revealed which will appal every sense with wonder and experience shall demonstrate its truth. But before you resign yourself to my power, let me apprize you that the purification you are about to undergo is sufficient to make the most courageous shudder. You must in a manner be committed to the flames and then to a raging torrent; your body must receive the most severe shocks and your mind for some instants distracted with a dreadful suspense. Thus I paint the enterprize you are willing to undertake; if it appears in its most gloomy colouring you have still the power of abandoning it; but if the constancy and firmness of your mind triumphs over the frailty and weakness of your body be assured that glory, refreshment both spiritual and corporeal will follow in a degree so sublime, so superior to mortality in general that you will exult in the remembrance of your sufferings. Be seated on that stone and ponder well your resolution.'

I obeyed; it was utterly impossible to retract. An enthusiasm that did not admit of fear had long possessed me. I was resolved and convincing the Bramin of the sincerity of my desire beseeched him to order me instantaneously to the trial. He complied and turning to Nouronihar said, 'Haste, my

[1] The Shastah is a Book written on the leaves of Palmtrees of very remote antiquity. Contains all the Learning and mythology of the Bramins. Its contents scarce ever reached Europe. Mr Bathurst, a Bookseller in London, possesses a few leaves of this inestimable treasure but none are sufficiently learned in the Sanscrit language to expound them. [Beckford's note]

daughter, to the interior grot; see that fuel be supplied to the consecrated hearth. Call Malich and Terminga.' She arose and casting on me a gracious glance cried, 'Adieu, stranger: Nouronihar will ever interest herself for one who defies so terrifying a prospect. We shall meet in the halls of the glorious.' The Persian language sounded inexpressibly melodious on her tongue.[1] She plunged into the darkness of the cave and left me immersed in thought. The Bramin favoured my mood and did not break the silence till in the fullness of my heart I begged him to believe the confidence I placed in him. 'Nothing,' continued I, 'can affright me; the opinion I entertain of the benevolence of your tribe has entirely banished suspicion; but, O my Father, pray that I may sustain the severity of this trial. May it please heaven to grant me strength to endure the shocks.'

'Doubtless heaven will,' answered the sage, 'and I will strive by my fervent prayers to obtain a consolation that shall sustain your sinking frame and fit you for the horrors of your trial.'

He prostrated himself before the mouth of the cave. Drops trickled from his aged head; his body seemed convulsed, but in the space of a few seconds it regained its former tranquillity. The clouds seemed to gather over the moon and shortly an entire gloom overspread the face of the heavens. It was then that I heard an aweful sound from above like thunder: to this succeeded the shrill sound of unknown instruments borne on the blasts of wind, violent gusts that sung in the cave. Next a full choir of clear loud harmony seemed to join in breathing an inspiration unfelt before and then to roll away in Æther. As I felt the influence of this musick, my senses were revived and strengthened in a tone of heroism.

A feeble glimmer at a vast distance in the cave attracted my sight. It augmented till I beheld two tall lucid forms advancing hand in hand; their white vesture was resplendent apparently without a cause and diffused a moonish lustre on the craggy arches which bent over the Grots.[2] They glided along till they stopped right opposite to the Bramin, who at that moment arose from the ground. 'Terminga,' (addressing himself to that which shone next me) 'is all prepared?'

'All waits the stranger,' replied the form with a faint voice like a distant flute.

'Malich,' (to the other) 'hast thou opened the iron portal?'

'The sacred grot may now be approached,' answered Malich.

'Nothing remains, my son,' said the Bramin, 'but the performance of your resolution. Follow these freely; commit yourself to them. Silently they must execute their orders. Silently they must be obeyed. I must retire. Expect no further encouragement. Rely on no supernatural interposition; seek consolation in our own bosom and you will find it. We shall meet again in splendour; think of that moment. Direct your thoughts to that point; let them dwell on

---

[1] In his teens, Beckford had taught himself Persian and Arabic.
[2] Grottoes.

expectation and repose on hope. Everything now depends on your conduct. Should you reluctantly linger on the brink of initiation or hesitate one instant the performance of what these will point out to you, never hope to behold the light of the sun. I will not mistrust my son,' continued the Bramin and retiring into a recess of the cavern left me between Malich and Terminga.

There was nothing ghastly in the countenances of my guides but the luminous quality with which their bodies was invested occasioned me to shrink back from them. My resolution soon returned and fluctuating between hope and fear I sincerely resigned myself to them. The moment I had inwardly determined this I found myself moving along with the same imperceptible motion as my guides whose feet did not seem to touch the pavement. In this manner we skimmed along the immense hollow space where the most uninterrupted silence prevailed. Now and then, indeed, I could just distinguish drops clear as crystals, dripping one by one from the icicles that hung over my head. The light which streamed on all sides from my guides illuminated the concave vault above and nothing perhaps can exceed the splendour of the appearance as we advanced farther and farther. Crystals of every form, of every colour, tinged with the rays from Malich and Terminga grew below, around and above us with the most luxuriant vegetation; minerals and ores of the most vivid hues were studded on the craggy arches which irregularly bent over our passage; some twinkled far, very far on high like stars in the firmament, others like the reflection of those luminaries in water shone on the pavement beneath. How shall I describe the lovely elegance of form with which nature has moulded these, her hidden production. Every grace, every beauty is lavished on the tall, slender wasted pillars of cristalization which cling to the sides and the roof of the cavern and then spread in bowers of web-like texture over the arches. The distance we had gone in the very womb of the mountain seemed prodigious, the time inconsiderable, such was the amazing swiftness of our motion.

The reflection of light glancing from crystal to crystal, streaming from arch to arch and from one brilliant mineral or spar to another, was exquisitely agreeable. The majestic roll of two distinct rivers, the one black, the other clear and receiving the play of the glittering ceiling above, added not a little to the enchantment of the scene. To give you an idea how I felt at seeing these objects would be without the circle of description. Let it suffice then to assure you that the outward appearance of the cave, its situation and the circumstances that attended my viewing it however striking were mean in comparison. The delight I experienced was very greatly tempered by the fears, the doubts, the apprehensions that continually tormented me with the idea of where I was going. This unpleasant thought was, as may easily be conceived, sufficient to check the perfection of my happiness nor indeed do I believe that there exists upon earth the circumstance of perfect enjoyment. Never in my life did I breathe with so much freedom or inhale such life as in the breezes of this cavern. I am convinced I was lifted above the rest of mortals. My motion, my sight that at once took in such extent and the spirit that invigorated my whole frame forced me to entertain that opinion. Thus was I wafted along to a spot where the grot extended and lengthening into aisles that looked boundless, all adorned in the same glittering manner, all producing groves of vegetable crystal and all glistening with rills of pure water trickling and oozing from every spar. The waters which flowed from every quarter formed labyrinths continually intersecting one another, would utterly have impeded or at least perplexed in a great degree the route of an unprotected mortal, were no obstructions to my way. We glided over them with the facility and elasticity of a feather borne up by the stream and advanced on their surface till we came to the edge of a torrent, a torrent of a magnitude that would have astonished an inhabitant of the banks of Niagara. Had I not been supported by extraordinary power, I should never have ventured a mere look down on this formidable deep from which arose a spray, at first sight like particles of rasped[1] diamonds, but on examination proved innumerable myriads of shining insects which the water dashes from its bosom. I found myself involved in this brilliant mist, when I recollected how we were to descend to the depths beneath as my guides directed their course apparently to that quarter, but before the recollection of an instant we shot down with the swiftness of a star beam and darkness for a moment screened my eyes from the splendours that had dazzled them. During this period my sense of hearing[2] was powerfully moved by the roar and complicated murmur of many waters, nor do I believe there is any sound on earth equal in loudness, the very echo was sufficient to deafen and when that echo was repeated again and again thro' the hollow caverns, grots and recesses of the mountain, imagine, if you dare, the sound. I cannot exactly tell how long my senses remained numbed. When they were unlocked I could distinguish, notwithstanding the winds and torrents that holloed in my ears, the hum and buzz of some sort of monstrous moths that whizzed by my ears; monstrous I call them, for surely the great noise they made could not proceed from small organs, and besides they were every second flapping full in my face and banging against my body with a violence that was far from inconsiderable. The light which had before proceeded from Malich and Terminga was extinguished the moment we entered these gloomy regions and as they observed the strictest silence I knew not whether they were with me or no; but I was grown callous with the wonders that had befallen me and, finding the supernatural motion I acquired in these caverns continue, supported myself with entire confidence. By degrees I proceeded till the noise of the waterfalls gradually lessened and my ears admitted the least sounds with the nicest exactitude. The flutter of some sort of wings, very high above, the cries and growling of animals that proceeded, I suppose, from the crevices in the rock and the very crawl and creeping of some kinds of reptiles underneath was plainly discernible. They seemed to swarm in great multitudes as I perceived a clammy crackling sound as they turned about one another, from

---

[1] Unpolished.
[2] It is remarkable that deaf people hear best during some great noise. Speak to them near a water mill and they will understand. [Beckford's note]

this reason I conjectured them to be of the serpent or lizard species. I may declare to have passed a great variety of climates, some hot, some wet, some cold, vapours strongly impregnated with sulphur and vitriol[1] wrapped round me like garments causing momentary pains and achings dreadfully acute. Others again conveyed the most heady fœtid smells and others grateful refreshing odours that restored me to life and vigour. The vapours continued for some time increasing in heat till they became so intense that I breathed with difficulty. They were clogged with a rich spicy perfume that made my head so giddy that I should have sunk under the oppression, had not I found myself sustained by something dense and soft. By this time I lamented with vehemence the privation of light, when suddenly a breeze of pure air restored me to every enjoyment. A vivid blaze of light flashed once more from the forms of Malich and Terminga who shone on each side of me with redoubled lustre. A heavenly radiance bright as the moon in full illuminated the spot I discovered with a silver light. I again regarded with pleasure the two rivers I observed before rolling along under an arched concave space blooming with groves of shining plants unlike any I had seen, some shooting in tall spires from the water, others bending in bowers over a little island formed by the streams and carpeted with a soft purple moss, spangled with innumerable white flowers, of a form, a texture and a delicacy you have no idea of on earth. These subterraneous productions have a finish, an elegance you can scarce conceive, much less execute. The roof seemed many hundred fathom high and towards the summit hovered several golden coloured clouds shot with vivid light and airy as muslin veils floating on the winds. Every gale (for many ranged thro'out this grot) shook the blossoms from the plants on the margin of the rivers and these blew about as the vehicles of insects that sucked their nourishment from their leaves. Conceive these clouds, these flowers, these insects in motion and surely you will delight in the brilliant flutter. When my eye had roved over these beautiful objects it directed itself to the termination of the scene where the arches, bowing down, seemed to touch the surface of the rivers which joining on the opposite side of the island looked as if they derived their common source from that quarter; but I had no time to observe, for my motion, which had subsided the instant I spent at gazing around, continued with repeated swiftness and brought me with my guides to the island. Here we once more stopped and my guides, reclining on the soft turf under the shade of a tall plant with broad leaves something like the banana, cropped some fruit and flowers with which it was braided at the same time and graciously presented them to me. I laid myself down at a respectful distance from them and with great humility received the present they tendered me. The smell of the flowers was reviving and the taste of the fruit and its effects exhilarating in a great degree. As I lay along the turf, I observed by the bright light which my guides cast immediately around them, various little animals of a beautiful form and covered with a soft down moving from flower to flower and tending their young which they concealed

---

[1] Sulphate of metal chemically combined with water.

in the white glossy leaves; they were so gentle and tame, that they suffered me to drop into their mouths, grain by grain, the seeds of the fruit I ate and expressed their gratitude by a low melodious sound accompanied by many little actions that expressed their confidence in me, such as uncovering their young and displaying to my sight their little magazines where they hoarded their provisions of seeds. I could observe also the broad leaves of the plant which waved over my head crowded with little beings so different from any you ever beheld that I despair of conveying an idea of them. The roots too of these plants which twisting together in fantastic forms hung over the water were not destitute of inhabitants. Here I discovered the nests of gigantic water fowl lined with their own feathers and teeming with a young brood as large and as white as swans. Their parents on the most distant shore of the river stalked about stately as ostriches and moved the sovereigns of their species. A variety of birds something like our swans, ducks and geese, but far more beautiful in their plumage swimming along the water brought roots, flowers and fruits to their respective young.

Malich roused me from my contemplations by kindly offering some liquid dew which was gathered in the ample flower of a large aloe[1] which sprouted out of the turf by his side. I quaffed the draught with great pleasure and soon after sunk into a profound repose. The time I slept, I am totally ignorant of, but when I awoke, judge of my surprize, when instead of the cheerful light, the busy animated scene, the lovely vegetation, the mild breeze and the soft moss, I found myself extended on the rough surface of a rugged rock in an immense gloomy cavern lofty but obscured by volumes of dark thick smoke rising in waving curls from an hearth of red hot iron on which burnt a tremendous fire fed with minerals distilling an oil which catching flame rolled its burning waves with a sullen fury along the hearth and then distilled in drops on the pavement. The red angry light which the fire diffused was just sufficient to shew the horrors which surrounded it, the black dingy vault, the uncouth crags of bare rock and the boiling waters of a rapid torrent which forming a frightful whirlpool in a gulph at the farther end of this dismal grot was there confounded with a darkness that looked substantial. I had every reason to imagine that I was in the neighbourhood of some volcano; the heat was more excessive than could be derived from the fire alone and in the channels and fissures of the rocks, down horrible chasms, flowed a fiery stream of molten gold, silver and other minerals indiscriminately mingled with ore and lava which sent forth black vapours that tinged the roof and the pavement with an infernal hue. My two companions, one at my head and the other at my feet, seemed to guard me as I lay on the sullied ground; their white raiment still retained its purity, but the glory which formerly played around them was obscured by the murky air of the place. The first reflection that entered my mind was how I was conveyed to this grot; no outlet, no entrance was visible, but after much search I perceived an iron grated door by

---

[1] I call it aloe; because it most resembled that plant amongst us; but it was very different. [Beckford's note]

which I imagine I was brought in, which I recollected the Bramin had mentioned before. 'What means this fire?' (cried I to myself) 'Surely the Bramin is an idolater and means to sacrifice me to his barbarous god.' As soon as I had thought those words, the countenances of my Malich and Terminga glowed with a flush of indignation. I saw my error and thought of the last words of the Sage. '*I will not mistrust my son.*' 'And what! shall I withdraw my confidence from him who reposed so much on me? shall I shrink? shall I doubt? shall I hesitate? Rather let me perish in the flames I dread. Yes, I behold the necessity of purification and I will meet it joyfully. It shall explode these vile mistrusts, these ungenerous fears.' The smile of approbation again returned and graced the features of my guides who instantly divesting me of my garments poured over me a balsamic oil which was to protect me in some measure from the fury of the flames. The struggle I own was violent. My arteries beat, my heart panted with unknown violence, my limbs refused to sustain me. I sought consolation in the countenances of the forms and found it. When I ventured to lift up my eyes, O horror of horrors! what objects did I behold on the farther side of the blazing hearth? Two ranks of ghastly spectres rose like exhalations from the vapours and formed a continued line from the fireside to the foaming whirlpool. Their tall meagre forms wrapped round with robes of a misty grey were calculated to inspire wonder, disgust and dread; their withered arms scarcely held the taper wands of steel with which they struck a multitude of sculls that sent forth a lamentable murmur that rung amongst the arches, and to this dire cadence they joined a mournful song that pierced my heart with despair and froze the current of my blood. Could you conceive all them at once opening their lank[1] wide mouths and from their scrannel[2] jaws sending forth dismal grating complaints in an unknown language and to a tune like the sound of an ancient portal which the winds turn on its hinges, you would shudder in a circle of the gayest pleasures. And yet there was sometimes a plaintive tone in their measures that inclined me to weep with compassion. Now they turned on me their hollow sockets, where their eyes gleamed feebly like expiring lamps and now they stretched forth their pale arms as if to implore that I would not pass. What this meant I could not well determine but a tremulous horror again threatened to overturn the resolute sentiments that had just before ruled. A look from Terminga that seemed to say 'And wilt thou then ...' made the scale of resolution again preponderate. The forms took advantage of this favourite moment and snatching me like a whirlwind wafted me thro' the flames. It would be vain to attempt describing the anguish that fired every pore; my blood seemed shrivelled; I felt.... Enough of these horrors! enough! more remain. The spectres vanished soon as I passed the hearth, but in what manner I cannot tell. I could distinguish or feel nothing but the present pain; every thing seemed fire and myself too, when by a violent and sudden transition I found myself committed to the whirlpool. Its eddies in an

---

[1] Empty, unfilled.
[2] Shrivelled.

instant almost totally deprived me of my senses, the waters seemed every-where to overpower me and with a gush that is inconceivable hurried me away seeming ten fathom deep and as precipitately dashed me against the low craggy roof that impended. How I escaped death is astonishing; at least I suffered all the horrors of its approach during the period before my senses were entirely gone. The current was bearing me away when the stupefaction[1] came on and what then became of me I cannot tell. When I awakened once more to life, I was cast upon a beach which felt like sand without the least glimmer of light. Here I lay a prey to every misery, my patience entirely exhausted, and for some moments destitute of every consolation, freezing with wet cold, covered with sharp pointed sands that some violent wind blew furiously against me and trickling with foetid unwholesome dews that fell one by one in large drops on my head. Yet, tho' attacked by a complication of calamities, the words of the Bramin shot into my mind; this dismal situation was perhaps the suspense I was to expect and that the happiness promised would soon follow was the hope that solaced the dreary hour, for so long do I imagine was the time I shivered on the beach. I could not help thinking my situation a little similar to that of the poor ghosts whom the ancients represented hovering on the banks of the Styx[2] whilst their bodies remained neglected and unhonoured with the rites of sepulchre.[3] Thank heaven I had not long to make any more reflections; an immense flow of water returned like the tides of the sea and washed me away under narrow craggy channels till at length the full blaze of that silver light which had delighted me before burst forth and a wave laid me gently on a shore which was carpeted with mossy herbage. A delicious refreshing slumber again made me sink down and reunited my wearied frame. Soon after I was called by a melodious voice. I looked up and beheld Malich and Terminga in all their radiance. These forms with looks of ineffable beneficence poured over me a balm which cast around a delicious odour. I arose, firm and unshaken, my mind clear, every sense restored and in a perfection I had never experienced, not even in the luminous cavern. Malich threw over me a robe of the purest white and shining with the same brilliancy as those which gleamed on him and his comrade. Terminga placed on my head a circle of light and with joy beaming in his eyes declared all performed.

'And now, young mortal,' continued the form, 'prepare thyself for those enjoyments of pure knowledge thou hast merited by thus daring the most formidable of elements. Now expect instruction from the lips of the good Moisasour[4] the master of our race. Behold the centre of the earth, its wonders, its sublimities: behold the influence of the all wise instinctive in the whole. Mark that silver radiance, which enlightens these abodes which ignorant men think enveloped in darkness, how goodly its effects on the

---

[1] Unconsciousness.
[2] River in Hades, the Greek mythological underworld.
[3] Burial rites.
[4] The name of the BRAMIN. [Beckford's note]

animals, the vegetation and the air. See how wonderfully adapted the least plant or insect to its situation. Cast your eyes to the horizon of rocks which terminates this particular valley. Do you observe that cloud of luminous insects, which hover near those distant caverns? They are destined to illuminate the plants and shrubs for the use of those white animals which you see cropping their flowers. Admire that uniform expanse of bright Æther, spread universally over the valley and judiciously concealing the craggy concave of the arching rocks, which laid open might appear disagreeably harsh and menacing to the sight. From this Æther which is composed of innumerable luminous particles, singly imperceptible, proceeds the serene mild light we enjoy. Often with a charming variety, meteors exhale from the mineral rocks that glide gently along for many hours gilding the rocks, the groves and the crystals with tints that no pencil can imitate. Some in the shape of smooth lucid globes of blueish fire roll down with the cataracts and hover over their streams, as they flow thro' the plain beneath. Others, something like your sun, shine amongst our bright clouds and for days and weeks regularly appear at the same hour and diffuse a gay, brilliant lustre, that enlivens every animal and every species of vegetation; but do not imagine they yield a more fervent degree of heat than we experienced in their absence. The temperate warmth we enjoy is occasioned by latent fires in the rocks tho' at a great distance. To the effect of these which answers to that of your sun, we owe that multitude of animals, and that luxuriant vegetation, with which we are blessed. It is their genial influence which cherishes the seeds of plants and the eggs of animals, which thaws those immense masses of ice which otherwise would choake up the hollows and concavities destined for inhabitants, and gives birth to rills which afford refreshment for the mossy turf and the many little reptiles that lurk under its covert. Altho' we have no sun to enlighten us by day or moon to direct our nocturnal hours, still we are not destitute of those divisions. At the same moment when your light declines and the day fades on the horizon, the Æther and the clouds which now glow with such lustre over your head equally lose their brightness, turn to deep blue which shortly darkens entirely. It is then that from the pores of every blossom and every flower, from under each leaf and each bud, issue myriads of fiery insects, whose wings quiver with a brilliancy like that of the diamond and whose continual flutterings produce a vivid light, of whose excellence and beauty you will soon be the witness. Sometimes indeed when the winds, which range thro' these subterraneous wilds, are violent, these insects fearing to encounter the fury of the blasts providently remain in their compact cells. How then will you demand are these gloomy hours enlightened? The evil brings with it the remedy. Vapours fresh from the distant volcanoes are wafted on the wings of the winds and being impregnated with the particles of our Æther occasion long lucid tracks of mild light, which remains during several nights in the same position.'

Whilst Terminga was relating the admirable disposition of this part of the globe a troop of shining forms like his own arose from behind a promontory and glided towards us by a winding path, shaded with a variety of shrubs. These forms gleamed behind the plants, which casually intervened like the noon when it twinkles thro' deep thickets. As they approached I could not refrain questioning my guide about them.

'And who are these beings' (said I) 'whose lustre eclipses the greatest splendour of mortality, whose graceful motion is never seen on the surface of the earth?'

'They are,' answered Malich, 'the inhabitants of these regions, a pure simple race unsullied by fraud or rapine, unconscious of the love of gold, jewels or any other baubles, which men so much esteem. Their hands are never embrued in blood, their stomachs never gorged with animal food, their conduct never influenced by ambition or injustice. Wonder not therefore that their bodies untainted with gross and foul particles should emit such lively rays nor suffer yourself any longer to be lost in admiration of their motion. Our atmosphere, which probably you may fancy cloggy by thick exhalations, is on the contrary thin untainted with imperceptible insects and purged by salutary vapours from the minerals. You have experienced the air we here breathe; it has the property of rendering your whole frame elastic and as you have skimmed whole leagues in an instant, our motion, unopposed by the least obstruction, is accelerated by every breeze and becomes fleet as the thistle blossoms on the gale. By a deception in vision which to your eyes may seem unaccountable, objects which from their distance would appear faint and misty on the surface of the earth, are here brought near in a manner it would be needless as yet for me to explain. How distant should you imagine yon caverns hollowed beneath those prodigious steeps where the shrubs, the colour of the flowers is even discernible and the animals which feed amongst them?' I answered perhaps a furlong. 'They are' (replied he) 'about nine leagues from this spot. Nay, check not that rising smile; you will shortly be convinced of things far more improbable.'

By this time the forms had advanced close to us and stood confest in all their splendour. Nothing can be conceived more placid than their countenances, nothing more delightful than the innocence and serenity which sat upon their brow; no wrinkles, the effects of care; no distortions, the produce of passion; every grace, every charm the result of candor was there conspicuous. They modestly cast their eyes on the ground and seemed to wait till Terminga addressed them, on which account I conjectured he was of a superior race. After a short silence during which I observed Terminga to gaze on the circle of forms with entire complacency, he enquired whither their course was destined.

'The wise Moisasour,' replied the whole troop, as it were with one voice, 'has ordered us to hasten to a remote region, where the mortals have just discovered a copious vein of gold. Our master foreseeing the baneful effects his discovery might produce amongst those discontented frail beings, wills that we should close the vein and spare by that act the mischiefs it might occasion amongst them.'

''Tis well,' answered Terminga, 'the will of Moisasour is ever the result of prudence. And next,' continued he, 'we must pursue our course. Moisasour awaits us in the halls of the glorious.'

No sooner had he spoke than the troop of forms glided away and were soon behind the rocks. Myself and my guides were wafted swift across the ample plain whose beauties passed like dreams before my eyes and seemed to fleet with equal celerity as our motion. In a few instants we gained the extremity of the valley where something that resembled human art was apparent in the structure of nine grand portals raised over the mouths of as many yawning caverns. On a nearer survey I perceived those portals to be no more than a sort of niche or entablature on which was engraved a variety of characters entirely unknown to me. The rocks above the caves [were] covered with the most flourishing growth of shrubs and aromatic plants that bespoke the fertility of the soil in which they grew. Some of these bowed their leafy branches quite over the mouths of the several grots they shaded and others retired amongst the nooks and crevices afforded their covert to these concealments. The heighth of the precipices was astonishing when I stood under them and looking upwards beheld grove above grove and peak above peak, I was lost in amazement. My motion, which had abated during a space just sufficient to allow my observing in the most cursory manner the objects which presented themselves around, again returned and hurried me together with my guides into one of the vast caverns I have mentioned. It was divided by at least three thousand massy columns into the most stately halls decorated with colonades of slender pillars inconceivably striking. The lesser order of pillars was formed of a clear white crystalisation, exquisitely beautiful. They supported neither frieze nor cornice, nor any ornament in the least degree consistent with the rules of architecture we observe on the surface of the earth, but sustained on their airy capitals a variety of glistening garlands composed of spars and intermixed like the branches which form our bowers. The pavement in some measure corresponded with the roof. Figure to yourself a variety of marble, agates, jaspers and other stones some of which you are utterly unacquainted with, all painted by the hand of nature with an infinity of elegant veins, all gleaming with the polish of a mirror and reflecting every object in the same manner. Mark how the pavement, like a lake of marble, extends amongst this spacious labyrinth of columns as far as your eye can reach. Deny, if you are able, the beauty of the scene. As we wound along the aisles, the sounds of harmony came pealing from the recesses of the subterrene.[1] I fancied I could distinguish the voice of Nouronihar. Terminga perceived my disturbance and willing to alleviate my impatience increased our motion with a rapidity that shortly left behind the halls and the pillars. We darted along a gallery of prodigious length, the pavement, roof, and walls entirely formed of polished agate which reflected our forms like a looking glass. We passed too hastily for me to observe with any degree of certainty the objects in the gallery; but I could not help being struck with two ranges of colossal statues placed regularly in niches one each side illuminated by a line of bright lambent flames which played about the sceptres they held in their hands. These fires blazed on innumerable golden altars with a vivacity

---

[1] I have made bold with this frenchified expression. [Beckford's note]

hat dazzled my eyes. Just as I was about to enquire the meaning of the culptures around me, we arrived at a vast arch closed by a portal of ebony, vhose valves flying open of a sudden with a sound that rung amongst the ltars, displayed an immensely spacious concave, unsupported by any visible ause and glowing with a refulgence that proceeded from an orb of the most rilliant hue suspended from the centre by chains that, almost imperceptible, vore the appearance of sunbeams. Under the orb I beheld a flight of many undred steps covered with a rich carpet of purple which imitated the mossy erbage of the subterraneous valleys. On every step sat a lucid form increasng in glory and stature the nearer they approached Moisasour who was eated on the summit of the steps while Nouronihar reclined at his feet.

'With this state the Bramin receives those,' said Terminga, 'who have nerited his protection by boldly contemning the terrors which encircle his bode. Advance and present yourself to him as initiated. Nouronihar will no onger fly your presence.'

As I ascended the steps in obedience to the directions of Terminga, the orb larted forth vivid flashes of light, the forms snatched each an instrument vhose shape and sound were equally new and joining in full accord hailed ne with harmony that lifted me to the very portal of heaven. How you would e enraptured could you behold those elegant forms sweeping the chords of heir golden instruments and rising of a sudden to a majestic stature, then vaving with an universal motion the luminous circle which tinged their rows with radiance, what would be your ecstasy could their sounds reach our ears. See how they lower the glories which surround them at the noment Moisasour quits his exalted seat and, leading Nouronihar, descends o meet me.

'Yes, I am not deceived,' exclaimed the Sage, 'my doubts are dissipated like he dreams of the night. Witness that orb, with what pleasure I behold the appy change resolution has effected. Away terrestrial prejudices. A moral of :urope has succeeded nor has he suffered hesitation to linger on his actions. 'o one purport they have tended and behold that end attained, to arrive at he goal, beheld as the termination of a long perspective. Look around, no rengui ever beheld the glories which the earth conceals in her centre. The nariner who after the experience of many years has traversed the oceans vhich encircle the surface of the globe exults with the thoughts of having urveyed the wide extended planet he inhabits, but how little doth he imagine hat nature veils in the caverns of the earth another world flourishing with as air a creation as that with which he is acquainted; but these wonders are arefully concealed from profane eyes. Had you not been inspired with a upernatural courage, the access of the cavern where you first beheld Nour-nihar and heard the melody of these beings which inhabit our region, would ave still remained enveloped in obscurity. In vain you would have clamber-d the Appenines and in vain presented yourself on the peak which overlooks ts entrance. You fancy in general that nature partial to your face has estowed her favors with unbounded liberality and that it is ye which she has laced at the summit of her works; but learn that these beings which you

have here beheld shining around are indued with faculties of which you hav
no idea. Their motion you have already observed and in some measur
required by breathing the air of our abode, so far you can form an idea; bu
think how glorious the power which invisibly can witness all the transaction
of men, can survey not only their outward actions but dive into the thought
of their hearts and trace them from their source. Recollect that the forms wh
conducted you, followed exactly the resolutions of your soul and without th
utmost sincerity on your part remained inactive. When on the brink of th
burning hearth you shrunk back with fear and at the moment you enter
tained suspicions injurious to my race, the visage of Malich was altered an
Terminga dreaded you would share the fate of others who had in vai
attempted the enterprize. Did you not remark also that instant your hear
dictated a contempt of danger, the initiation was effected and you wer
wafted thro' the flames? But let me dwell no longer on the agonies you hav
suffered. Let is suffice to assure you that these beings exceed in many respect
the race which bespreads your earth. Mark that they regard you withou
astonishment. Are you not surprized at this seeming indifference when a nev
object appears? Certainly you are, but know that they often fleet unsee
along your empires and silently contemplate the affairs of mankind. Lik
exhalations they rise from the depths of their caverns and vanish like depart
ing vapours. The regions they chiefly delight to visit are those luxurian
forests which shade the valleys of the Andes. Here they frequently hol
converse with the simple descendants of those former rulers of the West, th
mighty Incas.[1] Embosomed in these aromatic groves they teach them t
adore the power who formed the sun and directed his genial influence on th
planets he enlightens. Sometimes the traveller wandering amongst thos
silent regions is surprized by their lucid forms glancing amongst the meteor
and sporting in the rainbows he contemplates beneath. Towards the extrem
peak of Catopaxi in a climate where the atmosphere still finer than in th
luminous cavern you so lately beheld, is purified by eternal fires, our rac
have hollowed an entrance to their subterraneous habitations. These statel
caves which form in a manner the portals of our abode are never viewed b
any except the genuine natives of the valleys immediately beneath. Unknow
to the rest of mankind these wilds are never imprinted with their steps, fo
the material frames of mortals in general and especially those of Europe ar
almost incapable of breathing so refined an air. These Firenguis deterred b
sudden eruptions, furious cataracts and hurricanes that in a moment stre
their tracks with desolation, lurk in their confined districts without scarc
venturing a look on the tremendous mass which occasions such formidabl
convulsions; but the Peruvians on the contrary mildly give way to th
elemental war and abandoning themselves entirely to the dispensations o
Providence smile on the dangers which sometime menace their habitations
Far from murmuring or blaspheming against the will of heaven they regar
these tempests with religious reverence and venerate the power in all th

[1] Ancient inhabitants of Peru.

majesty of his anger. The elders of these happy tribes separating from the youth who lead an active life in the forests, ascend when age has in a manner consecrated them to us even to the verge of our glistening caverns and there lifted above the storms, the vapours and the concerns of humanity enjoy all the sublimity of meditation. In this region they remain till death delivers them to the Æther of souls. With what delight we dwell upon the genuine descendants of those patriarchs who in former times were esteemed worthy of the interposition of the creator of all things. These and these alone are conversant with the pure spirits that move at this instant around us.

'Oftentimes in a glittering train they issue from the very womb of the mountain and summoning a synod of the Peruvian sages lead them to the pinnacle of Catopaxi at the hour of midnight. From this elevation they point out the worlds that roll thro' the heavens, describe the track of planets and notice remote moons that revolve around stars of whose magnitude your astronomers are ignorant. The faculties of vision are enjoyed with an infinite superiority on such an elevation. No fogs, no vapours obstruct the sight. It is these lofty regions which the moon enlightens with all her splendour. A perfect tranquillity prevails on the peak of Catopaxi. The air never vexed by tempests enjoys a continual serenity free from change except when a mild dew descends and diffuses a refreshing coolness. Altho' the dense atmosphere which envelops the world beneath generally screens the prospects presented on its surface, yet what can be more glorious than the extent of the skies, those azure plains where myriads of objects offer themselves to view, all beaming with a radiance of which they seem divested when gazed at from the empires below. The moon and the luminary girdle which enlightens Saturn shine confest without the aid of mechanical instruments and in the same manner the satellites of various planets and others of which ye have no conception are discernible at the first glance. Wonder not therefore that sages are ambitious of such a residence; but an experienced age must have stamped their characters with wisdom before our beings conduct them to the highest pitch of exaltation. When this glorious period arrives, they quit their kindred in the vallies never to return and abandon themselves solely to divine contemplation. Nor ever more do they behold the habitations they have quitted unless the clouds and vapours as they fleet present a transitory gleam of the grove, the verdure and the charms of the regions below.

'Methinks at this moment I view them seated on the mountain brow under the serene expanse of Æther. At their feet many fathom down, the empire of the winds raging amongst the atmosphere of your world. Aweful thunders that roll for hours reecho along the precipices. Lightnings, flashing from the ocean of vapours and darting in forked streams, till lost amongst eternal fogs, precipitate their fire on the valleys. Now I perceive them stretched on the ground, hanging over the volumes of our sciences. Now I behold them encircled by forms far superior in every excellence to.... But let me cease nor crowd your senses with farther subjects of astonishment. Your frame has occasion for sustenance.

'Let us enter the recesses of my habitation. What you have as yet seen is but the portal. . . .' My attention had been so earnestly fixed by the conversation of the Bramin that I did not perceive for some time after he had finished speaking, the solitude of the immense dome. The forms had all left us and Nouronihar and the Bramin were the only beings visible in the vast space around. They were both reclined on the purple steps and seemed ruminating in silence. For my part I took advantage of the profound stillness to contemplate my present situation. 'And I am then sunk into the centre of the globe. Have I the prodigious chain of Alps piled over my head? Is it possible that I am awake? Can a mortal have penetrated thro' such spacious grottos? How can I have sustained the flames, the whirlpool and all their attendant horrors? Surely my frame must have been overcome by such repeated attacks and from such formidable elements? Yet all these circumstances seem fresh in my memory; my sense of feeling has been most uncommonly exquisite; I have seen, I have heard, I have tasted; and could I dream of these senses with like perfection? Is it possible that I could reason and reflect as I do at this very moment in my sleep? With what distinctness I survey this stupendous dome studded with glittering gems, that orb which flashes so clear a light, that pavement of agate with all its mazy veins, those steps, this purple carpet and more than all that elegant female and that venerable seer; and are they illusions? Do I not hear that rill which falls from one shell to another? Certainly I can distinguish the leaping of fish in its clear waters. Do I not also inhale the incense of those spice trees which are placed in vases on the edges of the steps? Can I enjoy these faculties and dream?'

VATHEK

AN ARABIAN TALE, 1786

Text established by Kenneth W. Graham as part of a doctoral thesis in the University of London, 1971. The editor's notes and the notes prepared by Kenneth Graham run in a single series at the foot of the page, Graham's notes distinguished by [K.G.]. A [B] in the text indicates a note approved by Beckford. Since Beckford always intended these notes to be read as part of the text, they are gathered at the end of it. The running head of the first edition was 'A History of the Caliph Vathek'.

VATHEK

Vathek,[1] ninth Caliph[B] of the race of the Abassides, was the son of Motassem, and the grandson of Haroun al Raschid. From an early accession to the throne, and the talents he possessed to adorn it, his subjects were induced to expect that his reign would be long and happy. His figure was pleasing and majestic; but when he was angry, one of his eyes became so terrible,[B] that no person could bear to behold it; and the wretch upon whom it was fixed, instantly fell backward, and sometimes expired. For fear, however, of depopulating his dominions and making his palace desolate, he but rarely gave way to his anger.

Being much addicted to women and the pleasures of the table, he sought by his affability, to procure agreeable companions; and he succeeded the better as his generosity was unbounded and his indulgencies unrestrained: for he did not think, with the Caliph Omar Ben Abdalaziz[B] that it was necessary to make a hell of this world to enjoy paradise in the next.

He surpassed in magnificence all his predecessors. The palace of Alkoremi, which his father, Motassem, had erected on the hill of Pied Horses, and which commanded the whole city of Samarah,[B] was, in his idea far too scanty: he added, therefore, five wings, or rather other palaces, which he destined for the particular gratification of each of the senses.

In the first of these were tables continually covered with the most exquisite dainties; which were supplied both by night and by day, according to their constant consumption; whilst the most delicious wines and the choicest cordials flowed forth from a hundred fountains that were never exhausted. This palace was called *The Eternal or unsatiating Banquet.*

The second was styled, *The Temple of Melody,* or *The Nectar of the Soul.* It was inhabited by the most skilful musicians and admired poets of the time; who not only displayed their talents within, but dispersing in bands without, caused every surrounding scene to reverberate their songs; which were continually varied in the most delightful succession.[B]

The palace named *The Delight of the Eyes,* or *The Support of Memory,* was one entire enchantment. Rarities, collected from every corner of the earth were there found in such profusion as to dazzle and confound, but for the order in which they were arranged. One gallery exhibited the pictures of the celebrated Mani,[B] and statues, that seemed to be alive. Here a well-

---

[1] Vathek was an historical figure, Caliph al-Wathik Bı'llah who died in 847 AD although Beckford's caliph shares the characteristics of other historical figures. See Boyd Alexander, *E.W.S.*, p. 91 ff.

managed perspective attracted the sight; there the magic of optics agreeably deceived it: whilst the naturalist on his part, exhibited in their several classes the various gifts that Heaven had bestowed on our globe. In a word, Vathek omitted nothing in this palace, that might gratify the curiosity of those who resorted to it, although he was not able to satisfy his own; for, of all men, he was the most curious.

The Palace of Perfumes, which was termed likewise *The Incentive to Pleasure*, consisted of various halls, where the different perfumes which the earth produces were kept perpetually burning in censers of gold. Flambeaux and aromatic lamps were here lighted in open day. But the too powerful effects of this agreeable delirium might be alleviated by descending into an immense garden, where an assemblage of every fragrant flower diffused through the air the purest odours.

The fifth[1] palace, denominated *The Retreat of Mirth*, or *The Dangerous*, was frequented by troops of young females beautiful as the Houris,[B] and not less seducing; who never failed to receive with caresses, all whom the Caliph allowed to approach them, and enjoy a few hours of their company.

Notwithstanding the sensuality in which Vathek indulged, he experienced no abatement in the love of his people, who thought that a sovereign giving himself up to pleasure, was as able to govern, as one who declared himself an enemy to it. But the unquiet and impetuous disposition of the Caliph would not allow him to rest there. He had studied so much for his amusement in the life-time of his father, as to acquire a great deal of knowledge, though not a sufficiency to satisfy himself; for he wished to know every thing; even sciences that did not exist. He was fond of engaging in disputes with the learned, but did not allow them to push their opposition with warmth. He stopped with presents the mouths of those whose mouths could be stopped; whilst others, whom his liberality was unable to subdue, he sent to prison to cool their blood; a remedy that often succeeded.

Vathek discovered also a predilection for theological controversy; but it was not with the orthodox that he usually held. By this means he induced the zealots to oppose him, and then persecuted them in return; for he resolved, at any rate, to have reason on his side.

The great prophet, Mahomet, whose vicars the caliphs are, beheld with indignation from his abode in the seventh heaven,[B] the irreligious conduct of such a vicegerent. 'Let us leave him to himself,' said he to the Genii,[B] who are always ready to receive his commands: 'let us see to what lengths his folly and impiety will carry him: if he run into excess, we shall know how to chastise him. Assist him, therefore, to complete the tower,[B] which, in imitation

---

[1] In the first edition the palace titles were set in small capitals. These were changed to italics in the second edition, but in the case of the palace of mirth the compositor extended his italics to include the conjunction, 'or', originally in lower case roman and not part of the palace title. It was not possible to take the same action with the title at 29:24 '*The Eternal or unsatiating Banquet*', since Henley's translation of what are two distinct titles in the French versions ('*le Festin éternel* ou *l'Insatiable*') draws them together into a single title. [K.G.]

of Nimrod,[1] he hath begun; not, like that great warrior, to escape being drowned, but from the insolent curiosity of penetrating the secrets of heaven: – he will not divine the fate that awaits him.'

The Genii obeyed; and, when the workmen had raised their structure a cubit in the day time, two cubits more were added in the night. The expedition, with which the fabric arose, was not a little flattering, to the vanity of Vathek: he fancied, that even insensible matter shewed a forwardness to subserve his designs; not considering, that the successes of the foolish and wicked form the first rod of their chastisement.

His pride arrived at its height, when having ascended, for the first time, the fifteen hundred stairs of his tower, he cast his eyes below, and beheld men not larger than pismires;[2] mountains, than shells; and cities, than bee-hives. The idea, which such an elevation inspired of his own grandeur, completely bewildered him: he was almost ready to adore himself; till, lifting his eyes upward, he saw the stars as high above him as they appeared when he stood on the surface of the earth. He consoled himself, however, for this intruding and unwelcome perception of his littleness, with the thought of being great in the eyes of others; and flattered himself that the light of his mind would extend beyond the reach of his sight, and extort from the stars the decrees of his destiny.

With this view, the inquisitive Prince passed most of his nights on the summit of his tower, till becoming an adept in the mysteries of astrology, he imagined that the planets had disclosed to him the most marvellous adventures, which were to be accomplished by an extraordinary personage, from a country altogether unknown. Prompted by motives of curiosity, he had always been courteous to strangers; but, from this instant, he redoubled his attention, and ordered it to be announced, by sound of trumpet through all the streets of Samarah, that no one of his subjects, on peril of his displeasure, should either lodge or detain a traveller, but forthwith bring him to the palace.

Not long after this proclamation, arrived in his metropolis a man so abominably hideous that the very guards, who arrested him, were forced to shut their eyes, as they led him along: the Caliph himself appeared startled at so horrible a visage; but joy succeeded to this emotion of terror, when the stranger displayed to his view such rarities as he had never before seen,[B] and of which he had no conception.

In reality, nothing was ever so extraordinary as the merchandize[3] this stranger produced; most of his curiosities, which were not less admirable for their workmanship than splendour, had, besides, their several virtues

---

[1] Babylonian prince, see *Genesis* X:8–9.
[2] Ants.
[3] So irregular are the two instances in the 1823 edition of the substitution of an -*ise* ending for a word printed -*ize* in the 1816 edition that nothing is to be gained from including the 1823 revision. Consequently, 'merchandize' and 'enterprize' at 49:3, retain their 1816 spellings. The spelling, *enterprize*, appears without alteration at 54:1 of the 1823 edition.

described on a parchment fastened to each. There were slippers, which, by spontaneous springs, enabled the feet to walk; knives, that cut without motion of the hand; sabres, that dealt the blow at the person they were wished to strike; and the whole enriched with gems, that were hitherto unknown.

The sabres, especially, the blades of which, emitted a dazzling radiance, fixed, more than all the rest, the Caliph's attention; who promised himself to decipher, at his leisure, the uncouth characters engraven on their sides. Without, therefore, demanding their price, he ordered all the coined gold to be brought from his treasury, and commanded the merchant to take what he pleased. The stranger obeyed, took little, and remained silent.

Vathek, imagining that the merchant's taciturnity was occasioned by the awe which his presence inspired, encouraged him to advance; and asked him, with an air of condescension, who he was? whence he came? and where he obtained such beautiful commodities? The man, or rather monster, instead of making a reply, thrice rubbed his forehead, which, as well as his body, was blacker than ebony; four times clapped his paunch, the projection of which was enormous; opened wide his huge eyes, which glowed like firebrands; began to laugh with a hideous noise, and discovered his long amber-coloured teeth, bestreaked with green.

The Caliph, though a little startled, renewed his inquiries, but without being able to procure a reply. At which, beginning to be ruffled, he exclaimed: – 'Knowest thou, wretch, who I am, and at whom thou art aiming thy gibes?' – Then, addressing his guards, – 'Have ye heard him speak? – is he dumb?' – 'He hath spoken,' they replied, 'but to no purpose.' 'Let him speak then again,' said Vathek, 'and tell me who he is, from whence he came, and where he procured these singular curiosities; or I swear, by the ass of Balaam,[1] that I will make him rue his pertinacity.'

This menace was accompanied by one of the Caliph's angry and perilous glances, which the stranger sustained without the slightest emotion; although his eyes were fixed on the terrible eye of the Prince.

No words can describe the amazement of the courtiers, when they beheld this rude merchant withstand the encounter unshocked. They all fell prostrate with their faces on the ground, to avoid the risk of their lives; and would have continued in the same abject posture, had not the Caliph exclaimed in a furious tone – 'Up, cowards! seize the miscreant! see that he be committed to prison, and guarded by the best of my soldiers! Let him, however, retain the money I gave him; it is not my intent to take from him his property; I only want him to speak.'

No sooner had he uttered these words, than the stranger was surrounded, pinioned and bound with strong fetters, and hurried away to the prison of the great tower; which was encompassed by seven empalements of iron bars, and armed with spikes in every direction, longer and sharper than spits. The Caliph, nevertheless, remained in the most violent agitation. He sat down

[1] Biblical prophet, *Numbers* XXII–XXIV.

indeed to eat; but, of the three hundred dishes that were daily placed before him, he could taste of no more than thirty-two.

A diet, to which he had been so little accustomed, was sufficient of itself to prevent him from sleeping; what then must be its effect when joined to the anxiety that preyed upon his spirits? At the first glimpse of dawn he hastened to the prison, again to importune this intractable stranger; but the rage of Vathek exceeded all bounds on finding the prison empty; the grates burst asunder, and his guards lying lifeless around him. In the paroxism of his passion he fell furiously on the poor carcases, and kicked them till evening without intermission. His courtiers and vizirs exerted their efforts to soothe his extravagance; but, finding every expedient ineffectual, they all united in one vociferation – 'The Caliph is gone mad! the Caliph is out of his senses!'

This outcry, which soon resounded through the streets of Samarah, at length reached the ears of Carathis, his mother, who flew in the utmost consternation to try her ascendancy on the mind of her son. Her tears and caresses called off his attention; and he was prevailed upon, by her intreaties, to be brought back to the palace.

Carathis, apprehensive of leaving Vathek to himself, had him put to bed; and, seating herself by him, endeavoured by her conversation to appease and compose him. Nor could any one have attempted it with better success; for the Caliph not only loved her as a mother, but respected her as a person of superior genius. It was she who had induced him, being a Greek herself, to adopt the sciences and systems of her country which all good Mussulmans hold in such thorough abhorrence.

Judiciary astrology was one of those sciences, in which Carathis was a perfect adept. She began, therefore, with reminding her son of the promise which the stars had made him; and intimated an intention of consulting them again. 'Alas!' said the Caliph as soon as he could speak, 'what a fool I have been! not for having bestowed forty thousand kicks on my guards, who so tamely submitted to death; but for never considering that this extraordinary man was the same that the planets had foretold; whom, instead of ill-treating, I should have conciliated by all the arts of persuasion.'

'The past,' said Carathis, 'cannot be recalled; but it behoves us to think of the future: perhaps, you may again see the object you so much regret: it is possible the inscriptions on the sabres will afford information. Eat, therefore, and take thy repose, my dear son. We will consider, to-morrow, in what manner to act.'

Vathek yielded to her counsel as well as he could, and arose in the morning with a mind more at ease. The sabres he commanded to be instantly brought; and, poring upon them, through a coloured glass, that their glittering might not dazzle, he set himself in earnest to decipher the inscriptions; but his reiterated attempts were all of them nugatory: in vain did he beat his head, and bite his nails; not a letter of the whole was he able to ascertain. So unlucky a disappointment would have undone him again, had not Carathis, by good fortune, entered the apartment.

'Have patience, my son!' said she: – 'you certainly are possessed of every important science; but the knowledge of languages is a trifle at best; and the accomplishment of none but a pedant. Issue a proclamation, that you will confer such rewards as become your greatness, upon any one that shall interpret what you do not understand, and what is beneath you to learn; you will soon find your curiosity gratified.'

'That may be,' said the Caliph; 'but, in the mean time, I shall be horribly disgusted by a crowd of smatterers, who will come to the trial as much for the pleasure of retailing their jargon, as from the hope of gaining the reward. To avoid this evil, it will be proper to add, that I will put every candidate to death, who shall fail to give satisfaction: for, thank Heaven! I have skill enough to distinguish, whether one translates or invents.'

'Of that I have no doubt,' replied Carathis; 'but, to put the ignorant to death is somewhat severe, and may be productive of dangerous effects. Content yourself with commanding their beards to be burnt[B]: – beards in a state, are not quite so essential as men.'

The Caliph submitted to the reasons of his mother; and, sending for Morakanabad, his prime vizir, said, – 'Let the common criers proclaim, not only in Samarah, but throughout every city in my empire, that whosoever will repair hither and decipher certain characters which appear to be inexplicable, shall experience that liberality for which I am renowned; but, that all who fail upon trial shall have their beards burnt off to the last hair. Let them add, also, that I will bestow fifty beautiful slaves, and as many jars of apricots from the Isle of Kirmith, upon any man that shall bring me intelligence of the stranger.'

The subjects of the Caliph, like their sovereign, being great admirers of women and apricots from Kirmith, felt their mouths water at these promises, but were totally unable to gratify their hankering; for no one knew what had become of the stranger.

As to the Caliph's other requisition, the result was different. The learned, the half learned, and those who were neither, but fancied themselves equal to both, came boldly to hazard their beards, and all shamefully lost them. The exaction of these forfeitures, which found sufficient employment for the eunuchs, gave them such a smell of singed hair, as greatly to disgust the ladies of the seraglio, and to make it necessary that this new occupation of their guardians should be transferred to other hands.

At length, however, an old man presented himself, whose beard was a cubit and a half longer than any that had appeared before him. The officers of the palace whispered to each other, as they ushered him in – 'What a pity, oh! what a great pity that such a beard should be burnt!'[1] Even the Caliph, when he saw it, concurred with them in opinion; but his concern was entirely needless. This venerable personage read the characters with facility, and

---

[1] This is an instance of the careful reproduction in successive editions of an error in the 1816 edition. The 1786 reading accords with Beckford's normal practice in the 1816 edition in recording the transition from direct to indirect speech. Beckford's practice in a similar situation may be seen at 37:33. [K.G.]

explained them verbatim as follows: 'We were made where every thing is well made: we are the least of the wonders of a place where all is wonderful and deserving the[1] sight of the first potentate on earth.'

'You translate admirably!' cried Vathek; 'I know to what these marvellous characters allude. Let him receive as many robes of honour and thousands of sequins of gold as he hath spoken words. I am in some measure relieved from the perplexity that embarrassed me!' Vathek invited the old man to dine, and even to remain some days in the palace.

Unluckily for him, he accepted the offer; for the Caliph having ordered him next morning to be called, said – 'Read again to me what you have read already; I cannot hear too often the promise that is made me – the completion of which I languish to obtain.' The old man forthwith put on his green spectacles, but they instantly dropped from his nose, on perceiving that the characters he had read the day preceding, had given place to others of different import. 'What ails you?' asked the Caliph; 'and why these symptoms of wonder?' – 'Sovereign of the world!' replied the old man, 'these sabres hold another language today from that they yesterday held.' – 'How say you?' returned Vathek: – 'but it matters not; tell me, if you can, what they mean.' – 'It is this, my lord,' rejoined the old man: 'Woe to the rash mortal who seeks to know that of which he should remain ignorant; and to undertake that which surpasseth his power!' – 'And woe to thee!' cried the Caliph, in a burst of indignation, 'to-day thou art void of understanding: begone from my presence, they shall burn but the half of thy beard, because thou wert yesterday fortunate in guessing: – my gifts I never resume.' The old man, wise enough to perceive he had luckily escaped, considering the folly of disclosing so disgusting a truth, immediately withdrew and appeared not again.

But it was not long before Vathek discovered[2] abundant reason to regret his precipitation; for, though he could not decipher the characters himself, yet, by constantly poring upon them, he plainly perceived that they every day changed; and, unfortunately, no other candidate offered to explain them. This perplexing occupation inflamed his blood, dazzled his sight, and brought on such a giddiness and debility that he could hardly support himself. He failed not, however, though in so reduced a condition, to be often carried to his tower, as he flattered himself that he might there read in the stars, which he went to consult, something more congruous to his wishes; but in this his hopes were deluded: for his eyes, dimmed by the vapours of his head, began to subserve his curiosity so ill, that he beheld nothing but a thick, dun cloud,[3] which he took for the most direful of omens.

---

[1] The reading in the first edition accords with common sense and corresponds to all French versions. Cf. Lausanne edition, p. 18: 'où tout est merveilleux & digne d'être vû....' [K.G.]

[2] In cases of end-of-line hyphenation the readings in the first, fourth and fifth editions are not applicable. [K.G.]

[3] Thundercloud.

Agitated with so much anxiety, Vathek entirely lost all firmness; a fever seized him and his appetite failed. Instead of being one of the greatest eaters, he became as distinguished for drinking. So insatiable was the thirst which tormented him, that his mouth, like a funnel, was always open to receive the various liquors that might be poured into it, and especially cold water, which calmed him more than any other.

This unhappy prince, being thus incapacitated for the enjoyment of any pleasure, commanded the palaces of the five senses to be shut up; forebore to appear in public, either to display his magnificence, or administer justice, and retired to the inmost apartment of his harem.[1] As he had ever been an excellent husband, his wives, overwhelmed with grief at his deplorable situation, incessantly supplied him with prayers for his health, and water for his thirst.

In the mean time the Princess Carathis, whose affliction no words can describe, instead of confining herself to sobbing and tears, was closetted daily with the vizir Morakanabad, to find out some cure, or mitigation, of the Caliph's disease. Under the persuasion that it was caused by enchantment, they turned over together, leaf by leaf, all the books of magic that might point out a remedy; and caused the horrible stranger, whom they accused as the enchanter, to be every where sought for, with the strictest diligence.

At the distance of a few miles from Samarah stood a high mountain, whose sides were swarded with wild thyme and basil, and its summit overspread with so delightful a plain, that it might have been taken for the Paradise destined for the faithful. Upon it grew a hundred thickets of eglantine[2] and other fragrant shrubs; a hundred arbours of roses, entwined with jessamine and honey-suckle; as many clumps of orange trees, cedar, and citron; whose branches, interwoven with the palm, the pomegranate, and the vine, presented every luxury that could regale the eye or the taste. The ground was strewed with violets, hare-bells, and pansies; in the midst of which numerous tufts of jonquils, hyacinths, and carnations perfumed the air. Four fountains, not less clear than deep, and so abundant as to slake the thirst of ten armies, seemed purposely placed here, to make the scene more resemble the garden of Eden watered by four sacred rivers. Here, the nightingale sang the birth of the rose, her well-beloved, and, at the same time, lamented its short-lived beauty: whilst the dove deplored the loss of more substantial pleasures; and the wakeful lark hailed the rising light that re-animates the whole creation. Here, more than any where, the mingled melodies of birds expressed the various passions which inspired them; and the exquisite fruits, which they pecked at pleasure, seemed to have given them a double energy.

To this mountain Vathek was sometimes brought, for the sake of breathing a purer air; and, especially, to drink at will of the four fountains. His attendants were his mother, his wives, and some eunuchs, who assiduously

---

[1] Part of Muslim house or palace appropriated to women where wives and concubines live.

[2] Sweet-briar.

employed themselves in filling capacious bowls of rock crystal, and emulous-ly presenting them to him. But it frequently happened, that his avidity exceeded their zeal, insomuch, that he would prostrate himself upon the ground to lap the water, of which he could never have enough.

One day, when this unhappy Prince had been long lying in so debasing a posture, a voice, hoarse but strong, thus addressed him: 'Why dost thou assimilate thyself to a dog, O Caliph, proud as thou art of thy dignity and power?' At this apostrophe,[1] he raised up his head, and beheld the stranger that had caused him so much affliction. Inflamed with anger at the sight, he exclaimed: – 'Accursed Giaour![B] what comest thou hither to do? – is it not enough to have transformed a prince, remarkable for his agility, into a water budget? Perceivest thou not, that I may perish by drinking to excess, as well as by thirst?'

'Drink then this draught,' said the stranger, as he presented to him a phial of a red and yellow mixture: 'and, to satiate the thirst of thy soul, as well as of thy body, know, that I am an Indian; but, from a region of India, which is wholly unknown.'

The Caliph, delighted to see his desires accomplished in part, and flattering himself with the hope of obtaining their entire fulfilment, without a moment's hesitation swallowed the potion, and instantaneously found his health restored, his thirst appeased, and his limbs as agile as ever. In the transports of his joy, Vathek leaped upon the neck of the frightful Indian, and kissed his horrid mouth and hollow cheeks, as though they had been the coral lips and the lilies and roses of his most beautiful wives.

Nor would these transports have ceased, had not the eloquence of Carathis repressed them. Having prevailed upon him to return to Samarah, she caused a herald to proclaim as loudly as possible – 'The wonderful stranger hath appeared again; he hath healed the Caliph; – he hath spoken! he hath spoken!'

Forthwith, all the inhabitants of this vast city quitted their habitations, and ran together in crowds to see the procession of Vathek and the Indian, whom they now blessed as much as they had before execrated, incessantly shouting – 'He hath healed our sovereign; – he hath spoken! he hath spoken!' Nor were these words forgotten in the public festivals, which were celebrated the same evening, to testify the general joy; for the poets applied them as a chorus to all the songs they composed on this interesting subject.

The Caliph, in the meanwhile, caused the palaces of the senses to be again set open; and, as he found himself naturally prompted to visit that of Taste in preference to the rest, immediately ordered a splendid entertainment, to which his great officers and favourite courtiers were all invited. The Indian, who was placed near the Prince, seemed to think that, as a proper acknow-ledgment of so distinguished a privilege, he could neither eat, drink, nor talk too much. The various dainties were no sooner served up than they vanished, to the great mortification of Vathek, who piqued himself on being the

---

[1] Exclamatory address.

greatest eater alive; and, at this time in particular, was blessed with an excellent appetite.

The rest of the company looked round at each other in amazement; but the Indian, without appearing to observe it, quaffed large bumpers to the health of each of them; sung in a style altogether extravagant; related stories, at which he laughed immoderately; and poured forth extemporaneous verses, which would not have been thought bad, but for the strange grimaces with which they were uttered. In a word, his loquacity was equal to that of a hundred astrologers; he ate as much as a hundred porters, and caroused in proportion.

The Caliph, notwithstanding the table had been thirty-two times covered, found himself incommoded by the voraciousness of his guest, who was now considerably declined in the Prince's esteem. Vathek, however, being unwilling to betray the chagrin he could hardly disguise, said in a whisper to Bababalouk, the chief of his eunuchs, 'You see how enormous his performances are in every way; what would be the consequence should he get at my wives! – Go! redouble your vigilance, and be sure look well to my Circassians, who would be more to his taste than all of the rest.'

The bird of the morning had thrice renewed his song, when the hour of the Divan[B] was announced. Vathek, in gratitude to his subjects, having promised to attend, immediately arose from table, and repaired thither, leaning upon his vizir who could scarcely support him: so disordered was the poor Prince by the wine he had drunk, and still more by the extravagant vagaries of his boisterous guest.

The vizirs, the officers of the crown and of the law, arranged themselves in a semicircle about their sovereign, and preserved a respectful silence; whilst the Indian, who looked as cool as if he had been fasting, sat down without ceremony on one of the steps of the throne, laughing in his sleeve at the indignation with which his temerity had filled the spectators.

The Caliph, however, whose ideas were confused, and whose head was embarrassed, went on administering justice at haphazard; till at length the prime vizir,[B] perceiving his situation, hit upon a sudden expedient to interrupt the audience and rescue the honour of his master, to whom he said in a whisper: – 'My lord, the Princess Carathis, who hath passed the night in consulting the planets, informs you, that they portend you evil, and the danger is urgent. Beware, lest this stranger, whom you have so lavishly recompensed for his magical gewgaws,[1] should make some attempt on your life: his liquor, which at first had the appearance of effecting your cure, may be no more than a poison, the operation of which will be sudden. – Slight not this surmise; ask him, at least, of what it was compounded, whence he procured it; and mention the sabres, which you seem to have forgotten.'

Vathek, to whom the insolent airs of the stranger became every moment less supportable, intimated to his vizir, by a wink of acquiescence, that he would adopt his advice; and, at once turning towards the Indian, said – 'Get

---

[1] Gaudy trifles.

up, and declare in full Divan of what drugs was compounded the liquor you enjoined me to take, for it is suspected to be poison: give also, that explanation I have so earnestly desired, concerning the sabres you sold me, and thus shew your gratitude for the favours heaped on you.'

Having pronounced these words, in as moderate a tone as he well could, he waited in silent expectation for an answer. But the Indian, still keeping his seat, began to renew his loud shouts of laughter, and exhibit the same horrid grimaces he had shewn them before, without vouchsafing a word in reply. Vathek, no longer able to brook such insolence, immediately kicked him from the steps; instantly descending, repeated his blow; and persisted, with such assiduity, as incited all who were present to follow his example. Every foot was up and aimed at the Indian, and no sooner had any one given him a kick, than he felt himself constrained to reiterate the stroke.

The stranger afforded them no small entertainment: for, being both short and plump, he collected himself into a ball, and rolled round on all sides, at the blows of his assailants, who pressed after him, wherever he turned, with an eagerness beyond conception, whilst their numbers were every moment increasing. The ball indeed, in passing from one apartment to another, drew every person after it that came in its way; insomuch, that the whole palace was thrown into confusion and resounded with a tremendous clamour. The women of the harem, amazed at the uproar, flew to their blinds to discover the cause; but, no sooner did they catch a glimpse of the ball, than, feeling themselves unable to refrain, they broke from the clutches of their eunuchs, who, to stop their flight, pinched them till they bled; but, in vain: whilst themselves, though trembling with terror at the escape of their charge, were as incapable of resisting the attraction.

After having traversed the halls, galleries, chambers, kitchens, gardens, and stables of the palace, the Indian at last took his course through the courts; whilst the Caliph, pursuing him closer than the rest, bestowed as many kicks as he possibly could; yet, not without receiving now and then a few which his competitors, in their eagerness, designed for the ball.

Carathis, Morakanabad, and two or three old vizirs, whose wisdom had hitherto withstood the attraction, wishing to prevent Vathek from exposing himself in the presence of his subjects, fell down in his way to impede the pursuit: but he, regardless of their obstruction, leaped over their heads, and went on as before. They then ordered the Muezins[B] to call the people to prayers; both for the sake of getting them out of the way, and of endeavouring, by their petitions, to avert the calamity; but neither of these expedients was a whit more successful. The sight of this fatal ball was alone sufficient to draw after it every beholder. The Muezins themselves, though they saw it but at a distance, hastened down from their minarets, and mixed with the crowd; which continued to increase in so surprising a manner, that scarce an inhabitant was left in Samarah, except the aged; the sick, confined to their beds; and infants at the breast, whose nurses could run more nimbly without them. Even Carathis, Morakanabad, and the rest, were all become of the party. The shrill screams of the females, who had broken from their apartments, and were unable to extricate themselves from the pressure of the crowd, together with those of the eunuchs jostling after them, and terrified lest their charge should escape from their sight; the execrations of husbands, urging forward and menacing each other; kicks given and received; stumblings and over-throws at every step; in a word, the confusion that universally prevailed, rendered Samarah like a city taken by storm, and devoted to absolute plunder. At last, the cursed Indian, who still preserved his rotundity of figure, after passing through all the streets and public places, and leaving them empty, rolled onwards to the plain of Catoul, and entered the valley at the foot of the mountain of the four fountains.

As a continual fall of water had excavated an immense gulph in the valley whose opposite side was closed in by a steep acclivity, the Caliph and his attendants were apprehensive, lest the ball should bound into the chasm, and, to prevent it, redoubled their efforts, but in vain. The Indian persevered in his onward direction; and, as had been apprehended, glancing from the precipice with the rapidity of lightning, was lost in the gulph below.

Vathek would have followed the perfidious Giaour,[1] had not an invisible agency arrested his progress. The multitude that pressed after him were at once checked in the same manner, and a calm instantaneously ensued. They all gazed at each other with an air of astonishment, and notwithstanding that the loss of veils and turbans, together with torn habits, and dust blended with sweat, presented a most laughable spectacle, yet there was not one smile to be seen. On the contrary, all with looks of confusion and sadness returned in silence to Samarah, and retired to their inmost apartments, without ever reflecting, that they had been impelled by an invisible power into the extrava-gance, for which they reproached themselves: for it is but just that men, who so often arrogate to their own merit the good of which they are but instru-ments, should also attribute to themselves absurdities which they could not prevent.

The Caliph was the only person who refused to leave the valley. He commanded his tents to be pitched there, and stationed himself on the very edge of the precipice, in spite of the representations of Carathis and Moraka-nabad, who pointed out the hazard of its brink giving way, and the vicinity to the magician, that had so cruelly tormented him. Vathek derided all their remonstrances; and, having ordered a thousand flambeaux[2] to be lighted, and directed his attendants to proceed in lighting more, lay down on the slippery margin, and attempted, by the help of this artificial splendour, to look through that gloom, which all the fires of the empyrean[3] had been insufficient to pervade. One while he fancied to himself voices arising from the depth of the gulph; at another, he seemed to distinguish the accents of the Indian; but all was no more than the hollow murmur of waters, and the din

---

[1] Term of reproach used by Muslims to describe infidels, especially Christians. In this case Giaour is an agent of Eblis, the Prince of Darkness.

[2] Torches.

[3] Celestial fieryness.

of the cataracts that rushed from steep to steep down the sides of the mountain.

Having passed the night in this cruel perturbation, the Caliph, at day-break, retired to his tent; where, without taking the least sustenance, he continued to doze till the dusk of evening began again to come on. He then resumed his vigils as before, and persevered in observing them for many nights together. At length, fatigued with so fruitless an employment, he sought relief from change. To this end, he sometimes paced with hasty strides across the plain; and, as he wildly gazed at the stars, reproached them with having deceived him; but, lo! on a sudden, the clear blue sky appeared streaked over with streams of blood, which reached from the valley even to the city of Samarah. As this awful phenomenon seemed to touch his tower, Vathek at first thought of repairing thither to view it more distinctly; but, feeling himself unable to advance, and being overcome with apprehension, he muffled up his face in the folds of his robe.

Terrifying as these prodigies were, this impression upon him was no more than momentary, and served only to stimulate his love of the marvellous. Instead, therefore, of returning to his palace, he persisted in the resolution of abiding where the Indian had vanished from his view. One night, however, while he was walking as usual on the plain, the moon and stars were eclipsed at once, and a total darkness ensued. The earth trembled beneath him, and a voice came forth, the voice of the Giaour, who, in accents more sonorous than thunder, thus addressed him: 'Wouldest thou devote thyself to me, adore[1] the terrestrial influences, and abjure Mahomet? On these conditions I will bring thee to the Palace of Subterranean Fire. There shalt thou behold, in immense depositories, the treasures which the stars have promised thee; and which will be conferred by those intelligences, whom thou shalt thus render propitious. It was from thence I brought my sabres, and it is there that Soliman Ben Daoud[B] reposes, surrounded by the talismans that control the world.'

The astonished Caliph trembled as he answered, yet he answered in a style that shewed him to be no novice in preternatural adventures: 'Where art thou? be present to my eyes; dissipate the gloom that perplexes me, and of which I deem thee the cause. After the many flambeaux I have burnt to discover thee, thou mayest, at least, grant a glimpse of thy horrible visage.' – 'Abjure then Mahomet!' replied the Indian, 'and promise me full proofs of thy sincerity: otherwise, thou shalt never behold me again.'

The unhappy Caliph, instigated by insatiable curiosity, lavished his prom-ises in the utmost profusion. The sky immediately brightened; and, by the

[1] The 1786 version reads: " 'Wouldest thou devote thyself to me: Adore then the terrest-rial influences....' " In his revision it seems likely that Beckford, intending to tighten the structure of the sentence, changed the question mark to a comma, began *adore* with the lower case, and marked out "then". The compositor included all revisions but the substitu-tion of a comma for a question mark. The editorial emendation brings the text into agreement with the Lausanne version which, in a similar structure, uses a comma rather than a question mark. [K.G.]

light of the planets, which seemed almost to blaze, Vathek beheld the earth
open; and, at the extremity of a vast black chasm, a portal of ebony, before
which stood the Indian, holding in his hand a golden key, which he sounded
against the lock.

'How,' cried Vathek, 'can I descend to thee? — Come,[1] take me, and
instantly open the portal.' — 'Not so fast,' replied the Indian, 'impatient
Caliph! — Know that I am parched with thirst, and cannot open this door, till
my thirst be thoroughly appeased; I require the blood of fifty children. Take
them from among the most beautiful sons of thy viziers and great men; or,
neither can my thirst nor thy curiosity be satisfied. Return to Samarah;
procure for me this necessary libation; come back hither; throw it thyself into
this chasm, and then shalt thou see!'

Having thus spoken, the Indian turned his back on the Caliph, who,
incited by the suggestions of demons, resolved on the direful sacrifice. — He
now pretended to have retained his tranquillity, and set out for Samarah
amidst the acclamations of a people who still loved him, and forbore not to
rejoice, when they believed him to have recovered his reason. So successfully
did he conceal the emotions of his heart, that even Carathis and Morakanabad were equally deceived with the rest. Nothing was heard of but festivals
and rejoicings. The fatal ball, which no tongue had hitherto ventured to
mention, was brought on the tapis.[2] A general laugh went round, though
many, still smarting under the hands of the surgeon, from the hurts received
in that memorable adventure, had no great reason for mirth.

The prevalence of this gay humour was not a little grateful to Vathek, who
perceived how much it conduced to his project. He put on the appearance of
affability to every one; but especially to his viziers, and the grandees of his
court, whom he failed not to regale with a sumptuous banquet; during
which, he insensibly directed the conversation to the children of his guests.
Having asked, with a good-natured air, which of them were blessed with the
handsomest boys, every father at once asserted the pretensions of his own;
and the contest imperceptibly grew so warm, that nothing could have with-
holden them from coming to blows, but their profound reverence for the
person of the Caliph. Under the pretence, therefore, of reconciling the dis-
putants, Vathek took upon him to decide; and, with this view, commanded
the boys to be brought.

It was not long before a troop of these poor children made their appearance, all equipped by their fond mothers with such ornaments, as might give
the greatest relief to their beauty, or most advantageously display the graces
of their age. But, whilst this brilliant assemblage attracted the eyes and hearts

[1] According to Beckford's fairly consistent usage, an interrogative statement is followed
by a question mark. In this case the capitalized "Come" would indicate that Beckford
intended to use a question mark rather than a semicolon, since he never follows a semicolon
with a new sentence beginning with a capital letter. Beckford altered this passage in the
1786 edition to conform with his French-language edition of 1815. In that version a
question mark is used. [K.G.]

[2] Patterned, coloured carpet.

of every one besides, the Caliph scrutinized each, in his turn, with a malignant avidity that passed from attention, and selected from their number the fifty whom he judged the Giaour would prefer.

With an equal shew of kindness as before, he proposed to celebrate a festival on the plain, for the entertainment of his young favourites, who, he said, ought to rejoice still more than all, at the restoration of his health, on account of the favours he intended for them.

The Caliph's proposal was received with the greatest delight, and soon published through Samarah. Litters, camels, and horses were prepared. Women and children, old men and young, every one placed himself as he chose. The cavalcade set forward, attended by all the confectioners in the city and its precincts; the populace, following on foot, composed an amazing crowd, and occasioned no little noise. All was joy; nor did any one call to mind, what most of them had suffered, when they lately travelled the road they were now passing so gaily.

The evening was serene, the air refreshing, the sky clear, and the flowers exhaled their fragrance. The beams of the declining sun, whose mild splendour reposed on the summit of the mountain, shed a glow of ruddy light over its green declivity, and the white flocks sporting upon it. No sounds were heard, save the murmurs of the four fountains; and the reeds and voices of shepherds calling to each other from different eminences.

The lovely innocents destined for the sacrifice, added not a little to the hilarity of the scene. They approached the plain full of sportiveness, some coursing butterflies, others culling flowers, or picking up the shining little pebbles that attracted their notice. At intervals they nimbly started from each other for the sake of being caught again, and mutually imparting a thousand caresses.

The dreadful chasm, at whose bottom the portal of ebony was placed, began to appear at a distance. It looked like a black streak that divided the plain. Morakanabad and his companions, took it for some work which the Caliph had ordered. Unhappy men! little did they surmise for what it was destined. Vathek unwilling that they should examine it too nearly, stopped the procession, and ordered a spacious circle to be formed on this side, at some distance from the accursed chasm. The body-guard of eunuchs was detached, to measure out the lists intended for the games; and prepare the rings for the arrows of the young archers. The fifty competitors were soon stripped, and presented to the admiration of the spectators the suppleness and grace of their delicate limbs. Their eyes sparkled with a joy, which those of their fond parents reflected. Every one offered wishes for the little candidate nearest his heart, and doubted not of his being victorious. A breathless suspence awaited the contests[1] of these amiable and innocent victims.

The Caliph, availing himself of the first moment to retire from the crowd, advanced towards the chasm; and there heard, yet not without shuddering, the voice of the Indian; who, gnashing his teeth, eagerly demanded: 'Where

[1] The 1823 revision accords with all French-language versions in using the plural. [K.G.]

are they? – Where are they? – perceivest thou not how my mouth waters?' – 'Relentless Giaour!' answered Vathek, with emotion; 'can nothing content thee but the massacre of these lovely victims? Ah! wert thou to behold their beauty, it must certainly move thy compassion.' – 'Perdition on thy compassion, babbler!' cried the Indian: 'give them me; instantly give them, or, my portal shall be closed against thee for ever!' – 'Not so loudly,' replied the Caliph, blushing. – 'I understand thee,' returned the Giaour with the grin of an Ogre;[B] 'thou wantest no presence of mind: I will, for a moment, forbear.'

During this exquisite dialogue, the games went forward with all alacrity, and at length concluded, just as the twilight began to overcast the mountains. Vathek, who was still standing on the edge of the chasm, called out, with all his might: – 'Let my fifty little favourites approach me, separately: and let them come in the order of their success. To the first, I will give my diamond bracelet; to the second, my collar of emeralds; to the third, my aigret[1] of rubies; to the fourth, my girdle of topazes; and to the rest, each a part of my dress, even down to my slippers.'

This declaration was received with reiterated acclamations; and all extolled the liberality of a prince, who would thus strip himself, for the amusement of his subjects, and the encouragement of the rising generation. The Caliph, in the meanwhile, undressed himself by degrees; and, raising his arm as high as he was able, made each of the prizes glitter in the air; but, whilst he delivered it, with one hand, to the child, who sprung forward to receive it; he, with the other, pushed the poor innocent into the gulph; where the Giaour, with a sullen muttering, incessantly repeated; 'more! more!'

This dreadful device was executed with so much dexterity, that the boy who was approaching him, remained unconscious of the fate of his forerunner; and, as to the spectators, the shades of evening, together with their distance, precluded them from perceiving any object distinctly. Vathek, having in this manner thrown in the last of the fifty; and, expecting that the Giaour, on receiving him, would have presented the key; already fancied himself, as great as Soliman,[2] and, consequently, above being amenable for what he had done: – when, to his utter amazement, the chasm closed, and the ground became as entire as the rest of the plain.

No language could express his rage and despair. He execrated the perfidy of the Indian; loaded him with the most infamous invectives; and stamped with his foot, as resolving to be heard. He persisted in this till his strength failed him; and, then, fell on the earth like one void of sense. His vizirs and grandees, who were nearer than the rest, supposed him, at first, to be sitting on the grass, at play with their amiable children; but, at length, prompted by doubt, they advanced towards the spot, and found the Caliph alone, who wildly demanded what they wanted? 'Our children! our children!' cried they. 'It is, assuredly, pleasant,' said he, 'to make me accountable for accidents.

---

[1] Spray.
[2] Monarch of the world or Jewish King famed for his wisdom and justice.

Your children, while at play, fell from the precipice, and I should have experienced their fate, had I not suddenly started back.'

At these words, the fathers of the fifty boys cried out aloud; the mothers repeated their exclamations an octave higher; whilst the rest, without knowing the cause, soon drowned the voices of both, with still louder lamentations of their own. 'Our Caliph,' said they, and the report soon circulated, 'our Caliph has played us this trick, to gratify his accursed Giaour. Let us punish him for perfidy! let us avenge ourselves! let us avenge the blood of the innocent! let us throw this cruel prince into the gulph that is near, and let his name be mentioned no more!'

At this rumour and these menaces, Carathis, full of consternation, hastened to Morakanabad, and said: 'Vizir, you have lost two beautiful boys, and must necessarily be the most afflicted of fathers; but you are virtuous; save your master.' − 'I will brave every hazard,' replied the vizir, 'to rescue him from his present danger; but, afterwards, will abandon him to his fate. Bababalouk,' continued he, 'put yourself at the head of your eunuchs: disperse the mob, and, if possible, bring back this unhappy prince to his palace.' Bababalouk and his fraternity, felicitating each other in a low voice on their having been spared the cares as well as the honour of paternity, obeyed the mandate of the vizir; who, seconding their exertions, to the utmost of his power, at length, accomplished his generous enterprize; and retired, as he resolved, to lament at his leisure.

No sooner had the Caliph re-entered his palace, then Carathis commanded the doors to be fastened; but perceiving the tumult to be still violent, and hearing the imprecations which resounded from all quarters, she said to her son: 'Whether the populace be right or wrong, it behoves you to provide for your safety; let us retire to your own apartment, and, from thence, through the subterranean passage, known only to ourselves, into your tower: there, with the assistance of the mutes[B] who never leave it, we may be able to make a powerful resistance. Bababalouk, supposing us to be still in the palace, will guard its avenue, for his own sake; and we shall soon find, without the counsels of that blubberer Morakanabad, what expedient may be the best to adopt.'

Vathek, without making the least reply, acquiesced in his mother's proposal, and repeated as he went: 'Nefarious Giaour! where art thou? hast thou not yet devoured those poor children? where are thy sabres? thy golden key? thy talismans?' − Carathis, who guessed from these interrogations a part of the truth, had no difficulty to apprehend, in getting at the whole as soon as he should be a little composed in his tower. This Princess was so far from being influenced by scruples, that she was as wicked, as woman could be; which is not saying a little; for the sex pique themselves on their superiority, in every competition. The recital of the Caliph, therefore, occasioned neither terror nor surprize to his mother: she felt no emotion but from the promises of the Giaour, and said to her son: 'This Giaour, it must be confessed, is somewhat sanguinary in his taste; but, the terrestrial powers are always terrible; nevertheless, what the one hath promised, and the others can confer, will prove a sufficient indemnification. No crimes should be thought too dear for such a reward: forbear, then, to revile the Indian; you have not fulfilled the conditions to which his services are annexed: for instance; is not a sacrifice to the subterranean Genii[1] required? and should we not be prepared to offer it as soon as the tumult is subsided? This charge I will take on myself, and have no doubt of succeeding, by means of your treasures, which as there are now so many others in store, may, without fear, be exhausted.' Accordingly, the Princess, who possessed the most consummate skill in the art of persuasion, went immediately back through the subterranean passage; and, presenting herself to the populace, from a window of the palace, began to harangue them with all the address of which she was mistress; whilst Bababalouk, showered money from both hands amongst the crowd, who by these united means were soon appeased. Every person retired to his home, and Carathis returned to the tower.

Prayer at break of day was announced,[B] when Carathis and Vathek ascended the steps, which led to the summit of the tower; where they remained for some time though the weather was lowering and wet. This impending gloom corresponded with their malignant dispositions; but when the sun began to break through the clouds, they ordered a pavilion to be raised, as a screen against the intrusion of his beams. The Caliph, overcome with fatigue, sought refreshment from repose; at the same time, hoping that significant dreams might attend on his slumbers; whilst the indefatigable Carathis, followed by a party of her mutes, descended to prepare whatever she judged proper, for the oblation of the approaching night.

By secret stairs, contrived within the thickness of the wall, and known only to herself and her son, she first repaired to the mysterious recesses in which were deposited the mummies[B] that had been wrested from the catacombs of the ancient Pharaohs. Of these she ordered several to be taken. From thence, she resorted to a gallery; where, under the guard of fifty female negroes mute and blind of the right eye, were preserved the oil of the most venomous serpents; rhinoceros' horns; and woods of a subtile and penetrating odour, procured from the interior of the Indies, together with a thousand other horrible rarities. This collection had been formed for a purpose like the present, by Carathis herself; from a presentiment, that she might one day, enjoy some intercourse with the infernal powers: to whom she had ever been passionately attached, and to whose taste she was no stranger.

To familiarize herself the better with the horrors in view, the Princess remained in the company of her negresses, who squinted in the most amiable manner from the only eye they had; and leered with exquisite delight, at the sculls and skeletons which Carathis had drawn forth from her cabinets; all of them making the most frightful contortions and uttering such shrill chatterings, that the Princess stunned by them and suffocated by the potency of the exhalations, was forced to quit the gallery, after stripping it of a part of its abominable treasures.

[1] Spirits. See Beckford's note *below*, p. 99.

Whilst she was thus occupied, the Caliph, who instead of the visions he expected, had acquired in these unsubstantial regions a voracious appetite, was greatly provoked at the mutes. For having totally forgotten their deafness, he had impatiently asked them for food; and seeing them regardless of his demand, he began to cuff, pinch, and bite them, till Carathis arrived to terminate a scene so indecent, to the great content of these miserable creatures: 'Son! what means all this?' said she, panting for breath. 'I thought I heard as I came up, the shrieks of a thousand bats, torn from their crannies in the recesses of a cavern; and it was the outcry only of these poor mutes, whom you were so unmercifully abusing. In truth, you but ill deserve the admirable provision I have brought you.' – 'Give it me instantly,' exclaimed the Caliph; 'I am perishing for hunger!' – 'As to that,' answered she, 'you must have an excellent stomach if it can digest what I have brought.' – 'Be quick,' replied the Caliph; – 'but, oh heavens! what horrors! what do you intend?' 'Come; come;' returned Carathis, 'be not so squeamish; but help me to arrange every thing properly; and you shall see that, what you reject with such symptoms of disgust, will soon complete your felicity. Let us get ready the pile, for the sacrifice of to-night; and think not of eating, till that is performed: know you not, that all solemn rites ought to be preceded by a rigorous abstinence?'

The Caliph, not daring to object, abandoned himself to grief and the wind that ravaged his entrails, whilst his mother went forward with the requisite operations. Phials of serpents' oil, mummies, and bones, were soon set in order on the balustrade of the tower. The pile began to rise; and in three hours was twenty cubits high. At length darkness approached, and Carathis, having stripped herself to her inmost garment, clapped her hands in an impulse of ecstacy; the mutes followed her example; but Vathek, extenuated with hunger and impatience, was unable to support himself, and fell down in a swoon. The sparks had already kindled the dry wood; the venomous oil burst into a thousand blue flames; the mummies, dissolving, emitted a thick dun[1] vapour; and the rhinoceros' horns, beginning to consume; all together diffused such a stench, that the Caliph, recovering, started from his trance, and gazed wildly on the scene in full blaze around him. The oil gushed forth in a plenitude of streams; and the negresses, who supplied it without intermission, united their cries to those of the Princess. At last, the fire became so violent, and the flames reflected from the polished marble so dazzling, that the Caliph, unable to withstand the heat and the blaze, effected his escape; and took shelter under the imperial standard.

In the mean time, the inhabitants of Samarah, scared at the light which shone over the city, arose in haste; ascended their roofs; beheld the tower on fire, and hurried, half naked to the square. Their love for their sovereign immediately awoke; and, apprehending him in danger of perishing in his tower, their whole thoughts were occupied with the means of his safety. Morakanabad flew from his retirement, wiped away his tears, and cried out

[1] Dull brownish.

for water like the rest. Bababalouk, whose olfactory nerves were more familiarized to magical odours, readily conjecturing, that Carathis was engaged in her favourite amusements, strenuously exhorted them not to be alarmed. Him, however, they treated as an old poltroon, and styled him a rascally traitor. The camels and dromedaries were advancing with water; but, no one knew by which way to enter the tower. Whilst the populace was obstinate in forcing the doors, a violent north-east wind drove an immense volume of flame against them. At first, they recoiled, but soon came back with redoubled zeal. At the same time, the stench of the horns and mummies increasing, most of the crowd fell backward in a state of suffocation. Those that kept their feet, mutually wondered at the cause of the smell; and admonished each other to retire. Morakanabad, more sick than the rest, remained in a piteous condition. Holding his nose with one hand, every one persisted in his efforts with the other to burst open the doors and obtain admission. A hundred and forty of the strongest and most resolute, at length accomplished their purpose. Having gained the stair-case, by their violent exertions, they attained a great height in a quarter of an hour.

Carathis, alarmed at the signs of her mutes, advanced to the stair-case; went down a few steps, and heard several voices calling out from below: 'You shall, in a moment have water!' Being rather alert, considering her age, she presently regained the top of the tower; and bade her son suspend the sacrifice for some minutes; adding, – 'We shall soon be enabled to render it more grateful. Certain dolts of your subjects, imagining no doubt that we were on fire, have been rash enough to break through those doors, which had hitherto remained inviolate; for the sake of bringing up water. They are very kind, you must allow, so soon to forget the wrongs you have done them; but that is of little moment. Let us offer them to the Giaour, – let them come up; our mutes, who neither want strength nor experience, will soon dispatch them; exhausted as they are, with fatigue.' – 'Be it so,' answered the Caliph, 'provided we finish, and I dine.' In fact, these good people, out of breath from ascending fifteen hundred stairs in such haste; and chagrined, at having spilt by the way, the water they had taken, were no sooner arrived at the top, than the blaze of the flames, and the fumes of the mummies, at once overpowered their senses. It was a pity! for they beheld not the agreeable smile, with which the mutes and negresses adjusted the cord to their necks: these amiable personages rejoiced, however, no less at the scene. Never before had the ceremony of strangling been performed with so much facility. They all fell, without the least resistance or struggle: so that Vathek, in the space of a few moments, found himself surrounded by the dead bodies of the most faithful of his subjects; all which were thrown on the top of the pile. Carathis, whose presence of mind never forsook her, perceiving that she had carcasses sufficient to complete her oblation, commanded the chains to be stretched across the stair-case, and the iron doors barricadoed, that no more might come up.

No sooner were these orders obeyed, than the tower shook; the dead bodies vanished in the flames; which, at once, changed from a swarthy crimson, to a bright rose colour: an ambient vapour emitted the most exquisite fragrance; the marble columns rang with harmonious sounds, and the liquified horns diffused a delicious perfume. Carathis, in transports, anticipated the success of her enterprize; whilst her mutes and negresses, to whom these sweets had given the cholic, retired grumbling to their cells.

Scarcely were they gone, when, instead of the pile, horns, mummies and ashes, the Caliph both saw and felt, with a degree of pleasure which he could not express, a table, covered with the most magnificent repast: flaggons of wine, and vases of exquisite sherbet reposing on snow. He availed himself, without scruple, of such an entertainment; and had already laid hands on a lamb stuffed with pistachios, whilst Carathis was privately drawing from a fillagreen urn, a parchment[B] that seemed to be endless; and which had escaped the notice of her son. Totally occupied in gratifying an importunate appetite, he left her to peruse it without interruption; which having finished, she said to him, in an authoritative tone, 'Put an end to your gluttony, and hear the splendid promises with which you are favoured!' She then read, as follows: 'Vathek, my well-beloved, thou hast surpassed my hopes: my nostrils have been regaled by the savour of thy mummies, thy horns; and, still more by the lives, devoted on the pile. At the full of the moon, cause the bands of thy musicians, and thy tymbals,[1] to be heard; depart from thy palace, surrounded by all the pageants of majesty; thy most faithful slaves;[2] thy best beloved wives; thy most magnificent litters; thy richest loaden camels; and set forward on thy way to Istakhar.[B] There, I await thy coming: that is the region of wonders: there shalt thou receive the diadem of Gian Ben Gian; the talismans[3] of Soliman;[B] and the treasures of the pre-adamite sultans:[B] there shalt thou be solaced with all kinds of delight. – But beware how thou enterest any dwelling[B] on thy route; or thou shalt feel the effects of my anger.'

The Caliph, notwithstanding his habitual luxury, had never before dined with so much satisfaction. He gave full scope to the joy of these golden tidings; and betook himself to drinking anew. Carathis, whose antipathy to wine was by no means insuperable, failed not to pledge him at every bumper he ironically quaffed to the health of Mahomet.[B] This infernal liquor completed their impious temerity, and prompted them to utter a profusion of blasphemies. They gave a loose to their wit, at the expense of the ass of Balaam, the dog of the seven sleepers, and the other animals admitted into the paradise of Mahomet.[B] In this sprightly humour, they descended the fifteen hundred stairs, diverting themselves as they went, at the anxious faces they saw on the square, through the barbacans[4] and loop-holes of the tower;

[1] Kettledrums.
[2] To correct each instance of the careless use of the comma and semicolon would not be to present an accurate version of Beckford's text. However, in this instance of a long series with each element save one separated by a semicolon, it seemed reasonable to remove the anomaly. [K.G.]
[3] Stones or rings engraved with characters and supposed to have occult powers. They appear in many oriental tales of the eighteenth century.
[4] Open spaces in the wall.

and, at length, arrived at the royal apartments, by the subterranean passage. Bababalouk was parading to and fro, and issuing his mandates, with great pomp to the eunuchs; who were snuffing the lights and painting the eyes of the Circassians.[B] No sooner did he catch sight of the Caliph and his mother, than he exclaimed, 'Hah! you have, then, I perceive, escaped from the flames: I was not, however, altogether out of doubt.' – 'Of what moment is it to us what you thought, or think?' cried Carathis: 'go; speed; tell Morakanabad that we immediately want him: and take care, not to stop by the way, to make your insipid reflections.'

Morakanabad delayed not to obey the summons; and was received by Vathek and his mother, with great solemnity. They told him, with an air of composure and commiseration, that the fire at the top of the tower was extinguished; but that it had cost the lives of the brave people who sought to assist them.

'Still more misfortunes!' cried Morakanabad, with a sigh. 'Ah, commander of the faithful, our holy prophet is certainly irritated against us! it behoves you to appease him.' – 'We will appease him, hereafter!' replied the Caliph, with a smile that augured nothing of good. 'You will have leisure sufficient for your supplications, during my absence: for this country is the bane of my health. I am disgusted with the mountain of the four fountains, and am resolved to go and drink of the stream of Rocnabad.[B] I long to refresh myself, in the delightful valleys which it waters. Do you, with the advice of my mother, govern my dominions, and take care to supply whatever her experiments may demand; for, you well know, that our tower abounds in materials for the advancement of science.'

The tower but ill suited Morakanabad's taste. Immense treasures had been lavished upon it; and nothing had he ever seen carried thither but female negroes, mutes and abominable drugs. Nor did he know well what to think of Carathis, who, like a cameleon, could assume all possible colours. Her cursed eloquence had often driven the poor mussulman to his last shifts. He considered, however, that if she possessed but few good qualities, her son had still fewer; and that the alternative, on the whole, would be in her favour. Consoled, therefore, with this reflection; he went, in good spirits, to soothe the populace, and make the proper arrangements for his master's journey.

Vathek, to conciliate the Spirits of the subterranean palace, resolved that his expedition should be uncommonly splendid. With this view he confiscated, on all sides, the property of his subjects; whilst his worthy mother stripped the seraglios[1] she visited, of the gems they contained. She collected all the sempstresses and embroiderers of Samarah and other cities, to the distance of sixty leagues, to prepare pavilions, palanquins,[2] sofas, canopies, and litters for the train of the monarch. There was not left, in Masulipatan,

---

[1] Appartments for wives and concubines.
[2] The reasoning used in 49:20 applies here. In this case each element in the series but one is set off by a comma. [K.G.]

a single piece of chintz; and so much muslin had been brought up to dress out Bababalouk and the other black eunuchs, that there remained not an ell[1] of it in the whole Irak of Babylon.

During these preparations, Carathis, who never lost sight of her great object, which was to obtain favour with the powers of darkness, made select parties of the fairest and most delicate ladies of the city: but in the midst of their gaiety, she contrived to introduce vipers amongst them, and to break pots of scorpions under the table. They all bit to a wonder, and Carathis would have left her friends to die, were it not that, to fill up the time, she now and then amused herself in curing their wounds, with an excellent anodyne of her own invention: for this good Princess abhorred being indolent.

Vathek, who was not altogether so active as his mother, devoted his time to the sole gratification of his senses, in the palaces which were severally dedicated to them. He disgusted himself no more with the divan, or the mosque. One half of Samarah followed his example, whilst the other lamented the progress of corruption.

In the midst of these transactions, the embassy returned, which had been sent, in pious times, to Mecca. It consisted of the most reverend Moullahs[B] who had fulfilled their commission, and brought back one of those precious besoms[2] which are used to sweep the sacred Cahaba:[B] a present truly worthy of the greatest potentate on earth!

The Caliph happened at this instant to be engaged in an apartment by no means adapted to the reception of embassies. He heard the voice of Bababalouk, calling out from between the door and the tapestry that hung before it: 'Here are the excellent Edris al Shafei, and the seraphic Al Mouhateddin, who have brought the besom from Mecca, and, with tears of joy, entreat they may present it to your majesty in person.' – 'Let them bring the besom hither, it may be of use,' said Vathek. 'How!' answered Bababalouk, half aloud and amazed. 'Obey,' replied the Caliph, 'for it is my sovereign will; go instantly, vanish! for here will I receive the good folk who have thus filled thee with joy.'

The eunuch departed muttering, and bade the venerable train attend him. A sacred rapture was diffused amongst these reverend old men. Though fatigued with the length of their expedition, they followed Bababalouk with an alertness almost miraculous, and felt themselves highly flattered, as they swept along the stately porticos, that the Caliph would not receive them like ambassadors in ordinary in his hall of audience. Soon reaching the interior of the harem (where, through blinds of Persian, they perceived large soft eyes, dark and blue, that came and went like lightning) penetrated with respect and wonder, and full of their celestial mission, they advanced in procession towards the small corridors that appeared to terminate in nothing, but, nevertheless, led to the cell where the Caliph expected their coming.

'What! is the commander of the faithful sick?' said Edris al Shafei, in a low

---

[1] A measure equivalent to 45 inches.
[2] Brooms made of twigs.

voice to his companion? – 'I rather think he is in his oratory,' answered Al Mouhateddin. Vathek, who heard the dialogue, cried out: – 'What imports it you, how I am employed? approach without delay.' They advanced, whilst the Caliph, without shewing himself, put forth his hand from behind the tapestry that hung before the door, and demanded of them the besom. Having prostrated themselves as well as the corridor would permit, and, even in a tolerable semicircle, the venerable Al Shafei, drawing forth the besom from the embroidered and perfumed scarves, in which it had been enveloped, and secured from the profane gaze of vulgar eyes, arose from his associates, and advanced, with an air of the most awful solemnity towards the supposed oratory; but, with what astonishment! with what horror was he seized! – Vathek, bursting out into a villainous[1] laugh, snatched the besom from his trembling hand, and, fixing upon some cobwebs, that hung from the ceiling, gravely brushed them away till not a single one remained. The old men, overpowered with amazement, were unable to lift their beards from the ground: for, as Vathek had carelessly left the tapestry between them half drawn, they were witnesses of the whole transaction. Their tears bedewed the marble. Al Mouhateddin swooned through mortification and fatigue, whilst the Caliph, throwing himself backward on his seat, shouted, and clapped his hands without mercy. At last, addressing himself to Bababalouk! – 'My dear black,' said he, 'go, regale these pious poor souls, with my good wine from Shiraz,[B] since they can boast of having seen more of my palace than any one besides.' Having said this, he threw the besom in their face, and went to enjoy the laugh with Carathis. Bababalouk did all in his power to console the ambassadors; but the two most infirm expired on the spot: the rest were carried to their beds, from whence, being heart-broken with sorrow and shame, they never arose.

The succeeding night, Vathek, attended by his mother, ascended the tower to see if every thing were ready for his journey: for, he had great faith in the influence of the stars. The planets appeared in their most favourable aspects. The Caliph, to enjoy so flattering a sight, supped gaily on the roof; and fancied that he heard, during his repast, loud shouts of laughter resound through the sky, in a manner, that inspired the fullest assurance.

All was in motion at the palace; lights were kept burning through the whole of the night: the sound of implements, and of artizans finishing their work; the voices of women, and their guardians, who sung at their embroidery: all conspired to interrupt the stillness of nature, and infinitely delighted the heart of Vathek who imagined himself going in triumph to sit upon the throne of Soliman. The people were not less satisfied than himself: all assisted to accelerate the moment, which should rescue them from the wayward caprices of so extravagant a master.

---

[1] Nothing is to be gained from adopting the 1823 spelling, *villanous*, to replace the more accepted form, *villainous*, used in the copy-text. The 1816 spelling of the same word is retained at 64:18 also. [K.G.]

The day preceding the departure of this infatuated Prince, was employed by Carathis, in repeating to him the decrees of the mysterious parchment; which she had thoroughly gotten by heart; and, in recommending him, not to enter the habitation of any one by the way: 'for, well thou knowest,' added she, 'how liquorish thy taste is after good dishes and young damsels; let me, therefore, enjoin thee, to be content with thy old cooks, who are the best in the world: and not to forget that, in thy ambulatory seraglio, there are at least three dozen of pretty faces which Bababalouk hath[1] not yet unveiled. I myself have a great desire to watch over thy conduct, and visit the subterranean palace, which, no doubt, contains whatever can interest persons, like us. There is nothing so pleasing as retiring to caverns: my taste for dead bodies, and every thing like mummy[2] is decided: and, I am confident, thou wilt see the most exquisite of their kind. Forget me not then, but the moment thou art in possession of the talismans which are to open the way to the mineral kingdoms and the centre of the earth itself, fail not to dispatch some trusty genius to take me and my cabinet: for the oil of the serpents I have pinched to death will be a pretty present to the Giaour who cannot but be charmed with such dainties.'

Scarcely had Carathis ended this edifying discourse, when the sun, setting behind the mountain of the four fountains, gave place to the rising moon. This planet, being that evening at full, appeared of unusual beauty and magnitude, in the eyes of the women, the eunuchs and the pages who were all impatient to set forward. The city re-echoed with shouts of joy, and flourishing of trumpets. Nothing was visible, but plumes, nodding on pavilions, and aigrets shining in the mild lustre of the moon. The spacious square resembled an immense parterre variegated with the most stately tulips of the east.[B]

Arrayed in the robes which were only worn at the most distinguished ceremonials, and supported by his vizir and Bababalouk, the Caliph descended the great staircase of the tower in the sight of all his people. He could not forbear pausing, at intervals, to admire the superb appearance which every where courted his view: whilst the whole multitude, even to the camels with their sumptuous burdens,[3] knelt down before him. For some time a general stillness prevailed, which nothing happened to disturb, but the shrill screams of some eunuchs in the rear. These vigilant guards, having remarked certain cages of the ladies[B] swagging somewhat awry, and discovered that a few adventurous gallants had contrived to get in, soon dislodged the enraptured culprits and consigned them, with good commendations, to the surgeons of the serail. The majesty of so magnificent a spectacle, was not,

---

[1] The 1786 reading seems to be the correct one. The parallel reading in all French-language versions employs the past indefinite rather than the pluperfect tense. [K.G.]

[2] If intended as a pun, unforgivable.

[3] The 1823 revision brings the spelling of this word into conformity with the usage at 56:28 of the copy-text. In both editions of 1816 and 1823, however, the spelling, *burthening*, is maintained at 85:14. [K.G.]

however, violated by incidents like these. Vathek, meanwhile, saluted the moon with an idolatrous air, that neither pleased Morakanabad, nor the doctors of the law, any more than the viziers and grandees of his court, who were all assembled to enjoy the last view of their sovereign.

At length, the clarions and trumpets from the top of the tower, announced the prelude of departure. Though the instruments were in unison with each other, yet a singular dissonance was blended with their sounds. This proceeded from Carathis who was singing her direful orisons to the Giaour, whilst the negresses and mutes supplied thorough base, without articulating a word. The good Mussulmans fancied that they heard the sullen hum of those nocturnal insects, which presage evil; and importuned Vathek to beware how he ventured his sacred person.

On a given signal, the great standard of the Califat was displayed; twenty thousand lances shone around it; and the Caliph, treading royally on the cloth of gold, which had been spread for his feet, ascended his litter, amidst the general acclamations of his subjects.

The expedition commenced with the utmost order and so entire a silence, that, even the locusts were heard from the thickets on the plain of Catoul.[B] Gaiety and good humour prevailing, they made full six leagues before the dawn; and the morning star was still glittering in the firmament, when the whole of this numerous train had halted on the banks of the Tigris, where they encamped to repose for the rest of the day.

The three days that followed were spent in the same manner; but, on the fourth, the heavens looked angry; lightnings broke forth, in frequent flashes; re-echoing peals of thunder succeeded; and the trembling Circassians clung with all their might, to their ugly guardians. The Caliph himself, was greatly inclined to take shelter in the large town of Ghulchissar, the governor of which, came forth to meet him, and tendered every kind of refreshment the place could supply. But, having examined his tablets, he suffered the rain to soak him, almost to the bone, notwithstanding the importunity of his first favourites. Though he began to regret the palace of the senses; yet, he lost not sight of his enterprize, and his sanguine expectation confirmed his resolution. His geographers were ordered to attend him; but, the weather proved so terrible that these poor people exhibited a lamentable appearance: and their maps of the different countries spoiled by the rain, were in a still worse plight than themselves. As no long journey had been undertaken since the time of Haroun al Raschid, every one was ignorant which way to turn; and Vathek, though well versed in the course of the heavens, no longer knew his situation on earth. He thundered even louder than the elements; and muttered forth certain hints of the bow-string which were not very soothing to literary ears. Disgusted at the toilsome weariness of the way, he determined to cross over the craggy heights and follow the guidance of a peasant, who undertook to bring him, in four days, to Rocnabad. Remonstrances were all to no purpose; his resolution was fixed.

The females and eunuchs uttered shrill wailings at the sight of the precipices below them, and the dreary prospects that opened, in the vast gorges of

ie mountains. Before they could reach the ascent of the steepest rock, night
vertook them, and a boisterous tempest arose, which, having rent the
wnings of the palanquins and cages, exposed to the raw gusts the poor
idies within, who had never before felt so piercing a cold. The dark clouds
iat overcast the face of the sky deepened the horrors of this disastrous night,
isomuch that nothing could be heard distinctly, but the mewling of pages
nd lamentations of sultanas.[1]

To increase the general misfortune, the frightful uproar of wild beasts
esounded at a distance; and there were soon perceived in the forest they
vere skirting, the glaring of eyes, which could belong only to devils or tigers.
'he pioneers, who, as well as they could, had marked out a track; and a part
f the advanced guard, were devoured, before they had been in the least
pprized of their danger. The confusion that prevailed was extreme. Wolves,
gers, and other carnivorous animals, invited by the howling of their com-
anions, flocked together from every quarter. The crashing of bones was
eard on all sides, and a fearful rush of wings over head; for now vultures
lso began to be of the party.

The terror at length reached the main body of the troops which sur-
ounded the monarch and his harem at the distance of two leagues from the
cene. Vathek (voluptuously reposed in his capacious litter upon cushions of
ilk, with two little pages[B] beside him of complexions more fair than the
iamel of Franguistan, who were occupied in keeping off flies) was soundly
sleep, and contemplating in his dreams the treasures of Soliman. The shrieks
owever of his wives, awoke him with a start; and, instead of the Giaour
vith his key of gold, he beheld Bababalouk full of consternation. 'Sire,'
xclaimed this good servant of the most potent of monarchs, 'misfortune is
rrived at its height, wild beasts, who entertain no more reverence for your
acred person, than for a dead ass, have beset your camels and their drivers;
hirty of the most richly laden are already become their prey, as well as your
onfectioners, your cooks,[B] and purveyors: and, unless our holy Prophet
hould protect us, we shall have all eaten our last meal.' At the mention of
ating, the Caliph lost all patience. He began to bellow, and even beat himself
for there was no seeing in the dark). The rumour every instant increased;
nd Bababalouk, finding no good could be done with his master, stopped
oth his ears against the hurly burly of the harem, and called out aloud:
Come, ladies, and brothers! all hands to work: strike light in a moment!
ever shall it be said, that the commander of the faithful served to regale
hese infidel brutes.' Though there wanted not in this bevy of beauties, a
ufficient number of capricious and wayward; yet, on the present occasion,
hey were all compliance. Fires were visible, in a twinkling, in all their cages.
'en thousand torches were lighted[B] at once. The Caliph, himself, seized a
arge one of wax: every person followed his example; and, by kindling ropes
nds, dipped in oil and fastened on poles, an amazing blaze was spread. The
ocks were covered with the splendour of sun-shine. The trails of sparks,

---

[1] Wives or concubines of a sultan or caliph.

wafted by the wind, communicated to the dry fern, of which there wa
plenty. Serpents were observed to crawl forth from their retreats, witl
amazement and hissings; whilst the horses snorted, stamped the ground
tossed their noses in the air, and plunged about, without mercy.

One of the forests of cedar that bordered their way, took fire; [B] and th
branches that overhung the path, extending their flames to the muslins an
chintzes, which covered the cages of the ladies obliged them to jump out, at th
peril of their necks. Vathek, who vented on the occasion a thousand blas
phemies, was himself compelled to touch, with his sacred feet, the naked earth

Never had such an incident happened before. Full of mortification, shame
and despondence, and not knowing how to walk, the ladies fell into the dirt
'Must I go on foot!' said one: 'Must I wet my feet!' cried another: 'Must I soi
my dress!' asked a third: 'Execrable Bababalouk!' exclaimed all: 'Outcast o
hell! what hast thou to do with torches! Better were it to be eaten by tigers
than to fall into our present condition! we are for ever undone! Not a porte
is there in the army not a currier[1] of camels; but hath seen some part of ou
bodies, and, what is worse, our very faces!'[B] On saying this, the most bashfu
amongst them hid their foreheads on the ground, whilst such as had more
boldness flew at Bababalouk; but he, well apprized of their humour and no
wanting in shrewdness, betook himself to his heels along with his comrades
all dropping their torches and striking their tymbals.

It was not less light than in the brightest of the dog-days, and the weathe
was hot in proportion; but how degrading was the spectacle, to behold the
Caliph bespattered, like an ordinary mortal! As the exercise of his faculties
seemed to be suspended, one of his Ethiopian wives (for he delighted ir
variety) clasped him in her arms; threw him upon her shoulder, like a sack o
dates, and, finding that the fire was hemming them in, set off, with no smal
expedition, considering the weight of her burden. The other ladies, who hac
just learnt the use of their feet, followed her; their guards galloped after; anc
the camel-drivers brought up the rear, as fast as their charge would permit.

They soon reached the spot, where the wild beats had commenced the
carnage, but which they had too much good sense not to leave at the
approaching of the tumult, having made besides a most luxurious supper
Bababalouk, nevertheless, seized on a few of the plumpest, which were unable
to budge from the place, and began to flea[2] them with admirable adroitness.
The cavalcade having proceeded so far from the conflagration, that the heat
felt rather grateful than violent, it was, immediately, resolved on to halt. The
tattered chintzes were picked up; the scraps, left by the wolves and tigers,
interred; and vengeance was taken on some dozens of vultures, that were too
much glutted to rise on the wing. The camels, which had been left unmolested to make sal ammoniac,[3] being numbered; and the ladies once more

---

[1] Man who looks after animals.

[2] Rid of fleas.

[3] Ammonium chloride was supposed to have been produced from the dung of camels
near the shrine of Jupiter of Ammon.

nclosed in their cages; the imperial tent was pitched on the levellest ground hey could find.

Vathek, reposing upon a mattress of down, and tolerably recovered from he jolting of the Ethiopian, who, to his feelings, seemed the roughest trotting ade he had hitherto mounted, called out for something to eat. But, alas! hose delicate cakes, which had been baked in silver ovens, for his royal nouth;[B] those rich manchets;[1] amber comfits; flaggons of Shiraz[2] wine; orcelain vases of snow; and grapes from the banks of the Tigris;[B] were all rremediably lost! — And nothing had Bababalouk to present in their stead, ut a roasted wolf; vultures à la daube; aromatic herbs of the most acrid oignancy; rotten truffles; boiled thistles: and such other wild plants, as must lcerate the throat and parch up the tongue. Nor was he better provided, in he article of drink: for he could procure nothing to accompany these rritating viands, but a few phials of abominable brandy which had been ecreted by the scullions in their slippers. Vathek made wry faces at so savage repast; and Bababalouk answered them, with shrugs and contortions. The Caliph, however, eat with tolerable appetite; and fell into a nap, that lasted ix hours.

The splendour of the sun, reflected from the white cliffs of the mountains, n spite of the curtains that inclosed Vathek, at length disturbed his repose. He awoke, terrified; and stung to the quick by wormwood-colour flies, which mitted from their wings a suffocating stench. The miserable monarch was erplexed how to act; though his wits were not idle, in seeking expedients, vhilst Bababalouk lay snoring, amidst a swarm of those insects that busily hronged, to pay court to his nose. The little pages, famished with hunger, ad dropped their fans on the ground; and exerted their dying voices, in itter reproaches on the Caliph; who now, for the first time, heard the anguage of truth.

Thus stimulated, he renewed his imprecations against the Giaour; and estowed upon Mahomet some soothing expressions. 'Where am I?' cried he: What are these dreadful rocks? these valleys of darkness! are we arrived at the orrible Kaf![B] is the Simurgh[B] coming to pluck out my eyes, as a punishment or undertaking this impious enterprize!' Having said this he turned himself owards an outlet in the side of his pavilion, but, alas! what objects occurred to is view? on one side, a plain of black sand that appeared to be unbounded; ind, on the other, perpendicular crags, bristled over with those abominable histles, which had, so severely, lacerated his tongue. He fancied, however, hat he perceived, amongst the brambles and briars, some gigantic flowers

---

[1] Fine wheaten bread rolls.

[2] The first appearance of this word (at 17:17 in the 1816 edition) is in the form, *Shiraz*, n all texts, English and French. In its second and subsequent appearances the spelling, *Schiraz*, is adopted in all English-language texts, whereas in the French editions the spelling, *Shiraz*, continues to be used. It appears to be a case of a variant spelling creeping into the irst edition through carelessness and religiously adopted in all subsequent editions. I have normalized the spelling to *Shiraz*, the accepted spelling of the Persian city denoted. [K.G.]

but was mistaken: for, these were only the dangling palampores[1] and variegated tatters of his gay retinue. As there were several clefts in the rock from whence water seemed to have flowed, Vathek applied his ear with the hope of catching the sound of some latent torrent; but could only distinguish the low murmurs of his people who were repining at their journey, and complaining for the want of water. 'To what purpose,' asked they, 'have we been brought hither? hath our Caliph another tower to build? or have the relentless afrits,[2][B] whom Carathis so much loves, fixed their abode in this place?'

At the name of Carathis, Vathek recollected the tablets he had received from his mother; who assured him, they were fraught with preternatural qualities,[B] and advised him to consult them, as emergencies might require. Whilst he was engaged in turning them over, he heard a shout of joy, and a loud clapping of hands. The curtains of his pavilion were soon drawn back and he beheld Bababalouk, followed by a troop of his favourites, conducted by two dwarfs[B] each a cubit high;[3] who brought between them a large basket of melons, oranges, and pomegranates. They were singing in the sweetest tones the words that follow: 'We dwell on the top of these rocks, in a cabin of rushes and canes; the eagles envy us our nest: a small spring supplies us with water for the Abdest,[4] and we daily repeat prayers,[B] which the Prophet approves. We love you, O commander of the faithful! our master, the good Emir Fakreddin, loves you also: he reveres, in your person, the vicegerent of Mahomet. Little as we are, in us he confides: he knows our hearts to be as good, as our bodies are contemptible; and hath placed us here to aid those who are bewildered on these dreary mountains. Last night, whilst we were occupied within our cell in reading the holy Koran, a sudden hurricane blew out our lights, and rocked our habitation. For two whole hours, a palpable darkness prevailed; but we heard sounds at a distance, which we conjectured to proceed from the bells of a Cafila,[B] passing over the rocks. Our ears were soon filled with deplorable shrieks, frightful roarings, and the sound of tymbals. Chilled with terror, we concluded that the Deggial,[B] with his exterminating angels, had sent forth his plagues on the earth. In the midst of these melancholy reflections, we perceived flames of the deepest red, glow in the horizon; and found ourselves, in a few moments, covered with flakes of fire. Amazed at so strange an appearance, we took up the volume dictated by the blessed intelligence, and, kneeling, by the light of the fire that surrounded us, we recited the verse which says: 'Put[5] no trust in any thing but the mercy

---

[1] Chintz Indian covers.

[2] Evil spirits: see Beckford's note.

[3] Beckford had a great fascination for dwarfs. At Fonthill Abbey, he kept one, Pierre Colas de Grailly from Evian, on his staff. Pierre was sketched by Benjamin West, President of the Royal Academy.

[4] Ablution. See Beckford's note following.

[5] In the one instance of a quotation appearing within a quotation in Beckford's *Azemia* (II, 155), the distinction is observed with single quotations marks as it is in the 1823 revision. [K.G.]

of Heaven: there is no help, save in the holy Prophet: the mountain of Kaf, itself, may tremble; it is the power of Alla only, that cannot be moved.' After having pronounced these words, we felt consolation, and our minds were hushed into a sacred repose. Silence ensured, and our ears clearly distinguished a voice in the air, saying: 'Servants of my faithful servant! go down to the happy valley of Fakreddin: tell him that an illustrious opportunity now offers to satiate the thirst of his hospitable heart. The commander of true believers is, this day, bewildered amongst these mountains and stands in need of thy aid.' – We obeyed, with joy, the angelic mission; and our master, filled with pious zeal, hath culled, with his own hands, these melons, oranges, and pomegranates. He is following us with a hundred dromedaries, laden with the purest waters of his fountains; and is coming to kiss the fringe of your consecrated robe, and implore you to enter his humble habitation which, placed amidst these barren wilds, resembles an emerald set in lead.' The dwarfs, having ended their address, remained still standing, and, with hands crossed upon their bosoms, preserved a respectful silence.

Vathek, in the midst of this curious harangue, seized the basket; and, long before it was finished, the fruits had dissolved in his mouth. As he continued to eat, his piety increased; and, in the same breath, he recited his prayers and called for the Koran and sugar.[B]

Such was the state of his mind, when the tablets, which were thrown by, at the approach of the dwarfs, again attracted his eye. He took them up; but was ready to drop on the ground, when he beheld in large red characters[B] inscribed by Carathis, these words; which were, indeed, enough to make him tremble; 'Beware of old doctors and their puny messengers of but one cubit high: distrust their pious frauds; and, instead of eating their melons, empale on a spit the bearers of them. Shouldest thou be such a fool as to visit them, the portal of the subterranean palace will shut in thy face with such force, as shall shake thee asunder: thy body shall be spit upon,[B] and bats will nestle in thy belly.'[B]

'To what tends this ominous rhapsody?' cries the Caliph: 'and must I then perish in these deserts, with thirst; whilst I may refresh myself in the delicious valley of melons and cucumbers? – Accursed be the Giaour with his portal of ebony! he hath made me dance attendance, too long already. Besides, who shall prescribe laws to me? – I, forsooth, must not enter any one's habitation! Be it so: but, what one can I enter, that is not my own!' Bababalouk, who lost not a syllable of this soliloquy, applauded it with all his heart; and the ladies, for the first time, agreed with him in opinion.

The dwarfs were entertained, caressed, and seated, with great ceremony, on little cushions of satin. The symmetry of their persons was a subject of admiration; not an inch of them was suffered to pass un-examined. Kicknacks and dainties were offered in profusion; but all were declined, with respectful gravity. They climbed up the sides of the Caliph's seat; and, placing themselves each on one of his shoulders, began to whisper prayers in his ears. Their tongues quivered, like aspen leaves; and the patience of Vathek was almost exhausted, when the acclamations of the troops announced the approach of Fakreddin, who was come with a hundred old grey-beards, and as many Korans and dromedaries. They instantly set about their ablutions, and began to repeat the Bismillah.[B] Vathek, to get rid of these officious monitors, followed their example; for his hands were burning.

The good emir, who was punctiliously religious, and likewise a great dealer in compliments, made an harangue five times more prolix and insipid than his little harbingers had already delivered. The Caliph, unable any longer to refrain, exclaimed: 'For the love of Mahomet, my dear Fakreddin, have done! let us proceed to your valley, and enjoy the fruits that Heaven hath vouchsafed you.' The hint of proceeding, put all into motion. The venerable attendants of the emir set forward, somewhat slowly; but Vathek, having ordered his little pages, in private, to goad on the dromedaries, loud fits of laughter broke forth from the cages; for, the unwieldy curvetting of these poor beasts, and the ridiculous distress of their superannuated riders, afforded the ladies no small entertainment.

They descended, however, unhurt into the valley, by the easy slopes which the emir had ordered to be cut in the rock; and already, the murmuring of streams and the rustling of leaves began to catch their attention. The cavalcade soon entered a path, which was skirted by flowering shrubs, and extended to a vast wood of palm trees, whose branches overspread a vast building of free stone. This edifice was crowned with nine domes, and adorned with as many portals of bronze, on which was engraven the following inscription: 'This is the asylum of pilgrims, the refuge of travellers, and the depositary of secrets from all parts of the world.'

Nine pages, beautiful as the day, and decently clothed in robes of Egyptian linen, were standing at each door. They received the whole retinue with an easy and inviting air. Four of the most amiable placed the Caliph on a magnificent tecthtrevan:[B] four others, somewhat less graceful, took charge of Bababalouk, who capered for joy at the snug little cabin that fell to his share; the pages that remained waited on the rest of the train.

Every man being gone out of sight, the gate of a large inclosure, on the right, turned on its harmonious hinges; and a young female, of a slender form, came forth. Her light brown hair floated in the hazy breeze of the twilight. A troop of young maidens, like the Pleiades,[1] attended her on tiptoe. They hastened to the pavilions that contained the sultanas: and the young lady, gracefully bending, said to them: 'Charming princesses, every thing is ready: we have prepared beds for your repose, and strewed your apartments with jasmine: no insects will keep off slumber from visiting your eye-lids; we will dispel them with a thousand plumes. Come then, amiable ladies, refresh your delicate feet, and your ivory limbs, in baths of rose water;[B] and, by the light of perfumed lamps, your servants will amuse you with tales.' The sultanas accepted, with pleasure, these obliging offers; and followed the young lady to the emir's harem; where we must, for a moment, leave them, and return to the Caliph.

---

[1] The seven stars.

Vathek found himself beneath a vast dome, illuminated by a thousand lamps of rock crystal: as many vases of the same material, filled with excellent sherbet, sparkled on a large table, where a profusion of viands were spread. Amongst others, were rice boiled in milk of almonds, saffron soups, and lamb à la crême;[B] of all which the Caliph was amazingly fond. He took of each, as much as he was able, testified his sense of the emir's friendship, by the gaiety of his heart; and made the dwarfs dance, against their will:[B] for these little devotees durst not refuse the commander of the faithful.[B] At last, he spread himself on the sofa,[1] and slept sounder than he ever had before.

Beneath this dome, a general silence prevailed; for there was nothing to disturb it but the jaws of Bababalouk, who had untrussed himself to eat with greater advantage; being anxious to make amends for his fast, in the mountains. As his spirits were too high to admit of his sleeping; and hating to be idle, he proposed with himself to visit the harem and repair to his charge of the ladies: to examine if they had been properly lubricated with the balm of Mecca;[B] if their eye-brows, and tresses, were in order; and, in a word, to perform all the little offices they might need. He sought for a long time together but without being able to find out the door. He durst not speak aloud for fear of disturbing the Caliph; and not a soul was stirring in the precincts of the palace. He almost despaired of effecting his purpose, when a low whispering just reached his ear. It came from the dwarfs, who were returned to their old occupation, and, for the nine hundred and ninety-ninth time in their lives, were reading over the Koran. They very politely invited Bababalouk to be of their party; but his head was full of other concerns. The dwarfs, though not a little scandalized at his dissolute morals, directed him to the apartments he wanted to find. His way thither lay through a hundred dark corridors, along which he groped as he went; and at last, began to catch, from the extremity of a passage, the charming gossiping of the women which not a little delighted his heart. 'Ah, ha! what not yet asleep?' cried he; and, taking long strides as he spoke, 'did you not suspect me of abjuring my charge?' Two of the black eunuchs, on hearing a voice so loud, left their party in haste, sabre in hand,[B] to discover the cause: but, presently, was repeated on all sides: ''Tis only Bababalouk! no one but Bababalouk!' This circumspect guardian, having gone up to a thin veil of carnation-colour silk that hung before the door-way, distinguished, by means of the softened splendor that shone through it, an oval bath of dark porphyry surrounded by curtains, festooned in large folds. Through the apertures between them, as they were not drawn close, groups of young slaves were visible; amongst whom, Bababalouk perceived his pupils, indulgingly expanding their arms, as if to embrace the perfumed water, and refresh themselves after their fatigues. The looks of tender languor; their confidential whispers; and the enchanting smiles with which they were imparted; the exquisite fragrance of

---

[1] This is the only instance of the spelling, *sopha*, in the copy-text. The adoption of the 1823 revision imposes consistency on the spelling of this word. [K.G.]

the roses: all combined to inspire a voluptuousness, which even Bababalouk himself was scarce able to withstand.

He summoned up, however, his usual solemnity, and in the peremptory[1] tone of authority, commanded the ladies, instantly, to leave the bath. Whilst he was issuing these mandates, the young Nouronihar, daughter of the emir, who was as sprightly as an antelope, and full of wanton gaiety, beckoned one of her slaves to let down the great swing[B] which was suspended to the ceiling by cords of silk: and whilst this was doing, winked to her companions in the bath: who, chagrined to be forced from so soothing a state of indolence, began to twist and entangle their hair to plague and detain Bababalouk; and teased him besides with a thousand vagaries.

Nouronihar perceiving that he was nearly out of patience accosted him, with an arch air of respectful concern, and said: 'My lord! it is not, by any means decent, that the chief eunuch of the Caliph our sovereign should thus continue standing: deign but to recline your graceful person upon this sofa which will burst with vexation, if it have not the honour to receive you.' Caught by these flattering accents, Bababalouk gallantly replied: 'Delight of the apple of my eye! I accept the invitation of your honied lips; and, to say truth, my senses are dazzled with the radiance that beams from your charms.' – 'Repose, then, at your ease,' replied the beauty; as she placed him on the pretended sofa which, quicker than lightning, flew up all at once. The rest of the women, having aptly conceived her design, sprang naked from the bath, and plied the swing, with such unmerciful jerks, that it swept through the whole compass of a very lofty dome, and took from the poor victim all power of respiration. Sometimes, his feet rased the surface of the water; and, at others, the skylight almost flattened his nose. In vain did he fill the air with the cries of a voice that resembled the ringing of a cracked jar; their peals of laughter were still predominant.

Nouronihar,[2] in the inebriety of youthful spirits, being used only to eunuchs of ordinary harems; and having never seen any thing so eminently disgusting, was far more diverted than all of the rest. She began to parody some Persian verses and sang with an accent most demurely piquant: 'Oh gentle white dove, as thou soar'st through the air, vouchsafe one kind glance on the mate of thy love: melodious Philomel,[3] I am thy rose;[B] warble some couplet to ravish my heart!'

The sultanas and their slaves, stimulated by these pleasantries, persevered at the swing, with such unremitted assiduity, that at length, the cord which had secured it, snapt suddenly asunder; and Bababalouk fell, floundering like a turtle, to the bottom of the bath. This accident occasioned an universal shout. Twelve little doors, till now unobserved, flew open at once; and the

---

[1] This spelling error, initiated in the second edition and repeated in the third, is one easily missed in proofreading. It is probably compositorial; Beckford was a competent Latinist. [K.G.]

[2] Beckford had used this name in *The Vision*, see above, p. 9.

[3] Daughter of Pandion who, according to legend, was turned into a nightingale.

ladies, in an instant, made their escape; but not before having heaped all the towels on his head and put out the lights that remained.

The deplorable animal, in water to the chin, overwhelmed with darkness, and unable to extricate himself from the wrappers that embarrassed him, was still doomed to hear, for his further consolation, the fresh bursts of merriment his disaster occasioned. He bustled, but in vain, to get from the bath; for, the margin was become so slippery, with the oil spilt in breaking the lamps,[B] that, at every effort, he slid back with a plunge which resounded aloud through the hollow of the dome.[1] These cursed peals of laughter, were redoubled at every relapse, and he, who thought the place infested rather by devils than women, resolved to cease groping, and abide in the bath; where he amused himself with soliloquies, interspersed with imprecations, of which his malicious neighbours, reclining on down, suffered not an accent to escape. In this delectable plight, the morning surprised him. The Caliph, wondering at his absence, had caused him to be sought for every where. At last, he was drawn forth almost smothered from under the wisp of linen, and wet even to the marrow. Limping, and his teeth chattering with cold, he approached his master; who inquired what was the matter, and how he came soused in so strange a pickle? – 'And why did you enter this cursed lodge?' answered Bababalouk, gruffly. – 'Ought a monarch like you to visit with his harem, the abode of a grey-bearded emir, who knows nothing of life? – And, with what gracious damsels doth the place too abound! Fancy to yourself how they have soaked me like a burnt crust; and made me dance like a jack-pudding,[2] the live-long night through, on their damnable swing. What an excellent lesson for your sultanas, into whom I had instilled such reserve and decorum!' Vathek, comprehending not a syllable of all this invective, obliged him to relate minutely the transaction: but, instead of sympathizing with the miserable sufferer, he laughed immoderately at the device of the swing and the figure of Bababalouk, mounted upon it. The stung eunuch could scarcely preserve the semblance of respect. 'Aye, laugh, my lord! laugh,' said he; 'but I wish this Nouronihar would play some trick on you; she is too wicked to spare even majesty itself.' These words made, for the present, but a slight impression on the Caliph; but they, not long after, recurred to his mind.

This conversation was cut short by Fakreddin, who came to request that Vathek would join in the prayers and ablutions, to be solemnized on a spacious meadow watered by innumerable streams. The Caliph found the waters refreshing, but the prayers abominably irksome. He diverted himself, however, with the multitude of calenders,[B] santons,[B] and derviches,[B] who were continually coming and going; but especially with the bramins,[3][B]

---

[1] At 62:24 the word is spelled correctly, *dome*. The repetition of this error in the Clarke editions is probably consequent upon the proofreader's losing the thread on turning the page. [K.G.]

[2] Clown.

[3] Voltaire had made the figure of the Brahmin a wise, sage-like person in *Histoire d'un Bon Bramin* (1761).

faquirs,[B] and other enthusiasts, who had travelled from the heart of India, and halted on their way with the emir. These latter had each of them some mummery peculiar to himself. One dragged a huge chain wherever he went; another an ouran-outang; whilst a third, was furnished with scourges; and all performed to a charm. Some would climb up trees, holding one foot in the air; others poise themselves over a fire, and, without mercy, fillip their noses. There were some amongst them that cherished vermin,[B] which were not ungrateful in requiting their caresses. These rambling fanatics revolted the hearts of the derviches, the calenders, and santons; however, the vehemence of their aversion soon subsided, under the hope that the presence of the Caliph would cure their folly, and convert them to the mussulman faith. But, alas! how great was their disappointment! for Vathek, instead of preaching to them, treated them as buffoons, bade them present his compliments to Visnow and Ixhora,[B] and discovered a predilection for a squat old man from the Isle of Serendib,[1] who was more ridiculous than any of the rest. 'Come!' said he, 'for the love of your gods, bestow a few slaps on your chops to amuse me.' The old fellow, offended at such an address, began loudly to weep; but, as he betrayed a villainous drivelling in shedding tears, the Caliph turned his back and listened to Bababalouk, who whispered, whilst he held the umbrella over him: 'Your majesty should be cautious of this odd assembly; which hath been collected, I know not for what. Is it necessary to exhibit such spectacles to a mighty potentate, with interludes of talapoins[B] more mangy than dogs? Were I you, I would command a fire to be kindled, and at once rid the estates of the emir, of his harem, and all his menagerie.' – 'Tush, dolt,' answered Vathek; 'and know, that all this infinitely charms me. Nor shall I leave the meadow, till I have visited every hive of these pious mendicants.'

Wherever the Caliph directed his course, objects of pity were sure to swarm round him;[B] the blind, the purblind, smarts without noses, damsels without ears, each to extol the munificence of Fakreddin, who, as well as his attendant grey-beards, dealt about, gratis, plasters and cataplasms[2] to all that applied. At noon, a superb corps of cripples made its appearance; and soon after advanced, by platoons, on the plain, the completest association of invalids that had even been embodied till then. The blind went groping with the blind, the lame limped on together, and the maimed made gestures to each other with the only arm that remained. The sides of a considerable water-fall were crowded by the deaf; amongst whom were some from Pegû, with ears uncommonly handsome and large, but who were still less able to hear than the rest. Nor were there wanting others in abundance with hump-backs; wenny necks; and even horns of an exquisite polish.

The emir, to aggrandize the solemnity of the festival, in honour of his illustrious visitant, ordered the turf to be spread, on all sides, with skins and

---

[1] Ceylon or Sri Lanka, according to legend, first terrestrial abode of Adam. Serendip also features in the work of Horace Walpole whose *The Three Princes of Serendip* appeared in 1754.

[2] Poultice or dressing.

table-cloths; upon which were served up for the good Mussulmans, pilaus[1] of every hue, with other orthodox dishes; and, by the express order of Vathek, who was shamefully tolerant, small plates of abominations[B] were prepared, to the great scandal of the faithful. The holy assembly began to fall to. The Caliph, in spite of every remonstrance from the chief of his eunuchs, resolved to have a dinner dressed on the spot. The complaisant emir immediately gave orders for a table to be placed in the shade of the willows. The first service consisted of fish, which they drew from a river, flowing over sands of gold at the foot of a lofty hill. These were broiled as fast as taken, and served up with a sauce of vinegar, and small herbs that grew on mount Sinai[B]: for every thing with the emir was excellent and pious.

The desert was not quite set on, when the sound of lutes, from the hill, was repeated by the echoes of the neighbouring mountains. The Caliph, with an emotion of pleasure and surprize, had no sooner raised up his head, than a handful of jasmine dropped on his face. An abundance of tittering succeeded the frolic, and instantly appeared, through the bushes, the elegant forms of several young females, skipping and bounding like roes. The fragrance diffused from their hair, struck the sense of Vathek, who, in an ecstacy, suspending his repast, said to Bababalouk: 'Are the peries[B] come down from their spheres? Note her, in particular, whose form is so perfect; venturously running on the brink of the precipice, and turning back her head, as regardless of nothing but the graceful flow of her robe. With what captivating impatience doth she contend with the bushes for her veil? could it be her who threw the jasmine at me!' – 'Aye! she it was; and you too would she throw, from the top of the rock,' answered Bababalouk; 'for that is my good friend Nouronihar, who so kindly lent me her swing. My dear lord and master,' added he, wresting a twig from a willow, 'let me correct her for her want of respect: the emir will have no reason to complain; since (bating what I owe to his piety) he is much to be blamed for keeping a troop of girls on the mountains, where the sharpness of the air gives their blood too brisk a circulation.'

'Peace! blasphemer,' said the Caliph; 'speak not thus of her, who, over these mountains, leads my heart a willing captive. Contrive, rather, that my eyes may be fixed upon her's: that I may respire her sweet breath as she bounds panting along these delightful wilds!' On saying these words, Vathek extended his arms towards the hill, and directing his eyes, with an anxiety unknown to him before, endeavoured to keep within view the object that enthralled his soul: but her course was as difficult to follow, as the flight of one of those beautiful blue butterflies of Cachemire,[B] which are, at once, so volatile and rare.

The Caliph, not satisfied with seeing, wished also to hear Nouronihar, and eagerly turned to catch the sound of her voice. At last, he distinguished her whispering to one of her companions behind the thickets from whence she had thrown the jasmine: 'A Caliph, it must be owned, is a fine thing to see;

---

[1] Rice dish with meat, spices and raisins, many coloured.

but my little Gulchenrouz is much more amiable: one lock of his hair is of more value to me than the richest embroidery of the Indies. I had rather that his teeth should mischievously press my finger, than the richest ring of the imperial treasure. Where have you left him, Sutlememe? and why is he not here?'

The agitated Caliph still wished to hear more; but she immediately retired with all her attendants. The fond monarch pursued her with his eyes till she was gone out of sight; and then continued like a bewildered and benighted traveller, from whom the clouds had obscured the constellation that guided his way. The curtain of night seemed dropped before him: every thing appeared discoloured. The falling waters filled his soul with dejection, and his tears trickled down the jasmines he had caught from Nouronihar, and placed in his inflamed bosom. He snatched up a few shining pebbles, to remind him of the scene where he felt the first tumults of love. Two hours were elapsed, and evening drew on, before he could resolve to depart from the place. He often, but in vain, attempted to go: a soft languor enervated the powers of his mind. Extending himself on the brink of the stream, he turned his eyes towards the blue summits of the mountain, and exclaimed, 'What concealest thou behind thee, pitiless rock? what is passing in thy solitudes? Whither is she gone? O heaven! perhaps she is now wandering in thy grottoes with her happy Gulchenrouz!'

In the mean time, the damps began to descend; and the emir, solicitous for the health of the Caliph, ordered the imperial litter to be brought. Vathek, absorbed in his reveries, was imperceptibly removed and conveyed back to the saloon, that received him the evening before. But, let us leave the Caliph immersed in his new passion: and attend Nouronihar beyond the rocks where she had again joined her beloved Gulchenrouz.

This Gulchenrouz was the son of Ali Hassan, brother to the emir: and the most delicate and lovely creature in the world. Ali Hassan, who had been absent ten years on a voyage to the unknown seas, committed, at his departure, this child, the only survivor of many, to the care and protection of his brother. Gulchenrouz could write in various characters with precision, and paint upon vellum the most elegant arabesques that fancy could devise. His sweet voice accompanied the lute in the most enchanting manner; and, when he sang the loves of Megnoun and Leilah,[B] or some unfortunate lovers of ancient days, tears insensibly overflowed the cheeks of his auditors. The verses he composed (for, like Megnoun, he, too, was a poet) inspired that unresisting languor, so frequently fatal to the female heart. The women all doated upon him; and, though he had passed his thirteenth year, they still detained him in the harem. His dancing was light as the gossamer waved by the zephyrs of spring; but his arms, which twined so gracefully with those of the young girls in the dance, could neither dart the lance in the chace,[B] nor curb the steeds that pastured in his uncle's domains. The bow, however, he drew with a certain aim, and would have excelled his competitors in the race, could he have broken the ties that bound him to Nouronihar.

The two brothers had mutually engaged their children to each other;[B] and

Nouronihar loved her cousin, more than her own beautiful eyes.[B] Both had the same tastes and amusements; the same long, languishing looks;[B] the same tresses; the same fair complexions; and, when Gulchenrouz appeared in the dress of his cousin, he seemed to be more feminine than even herself. If, at any time, he left the harem, to visit Fakreddin; it was with all the bashfulness of a fawn, that consciously ventures from the lair of its dam:[1] he was, however, wanton enough to mock the solemn old grey-beards, though sure to be rated without mercy in return. Whenever this happened, he would hastily plunge into the recesses of the harem; and, sobbing, take refuge in the fond arms of Nouronihar who loved even his faults beyond the virtues of others.

It fell out this evening, that, after leaving the Caliph in the meadow, she ran with Gulchenrouz over the green sward of the mountain, that sheltered the vale where Fakreddin had chosen to reside. The sun was dilated on the edge of the horizon; and the young people, whose fancies were lively and inventive, imagined they beheld, in the gorgeous clouds of the west, the domes of Shaddukian and Ambreabad,[B] where the Peries have fixed their abode. Nouronihar, sitting on the slope of the hill, supported on her knees the perfumed head of Gulchenrouz. The unexpected arrival of the Caliph and the splendour that marked his appearance, had already filled with emotion the ardent soul of Nouronihar. Her vanity irresistibly prompted her to pique the prince's attention; and this, she before took good care to effect, whilst he picked up the jasmine she had thrown upon him. But, when Gulchenrouz asked after the flowers he had culled for her bosom, Nouronihar was all in confusion. She hastily kissed his forehead; arose in a flutter; and walked, with unequal steps, on the border of the precipice. Night advanced, and the pure gold of the setting sun had yielded to a sanguine red; the glow of which, like the reflection of a burning furnace, flushed Nouronihar's animated countenance. Gulchenrouz, alarmed at the agitation of his cousin, said to her, with a supplicating accent – 'Let us begone; the sky looks portentous; the tamarisks[2] tremble more than common; and the raw wind chills my very heart. Come! let us begone; 'tis a melancholy night!' Then, taking hold of her hand, he drew it towards the path he besought her to go. Nouronihar, unconsciously followed the attraction; for, a thousand strange imaginations occupied her spirits. She passed the large round of honey-suckles, her favourite resort, without ever vouchsafing it a glance; yet Gulchenrouz could not help snatching off a few shoots in his way, though he ran as if a wild beast were behind.

The young females seeing them approach in such haste, and, according to custom, expecting a dance, instantly assembled in a circle and took each other by the hand: but, Gulchenrouz coming up out of breath, fell down at once on the grass. This accident struck with consternation the whole of this frolicsome party; whilst Nouronihar, half distracted and overcome, both by

---

[1] Mother.
[2] Small white or pink flowers.

the violence of her exercise, and the tumult of her thoughts, sunk feebly down at his side; cherished his cold hands in her bosom, and chafed his temples with a fragrant perfume. At length, he came to himself; and, wrapping up his head in the robe of his cousin, intreated that she would not return to the harem. He was afraid of being snapped at by Shaban his tutor; a wrinkled old eunuch of a surly disposition; for, having interrupted the wonted walk of Nouronihar, he dreaded lest the churl should take it amiss. The whole of this sprightly group, sitting round upon a mossy knoll, began to entertain themselves with various pastimes; whilst their superintendants, the eunuchs, were gravely conversing at a distance. The nurse of the emir's daughter, observing her pupil sit ruminating with her eyes on the ground, endeavoured to amuse her with diverting tales; to which Gulchenrouz, who had already forgotten his inquietudes, listened with a breathless attention. He laughed; he clapped his hands; and passed a hundred little tricks on the whole of the company, without omitting the eunuchs whom he provoked to run after him, in spite of their age and decrepitude.

During these occurrences, the moon arose, the wind subsided, and the evening became so serene and inviting, that a resolution was taken to sup on the spot. One of the eunuchs ran to fetch melons whilst others were employed in showering down almonds from the branches that overhung this amiable party. Sutlememe, who excelled in dressing a salad, having filled large bowls of porcelain with eggs of small birds, curds turned with citron juice, slices of cucumber, and the inmost leaves of delicate herbs, handed it round from one to another and gave each their shares with a large spoon of cocknos.[B] Gulchenrouz, nestling, as usual, in the bosom of Nouronihar, pouted out his vermillion little lips against the offer of Sutlememe; and would take it, only, from the hand of his cousin, on whose mouth he hung, like a bee inebriated with the nectar of flowers.

In the midst of this festive scene, there appeared a light on the top of the highest mountain, which attracted the notice of every eye. This light was not less bright than the moon when at full, and might have been taken for her, had not the moon already risen. The phenomenon occasioned a general surprize and no one could conjecture the cause. It could not be a fire, for the light was clear and bluish: nor had meteors ever been seen of that magnitude or splendour. This strange light faded, for a moment; and immediately renewed its brightness. It first appeared motionless, at the foot of the rock; whence it darted in an instant, to sparkle in a thicket of palm-trees: from thence it glided along the torrent; and at last fixed in a glen that was narrow and dark. The moment it had taken its direction, Gulchenrouz, whose heart always trembled at any thing sudden or rare, drew Nouronihar by the robe and anxiously requested her to return to the harem. The women were importunate in seconding the intreaty; but the curiosity of the emir's daughter prevailed. She not only refused to go back, but resolved, at all hazards, to pursue the appearance.

Whilst they were debating what was best to be done, the light shot forth so dazzling a blaze that they all fled away shrieking. Nouronihar followed them a few steps, but, coming to the turn of a little bye path, stopped, and went back alone. As she ran with an alertness peculiar to herself, it was not long before she came to the place, where they had just been supping. The globe of fire now appeared stationary in the glen, and burned in majestic stillness. Nouronihar, pressing her hands upon her bosom, hesitated, for some moments, to advance. The solitude of her situation was new; and silence of the night, awful; and every object inspired sensations, which, till then, she never had felt. The affright of Gulchenrouz recurred to her mind, and she, a thousand times turned to go back; but this luminous appearance was always before her. Urged on by an irresistible impulse, she continued to approach it, in defiance of every obstacle that opposed her progress.

At length she arrived at the opening of the glen; but, instead of coming up to the light, she found herself surrounded by darkness; excepting that, at a considerable distance, a faint spark glimmered by fits. She stopped, a second time: the sound of water-falls mingling their murmurs; the hollow rustlings among the palm-branches; and the funereal screams of the birds from their rifted trunks: all conspired to fill her soul with terror. She imagined, every moment, that she trod on some venomous reptile. All the stories of malignant Dives[1] and dismal Goules[B] thronged into her memory: but, her curiosity was, notwithstanding, more predominant than her fears. She, therefore, firmly entered a winding track that led towards the spark; but, being a stranger to the path, she had not gone far, till she began to repent of her rashness. 'Alas!' said she, 'that I were but in those secure and illuminated apartments, where my evenings glided on with Gulchenrouz! Dear child! how would thy heart flutter with terror, wert thou wandering in these wild solitudes, like me!' Thus speaking, she advanced, and, coming up to steps hewn in the rock, ascended them undismayed. The light, which was now gradually enlarging, appeared above her on the summit of the mountain, and as if proceeding from a cavern. At length, she distinguished a plaintive and melodious union of voices, that resembled the dirges which are sung over tombs. A sound, like that which arises from the filling of baths, struck her ear at the same time. She continued ascending, and discovered large wax torches in full blaze, planted here and there in the fissures of the rock. This appearance filled her with fear, whilst the subtile[2] and potent odour, which the torches exhaled, caused her to sink, almost lifeless, at the entrance of the grot.

Casting her eyes within, in this kind of trance, she beheld a large cistern of gold, filled with a water, the vapour of which distilled on her face a dew of the essence of roses. A soft symphony resounded through the grot. On the sides of the cistern, she noticed appendages of royalty, diadems and feathers of the heron, all sparkling with carbuncles.[B] Whilst her attention was fixed on this display of magnificence, the music ceased, and a voice instantly demanded: 'For what monarch are these torches kindled, this bath prepared,

---

[1] Evil spirits in Persian demonology.

[2] At 46:31 and 91:38, the spelling, *subtile*, is used. I have followed the 1823 text in imposing consistency on the spelling of this word. [K.G.]

and these habiliments[1] which belong, not only to the sovereigns of the earth, but even to the talismanick powers!' To which a second voice answered: 'They are for the charming daughter of the emir Fakreddin.' – 'What,' replied the first, 'for that trifler, who consumes her time with a giddy child, immersed in softness, and who, at best, can make but a pitiful husband?' – 'And can she,' rejoined the other voice, 'be amused with such empty toys, whilst the Caliph, the sovereign of the world, he who is destined to enjoy the treasures of the pre-adamite sultans; a prince six feet high; and whose eyes pervade the inmost soul of a female, is inflamed with love for her. No! she will be wise enough to answer that passion alone, that can aggrandize her glory. No doubt she will; and despise the puppet of her fancy. Then all the riches this place contains, as well as the carbuncle of Giamschid,[B] shall be her's.' – 'You judge right,' returned to the first voice; 'and I haste to Istakhar, to prepare the palace of subterranean fire for the reception of the bridal pair.'

The voices ceased; the torches were extinguished,[B] the most entire darkness succeeded; and Nouronihar recovering, with a start, found herself reclined on a sofa, in the harem of her father. She clapped her hands,[B] and immediately came together, Gulchenrouz and her women; who, in despair at having lost her, had dispatched eunuchs to seek her, in every direction. Shaban appeared with the rest, and began to reprimand her, with an air of consequence: 'Little impertinent,' said he, 'have you false keys, or are you beloved of some genius, that hath given you a picklock? I will try the extent of your power: come to the dark chamber, and expect not the company of Gulchenrouz: – be expeditious! I will shut you up, and turn the key twice upon you!' At these menaces, Nouronihar indignantly raised her head, opened on Shaban her black eyes, which, since the important dialogue of the enchanted grot, were considerably enlarged, and said: 'Go, speak thus to slaves; but learn to reverence her who is born to give laws and subject all to her power.'

Proceeding in the same style, she was interrupted by a sudden exclamation of, 'The Caliph! the Caliph!' All the curtains were thrown open, the slaves prostrated themselves in double rows, and poor little Gulchenrouz went to hide beneath the couch of a sofa. At first appeared a file of black eunuchs trailing after them long trains of muslin embroidered with gold, and holding in their hands censers, which dispensed, as they passed, the grateful perfume of the wood of aloes.[2] Next marched Bababalouk with a solemn strut, and tossing his head, as not overpleased at the visit. Vathek came close after, superbly robed: his gait was unembarassed and noble; and his presence would have engaged admiration, though he had not been the sovereign of the world. He approached Nouronihar with a throbbing heart, and seemed enraptured at the full effulgence of her radiant eyes, of which he had before caught but a few glimpses: but she instantly depressed them, and her confusion augmented her beauty.

---

[1] Clothes.
[2] Beckford was much taken with these plants, enjoying their profusion in Portugal. Also see *above*, p. 17 n.1.

Bababalouk, who was a thorough adept in coincidences of this nature, and knew that the worst game should be played with the best face, immediately made a signal for all to retire; and no sooner did he perceive beneath the sofa the little one's feet, than he drew him forth without ceremony, set him upon his shoulders, and lavished on him, as he went off, a thousand unwelcome caresses. Gulchenrouz cried out, and resisted till his cheeks became the colour of the blossom of pomegranates, and his tearful eyes sparkled with indignation. He cast a significant glance at Nouronihar, which the Caliph noticing, asked, 'Is that, then, your Gulchenrouz?' – 'Sovereign of the world!' answered she, 'spare my cousin, whose innocence and gentleness deserve not your anger!' – 'Take comfort,' said Vathek, with a smile: 'he is in good hands. Bababalouk is fond of children: and never goes without sweetmeats and comfits.' The daughter of Fakreddin was abashed, and suffered Gulchenrouz to be borne away without adding a word. The tumult of her bosom betrayed her confusion, and Vathek becoming still more impassioned, gave a loose to his frenzy; which had only not subdued the last faint strugglings of reluctance, when the emir suddenly bursting in, threw his face upon the ground, at the feet of the Caliph, and said: 'Commander of the faithful! abase not yourself to the meanness of your slave.' – 'No, emir,' replied Vathek, 'I raise her to an equality with myself: I declare her my wife; and the glory of your race shall extend from one generation to another.' – 'Alas! my lord,' said Fakreddin, as he plucked off a few grey hairs of his beard; 'cut short the days of your faithful servant, rather than force him to depart from his word. Nouronihar is solemnly promised to Gulchenrouz, the son of my brother Ali Hassan: they are united, also, in heart; their faith is mutually plighted; and affiances, so sacred, cannot be broken.' – 'What then!' replied the Caliph, bluntly, 'would you surrender this divine beauty to a husband more woman-ish than herself; and can you imagine, that I will suffer her charms to decay in hands so inefficient and nerveless? No! she is destined to live out her life within my embraces: such is my will: retire; and disturb not the night I devote to the worship of her charms.'

The irritated emir drew forth his sabre, presented it to Vathek, and, stretching out his neck, said, in a firm tone of voice: 'Strike your unhappy host, my lord! he has lived long enough, since he hath seen the prophet's vicegerent violate the rights of hospitality.' At his uttering these words, Nouronihar, unable to support any longer the conflict of her passions, sunk down in a swoon. Vathek, both terrified for her like, and furious at an opposition to his will, bade Fakreddin assist his daughter, and withdrew; darting his terrible look at the unfortunate emir, who suddenly fell back-ward, bathed in a sweat as cold as the damp of death.

Gulchenrouz, who had escaped from the hands of Bababalouk and was, that instant, returned, called out for help, as loudly as he could, not having strength to afford it himself. Pale and panting, the poor child attempted to revive Nouronihar by caresses; and it happened, that the thrilling warmth of his lips restored her to life. Fakreddin beginning also to recover from the look of the Caliph, with difficulty tottered to a seat; and, after warily casting round his eye, to see if this dangerous Prince were gone, sent for Shaban and Sutlememe; and said to them apart: 'My friends! violent evils require violent remedies; the Caliph has brought desolation and horror into my family; and, how shall we resist his power? Another of his looks will send me to the grave. Fetch, then, that narcotick powder which a dervish[1] brought me from Aracan. A dose of it, the effect of which will continue three days, must be administered to each of these children. The Caliph will believe them to be dead; for, they will have all the appearance of death. We shall go, as if to inter them in the cave of Meimouné,[2] at the entrance of the great desert of sand and near the bower of my dwarfs. When all the spectators shall be withdrawn, you, Shaban, and four select eunuchs, shall convey them to the lake; where provision shall be ready to support them a month: for, one day allotted to the surprize this event will occasion; five, to the tears; a fortnight to reflection; and the rest, to prepare for renewing his progress; will, according to my calculation, fill up the whole time that Vathek will tarry; and I shall, then, be freed from his intrusion.'

'Your plan is good,' said Sutlememe, 'if it can but be effected. I have remarked, that Nouronihar is well able to support the glances of the Caliph: and, that he is far from being sparing of them to her: be assured, therefore, that notwithstanding her fondness for Gulchenrouz, she will never remain quiet, while she knows him to be here. Let us persuade her, that both herself and Gulchenrouz are really dead; and, that they were conveyed to those rocks, for a limited season, to expiate the little faults, of which their love was the cause. We will add, that we killed ourselves in despair; and that your dwarfs, whom they never yet saw, will preach to them delectable sermons. I will engage that every thing shall succeed to the bent of your wishes.' – 'Be it so!' said Fakreddin, 'I approve your proposal: let us lose not a moment to give it effect.'

They hastened to seek for the powder which, being mixed in a sherbet, was immediately administered to Gulchenrouz and Nouronihar. Within the space of an hour, both were seized with violent palpitations; and a general numbness gradually ensued. They arose from the floor where they had remained ever since the Caliph's departure; and, ascending to the sofa, reclined themselves upon it, clasped in each other's embraces. 'Cherish me, my dear Nouronihar!' said Gulchenrouz: 'put thy hand upon my heart; it feels as if it were frozen. Alas! thou art as cold as myself! hath the Caliph murdered us both, with his terrible look?' – 'I am dying!' cried she, in a faultering voice: 'Press me closer; I am ready to expire!' – 'Let us die then, together,' answered

---

[1] There is an apparent inconsistency in the spelling of this word in all English editions. At this reference the spelling, *dervish*, is employed, whereas at 63:38 and 64:9 the plural form of the word is spelled, *derviches*. I have taken the ostensibly undifferentiated spelling to be characteristic of Beckford's usage and allowed the word to stand. [K.G.]

[2] This word is used four times in the 1816 edition, twice with the accent and twice without. In the only section of the edition set from manuscript, the passage extending from page 154 to 156 that Beckford translated for this edition to correct Henley's omission, the spelling, *Meimouné*, is used. I have taken this to be an indication of Beckford's conscious intent and normalized spellings accordingly. [K.G.]

the little Gulchenrouz; whilst his breast laboured with a convulsive sigh: 'let me, at least, breathe forth my soul on thy lips!' They spoke no more, and became as dead.

Immediately, the most piercing cries were heard through the harem; whilst Shaban and Sutlememe personated with great adroitness, the parts of persons in despair. The emir, who was sufficiently mortified, to be forced into such untoward expedients; and had now, for the first time, made a trial of his powder, was under no necessity of counterfeiting grief. The slaves, who had flocked together from all quarters, stood motionless, at the spectacle before them. All lights were extinguished, save two lamps; which shed a wan glimmering over the faces of these lovely flowers that seemed to be faded in the spring-time of life. Funeral vestments were prepared; their bodies were washed[B] with rose-water; their beautiful tresses were braided and incensed; and they were wrapped in symars[1] whiter than alabaster.

At the moment, that their attendants were placing two wreaths of their favourite jasmines, on their brows, the Caliph, who had just heard the tragical catastrophe, arrived. He looked not less pale and haggard than the goules that wander, at night, among the graves. Forgetful of himself and every one else, he broke through the midst of the slaves; fell prostrate at the foot of the sofa; beat his bosom; called himself 'atrocious murderer!' and invoked upon his head, a thousand imprecations. With a trembling hand he raised the veil that covered the countenance of Nouronihar, and uttering a loud shriek, fell lifeless on the floor. The chief of the eunuchs dragged him off, with horrible grimaces, and repeated as he went, 'Aye, I foresaw she would play you some ungracious turn!'

No sooner was the Caliph gone, than the emir commanded biers to be brought, and forbade that any one should enter the harem. Every window was fastened; all instruments of music were broken;[B] and the Imans began to recite their prayers.[B] Towards the close of this melancholy day, Vathek sobbed in silence; for they had been forced to compose, with anodynes, his convulsions of rage and desperation.

At the dawn of the succeeding morning, the wide folding doors of the palace were set open, and the funeral procession moved forward for the mountain. The wailful cries of 'La Ilah illa Alla!'[2] reached the Caliph, who was eager to cicatrize himself, and attend the ceremonial: nor could he have been dissuaded, had not his excessive weakness disabled him from walking. At the few first steps he fell on the ground, and his people were obliged to lay him on a bed, where he remained many days in such a state of insensibility as excited compassion in the emir himself.

When the procession was arrived at the grot of Meimouné, Shaban and Sutlememe dismissed the whole of the train, excepting the four confidential eunuchs who were appointed to remain. After resting some moments near the biers, which had been left in the open air; they caused them to be carried

---

[1] Loose garments for women.
[2] There is no God but God.

to the brink of a small lake, whose banks were overgrown with a hoary moss. This was the great resort of herons and storks which preyed continually on little blue fishes. The dwarfs, instructed by the emir, soon repaired thither; and, with the help of the eunuchs, began to construct cabins of rushes and reeds, a work in which they had admirable skill. A magazine also was contrived for provisions, with a small oratory for themselves, and a pyramid of wood, neatly piled to furnish the necessary fuel: for the air was bleak in the hollows of the mountains.

At evening two fires were kindled on the brink of the lake, and the two lovely bodies, taken from their biers, were carefully deposited upon a bed of dried leaves, within the same cabin. The dwarfs began to recite the Koran, with their clear, shrill voices; and Shaban and Sutlememe stood at some distance, anxiously waiting the effects of the powder. At length Nouronihar and Gulchenrouz faintly stretched out their arms; and, gradually opening their eyes, began to survey, with looks of increasing amazement, every object around them. They even attempted to rise; but, for want of strength, fell back again. Sutlememe, on this, administered a cordial, which the emir had taken care to provide.

Gulchenrouz, thoroughly aroused, sneezed out aloud: and, raising himself with an effort that expressed his surprize, left the cabin and inhaled the fresh air, with the greatest avidity. 'Yes,' said he, 'I breathe again! again do I exist! I hear sounds! I behold a firmament, spangled over with stars!' – Nouronihar, catching these beloved accents, extricated herself from the leaves and ran to clasp Gulchenrouz to her bosom. The first objects she remarked, were their long simars,[1] their garlands of flowers, and their naked feet: she hid her face in her hands to reflect. The vision of the enchanted bath, the despair of her father, and, more vividly than both, the majestic figure of Vathek, recurred to her memory. She recollected also, that herself and Gulchenrouz had been sick and dying; but all these images bewildered her mind. Not knowing where she was, she turned her eyes on all sides, as if to recognize the surrounding scene. This singular lake, those flames reflected from its glassy surface, the pale hues of its banks, the romantic cabins, the bullrushes, that sadly waved their drooping heads; the storks, whose melancholy cries blended with the shrill voices of the dwarfs, every thing conspired to persuade her, that the angel of death had opened the portal of some other world.[B]

Gulchenrouz, on his part, lost in wonder, clung to the neck of his cousin. He believed himself in the region of phantoms; and was terrified at the silence she preserved. At length addressing her; 'Speak,' said he, 'where are we? do you not see those spectres that are stirring the burning coals? Are they Monker and Nekir[B] who are come to throw us into them? Does the fatal bridge[B] cross this lake, whose solemn stillness, perhaps, conceals from us an abyss, in which, for whole ages, we shall be doomed incessantly to sink.'

---

[1] In the absence of evidence of Beckford's preference, the undifferentiated spellings, *simars* here – *symars* 73:15, have not been normalized. [K.G.]

'No, my children,' said Sutlememe, going towards them, 'take comfort! the exterminating angel, who conducted our souls hither after yours, hath assured us, that the chastisement of your indolent and voluptuous life, shall be restricted to a certain series of years,[B] which you must pass in this dreary abode; where the sun is scarcely visible, and where the soil yields neither fruits nor flowers. These,' continued she, pointing to the dwarfs, 'will provide for our wants; for souls, so mundane as ours, retain too strong a tincture of their earthly extraction. Instead of meats, your food will be nothing but rice; and your bread shall be moistened in the fogs that brood over the surface of the lake.'

At this desolating prospect, the poor children burst into tears, and prostrated themselves before the dwarfs; who perfectly supported their characters, and delivered an excellent discourse, of a customary length, upon the sacred camel;[B] which, after a thousand years, was to convey them to the paradise of the faithful.

The sermon being ended, and ablutions performed, they praised Alla and the Prophet; supped very indifferently; and retired to their withered leaves. Nouronihar and her little cousin, consoled themselves on finding that the dead might lay in one cabin. Having slept well before, the remainder of the night was spent in conversation on what had befallen them; and both, from a dread of apparitions, betook themselves for protection to one another's arms.

In the morning, which was lowering and rainy, the dwarfs mounted high poles, like minarets, and called them to prayers. The whole congregation, which consisted of Sutlememe, Shaban, the four eunuchs, and a few storks that were tired of fishing, was already assembled. The two children came forth from their cabin with a slow and dejected pace. As their minds were in a tender and melancholy mood, their devotions were performed with fervour. No sooner were they finished than Gulchenrouz demanded of Sutlememe, and the rest, 'how they happened to die so opportunely for his cousin and himself?' – 'We killed ourselves,' returned Sutlememe, 'in despair at your death.' On this, Nouronihar who, notwithstanding what had past, had not yet forgotten her vision said – 'And the Caliph! is he also dead of his grief? and will he likewise come hither?' The dwarfs, who were prepared with an answer, most demurely replied: 'Vathek is damned beyond all redemption!' – 'I readily believe so,' said Gulchenrouz; 'and am glad, from my heart, to hear it; for I am convinced it was his horrible look that sent us hither, to listen to sermons, and mess[1] upon rice.' One week passed away, on the side of the lake, unmarked by any variety: Nouronihar ruminating on the grandeur of which death had deprived her; and Gulchenrouz applying to prayers and basket-making with the dwarfs, who infinitely pleased him.

Whilst this scene of innocence was exhibiting in the mountains, the Caliph presented himself to the emir in a new light.[B] The instant he recovered the use of his senses, with a voice that made Bababalouk quake, he thundered out:

---

[1] Dine together.

'Perfidious Giaour! I renounce thee for ever! it is thou who has slain my beloved Nouronihar! and I supplicate the pardon of Mahomet; who would have preserved her to me, had I been more wise. Let water be brought, to perform my ablutions, and let the pious Fakreddin be called to offer up his prayers with mine, and reconcile me to him. Afterwards, we will go together and visit the sepulchre of the unfortunate Nouronihar. I am resolved to become a hermit, and consume the residue of my days on this mountain, in hope of expiating my crimes.' – 'And what do you intend to live upon there?' inquired Bababalouk: 'I hardly know,' replied Vathek, 'but I will tell you when I feel hungry – which, I believe, will not soon be the case.'

The arrival of Fakreddin put a stop to this conversation. As soon as Vathek saw him, he threw his arms around his neck, bedewed his face with a torrent of tears, and uttered things so affecting, so pious, that the emir, crying for joy, congratulated himself, in his heart upon having performed so admirable and unexpected a conversion. As for the pilgrimage to the mountain, Fakreddin had his reasons not to oppose it; therefore, each ascending his own litter, they started.

Notwithstanding the vigilance with which his attendants watched the Caliph, they could not prevent his harrowing his cheeks with a few scratches, when on the place where he was told Nouronihar had been buried; they were even obliged to drag him away, by force of hands, from the melancholy spot. However he swore, with a solemn oath, that he would return thither every day. This resolution did not exactly please the emir – yet he flattered himself that the Caliph might not proceed farther, and would merely perform his devotions in the cavern of Meimouné. Besides, the lake was so completely concealed within the solitary bosom of those tremendous rocks, that he thought it utterly impossible any one could ever find it. This security of Fakreddin was also considerably strengthened by the conduct of Vathek, who performed his vow most scrupulously, and returned daily from the hill so devout, and so contrite, that all the grey-beards were in a state of ecstasy on account of it.

Nouronihar was not altogether so content; for though she felt a fondness for Gulchenrouz, who, to augment the attachment, had been left at full liberty with her, yet she still regarded him as but a bauble that bore no competition with the carbuncle of Giamschid. At times, she indulged doubts on the mode of her being; and scarcely could believe that the dead had all the wants and the whims of the living. To gain satisfaction, however, on so perplexing a topic; one morning, whilst all were asleep, she arose with a breathless caution from the side of Gulchenrouz: and, after having given him a soft kiss, began to follow the windings of the lake, till it terminated with a rock, the top of which was accessible, though lofty. This she climbed with considerable toil; and, having reached the summit, set forward in a run, like a doe before the hunter. Though she skipped with the alertness of an antelope, yet, at intervals she was forced to desist, and rest beneath the tamarisks to recover her breath. Whilst she, thus reclined, was occupied with her little reflections on the apprehension that she had some knowledge of the place;

Vathek, who, finding himself that morning but ill at ease, had gone forth before the dawn, presented himself, on a sudden, to her view. Motionless with surprise, he durst not approach the figure before him trembling and pale, but yet lovely to behold. At length, Nouronihar, with a mixture of pleasure and affliction, raising her fine eyes to him, said: 'My lord! are you then come hither to eat rice and hear sermons with me?' – 'Beloved phantom!' cried Vathek, 'thou dost speak; thou has the same graceful form; the same radiant features: art thou palpable likewise?' and, eagerly embracing her, added: 'Here are limbs and a bosom, animated with a gentle warmth!' – What can such a prodigy mean?'

Nouronihar, with indifference answered: 'You know, my lord, that I died on the very night you honoured me with your visit. My cousin maintains it was from one of your glances; but I cannot believe him: for, to me, they seem not so dreadful. Gulchenrouz died with me, and we were both brought into a region of desolation, where we are fed with a wretched diet. If you be dead also, and are come hither to join us, I pity your lot: for, you will be stunned with the clang of the dwarfs and the storks. Besides, it is mortifying in the extreme, that you, as well as myself, should have lost the treasures of the subterranean palace.'

At the mention of the subterranean palace, the Caliph suspended his caresses, (which indeed had proceeded pretty far) to seek from Nouronihar an explanation of her meaning. She then recapitulated her vision; what immediately followed; and the history of her pretended death; adding, also, a description of the place of expiation, from whence she had fled; and all, in a manner, that would have extorted his laughter, had not the thoughts of Vathek been too deeply engaged. No sooner, however, had she ended, than he again clasped her to his bosom and said: 'Light of my eyes! the mystery is unravelled; we both are alive! Your father is a cheat, who, for the sake of dividing us, hath deluded us both: and the Giaour, whose design, as far as I can discover, is, that we shall proceed together, seems scarce a whit better. It shall be some time, at least, before he finds us in his palace of fire. Your lovely little person, in my estimation, is far more precious than all the treasures of the pre-adamite sultans; and I wish to possess it at pleasure, and, in open day, for many a moon, before I go to burrow under ground, like a mole. Forget this little trifler, Gulchenrouz: and' – 'Ah! my lord!' interposed Nouronihar, 'let me intreat that you do him no evil.' – 'No, no!' replied Vathek, 'I have already bid you forbear to alarm yourself for him. He has been brought up too much on milk and sugar to stimulate my jealousy. We will leave him with the dwarfs; who, by the bye, are my old acquaintances: their company will suit him far better than yours. As to other matters; I will return no more to your father's. I want not to have my ears dinned by him and his dotards with the violation of the rights of hospitality: as if it were less an honour for you to espouse the sovereign of the world, than a girl dressed up like a boy!'

Nouronihar could find nothing to oppose, in a discourse so eloquent. She only wished the amorous monarch had discovered more ardour for the carbuncle of Giamschid: for flattered herself it would gradually increase; and, therefore, yielded to his will, with the most bewitching submission.

When the Caliph judged it proper, he called for Bababalouk, who was asleep in the cave of Meimouné, and dreaming that the phantom of Nouronihar, having mounted him once more on her swing, had just given him such a jerk, that he, one moment, soared above the mountains, and the next, sunk into the abyss. Starting from his sleep at the sound of his master, he ran, gasping for breath, and had nearly fallen backward at the sight, as he believed, of the spectre, by whom he had, so lately, been haunted in his dream. 'Ah, my lord!' cried he, recoiling ten steps, and covering his eyes with both hands, 'do you then perform the office of a goul! have you dug up the dead? yet hope not to make her your prey: for, after all she hath caused me to suffer, she is wicked enough to prey even upon you.'

'Cease to play the fool,' said Vathek, 'and thou shalt soon be convinced that it is Nouronihar herself, alive and well, whom I clasp to my breast. Go and pitch my tents in the neighbouring valley. There will I fix my abode, with this beautiful tulip, whose colours I soon shall restore. There exert thy best endeavours to procure whatever can augment the enjoyments of life, till I shall disclose to thee more of my will.'

The news of so unlucky an event soon reached the ears of the emir, who abandoned himself to grief and despair, and began, as did his old grey-beards, to begrime his visage with ashes. A total supineness ensued; travellers were no longer entertained; no more plasters were spread; and, instead of the charitable activity that had distinguished this asylum, the whole of its inhabitants exhibited only faces of half a cubit long, and uttered groans that accorded with their forlorn situation.

Though Fakreddin bewailed his daughter, as lost to him for ever, yet Gulchenrouz was not forgotten. He dispatched immediate instruction to Sutlememe, Shaban, and the dwarfs, enjoining them not to undeceive the child, in respect to his state; but, under some pretence, to convey him far from the lofty rock, at the extremity of the lake,[1] to a place which he should appoint, as safer from danger, for he suspected that Vathek intended him evil.

Gulchenrouz, in the meanwhile, was filled with amazement, at not finding his cousin; nor were the dwarfs less surprised; but Sutlememe, who had more penetration, immediately guessed what had happened. Gulchenrouz was amused with the delusive hope of once more embracing Nouronihar, in the interior recesses of the mountains, where the ground, strewed over with orange blossoms and jasmines, offered beds much more inviting than the withered leaves in their cabin; where they might accompany with their voices, the sounds of their lutes, and chase butterflies. Sutlememe was far gone in this sort of description, when one of the four eunuchs beckoned her aside, to apprize her of the arrival of a messenger from their fraternity, who had explained the secret of the flight of Nouronihar, and brought the commands of

---

[1] To follow the 1823 text and omit the first comma in this line would be merely to add confusion where none before had existed. [K.G.]

the emir. A council with Shaban and the dwarfs was immediately held. Their baggage being stowed in consequence of it, they embarked in a shallop,[1] and quietly sailed with the little one, who acquiesced in all their proposals. Their voyage proceeded in the same manner, till they came to the place where the lake sinks beneath the hollow of a rock; but, as soon as the bark had entered it and Gulchenrouz found himself surrounded with darkness, he was seized with a dreadful consternation, and incessantly uttered the most piercing outcries; for he now was persuaded he should actually be damned for having taken too many little freedoms, in his life-time, with his cousin.

But let us return to the Caliph, and her who ruled over his heart. Bababa-louk had pitched the tents, and closed up the extremities of the valley, with magnificent screens of India cloth, which were guarded by Ethiopian slaves with their drawn sabres. To preserve the verdure of this beautiful inclosure in its natural freshness, white eunuchs went continually round it with gilt water vessels. The waving of fans was heard near the imperial pavilion; where, by the voluptuous light that glowed through the muslins, the Caliph enjoyed, at full view, all the attractions of Nouronihar. Inebriated with delight, he was all ear to her charming voice, which accompanied the lute; while she was not less captivated with his descriptions of Samarah, and the tower full of wonders; but especially with his relation of the adventure of the ball, and the chasm of the Giaour, with its ebony portal.

In this manner they conversed the whole day, and at night they bathed together, in a basin of black marble, which admirably set off the fairness of Nouronihar. Bababalouk, whose good graces this beauty had regained, spared no attention, that their repasts might be served up with the minutest exactness: some exquisite rarity was ever placed before them; and he sent even to Shiraz, for that fragrant and delicious wine which had been hoarded up in bottles, prior to the birth of Mahomet.[B] He had excavated little ovens in the rock,[B] to bake the nice manchets[2] which were prepared by the hands of Nouronihar, from whence they had derived a flavour so grateful to Vathek, that he regarded the ragouts of his other wives as entirely maukish: whilst they would have died of chagrin at the emir's, at finding themselves so neglected, if Fakreddin, notwithstanding his resentment, had not taken pity upon them.

The sultana Dilara, who, till then, had been the favourite, took this dereliction of the Caliph to heart, with a vehemence natural to her character: for, during her continuance in favour, she had imbibed from Vathek many of his extravagant fancies, and was fired with impatience to behold the superb tombs of Istakhar,[3] and the palace of forty columns; besides, having been

---

[1] Light, open boat.

[2] Fine wheaten bread rolls.

[3] In the first two appearances of this word in the first three English-language editions (at 49:22 and 70:13) the spelling used is *Istakhar*. Except for two instances in the Lausanne edition, the word is spelled *Istakhar* consistently in the first three French-language editions. I have normalized the spelling of this word, therefore, in accordance with these indications of Beckford's preference, ascribing the spelling, *Istakar*, to the unconscious repetition in successive editions of the usage introduced by Henley in the first edition. [K.G.]

brought up amongst the magi, she had fondly cherished the idea of the Caliph's devoting himself to the worship of fire: thus, his voluptuous and desultory life with her rival, was to her a double source of affliction. The transient piety of Vathek had occasioned her some serious alarms; but the present was an evil of far greater magnitude. She resolved, therefore, without hesitation, to write to Carathis, and acquaint her that all things went ill; that they had eaten, slept, and revelled at an old emir's, whose sanctity was very formidable; and that, after all, the prospect of possessing the treasures of the pre-adamite sultans, was no less remote than before. This letter was entrusted to the care of two woodmen, who were at work in one of the great forests of the mountains; and who, being acquainted with the shortest cuts, arrived in ten days at Samarah.

The Princess Carathis was engaged at chess with Morakanabad, when the arrival of these wood-fellers was announced. She, after some weeks of Vathek's absence, had forsaken the upper regions of her tower, because every thing appeared in confusion among the stars, which she consulted relative to the fate of her son. In vain did she renew her fumigations, and extend herself on the roof, to obtain mystic visions; nothing more could she see in her dreams, than pieces of brocade, nosegays of flowers, and other unmeaning gew-gaws. These disappointments had thrown her into a state of dejection, which no drug in her power was sufficient to remove. Her only resource was in Morakanabad, who was a good man, and endowed with a decent share of confidence; yet, whilst in her company, he never thought himself on roses.

No person knew aught of Vathek, and, of course, a thousand ridiculous stories were propagated at his expense. The eagerness of Carathis may be easily guessed at receiving the letter, as well as her rage at reading the dissolute conduct of her son. 'Is it so!' said she: 'either I will perish, or Vathek shall enter the palace of fire. Let me expire in flames, provided he may reign on the throne of Soliman!' Having said this, and whirled herself round in a magical manner, which struck Morakanabad with such terror as caused him to recoil, she ordered her great camel Alboufaki to be brought, and the hideous Nerkes, with the unrelenting Cafour, to attend. 'I require no other retinue,' said she to Morakanabad: 'I am going on affairs of emergency; a truce, therefore, to parade! Take you care of the people; fleece them well in my absence, for we shall expend large sums, and one knows not what may betide.'

The night was uncommonly dark, and a pestilential blast blew from the plain of Catoul, that would have deterred any other traveller however urgent the call: but Carathis enjoyed most whatever filled others with dread. Nerkes concurred in opinion with her; and Cafour had a particular predilection for a pestilence. In the morning this accomplished caravan, with the woodfellers, who directed their route, halted on the edge of an extensive marsh, from whence so noxious a vapour arose, as would have destroyed any animal but Alboufaki, who naturally inhaled these malignant fogs with delight. The peasants entreated their convoy not to sleep in this place. 'To sleep,' cried

Carathis, 'what an excellent thought! I never sleep, but for visions; and, as to my attendants, their occupations are too many to close the only eye they have.' The poor peasants, who were not overpleased with their party, remained open-mouthed with surprise.

Carathis alighted, as well as her negresses; and, severally stripping off their outer garments, they all ran to cull from those spots where the sun shone fiercest, the venomous plants that grew on the marsh. This provision was made for the family of the emir; and whoever might retard the expedition to Istakhar. The woodmen were overcome with fear, when they beheld these three horrible phantoms run; and, not much relishing the company of Alboufaki, stood aghast at the command of Carathis to set forward; notwithstanding it was noon, and the heat fierce enough to calcine even rocks. In spite however, of every remonstrance, they were forced implicitly to submit.

Alboufaki, who delighted in solitude, constantly snorted whenever he perceived himself near a habitation; and Carathis, who was apt to spoil him with indulgence, as constantly turned him aside; so that the peasants were precluded from procuring subsistence; for, the milch goats[1] and ewes, which Providence had sent towards the district they traversed to refresh travellers with their milk, all fled at the sight of the hideous animal and his strange riders. As to Carathis, she needed no common aliment; for her invention had previously furnished her with an opiate, to stay her stomach; some of which she imparted to her mutes.

At dusk, Alboufaki making a sudden stop, stampt with his foot; which, to Carathis, who knew his ways, was a certain indication that she was near the confines of some cemetery.[B] The moon shed a bright light on the spot, which served to discover a long wall with a large door in it, standing a-jar; and so high that Alboufaki might easily enter. The miserable guides, who perceived their end approaching, humbly implored Carathis, as she had now so good an opportunity, to inter them; and immediately gave up the ghost. Nerkes and Cafour, whose wit was of a style peculiar to themselves, were by no means parsimonious of it on the folly of these poor people; nor could any thing have been found more suited to their taste, than the site of the burying ground, and the sepulchres which its precincts contained. There were, at least, two thousand of them on the declivity of a hill. Carathis was too eager to execute her plan, to stop at the view, charming as it appeared in her eyes. Pondering the advantages that might accrue from her present situation, she said to herself, 'So beautiful a cemetery must be haunted by gouls! they never want for intelligence: having heedlessly suffered my stupid guides to expire, I will apply for directions to them; and, as an inducement, will invite them to regale on these fresh corpses.' After this wise soliloquy, she beckoned to Nerkes and Cafour, and made signs with her fingers, as much as to say: 'Go; knock against the sides of the tombs and strike up your delightful warblings.'

The negresses, full of joy at the behests of their mistress; and promising

---

[1] Goats kept for milk.

themselves much pleasure from the society of the gouls, went, with an air of conquest, and began their knockings at the tombs. As their strokes were repeated, a hollow noise was made[1] in the earth; the surface hove up into heaps; and the gouls, on all sides, protruded their noses to inhale the effluvia, which the carcases of the woodmen began to emit. They assembled before a sarcophagus of white marble, where Carathis was seated between the bodies of her miserable guides. The Princess received her visitants with distinguished politeness; and, supper being ended, they talked of business. Carathis soon learnt from them every thing she wanted to discover; and, without loss of time, prepared to set forward on her journey. Her negresses, who were forming tender connexions with the gouls, importuned her, with all their fingers, to wait at least till the dawn. But Carathis, being chastity in the abstract, and an implacable enemy to love intrigues and sloth, at once rejected their prayer; mounted Alboufaki, and commanded them to take their seats instantly. Four days and four nights, she continued her route without interruption. On the fifth, she traversed craggy mountains, and half-burnt forests; and arrived on the sixth, before the beautiful screens which concealed from all eyes the voluptuous wanderings of her son.

It was day-break, and the guards were snoring on their posts in careless security, when the rough trot of Alboufaki awoke them in consternation. Imagining that a group of spectres, ascended from the abyss, was approaching, they all, without ceremony, took to their heels. Vathek was, at that instant, with Nouronihar in the bath; hearing tales, and laughing at Bababalouk, who related them: but, no sooner did the outcry of his guards reach him, than he flounced from the water like a carp; and as soon threw himself back at the sight of Carathis; who, advancing with her negresses, upon Alboufaki, broke through the muslin awnings and veils of the pavilion. At this sudden apparition, Nouronihar (for she was not, at all times, free from remorse) fancied, that the moment of celestial vengeance was come; and clung about the Caliph, in amorous despondence.

Carathis, still seated on her camel, foamed with indignation, at the spectacle which obtruded itself on her chaste view. She thundered forth without check or mercy: 'Thou double-headed and four-legged monster! what means all

---

[1] The substitution in the 1823 edition of 'made' for 'heard' corrects a slight anomaly in the text arising from the translations of 'on entendoit un bruit sourd dans la terre'. Henley's practice was to render constructions using *on* into the passive voice, hence the reading of the 1786 and 1816 editions: 'a hollow noise was heard in the earth'. This translation introduces a problem in modification: the phrase, 'in the earth', appears to modify 'heard' rather than 'noise'. The positioning of elements in the French sentence avoids this ambiguity. As the account of the 1816 revisions indicates, Beckford was sensitive to ambiguous modifications. In this case he made the correction by changing the focus of the narrative from those listening *on* the earth to those making the noise *in* the earth. The revision introduces a logical parallelism: the noise in the earth was made in answer to the knockings on the earth. Given the logic of the revision, its resemblance to the pattern of revision in the 1816 edition, and the authorial nature of most of the 1823 revisions, I have adopted the 1823 reading as Beckford's final intention. [K.G.]

this winding and writhing? art thou not ashamed to be seen grasping this limber sapling; in preference to the sceptre of the pre-adamite sultans? Is it then, for this paltry doxy,[1] that thou hast violated the conditions in the parchment of our Giaour! Is it on her, thou hast lavished thy precious moments! Is this the fruit of the knowledge I have taught thee! Is this the end of thy journey? Tear thyself from the arms of this little simpleton; drown her, in the water before me; and, instantly follow my guidance.'

In the first ebullition[2] of his fury, Vathek had resolved to rip open the body of Alboufaki and to stuff it with those of the negresses and of Carathis herself, but the remembrance of the Giaour, the palace of Istakhar, the sabres, and the talismans, flashing before his imagination, with the simultaneousness of lightning, he became more moderate, and said to his mother, in a civil, but decisive tone; 'Dread lady! you shall be obeyed; but I will not drown Nouronihar. She is sweeter to me than a Myrabolan comfit;[B] and is enamoured of carbuncles; especially that, of Giamschid; which hath also been promised to be conferred upon her: she, therefore, shall go along with us; for, I intend to repose with her upon the sofas of Soliman: I can sleep no more without her.' – 'Be it so!' replied Carathis, alighting; and, at the same time, committing Alboufaki to the charge of her black women.

Nouronihar, who had not yet quitted her hold, began to take courage; and said, with an accent of fondness, to the Caliph: 'Dear sovereign of my soul! I will follow thee, if it be thy will, beyond the Kaf, in the land of the afrits.[3] I will not hesitate to climb, for thee, the nest of the Simurgh; who, this lady excepted, is the most awful of created beings.' – 'We have here then,' subjoined Carathis, 'a girl, both of courage and science!' Nouronihar had certainly both; but, notwithstanding all her firmness, she could not help casting back a thought of regret upon the graces of her little Gulchenrouz; and the days of tender endearments she had participated with him. She, even, dropped a few tears; which, the Caliph observed; and inadvertently breathed out with a sigh: 'Alas! my gentle cousin! what will become of thee!' – Vathek, at his apostrophe, knitted up his brows; and Carathis inquired what it could mean? 'She is preposterously sighing after a stripling with languishing eyes and soft hair, who loves her,' said the Caliph. 'Where is he?' asked Carathis. I must be acquainted with this pretty child: for,' added she, lowering her voice, 'I design, before I depart, to regain the favour of the Giaour. This is nothing so delicious, in his estimation, as the heart of a delicate boy palpitating with the first tumults of love.'

Vathek, as he came from the bath, commanded Bababalouk to collect the women, and other moveables of his harem; embody his troops; and hold himself in readiness to march within three days; whilst Carathis retired alone to a tent, where the Giaour solaced her with encouraging visions; but, at

---

[1] Reason or opinion.
[2] A state of agitation in the blood or humours due to heat.
[3] See *above*, p. 58 n. 2.

length, waking, she found at her feet, Nerkes and Cafour, who informed her, by their signs, that having led Alboufaki to the borders of a lake; to browse on some grey moss, that looked tolerably venomous; they had discovered certain blue fishes,^B of the same kind with those in the reservoir on the top of the tower. 'Ah! ha!' said she, 'I will go thither to them. These fish are past doubt of a species that, by a small operation, I can render oracular. They may tell me, where this little Gulchenrouz is; whom I am bent upon sacrificing.' Having thus spoken, she immediately set out, with her swarthy retinue.

It being but seldom that time is lost, in the accomplishment of a wicked enterprize, Carathis and her negresses soon arrived at the lake; where, after burning the magical drugs, with which they were always provided; they stripped themselves naked, and waded to their chins; Nerkes and Cafour waving torches around them, and Carathis pronouncing her barbarous incantations. The fishes, with one accord, thrust forth their heads from the water; which was violently rippled by the flutter of their fins: and, at length, finding themselves constrained, by the potency of the charm, they opened their piteous mouths, and said: 'From gills to tail, we are yours; what seek ye to know?' – 'Fishes,' answered she, 'I conjure you, by your glittering scales; tell me where now is Gulchenrouz?' – 'Beyond the rock,' replied the shoal, in full chorus: 'will this content you? for we do not delight in expanding our mouths.' – 'It will,' returned the Princess: 'I am not to learn, that you are not used to long conversations: I will leave you therefore to repose, though I had other questions to propound.' The instant she had spoken, the water became smooth; and the fishes, at once, disappeared. Carathis, inflated with the venom of her projects, strode hastily over the rock; and found the amiable Gulchenrouz, asleep, in an arbour; whilst the two dwarfs were watching at his side, and ruminating their accustomed prayers. These diminutive personages possessed the gift of divining, whenever an enemy to good Mussulmans approached: thus, they anticipated the arrival of Carathis; who, stopping short, said to herself: 'How placidly doth he recline his lovely little head! how pale, and languishing, are his looks! it is just the very child of my wishes!' The dwarfs interrupted this delectable soliloquy, by leaping, instantly, upon her; and scratching her face, with their utmost zeal. But Nerkes and Cafour, betaking themselves to the succour of their mistress, pinched the dwarfs so severely in return, that they both gave up the ghost; imploring Mahomet to inflict his sorest vengeance upon this wicked woman, and all her household.

At the noise which this strange conflict occasioned in the valley, Gulchenrouz awoke; and, bewildered with terror, sprung impetuously and climbed an old fig-tree that rose against the acclivity of the rocks; from thence he gained their summits, and ran for two hours without once looking back. At last, exhausted with fatigue, he fell senseless into the arms of a good old genius, whose fondness for the company of children, had made it his sole occupation to protect them. Whilst performing his wonted rounds through the air, he had pounced on the cruel Giaour, at the instant of his growling in the horrible chasm, and had rescued the fifty little victims which the impiety of Vathek had devoted to his voracity. These the genius brought up in nests still higher than the clouds, and himself fixed his abode, in a nest more capacious than the rest, from which he had expelled the Rocs that had built it.

These inviolable asylums were defended against the dives and the afrits,[1] by waving streamers; on which were inscribed in characters of gold, that flashed like lightning, the names of Alla and the Prophet. It was there that Gulchenrouz, who, as yet remained undeceived with respect to his pretended death, thought himself in the mansions of eternal peace. He admitted without fear the congratulations of his little friends, who were all assembled in the nest of the venerable genius, and vied with each other in kissing his serene forehead and beautiful eye-lids. – Remote from the inquietudes of the world; the impertinence of harems, the brutality of eunuchs, and the inconstancy of women; there he found a place truly congenial to the delights of his soul. In this peaceable society his days, months, and years glided on; nor was he less happy than the rest of his companions: for the genius, instead of burthening his pupils with perishable riches and vain sciences, conferred upon them the boon of perpetual childhood.

Carathis, unaccustomed to the loss of her prey, vented a thousand execrations on her negresses, for not seizing the child, instead of amusing themselves with pinching to death two insignificant dwarfs from which they gain no advantage. She returned into the valley murmuring; and, finding that her son was not risen from the arms of Nouronihar, discharged her ill-humour upon both. The idea, however, of departing next day for Istakhar, and of cultivating, through the good offices of the Giaour, an intimacy with Eblis himself, at length consoled her chagrin. But fate had ordained it otherwise.

In the evening as Carathis was conversing with Dilara, who, through her contrivance had become of the party, and whose taste resembled her own, Bababalouk came to acquaint her that the sky towards Samarah looked of a fiery red, and seemed to portend some alarming diaster. Immediately recurring to her astrolabes[B] and instruments of magic, she took the altitude of the planets, and discovered, by her calculations, to her great mortification, that a formidable revolt had taken place at Samarah, that Motavakel, availing himself of the disgust, which was inveterate against his brother, had incited commotions amongst the populace, made himself master of the palace, and actually invested the great tower, to which Morakanabad had retired, with a handful of the few that still remained faithful to Vathek.

'What!' exclaimed she; 'must I lose, then, my tower! my mutes! my negresses! my mummies! and, worse than all, the laboratory, the favourite resort of my nightly lucubrations, without knowing, at least, if my hair-brained son will complete his adventure? No! I will not be dupe! immediately will I speed to support Morakanabad. By my formidable art, the clouds shall pour grape-shot in the faces of the assailants and shafts of red-hot iron on their heads. I will let loose my stores of hungry serpents and torpedos, from beneath them; and we shall soon see the stand they will make against such an explosion!'

[1] See *above*, p. 58 n. 2.

Having thus spoken, Carathis hasted to her son who was tranquilly banqueting with Nouronihar, in his superb carnation-coloured tent. 'Glutton, that thou art!' cried she, 'were it not for me, thou wouldst soon find thyself the mere commander of savoury pies. Thy faithful subjects have abjured the faith they swore to thee. Motavakel, thy brother, now reigns on the hill of Pied Horses: and, had I not some slight resources in the tower, would not be easily persuaded to abdicate. But, that time may not be lost, I shall only add a few words: – Strike tent to-night; set forward; and beware how thou loiterest again by the way. Though, thou hast forfeited the conditions of the parchment, I am not yet without hope: for, it cannot be denied, that thou hast violated, to admiration, the laws of hospitality by seducing the daughter of the emir, after having partaken of his bread and his salt. Such a conduct cannot but be delightful to the Giaour; and if, on thy march, thou canst signalize thyself, by an additional crime; all will still go well, and thou shalt enter the palace of Soliman, in triumph. Adieu! Alboufaki and my negresses are waiting at the door.'

The Caliph had nothing to offer in reply: he wished his mother a prosperous journey, and ate on till he had finished his supper. At midnight, the camp broke up, amidst the flourishing of trumpets and other martial instruments; but loud indeed must have been the sound of the tymbals, to overpower the blubbering of the emir, and his grey-beards; who, by an excessive profusion of tears, had so far exhausted the radical moisture, that their eyes shrivelled up in their sockets, and their hairs dropped off by the roots. Nouronihar, to whom such a symphony was painful, did not grieve to get out of hearing. She accompanied the Caliph in the imperial litter; where they amused themselves, with imagining the splendour which was soon to surround them. The other women, overcome with dejection were dolefully rocked in their cages: whilst Dilara consoled herself, with anticipating the joy of celebrating the rites of fire, on the stately terraces of Istakhar.

In four days, they reached the spacious valley of Rocnabad. The season of spring was in all its vigour, and the grotesque branches of the almond trees, in full blossom, fantastically chequered with hyacinths and jonquils, breathed forth a delightful fragrance. Myriads of bees, and scarce fewer of santons,[1] had there taken up their abode. On the banks of the stream, hives and oratories[B] were alternately ranged; and their neatness and whiteness were set off, by the deep green of the cypresses, that spired up amongst them. These pious personages amused themselves, with cultivating little gardens, that abounded with flowers and fruits; especially, musk-melons, of the best flavour that Persia could boast. Sometimes dispersed over the meadow, they entertained themselves with feeding peacocks, whiter than snow; and turtles, more blue than the sapphire. In this manner were they occupied, when the harbingers of the imperial procession began to proclaim: 'Inhabitants of Rocnabad! prostrate yourselves on the brink of your

---

[1] Monks (European designation for monks or hermits among Muslims).

ure waters; and tender your thanksgivings to heaven, that vouchsafeth to
hew you a ray of its glory: for, lo! the commander of the faithful draws
ear.'

The poor santons, filled with holy energy, having bustled to light up wax
orches in their oratories, and expand the Koran on their ebony desks, went
orth to meet the Caliph with baskets of honey-comb, dates, and melons.
ut, whilst they were advancing in solemn procession and with measured
teps, the horses, camels, and guards, wantoned over their tulips and other
lowers, and made a terrible havoc amongst them. The santons could not
elp casting from one eye a look of pity on the ravages committing around
hem; whilst the other was fixed upon the Caliph and heaven. Nouronihar,
nraptured with the scenery of a place which brought back to her remem-
rance the pleasing solitudes where her infancy had passed, intreated
athek to stop: but he, suspecting that these oratories might be deemed, by
he Giaour, an habitation, commanded his pioneers to level them all. The
antons stood motionless with horror, at the barbarous mandate; and, at
ast, broke out into lamentations; but these were uttered with so ill a grace,
hat Vathek bade his eunuchs to kick them from his presence. He then
escended from the litter, with Nouronihar. They sauntered together in the
neadow; and amused themselves with culling flowers, and passing a
housand pleasantries on each other. But the bees, who were staunch
Mussulmans, thinking it their duty to revenge the insult offered to their
ear masters, the santons, assembled so zealously to do it with good effect,
hat the Caliph and Nouronihar were glad to find their tents prepared to
eceive them.

Bababalouk, who, in capacity of purveyor, had acquitted himself, with
pplause, as to peacocks and turtles; lost no time in consigning some dozens
o the spit; and as many more to be fricasseed. Whilst they were feasting,
aughing, carousing, and blaspheming at pleasure, on the banquet so liberally
urnished; the moullahs, the sheiks, the cadis,[B] and imans of Shiraz (who
eemed not to have met the santons) arrived; leading by bridles of riband,
nscribed from the Koran,[B] a train of asses which were loaded with the
hoicest fruits the country could boast. Having presented their offerings to
he Caliph; they petitioned him, to honour their city and mosques, with his
resence. 'Fancy not,' said Vathek, 'that you can detain me. Your presents I
ondescend to accept; but beg you will let me be quiet; for, I am not over-
ond of resisting temptation. Retire then: – Yet, as it is not decent, for
ersonages so reverend, to return on foot; and, as you have not the appear-
nce of expert riders, my eunuchs shall tie you on your asses with the
recaution that your backs be not turned towards me: for, they understand
tiquette.' – In this deputation, were some high-stomached sheiks who,
aking Vathek for a fool, scrupled not to speak their opinion. These, Bababa-
ouk girded with double cords; and having well disciplined their asses with
ettles behind, they all started, with a preternatural alertness; plunging,
icking, and running foul of one another, in the most ludicrous manner
maginable.

Nouronihar and the Caliph mutually contended who should most enjoy so degrading a sight. They burst out in peals of laughter, to see the old men and their asses fall into the stream. The leg of one was fractured; the shoulder of another, dislocated; the teeth of a third, dashed out; and the rest suffered still worse.

Two days more, undisturbed by fresh embassies, having been devoted to the pleasures of Rocnabad, the expedition proceeded; leaving Shiraz on the right, and verging towards a large plain; from whence were discernable, on the edge of the horizon, the dark summits of the mountains of Istakhar.

At this prospect, the Caliph and Nouronihar were unable to repress their transports. They bounded from their litter to the ground; and broke forth into such wild exclamations, as amazed all within hearing. Interrogating each other, they shouted, 'Are we not approaching the radiant palace of light? or gardens, more delightful than those of Sheddad?' – Infatuated mortals! they thus indulged delusive conjecture, unable to fathom the decrees of the Most High!

The good Genii, who had not totally relinquished the superintendence of Vathek; repairing to Mahomet, in the seventh heaven; said: 'Merciful Prophet! stretch forth thy propitious arms, towards they vicegerent; who is ready to fall, irretrievably, into the snare, which his enemies, the dives, have prepared to destroy him. The Giaour is awaiting his arrival, in the abominable palace of fire; where, if he once set his foot, his perdition will be inevitable.' Mahomet answered, with an air of indignation: 'He hath too well deserved to be resigned to himself; but I permit you to try if one effort more will be effectual to divert him from pursuing his ruin.'

One of these beneficent Genii, assuming, without delay, the exterior of a shepherd, more renowned for his piety than all the derviches and santons of the region, took his station near a flock of white sheep, on the slope of a hill; and began to pour forth, from his flute, such airs of pathetic melody, as subdued the very soul; and, wakening remorse, drove, far from it, every frivolous fancy. At these energetic sounds, the sun hid himself beneath a gloomy cloud; and the waters of two little lakes, that were naturally clearer than crystal, became of a colour like blood. The whole of this superb assembly was involuntarily drawn towards the declivity of the hill. With downcast eyes, they all stood abashed; each upbraiding himself with the evil he had done. The heart of Dilara palpitated; and the chief of the eunuchs, with a sigh of contrition, implored pardon of the women, whom, for his own satisfaction, he had so often tormented.

Vathek and Nouronihar turned pale in their litter; and, regarding each other with haggard looks, reproached themselves – the one with a thousand of the blackest crimes; a thousand projects of impious ambition; – the other, with the desolation of her family; and the perdition of the amiable Gulchenrouz. Nouronihar persuaded herself that she heard, in the fatal music, the groans of her dying father; and Vathek, the sobs of the fifty children he had sacrificed to the Giaour. Amidst these complicated pangs of anguish, they perceived themselves impelled towards the shepherd, whose countenance was so commanding that Vathek, for the first time, felt overawed; whilst Nouronihar concealed her face with her hands. The music paused; and the Genius, addressing the Caliph, said: 'Deluded prince! to whom Providence hath confided the care of innumerable subjects; is it thus that thou fulfillest thy mission? Thy crimes are already completed; and, art thou now hastening towards thy punishment? Thou knowest that, beyond these mountains, Eblis[B] and his accursed dives hold their infernal empire; and seduced by a malignant phantom, thou art proceeding to surrender thyself to them! This moment is the last of grace allowed thee: abandon thy atrocious purpose: return: give back Nouronihar to her father, who still retains a few sparks of life: destroy thy tower with all its abominations: drive Carathis from thy councils: be just to thy subjects: respect the ministers of the Prophet:[1] compensate for thy impieties, by an exemplary life:[B] and, instead of squandering thy days in voluptuous indulgence, lament thy crimes on the sepulchres of thy ancestors. Thou beholdest the clouds that obscure the sun: at the instant he recovers his splendour, if thy heart be not changed, the time of mercy assigned thee will be past for ever.'

Vathek, depressed with fear, was on the point of prostrating himself at the feet of the shepherd; whom he perceived to be of a nature superior to man: but, his pride prevailing, he audaciously lifted his head, and, glancing at him one of his terrible looks, said: 'Whoever thou art, withhold thy useless admonitions: thou wouldst either delude me, or art thyself deceived. If what I have done be so criminal, as thou pretendest, there remains not for me a moment of grace. I have traversed a sea of blood, to acquire a power, which will make thy equals tremble; deem not that I shall retire when in view of the port; or, that I will relinquish her, who is dearer to me than either my life, or thy mercy. Let the sun appear! let him illume my career! it matters not where it may end.' On uttering these words, which made even the Genius shudder, Vathek threw himself into the arms of Nouronihar; and commanded that his horses should be forced back to the road.

There was no difficulty in obeying these orders: for, the attraction had ceased: the sun shone forth in all his glory, and the shepherd vanished with a lamentable scream.

The fatal impression of the music of the Genius, remained, notwithstanding, in the heart of Vathek's attendants. They viewed each other with looks of consternation. At the approach of night, almost all of them escaped; and, of this numerous assemblage, there only remained the chief of the eunuchs, some idolatrous slaves, Dilara, and a few other women; who, like herself, were votaries of the religion of the Magi.[2]

The Caliph, fired with the ambition of prescribing laws to the powers of darkness, was but little embarrassed at this dereliction. The impetuosity of his blood prevented him from sleeping; nor did he encamp any more, as

---

[1] The substitution of a colon for a semicolon imposes consistency on the punctuation of this sentence. [K.G.]
[2] Persian priestly caste, especially skilled in astrology and magic.

before. Nouronihar, whose impatience, if possible exceeded his own, impor
tuned him to hasten his march, and lavished on him a thousand caresses, to
beguile all reflection. She fancied herself already more potent than Balkis,
and pictured to her imagination the Genii falling prostrate at the foot of he
throne. In this manner they advanced by moon-light, till they came withir
view of the two towering rocks that form a kind of portal to the valley, a
the extremity of which, rose the vast ruins of Istakhar. Aloft, on the moun
tain, glimmered the fronts of various royal mausoleums, the horror o
which was deepened by the shadows of night. They passed through tw
villages, almost deserted; the only inhabitants remaining being a few feebl
old men: who, at the sight of horses and litters, fell upon their knees, an
cried out: 'O Heaven! is it then by these phantoms that we have been, fo
six months tormented! Alas! it was from the terror of these spectres and th
noise beneath the mountains, that our people have fled, and left us at th
mercy of the malificent spirits!' The Caliph, to whom these complaints wer
but unpromising auguries, drove over the bodies of these wretched old men
and, at length, arrived at the foot of the terrace of black marble. There h
descended from his litter, handing down Nouronihar; both with beatin;
hearts, stared wildly around them, and expected, with an apprehensiv
shudder, the approach of the Giaour. But nothing as yet announced hi
appearance.

A death-like stillness reigned over the mountain and through the air. Th
moon dilated on a vast platform[1] the shades of the lofty columns whicl
reached from the terrace almost to the clouds. The gloomy watch-towers
whose number could not be counted, were covered by no roof; and thei
capitals, of an architecture unknown in the records of the earth, served as a
asylum for the birds of night, which, alarmed at the approach of sucl
visitants, fled away croaking.

The chief of the eunuchs, trembling with fear, besought Vathek that a fir
might be kindled. 'No!' replied he, 'there is no time left to think of sucl
trifles; abide where thou art, and expect my commands.' Having thus spoken
he presented his hand to Nouronihar; and, ascending the steps of a vas
staircase, reached the terrace, which was flagged with squares of marble, an
resembled a smooth expanse of water, upon whose surface not a blade o
grass ever dared to vegetate. On the right rose the watch-towers, ranged
before the ruins of an immense palace, whose walls were embossed witl
various figures. In front stood forth the colossal forms of four creatures
composed of the leopard and the griffin, and though but of stone, inspire
emotions of terror. Near these were distinguished by the splendour of th
moon, which streamed full on the place, characters like those on the sabre
of the Giaour, and which possessed the same virtue of changing ever;
moment. These, after vacillating for some time, fixed at last in Arabic letters
and prescribed to the Caliph the following words: – 'Vathek! thou has

---

[1] Because the inclusion of a comma after 'platform' renders a straightforward sentenc
confusing, I have followed the lead of the Bentley edition by omitting it. [K.G.]

violated the conditions of my parchment, and deserveth[1] to be sent back, but in favour to thy companion, and, as the meed[2] for what thou hast done to obtain it; Eblis permitteth that the portal of his palace shall be opened; and the subterranean fire will receive thee into the number of its adorers.'

He scarcely had read these words, before the mountain, against which the terrace was reared, trembled; and the watch-towers were ready to topple headlong upon them. The rock yawned, and disclosed within it a staircase of polished marble, that seemed to approach the abyss. Upon each stair were planted two large torches, like those Nouronihar had seen in her vision; the camphorated vapour of which ascended and gathered itself into a cloud under the hollow of the vault.

This appearance, instead of terrifying, gave new courage to the daughter of Fakreddin. Scarcely deigning to bid adieu to the moon, and the firmament; she abandoned, without hesitation, the pure atmosphere, to plunge into these infernal exhalations. The gait of those impious personages was haughty, and determined.

As they descended, by the effulgence of the torches, they gazed on each other with mutual admiration; and both appeared so resplendent, that they already esteemed themselves spiritual intelligences. The only circumstance that perplexed them, was their not arriving at the bottom of the stairs. On hastening their descent, with an ardent impetuosity, they felt their steps accelerated to such a degree, that they seemed not walking but falling from a precipice. Their progress, however, was at length impeded, by a vast portal of ebony which the Caliph, without difficulty, recognized. Here the Giaour awaited them, with the key in his hand. 'Ye are welcome!' said he to them, with a ghastly smile, 'in spite of Mahomet, and all his dependents. I will now usher you into that palace, where you have so highly merited a place.' Whilst he was uttering these words, he touched the enameled lock with his key; and the doors, at once, flew open with a noise still louder than the thunder of the dog days, and as suddenly recoiled, the moment they had entered.

The Caliph and Nouronihar beheld each other with amazement, at finding themselves in a place, which, though roofed with a vaulted ceiling, was so spacious and lofty, that, at first, they took it for an immeasurable plain. But their eyes, at length, growing familiar to the grandeur of the surrounding objects, they extended their view to those at a distance; and discovered rows of columns and arcades, which gradually diminished, till they terminated in a point radiant as the sun, when he darts his last beams athwart the ocean. The pavement, strewed over with gold dust and saffron, exhaled so subtile an odour, as almost overpowered them. They, however, went on; and observed an infinity of censers, in which, ambergrise[3] and the wood of aloes, were

---

[1] In altering 'deservest' to 'deserveth' Beckford committed an error in grammar, but since the change appears to have been consciously made, I am accepting the usage as characteristic of Beckford. [K.G.]

[2] Reward.

[3] A wax-like substance used in perfumery.

continually burning. Between the several columns, were placed tables; each, spread with a profusion of viands; and wines, of every species, sparkling in vases of crystal. A throng of Genii, and other fantastic spirits, of either sex, danced lasciviously, at the sound of music, which issued from beneath.

In the midst of this immense hall, a vast multitude was incessantly passing; who severally kept their right hands on their hearts; without once regarding any thing around them. They had all, the livid paleness of death. Their eyes, deep sunk in their sockets, resembled those phosphoric meteors, that glimmer by night, in places of interment. Some stalked slowly on; absorbed in profound reverie: some shrieking with agony, ran furiously about like tigers, wounded with poisoned arrows; whilst others, grinding their teeth in rage, foamed along more frantic than the wildest maniac. They all avoided each other; and, though surrounded by a multitude that no one could number, each wandered at random, unheedful of the rest, as if alone on a desert where no foot had trodden.

Vathek and Nouronihar, frozen with terror, at a sight so baleful, demanded of the Giaour what these appearances might mean; and, why these ambulating spectres never withdrew their hands from their hearts? 'Perplex not yourselves, with so much at once,' replied he bluntly; 'you will soon be acquainted with all: let us haste, and present you to Eblis.' They continued their way, through the multitude; but, notwithstanding their confidence at first, they were not sufficiently composed to examine, with attention, the various perspective of halls and of galleries, that opened on the right hand and left; which were all illuminated by torches and braziers, whose flames rose in pyramids to the centre of the vault. At length they came to a place, where long curtains brocaded with crimson and gold, fell from all parts in solemn confusion. Here, the choirs and dances were heard no longer. The light which glimmered, came from afar.

After some time, Vathek and Nouronihar perceived a gleam brightening through the drapery, and entered a vast tabernacle hung around with the skins of leopards. An infinity of elders with streaming beards, and afrits in complete armour, had prostrated themselves before the ascent of a lofty eminence; on the top of which, upon a globe of fire, sat the formidable Eblis. His person was that of a young man, whose noble and regular features seemed to have been tarnished by malignant vapours. In his large eyes appeared both pride and despair: his flowing hair retained some resemblance to that of an angel of light. In his hand, which thunder had blasted, he swayed the iron sceptre, that causes the monster Ouranbad,[B] the afrits, and all the powers of the abyss to tremble. At his presence, the heart of the Caliph sunk within him; and he fell prostrate on his face. Nouronihar, however, though greatly dismayed, could not help admiring the person of Eblis: for, she expected to have seen some stupendous giant. Eblis, with a voice more mild than might be imagined, but such as penetrated the soul and filled it with the deepest melancholy, said: 'Creatures of clay,[B] I receive you into mine empire: ye are numbered amongst my adorers: enjoy whatever this palace affords: the treasures of the pre-adamite sultans; their fulminating sabres; and those talismans, that compel the dives to open the subterranean expanses of the mountain of Kaf, which communicate with these. There, insatiable as your curiosity may be, shall you find sufficient objects to gratify it. You shall possess the exclusive privilege of entering the fortresses of Aherman,[B] and the halls of Argenk,[B] where are pourtrayed all creatures endowed with intelligence; and the various animals that inhabited the earth prior to the creation of that contemptible being whom ye denominate the father of mankind.'

Vathek and Nouronihar feeling themselves revived and encouraged by this harangue, eagerly said to the Giaour; 'Bring us instantly to the place which contains these precious talismans.' – 'Come,' answered this wicked dive, with his malignant grin, 'come and possess all that my sovereign hath promised; and more.' He then conducted them into a long aisle adjoining the tabernacle; preceding them with hasty steps, and followed by his disciples with the utmost alacrity. They reached, at length, a hall of great extent, and covered with a lofty dome; around which appeared fifty portals of bronze, secured with as many fastenings of iron. A funereal gloom prevailed over the whole scene. Here, upon two beds of incorruptible cedar, lay recumbent the fleshless forms of the pre-adamite kings, who had been monarchs of the whole earth. They still possessed enough of life to be conscious of their deplorable condition. Their eyes retained a melancholy motion: they regarded one another with looks of the deepest dejection; each holding his right hand, motionless, on his heart. At their feet were inscribed the events of their several reigns, their power, their pride, and their crimes; Soliman Daki; and Soliman, called Gian Ben Gian, who, after having chained up the dives in the dark caverns of Kaf, became so presumptuous as to doubt of the Supreme Power. All these maintained great state; though not to be compared with the eminence of Soliman Ben Daoud.

This king, so renowned for his wisdom, was on the loftiest elevation; and placed immediately under the dome. He appeared to possess more animation than the rest. Though, from time to time, he laboured with profound sighs; and, like his companions, kept his right hand on his heart;[B] yet his countenance was more composed, and he seemed to be listening to the sullen roar of a cataract visible in part through one of the grated portals. This was the only sound that intruded on the silence of these doleful mansions. A range of brazen vases surrounded the elevation. 'Remove the covers from these cabalistic depositaries,' said the Giaour to Vathek; 'and avail thyself of the talismans which will break asunder all these gates of bronze; and not only render thee master of the treasures contained within them, but also of the spirits by which they are guarded.'

The Caliph, whom this ominous preliminary had entirely disconcerted, approached the vases with faltering footsteps; and was ready to sink with terror when he heard the groans of Soliman. As he proceeded, a voice from the livid lips of the prophet articulated these words: 'In my life-time, I filled a magnificent throne;[B] having, on my right hand, twelve thousand seats of gold, where the patriarchs and the prophets heard my doctrines; on my left, the sages and doctors, upon as many thrones of silver, were present at all my decisions. Whilst I thus administered justice to innumerable multitudes, the birds of the air, hovering over me, served as a canopy against the rays of the sun. My people flourished; and my palace rose to the clouds. I erected a temple to the Most High, which was the wonder of the universe: but, I basely suffered myself to be seduced by the love of women, and a curiosity that could not be restrained by sublunary things. I listened to the counsels of Aherman, and the daughter of Pharaoh; and adored fire, and the hosts of heaven. I forsook the holy city, and commanded the Genii to rear the stupendous palace of Istakhar, and the terrace of the watch towers; each of which was consecrated to a star. There, for a while, I enjoyed myself in the zenith of glory and pleasure. Not only men, but supernatural beings were subject also to my will. I began to think, as these unhappy monarchs around had already thought, that the vengeance of Heaven was asleep; when, at once, the thunder burst my structures asunder, and precipitated me hither: where, however, I do not remain, like the other inhabitants, totally destitute of hope; for, an angel of light hath revealed that in consideration of the piety of my early youth, my woes shall come to an end, when this cataract shall for ever cease to flow. Till then I am in torments, ineffable torments! an unrelenting fire preys on my heart.'

Having uttered this exclamation, Soliman raised his hands towards heaven, in token of supplication; and the Caliph discerned through his bosom, which was transparent as crystal, his heart enveloped in flames. At a sight so full of horror, Nouronihar fell back, like one petrified, into the arms of Vathek, who cried out with a convulsive sob; 'O Giaour! whither hast thou brought us! Allow us to depart, and I will relinquish all thou hast promised. O Mahomet! remains there no more mercy?' – 'None! none!' replied the malicious dive.[1] 'Know, miserable prince! thou art now in the abode of vengeance and despair. Thy heart, also, will be kindled like those of the other votaries of Eblis. A few days are allotted thee previous to this fatal period: employ them as thou wilt; recline on these heaps of gold; command the infernal potentates; range, at thy pleasure, through these immense subterranean domains: no barrier shall be shut against thee. As for me, I have fulfilled my mission: I now leave thee to thyself.' At these words he vanished.

The Caliph and Nouronihar remained in the most abject affliction. Their tears were unable to flow, and scarcely could they support themselves. At length, taking each other, despondingly, by the hand, they went faltering from this fatal hall; indifferent which way they turned their steps. Every portal opened at their approach. The dives fell prostate before them. Every reservoir of riches was disclosed to their view: but they no longer felt the incentives of curiosity, of pride, or avarice. With like apathy they heard the chorus of Genii, and saw the stately banquets prepared to regale them. They

---

[1] See *above*, p. 69 n. 1.

went wandering on, from chamber to chamber; hall to hall; and gallery to gallery; all without bounds or limit; all distinguishable by the same louring gloom; all adorned with the same awful grandeur; all traversed by persons in search of repose and consolation; but, who sought them in vain; for every one carried within him a heart tormented in flames. Shunned by these various sufferers, who seemed by their looks to be upbraiding the partners of their guilt, they withdrew from them to wait, in direful suspense, the moment which should render them to each other the like objects of terror.

'What!' exclaimed Nouronihar; 'will the time come when I shall snatch my hand from thine!' – 'Ah!' said Vathek, 'and shall my eyes ever cease to drink from thine long draughts of enjoyment! Shall the moments of our reciprocal ecstasies be reflected on with horror! It was not thou that broughtest me hither; the principles by which Carathis perverted my youth, have been the sole cause of my perdition! it is but right she should have her share of it.' Having given vent to these painful expressions, he called to an afrit, who was stirring up one of the braziers, and bade him fetch the Princess Carathis from the palace of Samarah.

After issuing these orders, the Caliph and Nouronihar continued walking amidst the silent croud, till they heard voices at the end of the gallery. Presuming them to proceed from some unhappy beings, who, like themselves, were awaiting their final doom; they followed the sound, and found it to come from a small square chamber, where they discovered, sitting on sofas, four young men, of goodly figure, and a lovely female, who were holding a melancholy conversation by the glimmering of a lonely lamp. Each had a gloomy and forlorn air; and two of them were embracing each other with great tenderness. On seeing the Caliph and the daughter of Fakreddin enter, they arose, saluted, and made room for them. Then he who appeared the most considerable of the group, addressed himself thus to Vathek: – 'Strangers! who doubtless are in the same state of suspense with ourselves, as you do not yet bear your hand on your heart, if you are come hither to pass the interval allotted, previous to the infliction of our common punishment, condescend to relate the adventures that have brought you to this fatal place; and we, in return, will acquaint you with ours, which deserve but too well to be heard. To trace back our crimes to their source, though we are not permitted to repent, is the only employment suited to wretches like us!'

The Caliph and Nouronihar assented to the proposal; and Vathek began, not without tears and lamentations, a sincere recital of every circumstance that had passed. When the afflicting narrative was closed, the young man entered on his own. Each person proceeded in order; and, when the third prince had reached the midst of his adventurers, a sudden noise interrupted him, which caused the vault to tremble and to open.

Immediately a cloud descended, which, gradually dissipating, discovered Carathis on the back of an afrit,[B] who grievously complained of his burden. She, instantly springing to the ground, advanced towards her son, and said, 'What dost thou here, in this little square chamber? As the dives are become subject to thy beck, I expected to have found thee on the throne of the pre-adamite kings.'

'Execrable woman!' answered the Caliph; 'cursed be the day thou gavest me birth! Go, follow this afrit; let him conduct thee to the hall of the Prophet Soliman: there thou wilt learn to what these palaces are destined, and how much I ought to abhor the impious knowledge thou hast taught me.'

'Has the height of power, to which thou art arrived, turned thy brain?' answered Carathis: 'but I ask no more than permission to shew my respect for Soliman the prophet. It is, however, proper thou shouldest know that (as the afrit has informed me neither of us shall return to Samarah) I requested his permission to arrange my affairs; and he politely consented. Availing myself, therefore, of the few moments allowed me, I set fire to the tower, and consumed in it the mutes, negresses, and serpents, which have rendered me so much good service: nor should I have been less kind to Morakanabad, had he not prevented me, by deserting at last to thy brother. As for Bababalouk, who had the folly to return to Samarah, to provide husbands for thy wives, I undoubtedly would have put him to the torture; but being in a hurry, I only hung him, after having decoyed him in a snare, with thy wives: whom I buried alive by the help of my negresses; who thus spent their last moments greatly to their satisfaction. With respect to Dilara, who ever stood high in my favour, she hath evinced the greatness of her mind, by fixing herself near, in the service of one of the magi; and, I think, will soon be one of our society.'

Vathek, too much cast down to express the indignation excited by such a discourse, ordered the afrit to remove Carathis from his presence, and continued immersed in thoughts which his companions durst not disturb.

Carathis, however, eagerly entered the dome of Soliman, and, without regarding in the least the groans of the prophet, undauntedly removed the covers of the vases, and violently seized on the talismans. Then, with a voice more loud than had hitherto been heard within these mansions, she compelled the dives to disclose to her the most secret treasures, the most profound stores, which the afrit himself had not seen. She passed, by rapid descents, known only to Eblis and his most favoured potentates; and thus penetrated the very entrails of the earth, where breathes the sansar, or the icy wind of death. Nothing appalled her dauntless soul. She perceived, however, in all the inmates who bore their hands on their heart, a little singularity, not much to her taste.

As she was emerging from one of the abysses, Eblis stood forth to her view; but notwithstanding he displayed the full effulgence of his infernal majesty, she preserved her countenance unaltered; and even paid her compliments with considerable firmness.

This superb monarch thus answered: 'Princess, whose knowledge, and whose crimes, have merited a conspicuous rank in my empire; thou dost well to avail thyself of the leisure that remains: for, the flames and torments, which are ready to seize on thy heart, will not fail to provide thee soon with full employment.' He said, and was lost in the curtains of his tabernacle.

Carathis paused for a moment with surprise; but resolved to follow the advice of Eblis, she assembled all the choirs of genii, and all the dives, to pay her homage. Thus marched she, in triumph, through a vapour of perfumes, amidst the acclamations of all the malignant spirits; with most of whom she had formed a previous acquaintance. She even attempted to dethrone one of the Solimans, for the purpose of usurping his place; when a voice, proceeding from the abyss of death, proclaimed: 'All is accomplished!' Instantaneously, the haughty forehead of the intrepid princess became corrugated with agony: she uttered a tremendous yell; and fixed, no more to be withdrawn, her right hand upon her heart, which was become a receptacle of eternal fire.

In this delirium, forgetting all ambitious projects, and her thirst for that knowledge which should ever be hidden from mortals, she overturned the offerings of the genii; and, having execrated the hour she was begotten and the womb that had borne her, glanced off in a rapid whirl that rendered her invisible,[B] and continued to revolve without intermission.

Almost at the same instant, the same voice announced to the Caliph, Nouronihar, the four princes, and the princess, the awful, and irrevocable decree. Their hearts immediately took fire, and they, at once, lost the most precious gift of heaven: – HOPE.[B] These unhappy beings recoiled, with looks of the most furious distraction. Vathek beheld in the eyes of Nouronihar nothing but rage and vengeance; nor could she discern aught in his, but aversion and despair. The two princes who were friends, and, till that moment, had preserved their attachment, shrunk back, gnashing their teeth with mutual and unchangeable hatred. Kalilah and his sister made reciprocal gestures of imprecation; all testified their horror for each other by the most ghastly convulsions, and screams that could not be smothered. All severally plunged themselves into the accursed multitude, there to wander in an eternity of unabating anguish.

Such was, and such should be, the punishment of unrestrained passions and atrocious deeds! Such shall be, the chastisement of that blind curiosity, which would transgress those bounds the wisdom of the Creator has pre-scribed to human knowledge; and such the dreadful disappointment of that restless ambition, which, aiming at discoveries reserved for beings of a supernatural order, perceives not, through its infatuated pride, that the condition of man upon earth is to be – humble and ignorant.

Thus the Caliph Vathek, who, for the sake of empty pomp and forbidden power, had sullied himself with a thousand crimes, became a prey to grief without end, and remorse without mitigation: whilst the humble, the despised Gulchenrouz passed whole ages in undisturbed tranquillity, and in the pure happiness of childhood.

NOTES[1]

Page 29. *Caliph*
This title amongst the Mahometans implies the three characters of Prophet, Priest, and King: it signifies, in the Arabic, *Successor, or Vicar*; and, by appropriation, the *Vicar of God on Earth*. It is, at this day, one of the titles of the Grand Signior, as successor of Mahomet; and of the Sophi of Persia, as successor of Ali. *Habesci's State of the Ottoman Empire*, p. 9. *D'Herbelot*, p. 985.[2]

Page 29. *one of his eyes became so terrible*
The author of Nighiaristan hath preserved a fact that supports this account; and there is no history of Vathek, in which his *terrible eye* is not mentioned.

Page 29. *Omar Ben Abdalaziz*
This Caliph was eminent above all others for temperance and self-denial; insomuch, that, according to the Mahometan faith, he was raised to Mahomet's bosom, as a reward for his abstinence in an age of corruption. *D'Herbelot*, p. 690.

Page 29. *Samarah*
A city of the Babylonian Irak; supposed to have stood on the site where Nimrod erected his tower. Khondemir relates, in his life of Motassem, that this prince, to terminate the disputes which were perpetually happening between the inhabitants of Bagdat and his Turkish slaves, withdrew from thence, and, having fixed on a situation in the plain of Catoul, there founded Samarah. He is said to have had in the stables of this city, a hundred and thirty thousand *pied horses*; each of which carried, by his order, a sack of earth to a place he had chosen. By this accumulation, an elevation was formed that commanded a view of all Samarah, and served for the foundation of his magnificent palace. *D'Herbelot*, p. 752. 808. 985. *Anecdotes Arabes*, p. 413.

---

[1] The original notes to *Vathek* were compiled by Samuel Henley when he translated Beckford's original French version into English for the 1786 edition. Beckford subsequently edited these notes for the 1816 edition; he always regarded them as part of the text. For a detailed comparison of notes to different editions, see Lonsdale, p. 123 ff.

[2] Beckford and Henley relied heavily on B. d'Herbelot de Molainville's *Bibliothèque Orientale* ... (Paris, 1697) to which supplementary material was added by various orientalists.

Page 29. *In the most delightful succession*
The great men of the East have been always fond of music. Though forbidden by the Mahometan religion, it commonly makes a part of every entertainment. *Nitimur in vetitum semper.*[1] Female slaves are generally kept to amuse them, and the ladies of their harems.

Page 29. *Mani*
This artist, whom Inatulla of Delhi styles *the far-famed*, lived in the reign of Schabur, or Sapor, the son of Ardschir Babegan; and was, by profession, a painter and sculptor. It appears, from the Arabian Nights,[2] that Haroun al Raschid, Vathek's grandfather, had adorned his palace and furnished his magnificent pavilion, with the most capital performances of the Persian artists.

Page 30. *Houris*
The virgins of Paradise, called, from their large black eyes, *Hur al oyun*. An intercourse with these, according to the institution of Mahomet, is to constitute the principal felicity of the faithful. Not formed of clay, like mortal women, they are adorned with unfading charms, and deemed to possess the celestial privilege of an eternal youth. *Al Koran*; *passim*.

Page 30. *Mahomet in the seventh heaven*
In this heaven, the paradise of Mahomet is supposed to be placed contiguous to the throne of Alla. Hagi Khalfah relates, that Ben Iatmaiah, a celebrated doctor of Damascus, had the temerity to assert, that, when the Most High erected his throne, he reserved a vacant place for Mahomet upon it.

Page 30. *Genii*
It is asserted, and not without plausible reasons, that the words *Genn, Ginn* – *Genius, Genie, Gian, Gigas, Giant, Geant* proceed from the same themes, *viz.* Γῆ, *the earth*, and Γάω *to produce*; as if these supernatural agents had been an early production of the earth, long before Adam was modelled out from a lump of it. The Ὄντες and Εωντες of Plato, bear a close analogy to these supposed intermediate creatures between God and man. From these premises arose the consequence that, boasting a higher order, formed of more subtile matter and possessed of much greater knowledge than man, they lorded over this planet and invisibly governed it with superior intellect. From this last circumstance, they obtained in Greece, the title of Δαίμονες, Demons, from Δάημων, *Sciens*, knowing. The Hebrew word נְפִלִים Nephilim (Gen. Cap. vi. 4.) translated by *Gigantes*, giants, claiming the same etymon with Νεφέλη a cloud, seems also to indicate that these intellectual beings inhabited the void expanse of the terrestrial atmosphere. Hence the very ancient fable of men of enormous strength and size revolting against the Gods, and all the mythological lore relating to that mighty conflict; unless we

---

[1] We always strive for the forbidden. Ovid *Amores*, III.iv.17.
[2] The first European edition appeared in French, translated by A. Galland beginning in 1704. An English pirated version appeared in 1708. Henley used the 1783 edition.

trace the origin of this important event to the ambition of Satan, his revolt against the Almighty and his fall with the angels.

Page 30.   *Assist him to complete the tower*
The genii were famous for their architectural skill. The pyramids of Egypt have been ascribed to Gian Ben Gian their chief, most likely, because they could not, from records, be attributed to any one else. According to the Koran, ch. 34, the genii were employed by Solomon in the erection of his temple.

The reign of Gian Ben Gian, over the Peris, is said to have continued for two thousand years; after which, EBLIS was sent by the Deity to exile them, on account of their disorders, and confine them in the remotest region of the earth. *D'Herbelot*, p. 396. *Bailly sur l'Atlantide*, p. 147.

Page 31.   *the stranger displayed such rarities as he had never before seen*
That such curiosities were much sought after in the days of Vathek, may be concluded from the encouragement which Haroun al Raschid gave to the mechanic arts, and the present he sent, by his ambassadors, to Charlemagne. This consisted of a clock, which, when put into motion, by means of a clepsydra,[1] not only pointed out the hours, but also, by dropping small balls on a bell, struck them; and, at the same instant, threw open as many little doors, to let out an equal number of horsemen. *Ann. Reg. Franc. Pip. Caroli, &c. ad ann. 807. Weidler*, p. 205.

Page 34.   *their beards to be burnt*
The loss of the beard, from the earliest ages, was accounted highly disgraceful. An instance occurs, in the Tales of Inatulla, of one being *singed off*, as a mulet on the owner, for having failed to explain a question propounded; and, in the Arabian Nights, a proclamation may be seen similar to this of Vathek. Vol. I. p. 268. Vol. II. p. 228.

Page 37.   *Giaour means infidel*

Page 38.   *the Divan*
This was both the supreme council and court of justice, at which the caliphs of the race of the Abassides assisted in person, to redress the injuries of every appellant. *D'Herbelot*, p. 298.

Page 38.   *the prime vizir*
Vazir, vezir, or as we express it, vizir, literally signifies a *porter*; and, by metaphor, the minister who bears the principal burthen of the state, generally called the sublime Porte.

Page 39.   *The Muezins and their minarets*
Valid, the son of Abdalmalek, was the first who erected a *minaret*, or turret; and this he placed on the grand mosque at Damascus; for the *muezin*, or

---

[1] Water clock – measures time by discharge of water.

crier, to announce from it, the hour of prayer. This practice has constantly been kept to this day. *D'Herbelot*, p. 576.

Page 41. *Soliman Ben Daoud*
The name of *David* in Hebrew is composed of the letter ٦ *Vau* between two ٦ *Daleths* ٦٦٦; and according to the Massoretic points ought to be pronounced *David*. Having no U consonant in their tongue, the Septuagint substituted the letter B for V, and wrote Δαβιδ, *Dabid*. The Syriac reads *Dad* or *Dod*; and the Arabs articulate *Daoud*.

Page 44. *with the grin of an ogre*
Thus, in the history of the punished vizir: — 'The prince heard enough to convince him of his danger, and then perceived that the lady, who called herself the daughter of an *Indian* king, was an *ogress*; wife to one of the those *savage demons*, called ogre, who stay in remote places, and make use of a thousand wiles to surprize and devour passengers.' *Arab. Nights*, vol. I. p. 56.

Page 45. *mutes*
It has been usual, in eastern courts, from time immemorial, to retain a number of mutes. These are not only employed to amuse the monarch, but also to instruct his pages, in an art to us little known, that of communicating their thoughts by signs, lest the sounds of their voices should disturb the sovereign. — *Habesci's State of the Ottoman Empire*, p. 164.[1] — The mutes are also the secret instruments of his private vengeance, in carrying the fatal string.

Page 46. *Prayer announced at break of day*
The stated seasons of public prayer, in the twenty-four hours, were five: daybreak, noon, mid-time between noon and sun-set, immediately as the sun leaves the horizon, and an hour and half after it is down.

Page 46. *mummies*
Moumia (from *moum*, wax and tallow) signifies the flesh of the human body preserved in the sand, after having been embalmed and wrapt in cerements. They are frequently found in the sepulchres of Egypt; but most of the Oriental mummies are brought from a cavern near Abin, in Persia. *D'Herbelot*, p. 647.

Page 49. *a parchment*
Parchments of the like mysterious import are frequently mentioned in the works of the Eastern writers. One in particular, amongst the Arabians, is held in high veneration. It was written by Ali, and Giafar Sadek, in mystic characters, and is said to contain the destiny of the Mahometan religion, and the great events which are to happen previous to the end of the world. This parchment is of *camel's skin*.

---

[1] A. Ghiga, trans., *The Present State of the Ottoman Empire ... Translated from the French Manuscript of Elias Habesci* (1784).

Page 49. *Istakhar*
This city was the ancient Persepolis[1] and capital of Persia, under the kings of the three first races. The author of Lebtarikh writes, that Kischtab there established his abode, erected several temples to the element of fire, and hewed out, for himself and his successors, sepulchres in the rocks of the mountain contiguous to the city. The ruins of columns and broken figures which still remain, defaced as they were by Alexander, and mutilated by time, plainly evince that those ancient potentates had chosen it for the place of their interment.

Page 49. *the talismans of Soliman*
The most famous *talisman* of the East, and which could control even the arms and magic of the dives, or giants, was *Mohur Solimani*, the seal or ring of Soliman Jared, fifth monarch of the world after Adam. By means of it, the possessor had the entire command, not only of the elements, but also of demons, and every created being. *Richardson's Dissertat.* p. 272. D'Herbelot, p. 820.

Page 49. *pre-adamite sultans*
These monarchs, which were seventy-two in number, are said to have governed each a distinct species of rational beings, prior to the existence of Adam.

Page 49. *beware how thou enterest any dwelling*
Strange as this injunction may seem, it is by no means incongruous to the customs of the country. Dr Pocock[2] mentions his travelling with the train of the Governor of Faiume, who, instead of lodging in a village that was near, preferred to pass the night in a grove of palm-trees. *Travels*, vol. I. p. 56.

Page 49. *every bumper he ironically quaffed to the health of Mahomet*
There are innumerable proofs that the Grecian custom, συμπιειν κυαθιζομευος, prevailed amongst the Arabs; but had these been wanted, Carathis could not be supposed a stranger to it. The practice was to hail the gods, in the first place; and then, those who were held in the highest veneration.

Page 49. *the ass of Balaam, the dog of the seven sleepers, and the other animals admitted into the paradise of Mahomet*
It was a tenet of the Mussulman creed, that all animals would be raised again, and many of them honoured with admission to paradise. The story of the seven sleepers, borrowed from Christian legends, was this: – In the days of the Emperor Decius,[3] there were certain Ephesian[4] youths of a good family, who, to avoid the flames of persecution, fled to a secret cavern, and there

---

[1] In southern Persia, taken by Alexander the Great in 330 BC.
[2] R. Pococke, *A Description of the East, and Some Other Countries*, 2 Vols (London, 1743–5).
[3] Roman Emperor who persecuted the Christians, AD 249–51.
[4] From the Hellenistic city of Ephesus in Asia Minor.

slept for a number of years. In their flight towards the cave, they were followed by a dog, which, when they attempted to drive him back, said: '*I love those who are dear unto God; go sleep, therefore, and I will guard you.*' – For this dog the Mahometans retain so profound a reverence, that their harshest sarcasm against a covetous person, is, 'He would not throw a bone to the dog of the seven sleepers.' It is even said, that their superstition induces them to write his name upon the letters they send to a distance, as a kind of talisman to secure them a safe conveyance. *Religious Ceremonies*, vol. VII. page 74, n. *Sale's Koran*, chap. xviii. *and notes.*[1]

Page 50. *painting the eyes of the Circassians*
It was an ancient custom in the East, which still continues, to tinge the eyes of women, particularly those of a fair complexion, with an impalpable powder, prepared chiefly from crude antimony, and called *surmeh*. Ebni'l Motezz, in a passage translated by Sir W. Jones, hath not only ascertained its *purple* colour, but also likened the *violet* to it.

> Viola collegit folia sua, similia
> Collyric nigro, quod bibit lachyrmas die discessus,
> Velut si esset super vasa in quibus fulgent.
> Primae ignis flammulae in sulphuris extremis partibus.[2]

This pigment, when applied to the inner surface of the lids, communicates to the eye (especially if seen by the light of lamps) so tender and fascinating a langour, as no language is competent to express. Hence the epithet Ιοβλεφαρος, violet-colour eye-lids, attributed by the Greeks to the goddess of beauty.

Page 50. *Rocnabad*
The stream thus denominated, flows near the city of Shiraz. Its waters are uncommonly pure and limpid, and its banks swarded with the finest verdure. Its praises are celebrated by Hafez, in an animated song, which Sir W. Jones has admirably translated: –

> Boy, let yon liquid ruby flow,
> And bid thy pensive heart be glad,
> Whate'er the frowning zealots say:
> Tell them, their Eden cannot shew
> A stream so clear as Rocnabad,
> A bower so sweet as Mosella[3]

Mosella was an oratory on the banks of Rocnabad.

[1] G. Sale, *The Koran, Commonly Called The Alcoran of Mohammed, Translated into English* ... 1734; 2nd edn, 2 Vols (1764).

[2] 'The violet has folded up (?) its petals, like black eye salve which drinks tears on the day of departure (?) just as if it (?) were above the vessels in which gleam the first flamelets of fire in the tips (?) of sulphur.' W. Jones, *Poeseos Asiaticae Commentariorum Libri Sex* (1774), p. 193.

[3] W. Jones, 'A Persian Song of Hafiz' *Poems Consisting Chiefly of Translations from the Asiatic Languages* (Oxford, 1772).

Page 51. *Moullahs*
Those amongst the Mahometans who were bred to the law, had this title; and the judges of cities and provinces were taken from their order.

Page 51. *the sacred Cahaba*
That part of the temple at Mecca which is chiefly revered, and, indeed, gives a sanctity to the rest, is a square stone building, the length of which, from north to south, is twenty-four cubits; and its breadth, from east to west, twenty-three. The door is on the east side, and stands about four cubits from the ground, the floor being level with the threshold. The Cahaba has a double roof, supported internally by three octangular pillars of aloes-wood; between which, on a bar of iron, hangs a row of silver lamps. The outside is covered with rich black damask, adorned with an embroidered band of gold. This hanging, which is changed every year, was formerly sent by the caliphs. *Sale's Preliminary Discourse*, p. 152.

Page 52. *regale these pious poor souls with my good wine from Shiraz*[1]
The prohibition of wine in the Koran is so rigidly observed by the conscientious, especially if they have performed the pilgrimage to Mecca, that they deem it sinful to press grapes for the purpose of making it, and even to use the money arising from its sale. *Chardin, Voy. de Perse, tom.* II. p. 212. – *Shiraz* was famous in the East, for its wines of different sorts, but particularly for its *red*, which was esteemed more highly than even the white wine of *Kismische*.

Page 53. *the most stately tulips of the East*
The tulip is a flower of eastern growth, and there held in great estimation. Thus, in an ode of Mesihi: – 'The edge of the bower is filled with the light of Ahmed: among the plants, the fortunate *tulips* represent his companions.'

Page 53. *certain cages of ladies*
There are many passages of the Moallakat in which these *cages* are fully described. Thus, in the poem of Lebeid:
     'How were thy tender affections raised, when the damsels of the tribe departed; when they hid themselves in carriages of cotton, like antelopes in their lair, and the tents as they were struck gave a piercing sound!
     'They were concealed in vehicles, whose sides were well covered with awnings and carpets, with fine-spun curtains and pictured veils.'
     Again, Zohair: –
     'They are mounted in carriages covered with costly awnings, and with rose-coloured veils, the lining of which have the hue of crimson andemwood.' *Moallakat, by Sir W. Jones*, p. 46.35.[2] *See also Lady M. W. Montague*, Let. xxvi.[3]

[1] In Southern Persia.
[2] W. Jones, trans., *The Moallakat, Or Seven Arabian Poems Which were suspended at the Temple at Mecca* (1783).
[3] Lady Mary Wortley Montagu, Letters . . . Written during her Travels in Europe, Asia and Africa, 4 Vols (London, 1763).

Page 54. *the locusts were heard from the thickets, on the plain of Catoul*
These insects are of the same species with the τεττιξ of the Greeks, and the *cicada* of the Latins. The locusts are mentioned in Pliny, b. 11. 29. They were so called from *loco usto*, because the havoc they made wherever they passed left behind the appearance of a place desolated by fire. How could then the commentators of Vathek say that they are called *locusts*, from their having been so denominated by the first English settlers in America?

Page 55. *Vathek—with two little pages*
'All the pages of the seraglio are sons of Christians made slaves in time of war, in their most tender age. The incursions of robbers in the confines of Circassia, afford the means of supplying the seraglio, even in times of peace.' *Habesci's State of the Ottoman Empire*, p. 157. That the pages here mentioned were *Circassians*, appears from the description of their complexion: — *more fair than the enamel of Franguistan.*

Page 55. *Confectioners and cooks*
What their precise number might have been in Vathek's establishment, it is not now easy to determine; but, in the household of the present Grand Seignor, there are not fewer than a hundred and ninety. *Habesci's State*, p. 145.

Page 55. *torches were lighted, &c*
Mr Marsden relates, in his History of Sumatra,[1] that tigers prove most fatal and destructive enemies to the inhabitants, particularly in their journeys; and adds, that the numbers annually slain by those rapacious tyrants of the woods, is almost incredible. As these tremendous enemies are alarmed at the appearance of fire, it is usual for the natives to carry a splendid kind of torch, chiefly to frighten them; and, also, to make a blaze with wood, in different parts, round their villages, p. 149.

Page 56. *One of the forests of cedar, that bordered their way, took fire*
Accidents of this kind, in Persia, are not unfrequent. 'It was an ancient practice with the kings and great men to set fire to large bunches of dry combustibles, fastened round wild beasts and birds, which being then let loose, naturally fled to the woods for shelter, and caused destructive conflagrations.' *Richardson's Dissertation*, p. 185.

Page 56. *hath seen some part of our bodies; and, what is worse, our very faces*
'I was informed,' writes Dr Cooke,[2] 'that the Persian women, in general, would sooner expose to public view any part of their bodies than their faces.' *Voyages and Travels*, vol. II. p. 443.

---

[1] W. Marsden, *The History of Sumatra* (London, 1783).
[2] J. Cook, *Voyages and Travels through the Russian Empire, Tartary and Part of the Kingdom of Persia*, 2 Vols (Edinburgh, 1770).

Page 57.   *cakes baked in silver ovens for his royal mouth*
Portable ovens were a part of the furniture of eastern travellers. St Jerom (on
Lament. v. 10) hath particularly described them. The Caliph's were of the
same kind, only substituting silver for brass. Dr Pocock mentions his having
been entertained in an Arabian camp with cakes baked for him. In what the
peculiarity of the royal bread consisted, it is not easy to determine; but, in
one of the Arabian Tales, a woman, to gratify her utmost desire, wishes to
become the wife of the sultan's baker; assigning for the reason, that she
might have her fill of that bread, which is called the sultan's. Vol. IV. p. 269.

Page 57.   *vases of snow; and grapes from the banks of the Tigris*
It was customary in eastern climates, and especially in the sultry season, to
carry, when journeying, supplies of snow. These *aestivae nives* (as Mamer-
tinus styles them) being put into separate vases, were, by that means, better
kept from the air, as no more was opened at once than might suffice for
immediate use. To preserve the whole from solution, the vessels that contained it were secured in packages of straw. Gesta Dei, p. 1098. — Vathek's
ancestor, the CALIPH MAHADI, in the pilgrimage to Mecca, which he undertook from ostentation rather than devotion, loaded upon camels so prodigious a quantity as was not only sufficient for himself and his attendants,
amidst the burning sands of Arabia; but, also, to preserve, in their natural
freshness, the various fruits he took with him, and to ice all their drink whilst
he staid at Mecca: the greater part of whose inhabitants had never seen snow
till then. *Anecdotes Arabes*, p. 326.

Page 57.   *horrible Kaf*
This mountain, which, in reality, is no other than Caucasus, was supposed to
surround the earth, like a ring encompassing a finger. The sun was believed
to rise from one of its eminences, (as over Oeta, by the Latin poets) and to set
on the opposite; whence, *from Kaf to Kaf*, signified from one extremity of the
earth to the other. The fabulous historians of the East affirm, that this
mountain was founded upon a stone, called *sakhrat*, one grain of which,
according to Lokman, would enable the possessor to work wonders. This
stone is further described as the pivot of the earth; and said to be one vast
emerald, from the refraction of whose beams, the heavens derive their azure.
It is added, that whenever God would excite an earthquake, he commands
the stone to move one of its fibres, (which supply in it the office of nerves)
and, that being moved, the part of the earth connected with it, quakes, is
convulsed, and sometimes expands. Such is the philosophy of the Koran! —
    The Tarikh Tabari, written in Persian, analagous to the same tradition,
relates, that, were it not for this emerald, the earth would be liable to
perpetual commotions and unfit for the abode of mankind.
    To arrive at the Kaf, a vast region,
                Far from the sun and summer-gale,[1]

---

[1] Thomas Gray, *The Progress of Poesy* (1757), l. 83.

must be traversed. Over this dark and cheerless desart, the way is inextricable, without the direction of supernatural guidance. Here the dives or giants were confined after their defeat by the first heroes of the human race; and here, also, the peries, or faeries, are supposed in ordinary to reside. Sukrage, the giant, was King of Kaf, and had Rucail, one of the children of Adam, for his prime minister. The giant Argenk, likewise, from the time that Tahamurah made war upon him, reigned here, and reared a superb palace in the city of Aherman, with galleries, on whose walls were painted the creatures that inhabited the world prior to the formation of Adam. *D'Herbelot*, p. 230, &c. &c.

Page 57.   *the simurgh*
That wonderful bird of the East, concerning which so many marvels are told, was not only endowed with reason, but possessed also the knowledge of every language. Hence it may be concluded to have been a dive in a borrowed form. This creature relates of itself that it had seen the great revolution of seven thousand years, twelve times commence and close; and that, in its duration, the world had been seven times void of inhabitants, and as often replenished. The simurgh is represented as a great friend to the race of Adam, and not less inimical to the dives. Tahamurath and Aherman were apprised by its predictions of all that was destined to befal them, and from it they obtained the promise of assistance in every undertaking. Armed with the buckler of Gian Ben Gian, Tahamurath was borne by it through the air, over the dark desart, to Kaf. From its bosom his helmet was crested with plumes, which the most renowned warriors have ever since worn. In every conflict the simurgh was invulnerable, and the heroes it favoured never failed of success. Though possessed of power sufficient to exterminate its foes, yet the exertion of that power was supposed to be forbidden. – Sadi, a serious author, gives it as an instance of the universality of Providence, that the simurgh, notwithstanding its immense bulk, is at no loss for sustenance on the mountain of Kaf.

Page 58.   *afrits*
These were a kind of Medusae, or Lamiae, supposed to be the most terrible and cruel of all the orders of the dives. *D'Herbelot*, p. 66.

Page 58.   *Tablets fraught with preternatural qualities*
Mr Richardson[1] observes, 'that in the East, men of rank in general carried with them pocket astronomical tables, which they consulted on every affair of moment.' These tablets, however, were of the *magical* kind; and such as often occur in works of romance. Thus, in Boiardo,[2] Orlando receives, from the father of the youth he had rescued, 'a book that would solve all doubts:' and, in Ariosto,[3] Logistilla bestows upon Astolpho a similar directory.

[1] J. Richardson, *A Dissertation on the Languages, Literature and Manners of the Eastern Nations* (Oxford, 1777), p. 191.
[2] M. M. Boiardo (1441–94), Italian poet, author of *Orlando Innamorato* an epic about Charlemagne, I.v.67.
[3] L. Ariosto (1474–1533), Italian poet, inspired by Boiardo, he composed *Orlando Furioso*, XV.xiv.

Page 58. *dwarfs*
Such unfortunate beings, as are thus 'curtailed of fair proportion,' have been, for ages, an appendage of Eastern grandeur. One part of their office consists in the instruction of the pages, but their principal duty is the amusement of their master. If a dwarf happen to be a mute, he is much esteemed; but if he be also an eunuch, he is regarded as a prodigy; and no pains or expense are spared to obtain him. – *Habesci's State of the Ottoman Empire*, page 164, &c.

Page 58. *A small spring supplies us with water for the abdest, and we daily repeat prayers, &c*
Amongst the indispensable rules of the Mahometan faith, ablution is one of the chief. This rite is divided into three kinds. The first, performed before prayers, is called *abdest*. It begins with washing both hands, and repeating these words: 'Praised be Alla, who created clean water, and gave it the virtue to purify: he also hath rendered our faith conspicuous.' This done, water is taken in the right hand thrice, and the mouth being washed, the worshipper subjoins: – 'I pray thee, O Lord, to let me taste of that water, which thou hast given to thy Prophet Mahomet in paradise, more fragrant than musk, whiter than milk, sweeter than honey: and which has the power to quench for ever, the thirst of him that drinks it.' This petition is accompanied with sniffing a little water into the nose; the face is then three times washed, and behind the ears; after which, water is taken with both hands, beginning with the right, and thrown to the elbow. The washing of the crown next follows, and the apertures of the ear with the thumbs: afterward the neck with all the fingers; and, finally, the feet. In this last operation, it is held sufficient to wet the sandal only. At each ceremonial a suitable petition is offered, and the whole concludes with this: 'Hold me up firmly, O Lord! and suffer not my foot to slip, that I may not fall from the bridge into hell.' Nothing can be more exemplary than the attention with which these rites are performed. If an involuntary cough or sneeze interrupt them, the whole service is begun anew, and that as often as it happens. *Habesci*, p. 91, &c.

Page 58. *the bells of a cafila*
A cafila, or caravan, according to Pitts,[1] is divided into distinct companies, at the head of which an officer, or person of distinction, is carried in a kind of horse litter, and followed by a sumpter camel, loaded with his treasure. This camel hath a bell fastened to either side, the sound of which may be heard at a considerable distance. Others have bells on their necks and their legs, to solace them when drooping with heat and fatigue. – Inatulla[2] also, in his tales, hath a similar reference: – 'the bells of the cafila may be rung in the thirsty desert.' vol. II. p. 15. These small bells were known at Rome from the earliest times, and called from their sounds *tintinnabulum*. Phaedrus gives us

---

[1] J. Pitts, *A True and Faithful Account of the Religion and Manners of the Mohammetans* (Exeter, 1704), p. 106.
[2] A. Dow, *Tales, Translated from the Persian of Inatulla of Delhi*, 2 Vols (1768).

a lively description of the mule carrying the fiscal monies; *clarumque collo jactans tintinnabulum*. Book II. fabl. vii.[1]

Page 58.   *Deggial*
This word signifies properly a liar and impostor, but is applied, by Mahometan writers, to their *Antichrist*. He is described as having but one eye and eyebrow, and on his forehead the radicals of *cafer* or *infidel* are said to be impressed. According to the traditions of the faithful, his first appearance will be between Irak and Syria, mounted on an ass. Seventy thousand Jews from Ispahan are expected to follow him. His continuance on earth is to be forty days. All places are to be destroyed by him and his emissaries, except *Mecca or Medina*; which will be protected by angels from the general overthrow. At last, however, he will be slain by Jesus, who is to encounter him at the gate of Lud. *D'Herbelot*, p. 282. *Sale's Prelim. Disc.* p. 106.

Page 59.   *sugar*
Dr Pocock mentions the sugar-cane as a great desert in Egypt; and adds, that, besides coarse loaf sugar and sugar candy, it yields a third sort, remarkably fine, which is sent to the Grand Seignor, and prepared only for himself. *Travels*, vol. I. p. 183. 204. The jeweller's son, in the story of the third Calender, desires the prince to fetch some *melon* and *sugar*, that he might refresh himself with them. *Arab. Nights*, vol. I. p. 159.

Page 59.   *red characters*
The laws of Draco are recorded by Plutarch,[2] in his life of Solon, to have been written in blood. If more were meant by this expression, than that those laws were of a sanguinary nature, they will furnish the earliest instance of the use of *red characters*; which were afterwards considered as appropriate to supreme authority; and employed to denounce some requisition or threatening designed to strike terror.

Page 59.   *thy body shall be spit upon*
There was no mark of contempt amongst the Easterns so ignominious as this. *Arab. Nights*, vol. I. p. 115. Vol. IV. p. 275.

Page 59.   *bats will nestle in thy belly*
Bats, in those countries, were very abundant; and, both from their numbers and size, held in abhorrence. See what is related of them by Thevenot, Part I. p. 132, 3. *Egmont and Hayman*, vol. II. p. 87. and other travellers in the East.

Page 60.   *the Bismillah*
This word (which is prefixed to every chapter of the Koran, except the ninth)

---

[1] 'Shaking the clear bell on his neck', Phaedrus, Book II, *Fab.* VII.5.
[2] Plutarch (c. AD 46–120) wrote as many as fifty lives, concentrating on the moral character of his subjects. He tells how Solon abolished the Draconian Laws because he judged them to be too severe, *Life of Solon*, XVII.

signifies, 'in the name of the most merciful God.' – It became not the initiatory formula of prayer, till the time of Moez the Fatimite. *D'Herbelot*, p. 326.

Page 60.   *a magnificent teeth*
This kind of *moving throne*, though more common, at present, than in the days of Vathek, is still confined to persons of the highest rank.

Page 60.   *baths of rose water*
The use of perfumed waters for the purpose of bathing is of an early origin in the East, where every odoriferous plant breathes a richer fragrance than is known to our more humid climates. The rose which yields this lotion is, according to Hasselquist, of a beautiful pale bluish colour, double, large as a man's fist, and more exquisite in scent than any other species. The quantities of this water distilled annually at Fajhum, and carried to distant countries, is immense. The mode of conveying it is in vessels of copper, coated with wax. *Voyag.* p. 248.

Page 61.   *lamb à la crème*
No dish amongst the Easterns was more generally admired. The Caliph Abdolmelek, at a splendid entertainment, to which whoever came was welcome, asked Amrou, the son of Hareth, what kind of meat he preferred to all others. The old man answered: 'An ass's neck, well seasoned and roasted.' – 'But what say you,' replied the Caliph, 'to the leg or shoulder of a *LAMB à la crème*?' and added,
'How sweetly we live if a shadow would last!'
M.S. Baud. Numb. 161, *À, Ockley's Hist. of the Saracens*, vol. II. p. 277.[1]

Page 61.   *made the dwarfs dance against their will*
Ali Chelebi al Moufti, in a treatise on the subject, held that dancing, after the example of the derviches, who made it a part of their devotion, was allowable. But in this opinion he was deemed to be heterodox; for Mahometans, in general place dancing amongst the things that are forbidden. *D'Herbelot*, p. 98.

Page 61.   *durst not refuse the commander of the faithful*
The mandates of Oriental potentates have ever been accounted irresistible. Hence the submission of these devotees to the will of the Caliph. *Esther*, i. 19. *Daniel* vi. 8. *Ludeke Expos. brevis*, p. 60.

Page 61.   *properly lubricated with the balm of Mecca*
Unguents, for reasons sufficiently obvious, have been of general use in hot climates. According to Pliny, 'at the time of the Trojan war, they consisted of oils PERFUMED with the odours of flowers, and, chiefly, of ROSES.'[2] – Hasselquist[3] speaks of oil, impregnated with the tuberose and jessamine; but

---

[1] S. Ockley, *The History of the Saracens*, 2 Vols, 3rd edn (Cambridge, 1757).
[2] Pliny, *Natural History*, XIII, i.
[3] F. Hasselquist, *Voyages and Travels in the Levant* (Stockholm, 1766), p. 267.

the unguent here mentioned was preferred to every other. Lady M. W. Montagu, desirous to try its effects, seems to have suffered materially from having improperly applied it.

Page 61.   *black eunuchs, sabre in hand*
In this manner the apartments of the ladies were constantly guarded. Thus, in the story of the enchanted horse, Firouz Schah, traversing a strange palace by night, entered a room, 'and, by the light of a lanthorn, saw that the persons he had heard snoring, were black eunuchs with naked sabres by them; which was enough to inform him that this was the guard-chamber of some queen or princess.' *Arabian Nights*, vol. IV. p. 189.

Page 62.   *to let down the great swing*
The swing was an exercise much used in the apartments of the Eastern ladies, and not only contributed to their amusement, but also to their health. *Tales of Inatulla*, vol. I. p. 259.

Page 62.   *melodious Philomel, I am thy rose*
The passion of the nightingale for the rose is celebrated over all the East. Thus, Mesihi, as translated by Sir W. Jones:
> Come, charming maid, and hear thy poet sing,
> Thyself the rose, and he the bird of Spring:
> Love bids him sing, and Love will be obey'd,
> Be gay: too soon the flowers of Spring will fade.[1]

Page 63.   *oil spilt in breaking the lamps*
It appears from Thevenot, that illuminations were usual on the arrival of a stranger, and he mentions, on an occasion of this sort, two hundred lamps being lighted. The quantity of oil, therefore, spilt on the margin of the bath, may be easily accounted for, from this custom.

Page 63.   *calenders*
These were a sort of men amongst the Mahometans, who abandoned father and mother, wife and children, relations and possessions, to wander through the world, under a pretence of religion, entirely subsisting on the fortuitous bounty of those they had the address to dupe. *D'Herbelot, Suppl.* p. 204.

Page 63.   *santons*
A body of religionists who were also called *abdals*, and pretended to be inspired with the most enthusiastic raptures of divine love. They were regarded by the vulgar as *saints. Olearius*, tom. I. p. 971. *D'Herbelot*, p. 5.

Page 63.   *derviches*
The term *dervich* signifies a *poor man*, and is the general appellation by which a Mahometan monk is named. There are, however, discriminations that distinguish this class from the others already mentioned. They are bound by no vow of poverty, they abstained not from marriage, and, whenever disposed,

---

[1] W. Jones, 'A Turkish Ode of Mesihi', *Poems* (1772), p. 113.

they may relinquish both their blue shirt and profession. *D'Herbelot, Suppl.* 214. – It is observable that these different orders, though not established till the reign of Nasser al Samani, are notwithstanding mentioned by our author as coeval with Vathek, and by the author of the Arabian Nights, as existing in the days of Haroun al Raschid: so that the Arabian fabulists appear as inattentive to chronological exactness in points of this sort, as our immortal dramatist himself.

Page 63. *Bramins*
These constitute the principal caste of the Indians, according to whose doctrine *Brahma*, from whom they are called, is the first of the three created beings, by whom the world was made. This Brahma is said to have communicated to the Indians four books, in which all the sciences and ceremonies of their religion are comprized. The word Brahma, in the Indian language, signifies *pervading all things*. The Brahmins lead a life of most rigid abstinence, refraining not only from the use, but even the touch, of animal food; and are equally exemplary for their contempt of pleasures and devotion to philosophy and religion. *D'Herbelot*, p. 212. *Bruckeri Hist. Philosoph.* tom. I. p. 194.

Page 64. *faquirs*
This sect are a kind of religious anchorets, who spend their whole lives in the severest austerities and mortification. It is almost impossible for the imagination to form an extravagance that has not been practised by some of them, to torment themselves. As their reputation for sanctity rises in proportion to their sufferings, those amongst them are reverenced the most, who are most ingenious in the invention of tortures, and persevering in enduring them. Hence some have persisted in sitting or standing for years together in one unvaried posture; supporting an almost intolerable burden; dragging the most cumbrous chains; exposing their naked bodies to the scorching sun, and hanging with the head downward before the fiercest fires. *Relig. Ceremon.* vol. III. p. 264, &c. *White's Sermons*, p. 504.

Page 64. *some that cherished vermin*
In this attachment they were not singular. The Emperor Julian[1] not only discovered the same partiality, but celebrated, with visible complacency, the shaggy and *populous* beard, which he fondly cherished; and even 'The Historian of the Roman Empire' affirms 'that the little animal is a beast familiar to man, and signifies love.' Vol. II. p. 343.[2]

Page 64. *Visnow and Ixhora*
Two deities of the Hindoos. The traditions of their votaries are, probably,

[1] Julian, Roman Emperor (361–3 AD) enthusiastic Hellenist.
[2] Edward Gibbon, *The History of the Decline and Fall of the Roman Empire*, 6 Vols (London, 1774–78). Gibbon (1737–94) was one of the English community at Geneva who shunned Beckford when he went into exile there in 1785 with Lady Margaret. Later, in an act of revenge, Beckford bought Gibbon's library and locked it up for several years.

allegorical; but without a key to disclose their mystic import, they are little better than senseless jargon; and, with the key, downright nonsense.

Page 64. *talapoins*
This order, which abounds in Siam, Laos, Pegu, and other countries, consists of different classes, and both sexes, but chiefly of men. *Relig. Ceremon.* vol. IV. p. 62, &c.

Page 64. *objects of pity were sure to swarm around him*
Ludeke mentions the practice of bringing those who were suffering under any calamity, or had lost the use of their limbs, &c. into public, for the purpose of exciting compassion. On an occasion, therefore, of this sort, when Fakreddin, like a pious Mussulman, was publicly to distribute his alms, and the commander of the faithful to make his appearance, such an assemblage might well be expected. The Eastern custom of regaling a convention of this kind is of great antiquity, as is evident from the parable of the king, in the Gospels, who entertained the maimed, the lame, and the blind; nor was it discontinued when Dr Pocock visited the East. Vol. I. p. 182.

Page 65. *small plates of abominations*
The Koran hath established several distinctions relative to different kinds of food, in imitation of the Jewish prescriptions; and many Mahometans are so scrupulous as not to touch the flesh of any animal over which, *inarticulo mortis*,[1] the butcher had omitted to pronounce the *Bismillah*. *Relig. Cerem.* Vol. VII. p. 110.

Page 65. *Sinai*
This mountain is deemed by Mahometans the noblest of all others, and even regarded with the highest veneration, because the divine law was promulgated from it. *D'Herbelot*, p. 812.

Page 65. *Peries*
The word *Peri*, in the Persian language, signifies that beautiful race of creatures which constitutes the link between angels and men. *See note to page 6.*

Page 65. *butterflies of Cachemire*
The same insects are celebrated in an unpublished poem by Mesihi. Sir Anthony Shirley relates, that it was customary in Persia 'to hawke after butterflies with sparrows, made to that use, and stares.'[2] – It is, perhaps, to this amusement that our Author alludes in the context.

Page 66. *Megnoun and Leilah*
These personages are esteemed amongst the Arabians as the most beautiful, chaste, and impassioned of lovers; and their amours have been celebrated

---

[1] 'Silenced in death'.
[2] A. Sherley, *His Relation of His Travels into Persia ...* (London, 1613).

with all the charms of verse in every Oriental language. The Mahometans regard them, and the poetical records of their love, in the same light as the Bridegroom and Spouse, and the Song of Songs are regarded by the Jews. *D'Herbelot*, p. 573.

Page 66.   *dart the lance in the chace*
Throwing the lance was a favourite pastime with the young Arabians; and so expert were they in this practice (which prepared them for the mightier conflicts, both of the chace and war) that they could bear off a ring on the points of their javelins. *Richardson's Dissertat.* p. 198. 281.

Page 66.   *The two brothers had mutually engaged their children to each other*
Contracts of this nature were frequent amongst the Arabians. Another instance occurs in the Story of Noureddin Ali and Benreddin Hassan.

Page 67.   *Nouronihar loved her cousin, more than her own beautiful eyes*
This mode of expression not only occurs in the sacred writers, but also in the Greek and Roman. Thus Catullus says:
> Quem plus illa oculis suis amabat.[1]

Page 67.   *the same long languishing looks*
So Ariosto:
> — negri occhi, —
> Pietosi a riguardare, a mover parchi.[2]

Page 67.   *Shaddukian and Ambreabad*
These were two cities of the Peries, in the imaginary region of *Ginnistan*, the former signifies *pleasure* and *desire*, the latter *the city of Ambergris*. See *Richardson's Dissertat.* p. 169.

Page 68.   *a spoon of cocknos*
The cocknos is a bird whose beak is much esteemed for its beautiful polish, and sometimes used as a spoon. Thus, in the History of Atalmulck and Zelica Begum, it was employed for a similar purpose: — 'Zelica having called for refreshment, six old slaves instantly brought in and distributed *Mahramas*, and then served about in a great bason of Martabam, a salad *made of herbs of various kinds, citron juice, and the pith of cucumbers.* They served it first to the Princess in a *cocknos' beak:* she took a beak of the salad, eat it, and gave another to the next slave that sat by her on her right hand; which slave did as her mistress had done.'

Page 69.   *Goules*
Goul, or *ghul*, in Arabic, signifies any terrifying object, which deprives people of the use of their senses. Hence it became the appellative of that species of

---

[1] 'Dearer to her than her two eyes', Catullus, *Poems*, III.5.
[2] 'black eyes, compassionate of look, sparing of movement', Ariosto, *Orlando Furioso*, VII.XII.2–3.

monster which was supposed to haunt forests, cemeteries, and other lonely places; and believed not only to tear in pieces the living, but to dig up and devour the dead. *Richardson's Dissert.* p. 174. 274.

Page 69.   *feathers of the heron, all sparkling with carbuncles*
Panaches of this kind are amongst the attributes of Eastern royalty. *Tales of Inatulla*, vol. ii. p. 205.

Page 70.   *the carbuncle of Giamschid*
This mighty potentate was the fourth sovereign of the dynasty of the Pischalians, and brother or nephew to Tahamurath. His proper name was *giam* or *jem*, and *sched*, which in the language of the ancient Persians denominated the sun: an addition, ascribed by some to the majesty of his person, and by others to the splendour of his actions. One of the most magnificent monuments of his reign was the city of Istakhar, of which Tahamurath had laid the foundations. This city, at present called *Gihil-*, or *Tchil-minar*, from the forty columns reared in it by Homai, or (according to our author and others) by Soliman Ben Daoud, was known to the Greeks by the name of Persepolis: and there is still extant in the East a tradition, that, when Alexander[1] burnt the edifices of the Persian kings, seven stupendous structures of Giamschid were consumed with his palace.

Page 70.   *the torches were extinguished*
To the union here prefigured, the following lines may be applied:
>   Non *Hymenaeus* adest illi, non gratia lecto;
>   Eumenides tenuere faces de funere raptas:
>   Eumenides stravere torum.[2]

Page 70.   *She clapped her hands*
This was the ordinary method in the East of calling the attendants in waiting. *See Arabian Nights.* vol. I. p. 5. 106. 193, &c.

Page 73.   *Funeral vestments were prepared; their bodies washed, &c*
The rites here practised had obtained from the earliest ages. Most of them may be found in Homer[3] and the other poets of Greece. Lucian[4] describes the dead in his time as washed, perfumed, vested, and crowned, with the flowers most in season; or, according to other writers, those in particular which the deceased were wont to prefer.

Page 73.   *all instruments of music were broken*
Thus, in the Arabian Nights: 'Haroun al Raschid wept over Schemselnihar,

[1] Alexander the Great (356–323 BC), King of Macedon whose conquest of the East took him as far as India.
[2] 'Neither Hymen nor a Grace stands by that marriage bed; rather Eumenides held the bridal torches (snatched from a pyre), Eumenides pepared the couch', Ovid, *Metamorphoses*, VI.429–31.
[3] Greek epic poet (12c to 7c BC?) author of *Iliad* and *Odyssey*.
[4] Philosopher and satirist (AD c115–200) born at Samosata on Euphrates, lived in Athens.

and, before he left the room, ordered all the musical instruments to be broken.' Vol. II. p. 196.

Page 73. *Imans began to recite their prayers*
An iman is the principal priest of a mosque. It was the office of the imans to precede the bier, praying as the procession moved on. *Relig. Cerem.* vol. VII. p. 117.

Page 74. *the angel of death had opened the portal of some other world*
The name of this exterminating angel is *Azrael*, and his office is to conduct the dead to the abode assigned them; which is said by some to be near the place of their interment. Such was the office of Mercury[1] in the Grecian Mythology. *Sale's Prelim. Disc.* p. 101. *Hyde in notis ad Bobov.* p. 19. *R. Elias, in Tishbi. Buxtorf Synag. Jud. et Lexic. Talmud. Homer. Odyss.*

Page 74. *Monker and Nekir*
These are two black angels of a tremendous appearance, who examine the departed on the subject of his faith: by whom, if he give not a satisfactory account, he is sure to be cudgelled with maces of red-hot iron, and tormented more variously than words can describe. *Relig. Ceremon.* vol. VII, p. 59. 68. 118. vol. V. p. 290. *Sale's Prelim. Disc.* p. 101.

Page 74. *the fatal bridge*
This bridge, called in Arabick *al Siral*, and said to extend over the infernal gulph, is represented as narrower than a spider's web, and sharper than the edge of a sword. Yet the paradise of Mahomet can be entered by no other avenue. Those indeed who have behaved well need not be alarmed; mixed characters will find it difficult; but the wicked soon miss their standing, and plunge headlong into the abyss. *Pocock in Port. Mos.* p. 282, &c.

Page 75. *a certain series of years*
According to the tradition from the Prophet, not less than nine hundred, nor more than seven thousand.

Page 75. *the sacred camel*
It was an article of the Mahometan creed, that all animals would be raised again, and some of them admitted into paradise. The animal here mentioned appears to have been of the those *white-winged* CAMELS *caparisoned with gold*, which Ali affirmed would be provided to convey the faithful. *Relig. Cer.* vol. VII, p. 70. *Sale's Prelim. Disc.* p. 112. *Al Janheri. Ebno'l Athir,* &c.

Page 75. *the Caliph presented himself to the emir in a new light*
The propensity of a vicious person, in affliction, to seek consolation from the ceremonies of religion, is an exquisite trait in the character of Vathek.

Page 79. *wine hoarded up in bottles, prior to the birth of Mahomet*
The prohibition of wine by the Prophet materially diminished its consumption,

---

[1] Roman name for Hermes, messenger of the Gods and conductor of souls of the dead to Hades, the underworld.

within the limits of his own dominions. Hence a reserve of it might be expected, of the age here specified. The custom of hoarding wine was not unknown to the Persians, though not so often practised by them, as by the Greeks and the Romans.

'I purchase' (says Lebeid) 'the old liquor, at a dear rate, in dark leathern bottles, long reposited; or in casks black with pitch, whose seals I break, and then fill the cheerful goblet.'[1] *Moallakat*, p. 53.

Page 79. *excavated ovens in the rock*
As substitutes for the portable ovens, which were lost.

Page 81. *the confines of some cemetery*
Places of interment in the East were commonly situated in scenes of solitude. We read of one in the history of the first calender, abounding with so many monuments, that four days were successively spent in it without the inquirer being able to find the tomb he looked for: and, from the story of Ganem, it appears that the doors of these cemeteries were often left open. *Arabian Nights*, vol. II. p. 112.

Page 83. *a Myrabolan comfit*
The invention of this confection is attributed by M. Cardonne[2] to Avicenna,[3] but there is abundant reason, exclusive of our author's authority, to suppose it of a much earlier origin. Both the Latins and Greeks were acquainted with the balsam, and the tree that produced it was indigenous in various parts of Arabia.

Page 84. *blue fishes*
Fishes of the same colour are mentioned in the Arabian Nights; and, like these, were endowed with the gift of speech.

Page 85. *astrolabes*
The mention of the astrolabe may be deemed incompatible, at first view, with chronological exactness, as there is no instance of any being constructed by a Mussulman, till after the time of Vathek. It may, however, be remarked, to go no higher, that Sinesius, bishop of Ptolemais, invented one in the fifth century; and that Carathis was not only herself a Greek, but also cultivated those sciences which the good Mussulmans of her time all held in abhorrence. *Bailly, Hist. de l'Astronom. Moderne*, tom. I. p. 563. 573.[4]

Page 86. *On the banks of the stream, hives and oratories*
The bee is an insect held in high veneration amongst the Mahometans, it

---

[1] From W. Jones, trans., *The Moallakat, Or Seven Arabian Poems, Which were Suspended on the Temple At Mecca* (1783).

[2] D. Cardonne, *A Miscellany of Eastern Learning*, 2 Vols (1771).

[3] Ibn Sina (980–1037) who taught medicine and philosophy at Ispahan. Renowned for his medical knowledge, he was nevertheless an insatiable sybarite.

[4] J. S. Bailly, *Histoire de L'Astronomie moderne depuis la fondation de l'école d'Alexandre*, 3 Vols (Paris, 1779–82).

being pointed out in the Koran, 'for a sign unto the people that understand.
It has been said, in the same sense: 'Go to the ant, thou sluggard,' *Prov.* vi. 6
The santons, therefore, who inhabit the fertile banks of Rocnabad, are no
less famous for their hives than their oratories. *D'Herbelot*, p. 717.

Page 87.   *Shieks, cadis*
Shieks are the chiefs of the societies of derviches: cadis are the magistrates of
a town or city.

Page 87.   *Asses in bridles of riband inscribed from the Koran*
As the judges of Israel in ancient days rode on white asses, so amongst th
Mahometans, those that affect an extraordinary sanctity, use the same anima
in preference to the horse. Sir John Chardin observed in various parts of the
East, that their reins, as here represented, were of silk, with the name of God
or other inscriptions upon them. *Budeke Expos. brevis*, p. 49. *Chardin's MS*
cited by Harmer.[1]

Page 89.   *Eblis*
D'Herbelot supposes this title to have been a corruption of the Greek
Διαβολος *diabolos*. It was the appellation conferred by the Arabians upon
the prince of the apostate angels, and appears more likely to originate from
the Hebrew הבל, *hebel*, vanity, pride. – *See below the note*[1] *'creatures of
clay.'*

Page 89.   *compensate for thy impieties by an exemplary life*
It is an established article of the Mussulman creed, that the actions of
mankind are all weighed in a vast unerring balance, and the future condition
of the agents determined according to the preponderance of evil or good
This fiction, which seems to have been borrowed from the Jews, had prob
ably its origin in the figurative language of scripture. Thus, Psalm lxii. 9
Surely men of low degree are vanity, and men of high degree are a lie: to be
laid in the balance, they are altogether lighter than vanity: and, in Daniel, the
sentence against the King of Babylon, inscribed on the wall: Thou art
weighed in the balance, and found wanting.

Page 90.   *Balkis*
This was the Arabian name of the Queen of Sheba, who went from the south
to hear the wisdom and admire the glory of Solomon. The Koran represents
her as a worshipper of fire. Solomon is said not only to have entertained her
with the greatest magnificence, but also to have raised her to his bed and his
throne. *Al Koran*, ch. XXVII. and *Sale's notes. D'Herbelot*, p. 182.

Page 92.   *Ouranbad*
This monster is represented as a fierce flying hydra, and belongs to the same
class with the *rakshe* whose ordinary food was serpents and dragons; the
scham, which had the head of a horse, with four eyes, and the body of a

---

[1] Part of Chardin's manuscript was published in T. Harmer, *Observations on Divers
Passages of Scripture*, 2nd edn, 4 Vols (1776).

flame-coloured dragon; the *syl*, a basilisk with a face resembling the human, but so tremendous that no mortal could bear to behold it; the *ejder*, and others. See these respective titles in Richardson's Persian, Arabic and English Dictionary.[1]

Page 92.   *Creatures of clay*
Nothing could have been more appositely imagined than this compellation. Eblis, according to Arabian mythology, had suffered a degradation from his primeval rank, and was consigned to these regions, for having refused to worship Adam, in obedience to the supreme command: alledging in justification of his refusal, that himself had been formed of etherial fire, whilst Adam was only a creature of clay. *Al Koran*, c. 55, &c.

Page 93.   *the fortress of Aherman*
In the mythology of the easterns, Aherman was accounted *the Demon of Discord*. The ancient Persian romances abound in descriptions of this fortress, in which the inferior demons assemble to receive the behests of their prince; and from whom they proceed to exercise their malice in every part of the world. *D'Herbelot*, p. 71.

Page 93.   *the halls of Argenk*
The halls of this mighty dive, who reigned in the mountains of Kaf, contained the statues of the seventy-two Solimans, and the portraits of the various creatures subject to them; not one of which bore the slightest similitude to man. Some had many heads; others, many arms; and some consisted of many bodies. Their heads were all very extraordinary, some resembling the elephant's, the buffalo's and the boar's; whilst others were still more monstrous. *D'Herbelot*, p. 820. Some of the idols worshipped to this day in the Hindostan answer to this description.

Ariosto, who owes more to Arabian fable than his commentators have hitherto supposed, seems to have been no stranger to the halls of Argenk, when he described one of the fountains of Merlin: —

> Era una delle fonti di Merlino
> Delle quattro di Francia da lui fatte;
> D'intorno cinta di bel marmo fino,
> Lucido, e terso, e bianco più che latte.
> Quivi d' intaglio con lavor divino
> Avea Merlino immagini ritratte.
> Direste che spiravano, e se prive
> Non fossero di voce, ch' eran vive.
>
> Quivi una Bestia uscir della foresta
> Parea di crudel vista, odiosa, e brutta,
> Che avea le orecchie d'asino, e la testa

---

[1] J. Richardson, *A Dictionary, Persian, Arabic & English*, 2 Vols (Oxford, 1777–80).

Di lupo, e i denti, e per gran fame asciutta;
Branche avea di leon; l'altro, che resta,
Tutto era volpe.[1]

Page 93.　*holding his right hand motionless on his heart.*
Sandys observes, that the application of the right hand to the heart is the customary mode of eastern salutation; but the perseverance of the votaries of Eblis in this attitude, was intended to express their devotion to him both heart and hand.

Page 93.　*In my life-time, I filled, &c*
This recital agrees perfectly with those in the Koran, and other Arabian legends.

Page 95.　*Carathis on the back of an afrit*
The expedition of the afrit in fetching Carathis, is characteristic of this order of dives. We read in the Koran that another of the fraternity offered to bring the Queen of Saba's throne to Solomon, before he could rise from his place, c. 27.

Page 97.　*Glanced off in a whirl that rendered her invisible*
It was extremely proper to punish Carathis by a rite, and one of the principal characteristics of that science in which she so much delighted, and which was the primary cause of Vathek's perdition and of her own. The circle, the emblem of eternity, and the symbol of the sun, was held sacred in the most ancient ceremonies of incantations; and the whirling round deemed as a necessary operation in magical mysteries. Was not the name of the greatest enchantress in fabulous antiquity, Circe,[2] derived from Κιρκος, a circle, on account of her magical revolutions and of the circular appearance and motion of the sun her father? The fairies and elves used to arrange themselves in a ring on the grass; and even the augur, in the liturgy of the Romans, whirled round, to encompass the four cardinal points of the world. It is remarkable, that a derivative of the Arabic word (which corresponds to the Hebrew 7,76, and is interpreted *scindere secare se in orbem, inde notio circinandi, mox gyrandi et hinc à motu versatili, fascinavit, incantavit)*[3] *signifies, in the Koran, the glimmering of twilight*; a sense deducible from the shapeless glimpses of objects, when hurried round with the velocity here described, and very applicable to the sudden disappearance of Carathis, who,

----

[1] 'It was one of the four springs which Merlin had created in France. It was surrounded by fine, shining marble which was polished and whiter than milk. Here Merlin had, with divine workmanship, carved images – you would say they breathed, and if they were no mute, that they wee alive.
Here a beast appeared coming out of the forest; a cruel, hateful and ugly sight, having ass' ears and the head, thin with hunger and teeth of a wolf; it has lions claws and for the rest was all fox', Ariosto, *Orlando Furioso*, XXVI, xxx–xxxi.

[2] Figure of Greek mythology who had a son by Odysseus.

[3] 'to tear, cut oneself in a circular fashion, whence the idea of circular motion, then of gyration and thence from a whirling movement, betwitches, enchants.'

like the stone in a sling, by the progressive and rapid increase of the circular motion, soon ceased to be perceptible. Nothing can impress a greater awe upon the mind than does this passage in the original.

Page 97. *They at once lost the most precious gift of heaven – Hope*
It is a soothing reflection to the bulk of mankind, that the commonness of any blessing is the true test of its value. Hence, Hope is justly styled 'the most precious of the gifts of heaven,' because, as Thales long since observed – ὅις αλλο μηδεν, αυτη παρεςιν[1] – it abides with those who are destitute of every other. Dante's inscription over the gate of hell was written in the same sense, and perhaps in allusion to the saying of the Grecian sage: –

Per me si va nella città dolente:
Per me si va nell' eterno dolore:
Per me si va tra la perduta gente.
Giustizia mosse 'l mio alto fattore:
Fecemi la divina potestate,
La somma sapienza, e 'l primo amore.
Dinanzi a me non fur cose create,
Se non eterne, ed io eterno duro:
Lasciate ogni speranza, voi che 'ntrate.
CANTO III.[1]

Strongly impressed with this idea, and in order to complete his description of the infernal dungeon, Milton says,

—— where ——
———— hope never comes
That comes to all.
Paradise L. l. 66.

THE END

[1] She is there/present, for those who have nothing else (source in Thales cannot be found).

[2]   'THROUGH me you pass into the city of woe:
Through me you pass into eternal pain:
Through me among the people lost for aye.

Justice the founder of my fabric moved:
To rear me was the task of power divine,
Supremest Wisdom, and primeval Love.
Before me things create were none, save things
Eternal, and eternal I endure.
All hope abandon, ye who enter here.'
A. Dante, *Inferno*, Canto III, 1–9, H. F. Cary trans., *The Vision; or Hell, Purgatory and Paradise by Dante Alighieri*, 1814 2nd edn, 3 Vols (London, 1819), 1:20–1.

SATIRES

I

From *Biographical Memoirs of Extraordinary Painters*, London, 1780

ALDROVANDUS MAGNUS[1]

This illustrious artist was one of the first who brought the art of painting in oil to a degree of perfection. It is well known, that Hubert and John Van-eyck[2] in a manner discovered this admirable secret, the finding of which occasioned almost as much trouble as the researches after the philosopher's stone; but though the Van-eycks succeeded to the admiration of all Europe, still the most experienced colourists unanimously allow Aldrovandus to have exceeded them in every respect. His varnish (composed chiefly of nut-oil) gave a superior glow to his paintings, rendered the tints more mellow, and the nice strokes of his pencil far more discernable than those of the Van-eycks: this circumstance alone is sufficient to give the preference to our artist, had not his knowledge of the demi-tints raised him above all his predecessors. Bruges claims the honour of his birth, which happened on St Simon's day, 1473.[3] His parents, wealthy merchants trading to the Levant, intended to send him into those countries, that he might acquire the language and be serviceable in their commerce. Every thing was agreed upon, and the day fixed for his departure. Fortunately for the arts, Jean Hemmeline,[4] a disciple of the Van-eycks, chanced to pay a visit to the old Aldrovandus, his beloved friend, on the eve of his son's departure. Observing a number of loose papers covered with sketches of animals and figures, scattered about the apartment, Hemmeline was tempted to take up some of them, and sitting down began to examine them with attention. He had not long contemplated them, before he broke out into exclamations of surprize, and enquired hastily for their author. The father, who was writing at his desk by the fire side, paid little attention to his friend's enthusiasm, and it was not till Hemmeline had pulled him three times by the sleeve that he cared to give any answer. Being of a very phlegmatic disposition, he replied coolly, 'that they were his son's scratches, and that he believed he would ruin him in paper were he to live much longer in such an idle way.' 'Truly,' said his mother, who was knitting in a great chair opposite to his father, and who was resolved to put in her word, 'our child is very innocently employed, and although he doth marr a little paper, or so, there is no need of snubbing him as you always do.' 'Woman,' answered old Aldrovandus, 'cease thy garrulity, our son will be shipped off to-morrow, so there needs no farther words.' Upon this the mother burst into tears, and, as she was always averse to her son's voyage, took this opportunity to give vent to her sorrow, and with a piteous voice cried out, 'You will,

---

[1] A fictitious name.

[2] Eyck, Jan van (c.1390–1441) and Hubert (d. 1426) early Netherlands painters famous for their clarity and realism.

[3] The apostle's feast day is 28th October.

[4] A variant of Hans Memling (c.1433–94) painter born at Frankfurt but member of the Netherlands school and resident in Bruges.

then, barbarous man! Father without bowels! you will, then, expose our first born to dwell amongst a parcel of brutal circumcised Moors and infidels. You will, then, have him go over sea and be shipwrecked without christian burial. O Lord! O Lord! why cannot folks live every one under his own figtree, without roving and wandering through perils and dangers, that make my blood run cold to think of. And all this for the lucre of gain! Are we not blessed with a competence at home, without looking for superfluities abroad? Yes, my precious baby, you shall not be torn from me. Here take my ruby cross, my gold bodkins[1], and all my parafernalia, leave me but Anthony my son ... Anthony, my son, ... O!' – The poor lady pronounced these last words with such vehemence, that, her spirits failing her, she fell into a swoon; and whilst proper assistance was called for, Hemmeline, touched with her situation (for he was full of sensibility) drew his chair near old Aldrovandus, and held the following discourse: 'You know, my dear friend, that Providence has been bountiful unto me, and that under its protection my talents have procured me an affluent fortune, to which I have no heir; for to say truth, I have had no time to beget children, and matrimony I have always regarded as a gilded pill, fair to the eye and bitter to the palate; therefore I have been several times on the very point of making you a proposition, which perhaps may not be disagreeable.' There was a solemnity in this harangue very suitable to the genius of Aldrovandus; the mention of affluence too and fortune tickled his ears, and the proposition not yet explained rouzed his attention. So conveying his pen into his wig, and twirling his thumbs round each other, the merchant turned a very placid countenance towards Hemmeline, who continued: 'In good truth, I have fixed upon an heir; I have cast on Anthony the eyes of adoption, and if you will but consent, I will defray the expences you have incurred in equipping him for the voyage, then I will take him home, nourish him with parental tenderness, and next I will teach him the principles of my art; for his capacity is capacious, and if the blossoms of his genius are duly cultivated, they will produce such fruit as will astonish the world. After my death he shall inherit all my possessions. Go then unto his mother, and comfort her, for she is grievously afflicted.' That I may not detain my readers with unnecessary details, I will briefly acquaint them, that Anthony Aldrovandus was, after some deliberation, placed under the care of Hemmeline, and the project of his voyage abandoned. Those who, after having been restrained in their warmest inclinations, find themselves on a sudden free, may conceive the joy of young Aldrovandus, when he found himself at liberty to pursue his beloved studies.[2] He now applied himself with such intenseness, that the kind Hemmeline was obliged to check an ardour, which might have proved prejudicial to his health; but nothing could hinder our young artist from giving four hours in a day to chemistry, his favourite science. Hemmeline was very assiduous in the laboratory, and had some part

---

[1] Long, ornamental hair-pins.
[2] There is an echo here of Beckford's own experience of being prevented from pursuing his favourite Arabian themes in literature by his guardians.

in the discovery of many admirable compositions, which contributed to the perfection of Aldrovandus's colours, ever famous for their splendour and durability. The judicious Hemmeline, marking the progress of his disciple, thought him sufficiently grounded in his art to give his paintings to the public, and purposely to make his talents known quitted the village of Dammé which had been their residence for eight years, and travelled to Ghent, where they arrived the 6th of Sept. 1492. Hemmeline immediately hired a house and furnished it with his own and Aldrovandus's paintings, which soon attracted the admiration of the curious, who flocked in crouds to behold them. Adam Spindlemans, a rich burgher of Ghent, purchased five of the most capital performances, which he sent as presents to the Dukes of Parma and Placentia, princes who delighted in the encouragement of arts, and whose cabinets began to be filled with the choicest productions of the pencil. Such a genius as Aldrovandus could not long remain in obscurity. George Podebrac, Duke of Bohemia,[1] formerly the patron of Hemmeline, desired him to send his disciple to his court, at the same time promising the most ample encouragement. An offer like this was not to be rejected, especially as Hemmeline was under such obligations to the Bohemian monarch that he could hardly have refused it with decency. Besides he had other reasons, of no less consequence to his disciple's advancement. Aldrovandus was not insensible to the charms of the fair sex, and Ann Spindlemans, whose beauty and coyness had been fatal to many lovers, held him in her chains. In vain he presented her with eastern curiosities, which his mother had privately procured him. In vain he laid a pair of silk stockings at her feet, at that period a valuable rarity. Not all his assiduity could procure him the least favour, so far was he from hoping ever to garter his present above the knee. It is incredible what elegant closet[2] pictures he lavished upon this haughty beauty. It was for her he finished so exquisitely the adventure of Salmacis and Hermaphroditus,[3] a fable the very reverse of his own unhappy situation. It was at her desire he impiously changed the sacred story of Bell and the Dragon, began for the Benedictines, into the garden of the Hesperides,[4] guarded by a more sagacious monster. This *trait* scandalized his master, whose chastity had taken the alarm at several other of his proceedings, and, under pretence of visiting his parents, he found means to snatch him from the allurements of Ann Spindlemans; nor was it till after he had left Ghent ten leagues behind, that he perceived the deceit. Such are the reveries into which love-lorn passion plunges his votaries! – Hemmeline, who accompanied his disciple, tried by sage discourses to set his conduct in its proper light, and told him with his accustomed gravity, that what was right could not be wrong, and *vise versâ*. He added, 'that youth was the season of folly, and that

[1] Possibly George of Podebrady (1420–71) who became King of Bohemia in 1458.
[2] Small, private room.
[3] Salmacis was the water nymph who loved Hermaphroditus, son of Hermes. Her embrace led to a fusion of their bodies according to Greek mythology.
[4] Daughters of Hesperides guarded the apple tree helped by the dragon, Ladon, according to Greek mythology.

passion was like an unbridled horse, a torrent without a dike, or a candle with a thief in it, and ended by comparing Ann Spindlemans herself to a vinegar-bottle, who would deluge the sallad of matrimony with much more vinegar than oil.' He continued for two long hours in this figurative style, when observing his disciples' eyes nearly closed, he gave another fillip to his imagination, and attempted to excite his attention by more splendid ideas. Now he represented to him what golden advantages would spring from his residence at Prague, what honours, what emoluments; and next he brought to view Duke Podebrac, with great solemnity appointing him his painter, and holding forth chains and medals decorated with costly gems, as the reward of his labours. These chains and medals the sagacious painter took great care to wave frequently before the eye of his fancy, and this lessened, in some measure, the acuteness of his sorrow. These flattering dreams served to alleviate his grief during the journey, and before he arrived at Prague had almost effaced Ann Spindlemans from his memory. How inconstant is youth, how apt to change, how fond of roving! But let us return to our artists, who met with the most honourable reception from the Duke. He immediately gave them an apartment in his palace, appointed them a magnificent table, and officers to attend them.

Aldrovandus, delighted with the generous treatment he had received, resumed his employments with double alacrity, and began an altar-piece for the cathedral, in which he may be said to have surpassed himself. The subject, Moses and the burning bush, was composed in the most masterly manner, and the flames represented with such truth and vivacity, that the young Princess Ferdinanda Joanna Maria being brought by the Duchess, for a little recreation, to see him work, cried out, 'La! Mamma, I won't touch that bramble bush for fear it should burn my fingers!' This circumstance, which I am well aware some readers will deem trifling, gained our painter great reputation amongst all the courtiers, and not a little applause to her Serene Highness, for her astonishing discernment and sagacity. All the nurses and some of the ladies-in-waiting declared, she was too clever to live long, and they were not mistaken, for this admirable Princess departed this life Jan. 23d, 1493, and it was unanimously observed, that had she lived, she would have been indubitably the jewel of Bohemia. This may seem a digression; but as it was her Serene Highness who first gave her spotless opinion of our artist's merit, I could not dispense with mentioning these few words in relation to her, and consecrating a tear to her memory. Aldrovandus was sensibly afflicted at her loss, and painted her apotheosis with wonderful intelligence. He represented the heavens wide open, and the Blessed Virgin in a rich robe of ultramarine, seated, according to custom, on the back of the old serpent, whose scales were horribly natural. Mercury, poetically habited, was placed judiciously in the off-skip, with an out-stretched arm, receiving the royal infant from the city of Prague. She was draped in a saffron stole, which seemed to float so naturally in the air, that a spectator might have sworn the wind blew it into all its beautiful folds. Above were gods and goddesses, saints and angels. Below were forests and gilded spires, nymphs, fauns, dryads and hamadryads,[1] all classically adorned with emblems and symbols. This master-piece gained him the esteem of Podebrac and the whole court, to which was added a rich chain with the Duke's picture, and a purse containing 1000 rixdollars. Encouraged by this liberality, Aldrovandus exerted himself more and more. It is from this time we may date some of his most capital productions. The tower of Babel,[2] in which he expressed the confusion of languages, Lot's wife, the Duchess of Bohemia, and two highly finished landscapes, since lost in the confusion of war, were all dispersed among the Bohemian nobles, who vied with each other in loading him with presents. His genius was now in its full vigour, his touch spirited, his colours harmonious, and his drawing correct. Italy envied the Bohemian court the possession of such an artist, and several of her Princes tried all possible means to engage him to visit them; but notwithstanding the great desire he had to behold the lovely prospects of Italy, the magnificence of Rome, and the remains of ancient grandeur so interesting to a picturesque eye,[3] he refused every offer, and resolved never to quit a monarch, from whom he had experienced such generosity. Podebrac, charmed with these sentiments, decorated him with the order of the Ram, and gave him in marriage Joan Jablinouski, a young lady to whom nature and fortune had been lavish of their favours. Their nuptials were celebrated by torch light in one of the royal gardens, and their Majesties and the whole court graced the ceremony with their presence; but this entertainment was unfortunately interrupted by the sudden death of Hemmeline, who had long been troubled with a *boulomee*, or voracious appetite, which occasioned him to devour whatever was set before him with a frightful precipitation. He met his fate in a huge pike, which he soon reduced to a mere skeleton, and soon after feeling a death-like cold at his stomach, called feebly to Aldrovandus, squeezed his hand and expired. The bridegroom was dreadfully disconcerted by this event, for he sincerely esteemed his master, notwithstanding the reproofs he had often received from him; and indeed he had every reason to respect his memory, as all the wealth of Hemmeline now became his own.

Aldrovandus was now arrived at the summit of prosperity: universally esteemed and admired, caressed by a puissant Prince, solaced by the blandishments of a lovely spouse, this happy painter had not a wish unsatisfied. He now began to enjoy his opulence in a palace he had built, and there divided his time between the delights of his art and the pleasures of society. Disciples flocked from very remote parts to seek his instructions; but he dismissed them all with handsome presents, two only excepted, whose conduct particularly won his esteem. The two elect were Andrew Guelph and Og of Basan,[4] since so famous in the annals of painting. The assiduity of these young men

---

[1] Nymphs of the woods and trees in Greek mythology.

[2] A city, probably Babylon, where according to Genesis the builders of a great tower could not understand one another as a punishment for their vanity.

[3] See *above* p. xxviii ff on the picturesque in travel accounts.

[4] Og, King of Basan, *Deuteronomy* 3.

was incredible, and their talents astonished Aldrovandus, who used always to be saying, 'If Og had lived before the Deluge, he would certainly have obtained permission from Noah to have been of the party in the ark,' Andrew Guelph he allowed to possess great merit, surprizing fire of genius, and an imagination tempered by science, and consequently super-excellent. In conversing with his chosen friends, and instructing his disciples, Aldrovandus passed many happy years, diversified by the birth of four children, to whom Ferdinand gave letters of nobility. At length fortune, tired with lavishing on him her gifts, clouded the evening of his life by an unforeseen misfortune. As he and his disciples worked night and day at a suite of paintings which was to contain the whole history of the Goths and Vandals, canvas began to grow exceedingly rare, and Ferdinand, touched with the lamentations of his favourite, summoned a solemn council, at which he ordered him to assist, with Andrew Guelph and Og of Basan bearing the sketches of part of the great historical work. The council assembled; Podebrac ascended the throne; the trumpets sounded; the painters arrived, and the paintings were exposed to the admiration of this august assembly, who conferred on Aldrovandus the title of Magnus, *nem. con.*[1] Afterwards they proceeded to business, and voted a supply of canvas. Several of the nobles distinguished themselves by very elegant harangues, and his Highness issued forth a proclamation, whereby he declared it treason for any of his liege subjects to conceal, purloin, or alienate any roll, bundle, or fardel[2] of canvas within his dominions, thereby impeding the collection which the aforesaid Aldrovandus Magnus, Knight of the most noble order of the Ram, was empowered to make. Now waggons and sledges arrived from every quarter, bringing the tributary canvas to Aldrovandus's palace. He, transported with gratitude, and fired by that enthusiasm to which we owe so many capital works, resolved to outdo his former outdoings, on the subject of Prince Drahomire, who in the year 921 was swallowed up by an earthquake in that spot where now stands the palace of Radzen. Animated by this glorious subject, he cried aloud for canvas, but instead of canvas, his disciples, with singed beards, brought the news of the conflagration of his warehouse, in which every thread of it was consumed. What a disappointment to collected genius! A paroxysm of grief ensued; and calling out continually 'Drahomire! Canvas! and St Luke!' Aldrovandus Magnus expired. There was hardly a dry eye in Prague. The Duke groaned; the courtiers wept; his disciples painted his catastrophe; the people put on black; the university composed epitaphs, and Professor Clod Lumpewitz[3] exceeded them all. His performance happily escaped the wreck of time, and I have the pleasure of setting it before my readers, with a version, supposed to be made by the ingenious Master John Ogilby.[4]

---

[1] Unanimously.
[2] Bundle.
[3] From the German words for rascal (lump) and wit (witz).
[4] John Ogilby (1600–76), Scottish author and translator.

Pictor Alexandri titulum gerit Aldrovandus;
Pictor erat magnus; magnus erat Macedo.
Mortis erat similis (sic fertur) causa duobus:
   Huic regna, autem illi cannaba deficiunt.[1]

Magnus, the title of old Alexander,
Was also that of Painter Aldrovand' here:
The one for want of[2] worlds to conquer cried,
T'other for lack of canvas nobly died.

SUCREWASSER[3] OF VIENNA

Our readers must now be presented with scenes and occurrences widely
differing from those which last we placed before them. They will no longer
behold an artist, consumed by the fervour of his genius and bewildered by the
charms of his imagination; but the most prudent and sage amongst them will
admire the regular and consistent conduct of Sucrewasser, which forms a
striking contrast to the eccentricity of Og.

The family of the Sucrewassers had been long established at Vienna; they
had kept a grocer's shop, which descended from father to son thro' a course
of many generations. The father of our artist exercised his hereditary business with the same probity as his ancestors. His mother, the daughter of a
Lombard pawnbroker, was the best sort of woman in the world, and had no
other fault than loving wine and two or three men besides her husband.
Young Sucrewasser was invested, at the age of six years, with the family
apron, and after having performed errands for some time, was admitted to
the desk at twelve; but discovering a much greater inclination for designing
the passengers, which were walking to fro before the window where he was
doomed to sit, then noting the articles of his father's commerce in his book,
he was bound apprentice to an uncle of his mother, who painted heraldry for
the Imperial Court, and his brother was promoted to the desk in his room.
Sucrewasser took great delight in his new situation, and learnt, with success,
to bestow due strength on a lion's paw, and give a courtly flourish to a
dragon's tail. His eagles began to be remarked for the justness of their
proportions and the neatness of their plumage; in short, an Italian painter, by
name Insignificanti,[4] remarked the delicacy of his pencil, and was resolved to

---

[1] 'The painter Aldovandrus has the claim to fame of Alexander;
     The painter was great; great was the Macedonian.
The cause of death for the two was similar, so the story goes:
     The one ran out of kingdoms, but the other of canvasses.'

[2] It is remarkable that the learned Professor Clod Lumpewitz ever maintained that this
renowned Conqueror was cruelly aspersed, by those who have killed him by drinking; and
instead of merely crying for more worlds to conquer, he insisted that he died solely on that
account. The critical reader will observe, that the admirable Ogilby, in conformity with the
general opinion, has taken a small liberty with his author. [Beckford's note]

[3] Sugar-water.

[4] Insignificant, petty.

obtain him for his scholar. The youth, finding himself in a comfortable habitation with a kind uncle, who was in a thriving way, and who offered him a share in his business when the time of his apprenticeship should expire, expressed no great desire to place himself under the tuition of Insignificanti; but as that painter had acquired a very splendid reputation, and was esteemed exceedingly rich, his parents commanded him to accept the offer, and Sucrewasser never disobeyed. He remained two or three years with this master, which he employed in faithfully copying his works; generally small landscapes, with shepherds and shepherdesses feeding their flocks, or piping under Arcadian shades.[1] These pieces pleased the world in general and sold well, which was all Insignificanti desired, and Sucrewasser had no other ambition than that of his master. The greatest harmony subsisted between them till three years were expired.

About this time the Princess Dolgoruki,[2] then at the Court of Vienna, selected Insignificanti and his pupil to paint her favourite lap dog, whose pendent ears and beautifully curling tail seemed to call loudly for a portrait. Insignificanti, before he began the picture, asked his pupil, with all the mildness of condescension, Whether he did not approve his intentions of placing the dog on a red velvet cushion. Sucrewasser replied gently, that he presumed a blue one would produce a much finer effect. His master, surprized to find this difference of opinion, elevated his voice, and exlaimed, 'Aye, but I propose adding a gold fringe, which shall display all the perfection of my art; all the feeling of delicacy of my pencil; but, hark you! I desire you will abstain from spoiling this part of the picture with your gross touch, and never maintain again that blue will admit of half the splendor of red.' These last words were pronounced with such energy, that Sucrewasser laid down his pencil, and begged leave to quit his master; who soon consented, as he feared Sucrewasser would surpass him in a very short space of time. The young man was but coolly received by his parents, who chided him for abandoning his master; but when they perceived his performances sold as well as before this rupture, their anger ceased, and they permitted him to travel to Venice, after having bestowed on him their benediction with the greatest cordiality.

His route lay through some very romantic country, which he never deigned to regard, modestly conjecturing he was not yet worthy to copy nature; so without straying either to the right or to the left, he arrived at Venice in perfect health, and recommended himself first to the public by painting in fresco on the walls of some casinos. The subjects were either the four Seasons or the three Graces.[3] Now and then a few blind Cupids,[4] and sometimes a lean Fury,[5] by way of variety. The colouring was gay and tender, and the drawing correct. The faces were pretty uniform and had all the most delightful smirk

---

[1] Arcadia, a region in the centre of the Peloponnese, associated in Greek mythology with the home of the gods.

[2] Probably Russian noble family of Dolgorukov.

[3] Three goddesses who personify beauty and ugliness according to Greek mythology.

[4] God of love in Roman religion.

[5] Primeval beings, represented as winged women with snakes about them.

imaginable; even his Furies looked as if they were half inclined to throw their torches into the water, and the serpents around their temples were as mild as eels. Many ladies stiled him *Pittore amabile*,[1] and many gentlemen had their snuff-boxes painted by his hand. He lived happily and contentedly till he became acquainted with Soorcrout,[2] who was a great admirer of Titian,[3] and advised him by all means to copy his performances; and as he generally followed the advice of those who thought it worth their while to give him any, he immediately set about it, but did not profit so much as he expected. It was Soorcrout who engaged him in that unlucky dispute with Og of Basan and Andrew Guelph; a controversy which lowered them considerably in the eyes of the world, and forfeited them the protection of Signor Boccadolce.[4]

After this disgrace, Soorcrout went to England, and Sucrewasser loitered in the environs of Venice till the storm was blown over. He then returned, lived peaceably there many years, and died at length of a cold he caught at a party on the water. His most splendid performance, Salome,[5] mother of the Maccabees, which he imitated from Titian, was sold by Soorcrout in England.

BLUNDERBUSSIANA

It was with difficulty we can ascertain the place or even the country where this artist was born; but we have most reason to imagine it was in Dalmatia,[6] towards the confines of Croatia. Rouzinski Blunderbussiana, father of him whose adventures will be the subject of the following pages, was captain of some banditti, for many years the terror of Dalmatia and the neighbouring countries. This formidable band exercised the most unlimited depredations, and as they were very numerous, nothing but an army could oppose them. Finding, however, security in defiles amongst the mountains, known but to themselves, the Venetian and Hungarian soldiery attempted their extirpation in vain. Rouzinski, their leader, was one of the haughtiest of mankind; his uncommon stature, matchless intrepidity, and wonderful success, had raised him to the despotic command of these brave savages, to whom no enterprize seemed impossible, and who executed their projects almost as soon as they were conceived. The caves in which they resided were hollowed in the rocks, forming the summit of a mountain in the wild province of the Morlakes, which they had in a manner subdued; no one daring to approach the spot where they had established their habitations. The peak of this mountain, seen from afar, was regarded by the Dalmatians with horror. Had they known

[1] The sweet painter.
[2] Sauercrout – a German dish of cabbage.
[3] Tiziano Vecellio (c. 1487–1576), Venetian painter whose art, in the grand style, dominated the school.
[4] Sweet mouth.
[5] Daughter of King Herod who danced for the head of St John the Baptist.
[6] Mountainous area of coastal Yugoslavia.

what scenes it concealed, they would have trembled indeed. The plan of this work will not admit a particular description of this mountain and its caves, or else I should certainly have lain before my readers some particulars concerning the residence of these banditti, which, perhaps, might have been worthy their attention; but at present I must confine myself merely to what relates to the life of Blunderbussiana. His father returning with a rich booty from Turky, brought with him a lady of some distinction, who had fallen unfortunately into his hands. He conveyed her to his cave, attempted to amuse her with the sight of those magazines (immense grottos) which contained his treasures, and by degrees falling deeply in love with her, laid them all at her feet.

The young Turk, who had seen but little of the world, was charmed with the manly aspect of her admirer, and dazzled by his liberality, after some time forgot the disgust his savage profession inspired. She at length consented to make him happy; and our hero sprung from this connection, which was celebrated with tumultuous festivity throughout all the subterraneous empire. Blunderbussiana's first ideas, caught from the objects around, cannot be supposed of the gentlest nature. He beheld gloomy caverns hollowed in craggy rocks, which threatened every instant to fall upon his head. He heard each night dreadful relations of combats which had happened in the day, and often, when wandering about the entrance of the caves, he spied his father and his companions stripping the slain, and letting down their bodies into pits and fissures which had never been fathomed. Being long inured to such ghastly sights, he by degrees grew pleased with them, and his inclination for painting first manifested itself in the desire he had of imitating the figures of his father's warriors.

Rouzinski, as soon as his son was able to dart a javelin or bear a musket, led him to the chace, and exulted in the activity with which he pursued the boar, and the alacrity with which he murdered the trembling stag.[1] After he had spent a year in these sanguinary amusements, his father thought him worthy to partake his expeditions, and led him first to the rencounter of a pretty large body of Turks, who escorted some Hungarian merchants. 'Such for the future must be your game,' said the ruthless robber to his son, who performed prodigies of cruelty and valour. But let me draw a veil over such frightful pictures. Though the truth forbids me entirely to conceal them, humanity pleads strongly for the abridgment of their relation. Two summers passed away in continual rapines and eternal scenes of active oppression. The winter was the season of repose, and the young Rouzinski employed it in recollecting the adventures of the summer months and fixing them by his pencil. Sometimes he read a treatise upon painting, found amongst the spoils of some Italians, which assisted him infinitely. They much recommended the study of anatomy, and he did not hesitate to follow the advice they gave. His father's band frequently bringing bodies to their caves, he amused himself

[1] In later years at Fonthill, Beckford had a wall built around his estate to keep the hunters out.

with dissecting and imitating the several parts, till he attained such a perfection in muscular expression as is rarely seen in the works of the greatest masters. His application was surprizing; for his curiosity to examine the structure of the human frame being inflamed, he pursued the study with such eagerness as those who are not *amateurs* cannot easily imagine. Every day discovered some new artery, or tendon to his view; every hour produced some masterly design, and though without any person to guide him, he made a progress which would have done credit to the most eminent artists. He now began to put his figures together in a great manner, and to group them with judgment; but colours were wanting, and without materials, Michael Angelo would have conceived the dome of St Peter's in vain.[1] He had read in his treatise of the works of Italian painters, which he languished to behold, and was determined, if possible, in the ensuing summer, to escape from his father and fly to a country, where he might indulge his inclinations; however, for the present he was charmed with the opportunities of perfecting himself in anatomy, and that occupation diverted his intention of taking flight for some time. In the spring he used early in the morning to quit his cave, and frequently trussing a body over his shoulders, repaired to a wood, and delighted himself in exploring it. Instead of carrying with him, in his walks, a nice pocket edition of some Elzevir[2] classic, he never was without a leg or an arm, which he went slicing along, and generally accompanied his operations with a melodious whistling; for he was of a chearful disposition, and, if he had had a different education, would have been an ornament to society.

Summer came, and he was called to attend his father, and a select detachment of the band, on an expedition into the Hungarian territories; but some regular troops being aware of their intentions, lay in ambush for their coming, sallied upon them, and left the old Rouzinski, with thirty of his comrades, dead upon the field. Blunderbussiana escaped, and made the best of his way thro' forests deemed impenetrable, and mountains, where he subsisted on wild fruit and the milk of goats. When he reached the borders of cultivation, his savage mien and the barbarous roll of his eyes, frighted every villager that beheld him;[3] and so strange was his appearance, that some said he could be nothing but the Antichrist, and others believed him to be the Wandering Jew.[4] After having experienced numerable hardships, which none but those accustomed from their infancy to fatigues could have sustained, he arrived at Friuli; where he was employed in cutting wood, by a Venetian surgeon, who had retired there to enjoy an estate which had been lately bequeathed him. One day, after he had worked very hard, he seized a cat that was frisking about near him, and, by way of recreation, dissected the animal with such skill, that his master, who happened to pass by, was quite surprized,

---

[1] Michelangelo Buonarroti (1475–1564), Italian sculptor, painter, architect and poet whose Sistine Chapel frescoes were begun in 1508.
[2] Books published in Leiden until 1712, renown for editions in small format.
[3] Later Beckford was to give Caliph Vathek a terrifying look. See *above*, pp. 29 and 98.
[4] Legendary character condemned to roam the world until Doomsday.

and mentioned this circumstance to several of his friends at dinner, amongst whom the famous Joseph Porta[1] chanced to be present. This painter, who was a great admirer of anatomy, wished to see the young proficient, and being struck with his uncouth figure, began to sketch out his portrait on some tablets he carried about him. Blunderbussiana was in raptures during the performance, and begging earnestly to examine it more narrowly, snatched the pencil from Porta's hand, and in a few strokes corrected some faults in the anatomy with such boldness and veracity, as threw the painter into amazement. Happening to want a servant at this time, Porta desired his friend to permit Blunderbussiana's returning with him to Venice; a request he granted without delay, and the young man joyfully accompanied him. He did not long remain with his master as a servant, being soon considered in the light of a disciple. All possible advantages were procured him, and after a year's study he gave several pieces to the public, in which the *clair obscure*[2] was finely observed. The scenes of his former life were still fresh in his memory, and his pictures almost always represented vast perspective caverns red with the light of fires, around which banditti were carousing; or else dark valleys between shaggy rocks strewed with the spoils of murder'd travellers. His father, leaning on his spear, and giving orders to his warriors, was generally the principal object in these pieces, characterised by a certain horror, which those ignorant of such dreadful scenes fancied imaginary. If he represented waters, they were dark and troubled; if trees, deformed and withered. His skies were lowering, and his *clair obscure* in that style the Italians call *sgraffito* (a greyish melancholy tint) which suited the gloominess of his subjects. It might be conjectured from this choice of subjects, that Blunderbussiana was a very dismal personage. On the contrary, he was, as we hinted before, of a social disposition, and much relished by those with whom he spent the hours he dedicated to amusement. His pleasures, to be sure, were singular, and probably will not be styled such by many of our readers. For example; after a chearful repast, which he never failed to enliven by his sallies, he would engage some of his friends to ramble about at midnight, and leading them slily to some burying grounds, entice them, by way of frolick, to steal some of the bodies, which he bore off with the greatest glee; exulting more than if he had carried alive in his arms the fairest ladies in the environs. This diversion proved fatal to him at length; for he caught a violent fever in consequence of a drinking match, which was to precede one of these delicious[3] excursions. The disorder, attacking his robust constitution, reduced him in two days to a very critical situation; and, burning with heat, he plunged into a cold bath, out of which he was taken delirious, and being conveyed to his bed, began to rave in a frightful manner. Every minute he seemed to behold the mangled limbs of those he had anatomized, quivering

[1] Joseph Porta (Salviati the Younger) (1520–70), Venetian painter who also worked in Rome.
[2] *Chiaroscuro*: light and shade.
[3] Affording great pleasure.

in his apartment. 'Haste, give me my instruments,' cried he, 'that I may spoil the gambols of three cursed legs, that are just stalked into the room, and are going to jump upon me. Help! help! or they will kick me out of bed. There again; only see those ugly heads, that do nothing but roll over me! – Hark! what a lumbering noise they make! now they glide along as smoothly as if on a bowling-green. – Mercy defend me from those gogling eyes! – Open all the windows, set wide the doors, – let those grim cats out that spit fire at me and lash me with their tails. O how their bones rattle! – Help! – Mercy! – O!' – The third day released him from his torments, and his body, according to his desire, was delivered, with all his anatomical designs, to the college of surgeons. Such was the end of the ingenious Blunderbussiana, whose skeleton the faculty have canonized, and whose paintings, dispersed in most of the Venetian palaces, still terrify the tender-hearted.

WATERSOUCHY[1]

We will now change our scenery from the rocks of Dalmatia to the levels of Holland, and instead of sailing on the canals of Venice saunter a little by those of Amsterdam. It was in the Kalverstraat, opposite to the hotel of Etanshasts, next door to the Blue Lion, that Watersouchy, whose delicate performances are so eagerly sought after by the curious, first drew his breath. The name of Watersouchy had been known in Amsterdam since the first existence of the republic. Two wax-chandlers, and at least twelve other capital dealers in grease, had rendered it famous, and the head of the family can never be forgotten, since he invented that admirable dish from which his descendents derived their appellation. Our artist's father, from humbly retailing farthing candles,[2] rose, by a monopoly on tallow, to great affluence, and had the honour of enlightening half the city. He was a thrifty diligent man, loved a pipe of reflection in the evening, and invented *save-alls*; but it was for the sole use of his own family. This prudent character endeared him so much to Mynheer Bootersac, a rich vintner, his next door neighbour, that he proposed to him his only daughter in marriage, and from this alliance, which happily took place on the 3d of May, 1640, sprung the hero of these memoirs.

The birth of young Watersouchy was marked by a decent though jovial meeting of his kindred on both sides. Much wine was drank, and ten candles assigned for home consumption. Such festivity had not been displayed in the family since it first began. Nor were these rejoicings without other foundation, as old Watersouchy, who had hitherto toiled and moiled from morn till eve, resolved, at the birth of his child to leave off business, and enjoy at ease the fortune he had acquired. It will be needless to mention particularly the

[1] Old Dutch for boiled fish.
[2] Candles costing a farthing each.

great care that was taken of the young Jeremy (for so he was baptized). Let it suffice to relate, that two years elapsed before he was weaned – so great was the tenderness of his parents, and such their fears lest a change of diet might endanger his constitution. It was no wonder that this child inspired such affectionate sentiments in his parents, so winning was his appearance. How could they fail to be struck with the prettiest, primmest mouth in the world, a rose-bud of a nose, large rolling eyes, and a complexion soft and mellow like his paternal candles? This sweet baby gave early signs of delight in rich and pleasing objects. The return of his parents from church in their holiday apparel ever attracted his attention and excited a placid smile, and any stranger garnished with lace might place him on his knee with impunity. He seemed to feel peculiar pleasure at seeing people bow to each other, and learnt sooner than any child in the street to handle his knife, to spare his bib and kiss his hand with address. This promising heir of the Watersouchies had just entered into his fifth year, when his father ventured for the first time to take him about to the Bootersacs and his other relations. These good people, enchanted with the neatness of his person and the correctness of his behaviour, never failed to load him with toys, sugar plumbs, and gingerbread; but a spruce set of Æsop's Fables,[1] minutely engraved, and some designs for Brussels point, were the presents in which he chiefly delighted. These delicate drawings drew his whole attention, and they were not long in his hands before he attempted to imitate them, with a perseverance and exactness, surprizing at his years. These infantine performances were carefully framed and glazed, and hung up in Madam Watersouchy's apartment, where they always produced the highest admiration. Amongst those who were principally struck with their merit was the celebrated Francis Van Cuyck de Mierhop,[2] a noble artist from Ghent, who, during his residence at Amsterdam, frequently condescended to pass his evenings at Watersouchy's. Mierhop could boast illustrious descent, to which his fortune was by no means equal, and having a peculiar genius for painting eatables, old women, and other pieces of still life, applied himself to the art, and made a considerable figure. Watersouchy's table was quite an academy in the branches he wished to cultivate, daily exhibiting the completest old women, the most portly turbots, the plumpest soles, and, in a word, the best conditioned fish imaginable, of every kind. Mierhop availed himself of his friend's invitations to study legs of mutton, sirloins of beef, and joints of meat in general. It was for Madam Watersouchy he painted the most perfect fillet of veal, that ever made the mouth of man to water, and she prided herself not a little upon the original having appeared at her table.

The air of Amsterdam agreeing with Mierhop's constitution and Watersouchy's table not less with his palate, he was quite inspired during his residence there, and took advantage of these circumstances to immortalize

---

[1] Aesop, composer of Greek fables about animals, was said to have lived in the middle of the sixth century BC.

[2] Francis Van Cuyck de Mierhop (1640–89), Dutch still-life painter.

himself, by an immense and most inviting picture, in which he introduced a whole entertainment. No part was neglected. – The vapour smoking over the dishes judiciously concealed the extremities of the repast, and gave the finest play to the imagination. This performance was placed with due solemnity in the Butchers-hall at Ghent, of which respectable corps he had been chosen protector.

Whilst he remained at Amsterdam, young Watersouchy was continually improving, and arrived to such perfection in copying point lace, that Mierhop entreated his father to cultivate these talents, and to place his son under the patronage of Gerard Dow,[1] ever renowned for the exquisite finish of his pieces. Old Watersouchy stared at the proposal, and solemnly asked his wife, to whose opinion he always paid a deference, whether painting was a genteel profession for their son. Mierhop, who overheard their conversation, smiled disdainfully at the question, and Madam Watersouchy answered, that she believed it was one of your liberal arts. In few words, the father was persuaded, and Gerard Dow, then resident at Leyden, prevailed upon to receive the son as a disciple.

Our young artist had no sooner set his foot within his master's apartment, than he found every object in harmony with his own dispositions. The colours finely ground, and ranged in the neatest boxes, the pencils so delicate as to be almost imperceptible, the varnish in elegant phials, the easel just where it ought to be, filled him with agreeable sensations, and exalted ideas of his master's merit. Gerard Dow on his side was equally pleased, when he saw him moving about with all due circumspection, and noticing his little prettinesses at every step. He therefore began his pupil's initiation with great alacrity, first teaching him cautiously to open the cabinet door, lest any particles of dust should be dislodged and fix upon his canvas, and advising him never to take up his pencil without sitting motionless a few minutes, till every mote casually floating in the air should be settled. Such instructions were not thrown away upon Watersouchy: he treasured them up, and refined, if possible, upon such refinements.[2]

Whilst he was thus learning method and arrangement, the other parts of his education were not neglected. A neighbouring schoolmaster instructed him in the rudiments of Latin, and a barber, who often served as a model to Gerard Dow, when composing his most sublime pieces, taught him the management of the violin. With the happiest dispositions we need not be surprized at the progress he made, nor astonished when we hear that Gerard Dow, after a year's study, permitted him to finish some parts of his own choicest productions. One of his earliest essays was in a large and capital perspective, in which a christening entertainment was displayed in all its glory. To describe exactly the masterly group of the gossips, the demureness

---

[1] Gerard Dou (1613–75), Dutch painter with an ultra-realist style.
[2] Robert Gemmett has identified this passage as being taken from J. B. Descamps' book *La vie des peintres flamands, allemands, et hollandois ...*, 4 Vols (Paris, 1753–64), 2:217–18; see Gemmett, *Memoirs*, p. 4.

of the maiden aunts, the puling infant in the arms of its nurse, the plaits of its swaddling-cloaths, the gloss of its ribbons, the fringe of the table-cloth, and the effect of light and shade on a salver adorned with custard-cups and jelly-glasses, would require at least fifty pages. In this space, perhaps, those details might be included; but to convey a due idea of that preciseness, that air of decorum, which was spread over the whole picture, surpasses the power of words. The collar of a lap-dog, a velvet bracelet, and the lace round the caps of the gossips, were the parts of this *chef d'oeuvre*, which Watersouchy had the honour of finishing, and he acquitted himself with a truth and exactness that enraptured his master, and brought him to place unbounded confidence in the hair strokes of his pencil. By degrees he rose to the highest place in the esteem of that incomparable artist, who, after eight years had elapsed, suffered him to group without assistance. An arm chair of the richest velvet, and a Turkey carpet, were the first compositions of which he claimed the exclusive honour. The exquisite drawing of these pieces was not less observable than the softness of their tints and the absolute nature of their colouring. Every man wished to sit down in the one, and every dog to repose on the other.

Whilst Watersouchy was making daily advances in his profession, his father was attacked by a lethargy, that, insensibly gaining ground, carried him off, and left his son in the undisturbed possession of a considerable sum of money. No sooner was he apprized of this event than he took leave of Gerard Dow, and arrived at his native city time enough to attend the funeral procession, and to partake of the feast which followed it; where his becoming sorrow and proper behaviour fixed him in the esteem of all his relations. This good opinion he took care to maintain, never shewing more attention to one than to another, but as it were portioning out his compliments into equal shares. Having passed the usual time without frequenting the world, and having closed the account of condolence, he began to take pleasure in society, and make himself known. His scrupulous adherence to form and propriety procured him the *entré* of many considerable houses, and recommended him to the particular notice of some of the principal magistrates of Amsterdam. These grave personages thought he would do honour to their city in foreign parts, and therefore advised his going to Antwerp for the advancement of his reputation.

Antwerp was at this period the centre of arts and manufactures; its public buildings were numerous and magnificent; its citizens wealthy; strangers from every quarter resorted thither for business, or for pleasure. Rubens[1] had introduced a fondness for painting, and had ornamented his cabinet with the most valuable productions of the pencil. This example was followed, and collections began to be formed by the opulent inhabitants. Where then could a painter, blessed with such talents as Watersouchy, expect a more favourable reception? He soon resolved to follow the advice of his respectable friends, and having settled his affairs and passed a month or two in taking

---

[1] Peter Paul Rubens (1577–1640), Flemish painter who made his home in Antwerp.

leave of his acquaintance with due form, he began his journey. Many recommendatory letters were given him, and particularly one to Monsieur Baise-la-main,[1] a banker of the first eminence, and an encourager of the fine arts, who united the greatest wealth with the most exemplary politeness. All the way he amused himself in the trackskuit[2] with looking over the stock of compliments he had treasured up from his youth, in order to perfect himself in all the rules of that good breeding, he purposed to display at Antwerp. 'Consider,' said he to himself, 'before whom you are to appear; reflect that you are now almost arrived at the zenith of propriety. Let all your actions be regular as the strokes of your pencil, and let the varnish of your manners shine like that of your paintings. Regulate your conduct by the fair example of those you will shortly behold, and do not the smallest thing but as if Monsieur Baise-la-main were before you.' Full of these resolutions he drew near to Antwerp. Advancing between spruce gardens and trim avenues he entered the city, not without some presentiment of the fame he was to acquire within its walls. Every mansion with high chequered roofs and mosaic chimnies, every fountain with elaborate dolphins and gothic pinnacles, found favour in his eyes. He was pleased with the neat perspectives continually presenting themselves, and augured well from a regularity so consonant to his own ideas. After a few hours repose at an inn, arranging each part of his dress with the utmost precision, he sallied forth in the cool of the evening, (for it was now the midst of summer) to deliver his recommendatory letters. The first person to whose acquaintence he aspired was Monsieur Baise-la-main, who occupied a sumptuous hotel near the cathedral. Directing his steps to that quarter, he passed through several lanes and alleys with slowness and caution, and arrived in a spotless condition at the area of that celebrated edifice, which was enlivened by crouds of well dressed people passing and repassing each other, with many courteous bows and salutations, whilst two sets of chimes in the spire above them filled the air with sober psalmody. Watersouchy was charmed when he found himself in this region of smirking faces, and stepping forwards amongst them, enquired for Monsieur Baife-la-main. Every body pointed to a gentleman in a modish perruque, blue coat with gold frogs,[3] and black velvet breeches. To this prepossessing personage he advanced with his very best bow, and delivered his letter. No sooner did the gentleman arrange his spectacles, and glance over the first lines of the epistle, then he returned the greeting fourfold. Watersouchy was as prodigal of salutations, and could hardly believe his ears when they were saluted with these flattering expressions. 'Your arrival, Mr Watersouchy, is an event I shall always have the honour to remember. And, Sir, permit me to assure you, from the bottom of my heart, that nobody can feel more thoroughly the obligations I have to my most estimable friends at Amsterdam, for the opportunity, Sir, they give me, of shewing any little, trifling, miserable

---

[1] Mr Kiss-the-hand.
[2] Canals for shipping.
[3] Attachments to waist belt for carrying a sword.

attentions in my power, to a disciple of Gerard Dow. Let me intreat you to tarry some time in my poor mansion: Indeed, Sir, you must not refuse me – I beg, my dear and respectable Sir, – I beseech' – It was impossible to resist such a torrent of civility. Watersouchy prepared to follow the courteous banker, who, taking him by the hand, led him, with every demonstration of kindness, to the door of his hotel.

Its frontispiece, rich with allegorical figures, of which I never could obtain a satisfactory explanation, was distinguished from more vulgar entrances, and seats of coloured marble on each side added to its magnificence. Let my readers figure to themselves Monsieur Baise-le-main leading the obsequious Watersouchy thro' several large halls and long passages, 'till they entered a rich apartment, where a circle of company, very splendidly attired, rose up to receive them. Half an hour was spent in presenting the artist to every individual. At length a pause in this ceremony ensued, and then the congratulations, with which he had been first received, were begun anew with redoubled ardour. Watersouchy, finding himself surrounded by so many solemn ruffs and consequential farthingales,[1] was penetrated with the sublimity of etiquette, and thought himself in the very Athens of politeness. This service of rites and ceremonies, with which strangers in those times were ushered into Antwerp, being hardly ended, the company began at length to relax into some degree of familiarity.

Mieris[2] and Sibylla Merian[3] were now announced. These two exquisite artists had carried the minute delicacy of the pencil to the highest pitch, and were pleased with an opportunity of conversing with one of the most promising disciples of Gerard Dow. Our artist was equally happy in their society, and a conversation was accordingly set on foot, in which Mons. Baise-le-main joining displayed infinite knowledge and precision. Having disserted previously upon his own collection, this great patron of the arts led them into his interior cabinet, where Elsheimers, Rowland Saveries, Albert Dürers, Brughels, and Polemburgs, collected at an immense expence, appeared on all sides. Mieris and Merian had also contributed to render it the most complete in the Netherlands. Their performances entirely engrossed the choicest corner in an apartment, which a profusion of gilding and carved work rendered superlatively fine. The chimney-piece was encrusted with the right old porcelain of China, and its aperture, in this season, was closed by a capital *Pietâ* of Julio Romano,[4] which immediately struck Watersouchy as an eye sore. He detested such colossal representations, such bold limbs and woeful countenances: conscious they were out of his reach, he condemned them as out of nature. With such sentiments, we may suppose he did not bestow much attention of the *Pietâ*, but expatiated with delight on the

[1] Hooped petticoats.
[2] Franz van Mieris the Elder (1635–81), Dutch portrait painter and engraver, famous for his treatment of silks, satins and jewelry.
[3] Maria Sibylla Merian (1647–1717), Dutch painter.
[4] Giulio Romano (1492–1546), pupil of Raphael, Mannerist painter.

faithful representation of an apothecary's shop by Mieris, and a cupid, holding a garland of flowers, by Merian. This ingenious lady was high in his esteem. He adored the extreme nicety of her touch, and not a little admired that strict sense of propriety which had induced her to marriage; for it seems she had chosen Jean Graff of Nuremburg[1] for her husband, merely to study the *Nud* in a modest way. After he had felicitated Madam Merian and Mieris upon their innumerable perfections, he took a cursory survey of the rest of the collection. He commended Albert Durer,[2] but could not help expressing some discontent at Polemburg.[3] The woody landscapes, which this painter imagined with so much happiness, were in general interspersed with the remains of antique temples, with rills and bathing nymphs in a style our artist could never taste. He liked their minuteness, but condemned the choice of subjects. 'O!' said Monsieur Baise-la-main, 'I love Polemburg; he is the essence of smoothness and suavity. But I agree, that there is something rather confused and unintelligible in his buildings, far unlike those comfortable habitations which our friend Mieris represents with such meritorious accuracy.' Mieris bowed, and Watersouchy, encouraged by Monsieur Baise-la-main's coincidence with his opinion, continued his critique. He shook his head at a picture wherein Polemburg had introduced a group of ruins, and exclaimed – 'Why not substitute, for example, the great church of Antwerp flourishing in the height of its perfection, in the room of those Roman lumps of confusion and decay? – Instead of representing the flowers of the parterre, he crouds his foreground with all manner of woods, and bestows as much pains on a dock leaf as I should on the most estimable carnation in your garden. Naked figures too I abhor: Madam Merian's cupids excepted, they are unfit to be viewed by the eye of decorum. And what opportunities does an artist lose by the banishment of dress! In dress and drapery are displayed the glory of his pencil! In ear-rings and bracelets the perfection of his touch – in a carpet all his science is united – grouping, colouring, shading, effect, every thing! Polemburg might have been a delightful master, had he remained with us; but he removed to Italy, and quitting the manner of Elsheimer[4] for the caprices of Raphael, no wonder his taste should have been corrupted.' Monsieur Baise-la-main and the artists listened attentively to this harangue, and conceived great ideas of Watersouchy's taste and abilities. The banker thought himself possessed of the eighth wonder of the world, and from this moment resolved to engross it entirely.

Supper being served up, the company left the cabinet and entered a large

[1] Johann Andreas Graff (1637–1701), painter and engraver of landscapes and figure subjects.

[2] Albrecht Dürer (1471–1528), German painter, engraver and designer of woodcuts, also from Nuremburg.

[3] Cornelius van Poelenburgh (c. 1586–1667), Dutch landscape painter who also worked in England and Rome.

[4] Adam Elsheimer (1580–1610), a German painter who lived in Rome and influenced the development of landscape painting.

hall, ornamented with the decollation of Holophernes by Mabuse,[1] and a brawn's[2] head by Mierhop. – In the midst appeared a table covered with dainties, in dishes of massive plate, and illuminated by innumerable wax lights, around which the company was assembled. Watersouchy was placed betwixt Monsieur Baise-la-main and the Burgomaster Van Gulph, a solemn upright man of glowing nose and fair complexion. Our artist could not for some time take his eye from off the Burgomaster's band, which was edged with the finest lace, and took an opportunity, whilst the other guests were closely engaged with the entertainment, to make a sketch from it, that did him honour and served to confirm him in his patron's good opinion.

The repast was conducted in the most orderly manner. By the time the Hippocras and Canary wines were handed about, universal satiety and good humour prevailed. The little disappointments of those, who were too late for one dish, or too full to taste another, were forgotten, and the respectable Van Gulph, having swallowed his usual portion of the good things of this world, began to expand, and pledged Watersouchy with much affability, who loudly descanted on the taste and discernment of Monsieur Baise-la-main, so apparent in his rare collection. Mieris taking the hint, seconded the observation, which was enforced by Madam Merian, whose example was followed by the rest of the ladies – Every one vied with his neighbour in steeping sugar'd cakes in sweet wine, and bestowing the amplest commendations on the cabinet of Monsieur Baise-la-main, who, in the midst of transport, exclaimed, 'Now truly my pictures pay me interest for my money!' The desert was ushered in with profusion of applause: All was smirk and compliment, whilst this sweetmeat was offered and that declined. At length it grew late, and the company separated after the accustomed formalities. – Watersouchy was conducted to his apartment, which corresponded with the magnificence of the mansion; and lulled asleep by the most flattering reflections, dreamt all the night of nothing but of painting the Burgomaster and his band. At breakfast next morning, he expressed to Monsieur Baise-la-main the ambition he had of distinguishing himself at Antwerp, and begged to seclude himself a small space from the world, that he might pursue his studies. Monsieur Baise-la-main approved of this idea, and assigned a room for his reception, where he soon arranged his pallet, pencils, &c. with all the precision of Gerard Dow. Nobody but the master of the house was allowed to enter this sanctuary. Here our artist remained six weeks in grinding his colours, composing an admirable varnish, and preparing his canvass, for a performance he intended as his *chef d'oeuvre*. A fortnight more passed before he decided upon a subject. At last he determined to commemorate the opulence of Monsieur Baise-la-main, by a perspective of his counting-house. He chose an interesting moment, when heaps of gold lay glittering on the counter, and citizens of distinction were soliciting a secure repository for

---

[1] Jan Gossaert (c.1470–1533) (also known as Mabuse), Flemish painter who visited Rome and was influenced by the Italian style.
[2] Boar.

their plate and jewels. A Muscovite wrapped in fur, and an Italian glistening in brocade, occupied the foreground. The eye glancing over these figures highly fininished, was directed thro' the windows of the shop into the area in front of the cathedral; of which, however, nothing was discovered, except two sheds before its entrance, where several barbers were represented at their different occupations. An effect of sunshine upon the counter discovered[1] every coin that was scattered upon its surface. On these the painter had bestowed such intense labour, that their very legends were distinguishable. It would be in vain to attempt conveying, by words, an idea adequate to this *chef d'oeuvre*, which must have been seen to have been duly admired. In three months it was far advanced; during which time our artist employed his leisure hours in practising jigs and minuets on the violin, and writing the first chapter of Genesis on a watch paper, which he adorned with a miniature of Adam and Eve, so exquisitely finished, that every ligament in their fig-leaves was visible. This little *jeu d' esprit* he presented to Madam Merian.

When the hour of publicity displaying his great performance was drawing near, Monsieur Baise-la-main invited a select party of connoisseurs to a splendid repast, and after they had well feasted, all joined in extolling the picture as much as they had done the entertainment itself. Were I not afraid of fatiguing my readers more than I have done, I should repeat, word for word, the exuberant encomiums this master-piece received upon this occasion; but I trust it will be fully sufficient to say, that none of the connoisseurs were uninterested, and every one had a pleasure in pointing out some new perfection. The ladies were in extasies. The Burgomaster Van Gulph was so charmed that he was resolved to have his portrait by this delicate hand, and Monsieur Baise-la-main immediately settled a pension upon the painter, merely to have the refusal of his pieces, paying largely at the same time for those he took.

These were the golden days of Watersouchy, who, animated by so much encouragement, was every week producing some agreeable novelty. Attaching himself strongly to the manner of Mieris, he, if possible, excelled him: his lillies were more glossy, and his carnations softer, and so harmonious, that the Flemish ladies, ever renowned for their fresh complexions, declared they had now found a painter worthy of portraying their beauty. Thus our happy artist, blown forwards by a continued gale of applause, reached a degree of merit unknown to his contemporaries, and soon left Gerard Dow and Mieris behind him. His pictures were eagerly sought after by the first collectors, and purchased at so extravagant a rate, that he refused sketching a slipper, or designing an ear-ring under the sum of *two hundred florins*. Every body desirous of possessing one of these treasures approached him with purses of gold, and he was so universally caressed and admired, that I (as a faithful biographer) am obliged to say, he soon mistook his rank among the professors of the art, and grew intolerably vain.

Become thus confident, he embraced, without hesitation, the proposal of

[1] Showed up.

drawing the Burgomaster Van Gulph. All his skill, all his minuteness was exhausted upon this occasion. The Burgomaster was presented in his formalities, sitting in his magisterial chair: his band was not forgotten; it was finished to the superlative degree. The very hairs of his eyelashes were numbered, and the pendent carbuncle below his nose, which had baffled Mieris and the first artists, was at length rendered with perfect exactitude and splendour. During the execution of this incomparable portrait, he absented himself from Monsieur Baise-la-main, and established his abode at Van Gulph's, whose inflexible propriety surpassed even that of the banker. Watersouchy, flattered by the pomp and importance of this great character, exclaimed, 'You are truly worthy to possess me!' The Burgomaster's lady, who was a witness to his matchless talents, soon expressed an ambition of being immortalized by his pencil, and begged to be honoured the next with his consideration. He having almost determined never to undertake another portrait after this *chef d'oeuvre* of her consort, with difficulty consented.

At length he began. Ambitious of shewing his great versatility, and desirous of producing a contrast to the portrait just finished, he determined to put the lady in action. She was represented watering a capsacum, with an air of superior dignity mingled with ineffable sweetness. Every part of her dress was minutely attended to; her ruffle was admirable; but her hands and arms exceeded all idea. Gerard Dow had bestowed five days[1] labour on this part of Madam Spiering's person, whose portrait was one of his best performances. Watersouchy, that he might surpass his master, spent a month in giving only to his patroness's fingers the last touch of perfection. Each had its ring, and so tinted, as almost at first sight to have deceived a discerning jeweller.

When he had finished this last masterpiece, he found himself quite weak and exhausted. The profound study in which he had been absorbed, impaired his health, and his having neglected exercise for the two last years brought on a hectic and feverish complaint. The only circumstance that now cheared his spirits was the conversation of a circle of old ladies; the friends of Madame Gulph. These good people had ever some little incident to entertain him, some gossiping narration that soothed and unbended his mind. But all their endeavours to restore him could not prevent his growing weaker and weaker. At last he took to cordials by their recommendation, become fond of news and tulips, and for a time was a little mended; so much indeed, that he resumed his pallet, and painted little pieces for his kind comforters; such as a favourite dormouse for Madam Dozinburg, and a cheese in a China dish with mites in it for some other venerable lady, whose name has not descended to us. But these performances were not much relished by Monsieur Baise-la-main, who plainly saw in them the approaching extinction of his genius. One day at the Burgomaster's, he found him laid on a couch, and wheezing from under a brocade nightgown. 'I have been troubled with an asthma for some time,' said the artist in a

---

[1] See Vies des Paintres Flamands, vol. 2, 217. [Beckford's note]

faint voice. 'So I perceive,' answered M. Baise-la-main. More of this interesting conversation has not been communicated to me, and I find an interval of three months in his memoirs, marked by no other occurrence than his painting a flea. After this last effort of genius, his sight grew dim, his oppression increased, he almost shrunk away to nothing, and in a few weeks dropped into his grave.

SATIRES

II

From *Modern Novel Writing or the Elegant Enthusiast*, by Lady Harriet Malowy [i.e. William Beckford], 2 Vols, London, 1796. The extracts are given the volume number and the page reference.

SENSIBILITY:

THE GENERAL'S GRANDMOTHER DIES

The grief, the anguish of the General, is not to be described: that heart alone can sympathize with such sensations, which has experienced such a loss. The revival of his grandmother's virtues obliterated the impression of her failings: — he remembered only the dignity of her form, and the graces of her mind! — nor could all his philosophic resolution support with fortitude, this unexpected stroke of fortune! He felt, bereaved of every social joy, the comfort of his life — deserted and forlorn! Thus the fair blooming branches cropped from the venerable tree, are left unsheltered, to the rude elements and boisterous tempest!

Scarce could the gentle force of friendship drag this heart-stricken General from the deformed remains of what was once his grandmother. Fixed like a statue, he gazed upon her face! then smote his gallant breast, and with a smile of anguish thus exclaimed.

'Yes, it is past! the only tie of nature that remained to attach me to existence, is now dissolved! — Life has no more a charm, nor death a pang for me! O thou who lately wert so kind, so talkative, so venerable! — thou art fled for ever — the ravages of sickness have defaced thine awe-inspiring wrinkles, and left thee a spectacle of horror! O my grandmother! my grandmother!'

Thus did the afflicted General vent his soul's anguish; neither when borne from this scene of desolation, did his piercing lamentation cease: — still he addressed the invisible object of his sorrows, till overwhelmed with grief, he sunk into a silent stupor.

[Vol. I, pp. 153–5]

A SONG OF DEATH

With blushing modestly she glows,
And from her bosom takes a rose,
Accept my Corydon![1] she cries,
With sweetest look, and downcast eyes,
Accept from me this fading flower —
He scarce can live another hour,
Yet while 'tis fresh, O let it be
A dear remembrancer of me!
        Rash sleep,
        Slash deep,
        Loory loory loo.

[1] Rustic person, shepherd.

A loud and general applause testified the company's delight at this song and in a little time afterwards, the principal male figure chaunted with a bas voice the ensuing stanza.

The Muses nine,[1] and Graces three,[2]
Do all unanimous agree:
The Muses first, that all they can impart
Of excellence is in your heart;
That all their wit and sense is in your mind
Pure as the golden ore, and as refined:
The Graces next, with reverence declare,
By merit you have ta'en their shape and air,
Thus the Nine Muses in your mind we see,
And in your lovely form the Graces, Three.
          Ever dare,
          Never spare,
          Hooly, cooly, kill.

[Vol. I, pp. 115–7]

SONNET

O Wilhelmina! 'tis with double joy,
   I see thee here, both as my friend and wife,
My future hours, my dear! I will employ,
   To make thee blest, I will upon my life.

Ah! should'st thou nine months hence, produce a boy;
   To sing the cherub, I'd resume my fife,
For then my happiness could never cloy,
   And then I'd bid adieu to war and strife.

The Marquis, too, should listen to my song,
   Thy worthy father, and the best of men!
While beef and beer should cheer the peasant throng.
   But I will now a moment drop my pen,
And wait the time, for which I so much long,
   When, without fail, I'll take it up agen.

[Vol. I, p. 235]

---

[1] In Greek mythology, Goddesses of literature and the arts.
[2] In Greek mythology, Goddesses embodying beauty and loveliness.

MRS DE MALTHE: A CHARACTER

MRS DE MALTHE[1] was a Lady of very shining qualities, and the finest aristocratic sensations; her noble ambition was to form splendid connections, and to be admitted into the society of the great. To gratify this wise wish, she sacrificed all other considerations. She wrote books, she gave balls and concerts, and she dressed, for no other purpose, but the attainment of this her favourite object. She was fully and properly persuaded that kings can do no wrong,[2] and that they were authorized by heaven to massacre and plunder their own subjects, and to desolate the world at their pleasure. She professed herself the most loyal of all human Beings; was a praise-worthy, orthodox believer, yet with religious enthusiasm she would have doomed all men to the flames, who even suffered themselves to doubt on any article of faith which she had adopted. For the majority of mankind, who languish in hovels, and wither away by hard labour, she had little compassion. She thought that they were only sent into the world to pay tithes and taxes, and by their incessant exertions to procure luxuries and amusements for the rich and powerful. To be distinguished as a woman of learning, she had ransacked all the indexes of books of science, and of the classics; her writings and discourse were larded with scraps of Latin and Greek, with far-fetched allusions, and obsolete quotations. Her manners were affectedly easy, and vulgarly refined; she was also more remarkable for her professions of sincerty, than for the sincerity of her professions. In her conversation she was frequently lively and sometimes entertaining, and at all times knew better how to please than to attach. She had confirmed all her old prejudices by travelling, and had acquired new ones, and hated a philosopher as much as she feared the devil.

[Vol. I, pp. 159–61]

A RECOGNITION

The general joy, however, was suddenly dissipated by the Countess, who fell senseless to the floor; delight yielded to surprise, and to the business of assistance. On recovering, the Countess looked wildly around her, and Doctor Philbert took a cup of coffee. This giving the whole company breathing time, Lord Damplin objected to the manœuvre, and her Ladyship

[1] Mrs de Malthe is probably a satirical sketch of Hester Lynch Piozzi (1741–1821) (Mrs Thrale from her first marriage), a lively, intelligent woman, friend of Dr Johnson and author of anecdotes about him.
[2] She subscribed to the Tory theory of passive obedience to the monarch.

exclaimed, 'Was it a vision that I saw, or a reality?' Every body put on thei spectacles, but could not discover any thing extraordinary. 'It was M Bloomville himself, my first husband, his very hair, his features, under female form; that benign countenance which I have so often contemplated i imagination.' Her fine eyes still seemed in search of some ideal object, an they began to doubt whether a sudden frenzy had not seized her brain. 'Ah again!' said she, and instantly relapsed, with an engaging motion of her head Their eyes were now turned towards Arabella, who was bringing a glass o water for the Countess's parrot, and on *her* the attention of all present wa now centered. She approached, ignorant of what had happened, and he surprise was great, when the Countess, reviving, fixed her eyes mournfull upon her, and asked her to take off her glove. 'It is, – it is my Arabella!' sai she, with a strong emotion; 'I have, indeed, found my long lost child; tha strawberry[1] on her arm confirms the decision.' The whole company crowde round them, and Jack Deepley crammed his hankerchief in his mouth Arabella fell at the feet of her new Mamma, and bathed her hand with tears 'Gracious me! for what have I been reserved!' She could say no more. Th Countess raised, and pressed her to her heart. It was upwards of seve minutes and a half, before either of them could speak, and all present wer too much affected to interrupt the silence. At length the Countess gazin tenderly upon Arabella said 'My beloved girl, within these last fiftee months, I have taught myself German.'

[Vol. II, pp. 4–7

AN ALPHABETICAL PARTY

On account of this happy discovery[2] the Countess ordered her house to b thrown open; mirth and festivity resounded through the walls; and th evening closed by a plentiful supper given to all her Ladyship's tradespeople who, to promote gaiety, were arranged at a long table in the servant's hall, i alphabetical order as follows: an attorney, a baker, a cheesemonger, dustman, an engraver, a fishwoman, a grocer, a haberdasher, an informer, joiner, a kitchen-maid, a lapidary,[3] a mercer, a nightman, an optician, poulterer, a quack, a reviewer, a silversmith, a taylor, a vintner, an undertak er, a writing-master, an xciseman, a yeoman, and a Zealander, who ha emigrated with the Stadtholder from Holland, and was a maker of Dutc tiles.

[Vol. II, pp. 14–5

---

[1] Birthmark.
[2] Of her daughter.
[3] Stone-cutter, engraver, polisher.

A POLITICAL FABLE

The Dream

'Methought I was thrown upon an island in the Atlantic ocean which was crowded with inhabitants, and the ports of which were full of vessels from all parts of the world. Its surface was covered with abundance, and every countenance I saw denoted chearfulness, prosperity, and content: But after a little time I beheld a band of ruffians possess themselves of all the power of government, and divide amongst themselves the riches of the land. The liberties of the people were speedily annihilated, they were plunged into destructive wars to gratify the selfishness and ambition of their rulers, they were reduced to famine by every species of the basest monopoly, and the honest and industrious poor were consigned to ignomity and treated with contempt. Then the people assembled in great multitudes to complain, and petitioned their oppressors to grant them some relief, but they found none, their just remonstrances were deemed seditious and treasonable, and the men who had thus seized the reigns of authority, published an order forbidding all persons to assemble, or even to murmur; and afterwards a decree was passed that all the tongues of all the complainants should be cut out as a proper punishment for their audacity. When this *strong measure* was carried into execution, there was a dead silence throughout the nation, and order and tranquility were pretty generally restored. Now methought the name of this stange country was, THE ISLAND OF MUM.

[Vol. II, pp. 99–101]

PRUNING THE DRAMATIS PERSONAE

There is however no accounting for accidents as we all know by fatal experience, for on the third day after the arrival of the party, owing to a copper stew-pan in which some celery had been cooked; every person present was seized with convulsions about eleven o'clock at night, and the following Ladies and Gentlemen departed this life in the course of twenty four hours; Amelia de Gonzales, General Barton, Lady Langley, Major Pemberton, the Marchioness of Oakley, Lord Charles Oakley, Doctor Philberd, Miss Warley, the two Miss Pebleys, Miss Maleverer, and Sir Sidney Walker. This terrible catastrophe occasioned much bustle throughout the county, and various opinions were formed upon the subject; however, as the coroner's inquest brought them all in lunatics, so that affair went off with more spirit and decorum than could at first have been imagined. Fortunately none of the great political personages were present at this fatal dinner, otherwise the country at large would have suffered an irreparable loss.

[Vol. II, pp. 110–1]

A VISIT TO MR PITT

As Henry, by the death of the Marchioness of Oakley, was become a man of immense property, with two Boroughs at his command, so the heaven-born minister[1] received him with more than his common candour, and presented him with a goblet of sherry and two macaroons. Henry, overcome by such a testimony of regard, and captivated by the condescension of so great a man, politely offered him in return a pinch of snuff, and with pleasing diffidence demanded if THE ACT FOR GENERAL SILENCE was passed. The great Rose assured him it was, and that Lord Grenville, Lord Mansfield, Mr Windham[2] and himself were the happiest of men, in spite of the high price of bread, and the encreasing weight of taxes, which he jocularly observed did not affect them. Henry getting more intimate, and more easy in the presence of such sublime personages, earnestly entreated to have a bason of pea soup, but this Pitt absolutely refused, because he was under the necessity of going to the house.[3]

TO THE HEAVENLY
MISS ARABELLA BLOOMVILLE

What proof shall I give of my passion,
　　Or how shall I struggle with fate?
Arabella! Since cards came in fashion,
　　You've mark'd me an object of hate.

I'd have willingly fought with the devil,
　　And grateful have been, to be slain,
For I suffer indefinite evil,
　　And warble alone to complain.

Like a madman I scour o'er the vallies,
　　Unobserv'd like a mite in a cheese,
For 'tis the criterion of malice
　　To laugh at my efforts to please.

---

[1] William Pitt the Younger. See *above*, p. xi n. 2.
[2] Members of the administration.
[3] i.e. The House of Commons.

Now I snuff the fresh air of the morning,
In a transport of sorrow – because
You treat me with flouting and scorning,
But hold, it is time I should pause.

Endymion

(Vol. II, pp. 30–1]

ELEVATION TO THE PEERAGE

Henry Lambert rushed into the room in a delirium of joy – 'O my Arabella, my angel, my life! what do you think has happened, the greatest good fortune has come to us, we shall no longer wither in plebeian vulgarity – no my dearest wife – we are now *noble* – my uncle the Earl of Frolicfun is dead, he is upon my soul, and I inherit the ancient barony of the family – I am now, *my Lord*, and you are, *your Ladyship* – we shall have a coronet in our coach, and we shall have precedence, O what a glorious advantage it is to be a Lord, to fit in the House of Peers in one's robes, and to make fine speeches, and to be called the *Nubble Lud* – I think I shall run mad with pleasure.'[1]

[Vol. II, p. 213]

AN HUMBLE ADDRESS TO THE DOERS
OF THAT EXCELLENT AND IMPARTIAL REVIEW, CALLED
THE BRITISH CRITIC[2]

Ladies and Gentlemen,
As I am well assured that your invaluable criticisms on the various literary productions of the present day, proceed from the joint labours of many ingenious men, and respectable old women, so I feel myself deeply interested in your decision on the merits of the foregoing work. It is therefore my most ardent wish to deprecate your vengeance, it is my most anxious hope to obtain your praise.

O do not break a fly upon a wheel!

But surely I shall not be deemed too vain, or unpardonably presumptuous, when I express a lively confidence in your approbation of this my first essay as a novelist – I am certain I have spared no pains in the composition, and I

---

[1] Ironic in view of Beckford's life long ambition, never realized, to obtain a peerage. See *above* p. cxiv and *below* p. 234 n. 2.
[2] A pro-Pitt magazine said to be financed by secret service funds. See V. Sage, ed., *The Gothick Novel* (London, 1990), p. 15. See *below* p. 189 n. 1.

have carefully avoided all those allusions and remarks which might tend to produce an overflow of your bile, or excite your laudable indignation. As I well know your noble natures never can forgive those scandalous sentiments of obsolete liberty, which our ridiculous ancestors were so eager to disseminate, but which all moderate, honorable, and enlightened persons now hold in just execration and contempt; so my principal care has been to keep clear of all such objects, as could give the slightest umbrage to your ingenuous minds, and extensive understandings. You also may conclude, that as far as silence gives consent, I perfectly approve of the two restraining bills[1] which have lately passed into laws, that I am a decided enemy to all improvement in political science, and wish to hear in the course of the ensuing campaign, that the British grenadiers shall have marched triumphantly into Paris.[2]

Do me the favor to erect your magnificent ears with attention while I recite to you a fable that shall fascinate you.

A screech Owl, an Ass, a Peacock, and a Boar, formed themselves into a critical Junto to decide upon the harmony of the groves, and the modulations of the forest. The roaring of the Lion was voted *nem. con.* to be bombast, the neighing of the Horse vapid and jejune, the song of the Nightingale miserable affectation, and the notes of the Linnet, the Goldfinch, and the Lark, namby-pamby nonsense. In short, they unanimously agreed that, (not including themselves) no living creature possessed any genius, musical powers, or natural melody, but THE MULE; his voice and abilities, therefore, they candidly acknowledged to be capital. These four animals now endeavoured to convince all the beasts and birds that their decision was a just one, and that in consequence, the mule ought to be the hero of the day.

With your permission 'most potent, grave, and reverend Signors!' I will defer the moral, and the application, to some more favorable opportunity.

But to lay aside all levity, it is impossible to deny that you waste your midnight oil, to save the present race from the horrors of licentiousness and the encroachments of philosophy, and when it is considered that

> The evil which men do, lives after them:
> The good oft lies interred with their bones.

Your disinterestedness must be most striking, for posterity, perhaps, may not pay to the pious memories of you or your employers, those honours which you have so assiduously struggled to deserve. You will, however, during your lives, find sufficient consolation from the idea, that you have supported to the best of your abilities, the good cause of GENERAL RESTRAINT and that you have laboured in your vocation with unabated ardor. If indeed the reflections of the fallen Adam should occasionally cross your minds, who on contemplating the miseries he had prepared for his descendants exclaimed,

---

[1] Probably Traitorous Correspondence Act (making it treasonable to reside in enemy territory) and the suspension of habeas corpus.

[2] France had declared war on England in 1793. By 1797 Pitt's administration was in serious trouble with war failures and bad harvests.

Who of all ages to succeed, but feeling
The evil on him brought by me, shall curse
My head, ill fare our ancestor impure
For this we may thank Adam.

Yet a proper sense of the immediate good enjoyed, must stiffle every sensation of remorse, while you rank in public opinion with the PITTS, the WINDHAMS, the DUNDASSES, the GRENVILLES, and the REEVESES of the day.

Go on then great and generous arbitrators of national taste! in your glorious and splendid career, direct the thunderbolts of your rage at the heads of those infamous and audacious libellers, who degrade literature by their free discussions, and philosophical remonstrances; and who even insult religion by their pernicious doctrines of toleration. Be it yours 'to stand in ᵗhe gap' between error and truth, between vice and virtue, be it yours to shake a flaming scourge, and to chastize those literary monsters who dare to push their researches beyond the sacred line of demarcation you have drawn.

To your virtues, liberality, and candour, the whole nation can bear testimony, for I defy the most impudent of your detractors to shew a single instance amongst all your writings, where you have spoken favorably of any work that was base enough to vindicate the hoggish herd of the people, that was mean enough to object to any measures of the present wise and incorruptible administration, or that was cowardly enough to censure the just and necessary war in which the nation is no so fortunately engaged. No, ye worthy magistrates of the mind! you have exerted your civil jurisdiction with meritorious perseverance, and if at any time you have stepped forth as warriors to defend the exclusive privileges of the FEW, against the vulgar attacks of the MANY, your demeanour has been truly gallant, you have thrown your lances with a grace, becoming the most renowned knights of chivalry, and have hurled your anathemas[1] at the murmuring multitude with a dignified fury that would have done honour to Peter the Hermit,[2] or to the chief of the Holy Inquisition.

Owing to your animated exertions, and the vigorous measures of your *patrons*, you may soon hope to see the happy inhabitants of this prosperous island express but one opinion, and act with one accord, the rich and the powerful shall be tranquilly triumphant, the low and the wretched patiently submissive, great men shall eat white bread in peace, and the poor feed on barley cakes in silence. Every person in the kingdom shall acknowledge the blessings of a strong regular government; while the absurd doctrine of the Rights of Man, shall be no more thought of, or respected, than the rights of horses, asses, dogs, and dromedaries.

That your enemies may speedily be cast into dungeons, or sent to Botany

---

[1] Furious denunciations, curses.
[2] Peter of Alcántara (1499–1562), founder of reformed Franciscan order; retired as a hermit in Arrábida near Lisbon.

Bay,[1] and that yourselves may become placemen, pensioners, peeresses, loan-mongers, bishops and contractors, is the constant wish and earnest prayer of,

Ladies and Gentlemen,
Your devoted humble servant,

HARRIET MARLOW

[Vol. II, pp. 217–32]

---

[1] Penal establishment in Australia.

SATIRES

III

From *Azemia, a Description or Sentimental Novel*, by J. A. M. Jenks [i.e. William Beckford], 2 Vols, London, 1797. The extracts are given the volume number and page reference.

AZEMIA

ANOTHER BLUE-BEARD!

An authentic history well known in Lincolnshire

In the year 1709, the manorhouse of Marsh Barton was inhabited by a gentleman of the name of Grimshaw, who possessed, besides that estate, other considerable property in this and the next county. He was a man of violent temper, and rough harsh manners, but his money made him to be feared; yet he was a very covetous, and kept but few servants for one of his estates. His mother lived to a good old age in the house with him, but, being bed-ridden, knew nothing of what passed in his house more than he pleased to tell her; so that his marriage with a pretty young woman, named Mrs Anne Lilburne, was kept a secret from her, under pretence that she would be displeased thereat, inasmuch as Mrs Anne, being the daughter of an officer killed in Spain a few years before, had no portion but her beauty. The old lady at last died; but after that the 'Squire seemed no more desirous of shewing his wife than he was before, so that hardly any of the neighbours or tenants that used to go to the house knew her by sight; and none but a woman servant, of no good repute, that had lived with Mr Grimshaw before he was married, was allowed to be about her although it was often given out that she was sickly and ailing.

Strange suspicions were sometimes harboured by the people of the country, for Mr Grimshaw led an odd sort of life. Sometimes he was gone away for a great many weeks together, none knew whither; and at other times he brought home with him, and generally in the middle of the night, certain strangers, who, if by chance they were seen seemed to the neighbours to be suspicious persons. They sat up, it was said, late, and sometimes all night long, drinking hard, and were always waited upon by that woman servant that was in her master's confidence. As to the poor young lady, she was less and less heard of and nobody dared to say what they thought; for all the parish belonged to the 'Squire, and he would have ruined any body that had talked against him; for he was vindictive and revengeful, and had put some poor men to prison that had offended him about the game, and others had been obliged to quit the country on his account. The then rector of the parish was of a quiet and somewhat indolent temper, and the fierce and violent lord of the manor was not one with whom he chose to contend.

Some time about the year 1715 it was given out that the young lady he had married two or three years before was dead; and to all appearance she was buried in the same vault where his mother had been laid some eighteen or twenty months before, and no more questions were asked about her.

The 'Squire went away soon afterwards, and staid some months. It was always a joyous time for the people who had any dealings with him when he was absent; for he was of such a hard and cruel nature, that his dependents trembled before him.

After being absent eighteen or twenty months he came home with a lady, quite a young creature, whom he had married in London; and then it was given out that he intended to live more sociable among his neighbours, and that his lady would keep such company as the country afforded. But the man himself was so hated and disliked, that none of the better sort of people round would go to see him.[1] The Rector dined with him twice, and saw the young lady, his new-married wife. She was a very pretty and agreeable person; but seemed so low-spirited and dejected, that it made his heart ache to see her. She looked, while she sat at the head of the table, like one who was suffering without daring to complain; and every now and then her husband seemed to fix his fierce and angry eyes on her, as if he was not willing her sorrowfulness should be remarked by the stranger.

The Rector liking the ways of Grimshaw less and less, went no more; and the same gloomy silence and seclusion reigned about the house as was seen there before. Hardly any body ever appeared in the family but the favourite housekeeper, who still governed every thing; and whenever the 'Squire was seen, it was only in some act of tyranny, or in a storm of passion and fury, and he seemed to grow worse and worse every day; so that his house was looked upon like the den of a wild beast, which all people were afraid to enter.

In 1715 was the rebellion,[2] and it was said that the 'Squire was gone out to join one of the associations that were made: there was not a soul in the neighbourhood for twenty miles about, but what would have been glad to have heard that he had met the rebels, and that they had knocked him on the head. As to the poor lady, his wife, she appeared no more; and there were people who scrupled not to say, that she was unfairly dealt by, or spirited away as the other unhappy young gentlewoman had been before.

One dark night, towards the end of November, Mr Jackson, rector, who was going on a journey the next day, went to the window of his room at the rectory to look at the weather, when he thought he saw something white move among the trees in the orchard: – he opened the casement and spoke: nobody answered: he spoke louder, saying, 'Who is there?' A low murmuring voice was heard, as of a person endeavouring in vain to utter the complaints that pain or terror would have extorted. Mr Jackson held the candle out of the window, and, looking earnestly down thought he saw a female kneeling on the ground, with lifted hands in the attitude of imploring succour. He spoke again, and the effort to answer was repeated by the person beneath him.

Mr Jackson was a timid and retired man, an invalid for many years: he had another living in a pleasanter part of the country, near Lincoln, and never

---

[1] Beckford had direct experience of social ostracism at Fonthill in later years.
[2] Jacobite rising in Scotland in 1715.

resided here longer than he was compelled to do, by the ill-natured attempts made by some of his parishioners to deprive him of his benefice for non-residence.... His feeble spirits were strangely alarmed by the general appearance of the figure on which the light fell, but the features he could not discern. He trembled, he hesitated, and then he heard again a sort of stifled sound of moaning; and not having courage to open his door, though he hardly knew of what he was afraid, he rang the bell at the head of his bed, and at the same time knocked loudly against the wainscot[1] with a stick. His only servants, a woman who had long had the care of his house, and her husband who worked in the garden and took care of the horse, were presently roused and came to the door, demanding to know what was the matter? Their master, having let them in, directed them to look from the window, where they both saw the same figure; but now, instead of its former attitude of supplication, it seemed to have fallen against the wall of the house, where motionless it lay half stretched on the ground.

'Tis a woman!' said James Walling, the labourer, 'and, to my thinking, she is dead!'

'Some traveller, I warrant,' cried his wife: 'there a been two or three to our door to-day.'

The man of peace and charity felt for a moment that it was his duty, as a clergyman and a christian, to shelter and relieve her whatever she might be; but fears, of he knew not what, among which some apprehensions of expence failed not to mingle themselves, half deterred him. The servant man had more bowels and fewer scruples; and though his wife muttered some half sentence against it, he went down unbidden, and, approaching the unhappy object on the ground, while Mr Jackson and the woman looked at him from the open window, he cried out to them, that it was no traveller nor beggar, but looked somewhat like a lady, but she was quite cold and senseless, and he believed dead. However, without staying for orders, which Mr Jackson seemed still but half disposed to give, he took her up in his arms and carried her into the kitchen, where he placed her before the covered embers, on the hearth. His master and the woman now descended, the care of the first was immediately directed to the door, which he carefully fastened within side, while James said to his wife, 'Why don't you look at the poor young gentlewoman, and see what help you can give her if she isn't quite dead? How can you have such a heart? I think I have seen this poor woman before, I don't know where but be that how 'twill, don't let her die without help.'

This awakened something like humanity; and indeed, what little could ever be produced in the half-petrified bosom of the woman, could not but be engaged on contemplating the piteous object before her. She now began to rub the palms of her hands, and, taking some brandy from a cupboard, chafed her temples and applied it to her nose.

After a while the young person opened her eyes; and the first use she made of her speech was to conjure Mr Jackson, in a feeble voice, not to let her be

---

[1] Wooden panelling of wall.

carried back to Barton-Marsh House. It proved to be the poor young lady, wife to 'Squire Grimshaw, who, in a dying condition, had escaped from the den of her merciless tyrant, and entreated Mr Jackson to afford her his protection; as the horrors she underwent at the manor house (not only from his cruelty and her extreme detestation of him, and from the insolence and inhumanity of the woman set over her, but from an apparition that continually disturbed her and prevented her ever sleeping, when her barbarous persecutors left her any repose), were so great, her misery became such, that it was impossible to endure it any longer. Mr Jackson, timid and cautious in his nature, was, from habits of interested compliance, abjectly afraid of offending any rich or powerful man; he therefore hesitated whether he should receive and protect the unhappy young creature who had thus thrown herself upon his mercy: yet he could not look upon her, nor listen to the plaintive and trembling voice in which she attempted incoherently to relate her wretched condition, without feeling it to be his duty, as a christian and a man, to defend her. His natural cowardice, however, and the extreme fear that Grimshaw inspired in the neighbourhood, would have prevented the good effects of these feelings, if his servant, who had more spirit and humanity than himself, and by whom he was very much governed, had not declared, that 'while he had a drop of blood left the poor gentlewoman should not be forced back by no such hard-hearted tyrant as the 'Squire.' His wife praised his resolution; and their master considering that he was to go away in the morning, and of course might escape being any party in the business if Grimshaw should be troublesome, consented to let the poor young woman be led by the female servant to a bed, where he left her without farther enquiry, and at day-break set forward as he had intended on his journey.

The woman, though of a harsh, cold, and covetous disposition, was moved by the wretched situation of the unfortunate young person; and her interest came in aid of her compassion, when she learned that the family of Mrs Grimshaw were rich tradesmen in London; and that though she had been sacrificed to her wicked and cruel husband, in order to leave more money at the disposal of her father for a favourite son; yet, her father being as she believed dead, her mother and an uncle, as well as that brother himself to whose advantage her father had made her a victim, would now, she was sure, not only receive and protect her, but handsomely reward the humane people who should be the means of her preservation.

She wrote a few lines to her mother as soon as she had strength to hold a pen; but from long disuse and great feebleness in her hands she could hardly make what she wrote legible. Walling set out with the letter, and put it himself into the post at the next market town, giving his wife a strict caution not to say a word to any of their few neighbours, as to their having a stranger in their house; for he observed, that though the 'Squire was gone from the Marsh House, yet Madam Hannah, as she was called, would soon set out after her mistress, and try to be sure to hinder her from telling tales – perhaps by killing her for good and all. 'I know well enough,' said the honest clown, 'that there have been desperate bad doings in that there house, and I warrant they wou'd not stick at nothing. This poor young gentlewoman is much to be pitied, and if I can help it she shall not be delivered no more into such wicked hands, for to be certain it is well known that t'other pretty young creature did not come fairly by her end, and I warrant the lady here knows that by more tokens than one.'

Mrs Walling had an old grudge against the 'Squire for having destroyed a whole litter of her pigs with his hounds in mere wantonness as he returned from hunting, for which he had refused to make the least reparation: she assented, therefore, to all her husband said, and promised to conceal from all her neighbours that Mrs Grimshaw had taken refuge in their house.

To this unhappy young lady she now set about administering such relief as was in her power but so great had been her sufferings, her small and feeble frame was so emaciated from the effects of terror, famine, and want of rest, that she appeared unlikely ever to recover, or even to live till her friends could come to her. Honest Walling now began to hope, that, since three days were passed, her persecutors were afraid of making any enquiries after her; and as she seemed to him, as well as to his wife, to be in a dying condition, he determined not to wait for news from London, but to apply to some of the the nearest gentlemen for their advice, and to fetch an apothecary from the next town. Regardless, therefore, of the cautious fears of his wife, who recurred now and then to her former apprehensions of their getting into trouble, he once more set forth on his benevolent purpose of procuring relief for the sick lady.

The first gentleman to whom he applied, and who lived at the distance of eleven miles, was even more the enemy of Mr Grimshaw than the other magistrates and people of fortune in the county; for he was quite of another party, and a great sportsman, in both of which characters the politics and pursuits of Grimshaw grievously interfered with him. He listened eagerly, therefore, to the melancholy tale told him by Walling; and delighted with the occasion, which he thought presented itself, of crushing a man he hated, he promised Walling all the assistance that could be given to the lady but, with more prudence than he generally possessed, advised, that another gentleman who lived nine or ten miles the other way, and who was remarkable for his benevolence, as well as knowledge of the law, might be applied to also. Walling again set forth, and obtained not only an hearing from this worthy man, but an assurance of the most immediate and effectual steps being taken towards the relief of the poor lady, for Mrs Bargrove, the lady of this gentleman, proposed setting out herself, and bringing the unfortunate Mrs Grimshaw to her house; while Mr Bargrove himself took measures for a proper enquiry into the ill-treatment she had received, to which he imputed the strange conversation she had told; imagining, as was indeed very probable, that weakness and terror had alienated her reason.

On the arrival of Mrs Bargrove at the parsonage house, attended by Walling, whom she had directed to be assisted by the loan of a horse; the woman, Mrs Walling, was found surrounded in the kitchen by all the gossips in the neighbourhood, and four stout clowns, who, till they discovered who the party were, had resisted their admission. They no sooner saw the good and benevolent Mrs Bargrove was come to direct them, than she was surrounded by the rustic group; and while some of the women bustled about to make a fire in the best room, and get the best accommodations ready for Madam, Mrs Walling, who could not resist the pleasure of relating all she knew, began to tell how (almost as soon as her husband was gone) they were alarmed by a visit from Mistress Hannah from the great house; 'who, first of all, Madam,' said Mrs Walling, 'came all at once upon me, as I was a ierning in our kitchen. Lord! when I see her I was in such a way, one mid have a knock'd me down wi a straw! – So up she comes, and says she, "So, Dame Wallings, how do you?" – Says I, but I'm sure I was as white as that there wall, "Pretty well, thank you, Madam Hannah; how be all you?" – "Oh!" said she, "much as one; master ben't at home. – These are troublesome times, Dame Wallings." – "Aye, Ma'am," said I, "the be so indeed – but the worse luck's ours." – "So the 'Squire's at the wars, I suppose." – "Yes; he's a Captain now, Dame," said she, "and gone to fight the Scotch rebuls agin his king and country."[1] So I took no notice, but went on ierning; and I minded that she looked about the room, and about the room, and at last she said, "This here house seems to me to be a better house than I thoft: I should like to see your bed chambers, Dame." – "There's nothing to see, Mrs Hannah," I answered, but I was read to drop, I was in such a fright; "and beside," said I, "Master have guied[2] me orders not to shew nobody them rooms on no account." – "Never mind," cried the bold hussey; so she slipped by me, and up she went, and without more ado popped into the room where the poor young lady was lying on the bed, in some poor clothes of mine that I had lent her while her own were washed. O dear! if you had but seen her, poor young thing! she gave a shriek, and then fell back dead on the bed, all one as if she had been shot. So with that I told Madam Hannah that she should not stay there, let what would come of it; and our Sam and Jack Pilcocks at Mill coming in just then, which was lucky enough, I bid um come up; and giving them to understand what was the matter, they turned the impudent woman down stairs, and out of the house; and Pilcocks he was in such a passion wi her, that he swore if she did not tramp off he would roll her in the ditch without more ado: aye, and drag her through the horse-pond – for he knew her, he said, of old. Well! so when we'd got her out of the house, and bolted all the doors, I went up again to the poor lady, who came by little and little out of her fit; but the minnut she opened her eyes she screamed out again – "Oh! save me, save me – Oh! there is Hannah – Oh! cruel, cruel! – " and so she went on, and have gone on ever since – quite gone and lost as one may say: and every now and then she frights me so that I think I shall be as bad as she; for she cries out, that there's the spectre of the murder'd somebody and her child; and then she speaks to something she fancies she sees, and says, "No, no, poor Gertrude; I am not gone – I am coming to you – the monster still holds me; Oh! don't help him! poor Gertrude!" And so she goes on from time

[1] See *above*, p. 164 n. 2.
[2] Guided: directed or given.

to time; but never has she spoke one word reasonable, as one may say, ever since Hannah's visit; and I'm certain, that if she was to see her again, or if the 'Squire himself was to attempt for to see her, she would die that very moment upon the spot.'

From this account, which, though it was very tedious, Mrs Bargrove patiently listened to, she found it would be very difficult to introduce herself, a stranger as she was, to the poor sufferer, without a great risk of making her worse. However, by the help of a skilful apothecary, and the great care and goodness of Mrs Bargrove, who attended her with the utmost care and humanity, she was well enough at the end of three days to be moved to Mr Bargrove's house; and the same day of her removal her brother came with two friends from London, determined to rescue her at all events from the hands of her wicked husband, whose conduct her surviving friends had always suspected to be bad towards her, though they had no idea how bad it was, nor how much she had suffered. It was not before a considerable time, and only by degrees, that Mrs Bargrove heard the following account of all the terrors she had gone through; which, though she heard it only at intervals, as the poor young lady could relate it, she collected in a narrative:

'I am sure,' said the poor young woman, who was hardly nineteen, 'that had my father known three years ago, when he married me to Mr Grimshaw, the wretchedness to which he condemned me, nothing would have induced him to have so sacrificed me.'

Mrs Bargrove tenderly enquired to what family she belonged?

'My father, Madam,' said Mrs Grimshaw, 'was a substantial tradesman in London, my mother, the daughter of a wealthy citizen. I was well brought up; and we might all have lived in competence if my father had not thought proper to take up an opinion that his son only must be amply provided for, and that his daughters must do as well as they could. He hoped he said to see his son Lord Mayor;[1] his daughters must marry whoever would have them. It was in pursuance of this plan that I was, I believe, sent to the house of the person who had married one of my sisters, when it was known Mr Grimshaw was to be there. He passed for a widower, and a country gentleman of large fortune. Unhappily, he took a liking to me; while I, the moment I saw him, felt myself tremble, and a deadly cold seemed to strike my heart. I shrunk from his civilities with terror and disgust; and when he was gone, my brother-in-law rallying me upon the conquest, as he called it, that I had made, I burst into tears. The next day, however, he came to my father's house, and again the sight of him made me shudder, and his voice struck cold to my heart.

Indeed, Madam, had I then dreamed that this man was to be my husband, I must I think have died; but our misfortunes come upon us by degrees, or else I suppose they could not be borne at all.

In three or four days he made his offer to my father, who accepted of him with eagerness as his son-in-law: the settlements were then agreed upon between them, and even the day was fixed without my being once consulted.

---

[1] Beckford's father, the Alderman, had been Lord Mayor of London twice.

My mother was ordered to tell me of it, and she bade me not say one word of opposition, or even one word that might demand delay. The fatal wedding was settled for that day fe'nnight[1] it was in vain I knelt to my mother – it was in vain that, on the ground, prostrate at his feet, I implored my father to have mercy upon me – nay, if they were determined to get rid of their poor Eleanor, to kill me, rather than to compel me to marry a man I could not help hating.

They both treated me as a silly child, that did not know what was for her own good; and my father, suspecting that one of his shopmen had some regard for me, turned the poor young man away at a moment's notice; while my mother sent me to my eldest sister, who was as hard-hearted as herself, and had never loved me: there I was ordered to remain in an upper chamber, where I was teased all day during this sad week, by my sister and brother-in-law's advice; and my mother in the mean time got my wedding-clothes made for me, and, the day before the dreadful one of my marriage, came to tell me that the next was fixed for my becoming the wife of Mr Grimshaw. She then shewed me the clothes she had prepared, in a way as if she thought such things would reconcile me to my lot, when she told me that Polly Such-a-one, and Betsy Such-a-one, had neither of them half as much, or half as good clothes on their wedding as mine were; and that *they* were only married to tradesfolks, whereas my intended husband was a gentleman of fortune, an Esquire, and had a fine seat in the country.

Never in my life had I been allowed the least will of my own; for though I was the youngest, I was not a favourite, and had been used to be ordered by my brother and sisters, and all the family, I had nobody to help me to resist this cruel tyranny. Mr Grimshaw, I thought, when I dared to look in his face, liked me the better for not liking him, and seemed to survey me, just as I can fancy a wild beast looks at the prey he is sure to have in his power. – Ah! Madam, the dreadful day came – I was carried to church more dead than alive; and though I never I believe moved my lips, for I was half insensible, yet I was congratulated on my marriage by my family, and put into a hired chariot and four, which Mr Grimshaw had provided, and, without any friend with me, brought to the manor house.

As I entered it, I felt sure that it would be my tomb: if it had been so directly, how many miseries should I have escaped from!

The first person I saw when I entered the house, was Mrs Hannah, who was dressed out to receive me, as if she had been the mistress of it, and I only an inferior visitor.

She surveyed me with scrutinizing eyes; but I saw a great deal of malice and ill nature mixed with her curiosity, as she from time to time spoke to her master in a sneering tone, and appeared hardly able to command herself from speaking the displeasure her looks expressed. Oh! Madam, when, in addition to such a reception, I considered myself at such a distance from my friends, and in the power of such a person as Mr Grimshaw, whom I had, during our

[1] Fortnight.

journey, found to be the most ill-tempered and fierce man I had ever seen (for he had sworn and scolded the whole way like a lunatic), and in that dismal great house, it is impossible to describe how my heart sunk, and how earnestly I wished, that, young as I was, I might go to my death-bed rather than remain the wretch I was. But, bad as my condition then seemed to be, it was, even when I made the worst of it, far, far short of that I found it really to be afterwards.

Mrs Hannah, or, as I was desired to call her, Mrs Pegham, was our companion at table, and directed every thing in the house, where I was never consulted; for both she and the man whom it was my misery to call my husband, treated me like a child too insignificant to be noticed. I was very glad of that; for I did not desire to interfere in Mr Grimshaw's family, and was obliged to them for letting me at any time escape from the necessity of hearing their voices, or staying in the room with them. Mrs Pegham took upon her to treat me with great insolence: she ordered even what clothes I should wear, and locked up the rest, saying to me, "that such a silly young thing was no judge of what was proper." I did not complain, because I knew it would have been useless, or even worse than useless, because Mr Grimshaw would only have laughed at me if he had been in a good humour, or sworn at me if he had been in a bad temper, which much oftener happened; and besides, I did not care for my appearance, and wished, that, except being clean, I might never look well in his eyes again: so that, far from caring about the fineries that were taken from me, I had no satisfaction so great as being suffered to stay up in a closet at the end of the house, where I heard nothing of what was passing; and there I used to remain and cry for hours together. My amusement, when I could take resolution to dry my eyes, was to write out of a bible, the only book I had for some time, such sentences as seemed to suit my sad condition; and this occupied more of my time than one would imagine, because I had not had much learning, and wrote very slow: but by degrees, and as I took a pleasure in it, I began to make out a little better, and the first want I found, was of materials for writing. I now and then took a sheet or two of paper out of an old leather case that lay about the parlour, when nobody saw me; for I dared not ask for any, Mr Grimshaw having told me once, when I expressed some wish to write to my mother, that he never suffered gossiping letters to be sent out of his house that my mother did not want to hear more of me than *he* told her, that I was very well, and he forbade my ever sending letters to any body. I said nothing at the time, but felt a strong desire to write from that moment; and I was now so much alone that I had plenty of time; for Mr Grimshaw, to my great satisfaction, was sometimes absent for a week, a fortnight, or even longer; and though when he came home he was generally in such a terrible humour that nobody but Mrs Pegham could endure the house, my comfort was, that he seemed to care less and less for this unfortunate person of mine which had occasioned all my misfortunes. Yet, when he had driven all his servants away by ill humour (for he used to abuse and beat the men so that he had actions brought against him continually), he would come up into the room where I was allowed to sit, and ask me what I did there? And whatever answer I gave, it was all the same; he either stood raving in the room till I fell senseless with terror, or dragged me down to the room where he and Mrs Pegham sat, and there he seemed to take an unaccountable pleasure in tormenting me; though, as I was so patient, and he had no one fault to accuse me of, it required some ingenuity to find topics of reproach and wrath. One of these however constantly was, that I was grown ugly. Far from that making me uneasy, I rejoiced at it, and wished to be the most odious and loathsome of human creatures, rather than ever appear in his eyes an object of what he called love. So passed the first wretched year of my marriage: at the beginning of that time I had been sometimes shewn to the few people whom he could not avoid seeing, as his wife, and had sat at the head of the table. I thought that once or twice some of the guests looked upon me with pity and concern: but as soon as the table-cloth was removed, I always had a hint from Mr Grimshaw to retire; and I never had an opportunity of speaking a word to any of these good people, who, if I had, could not perhaps have done me any service.

Autumn came on, and Mr Grimshaw, who affected to be very fond of field sports, went away into the North a-shooting. I knew the time he was to go, for I was lucky enough then to sleep in a room by myself; and I remember, that in a dark morning in October I softly opened the casement, from which, over an old wall, I could see into the stable yard; and when I heard him go out, swearing at his servants, my heart beat with apprehension, lest, as it was a bad morning, he should delay his journey; for he was very capricious, and often took it into his head to return after he had set out, or find some excuse for not going. He seemed always pursued by some tormenting thoughts, that never suffered him to rest contented any where many days together.

However, this time he went, I heard him depart, followed by a servant with his gun; and as the noise of their horses feet, and of the man whistling to the dogs, became fainter and fainter, I felt quite relieved; so great was the horror of his presence, and, alas! such sort of negative comfort was all I could now ever hope to have.

Mrs Pegham, who perhaps hates him in her heart, was that day in a rather better humour than usual. She had some friends, she said, out of Yorkshire, who were to dine with her, and she desired I would dine in my own room, as I had often of late been suffered to do. I was very glad to do so now, and had not the least curiosity to see her friends, or wish to be a party in the merriment that seemed to go on in the best parlour, which I heard as I stepped across the landing-place of the great stairs, to go down as soon as I had dined to walk in what is called the lower garden. I had always chosen this place when I was allowed to go out, because it was hid from the windows of the house by the great garden walls. On one side of this second garden was a row of old fir trees, and a high cut holly hedge beyond them: the walk between led up to a sort of bower or arbour made of yew, cut also, and a wooden table in the middle of it; and shrubs, such as holly and laurustinus, grew about it, so that it was open no way but that which looked down a grass walk, between the holly hedge and the fir trees. There were table vegetables grew in the middle of the plot of ground, and on the other side was a long double row of filbert trees,[1] so old that they met at the top, and formed a sort of arbour all the length of the garden.

The evening I speak of was cold and gloomy, though there was but little wind. I walked to the end of the fir-tree walk, and sat down in the yew arbour. It was nearly dusk and every thing was quite silent about the garden. I fell into reflections on the different situation I was in now from that when I was in my father's cheerful house in the midst of a great city, with the bustle of commerce always about me, and where every body seemed so busy, that none had time to think themselves unhappy. Now, in this cheerless solitude the cessation of the actual misery I suffered in Mr Grimshaw's presence gave me but time to consider how dreadful my fate was.

As I thus gave myself up to melancholy thoughts, my eyes were insensibly fixed on the end of the long dark walk that was before me when a figure, not distinctly seen through the gloom, appeared there, and I could just discern that it seemed to be a woman, and was clad in some light colour. I felt no alarm, for I thought it was Mrs Pegham, or one of the maids; I looked steadily, and saw that she waved her hand as beckoning me towards her. My heart misgave me; I feared that Mr Grimshaw was returned, and that I was sent for in. I arose with this idea, and walked towards the person, who seemed to me to wait for me at the end of the walk; but as I approached, the form became more and more indistinct, till it seemed dissolved in air; and when I found myself close to the spot where I had imagined it to be, there was nothing. I looked round me in amaze,[2] but still without terror – I listened. It was, I thought, surely my sight that deceived me, or some reflection of the trees in the declining light. I felt rather relieved than alarmed; for any thing was preferable in my opinion to what I had dreaded as the cause of this summons, the return of Mr Grimshaw. But the evening was become very cold, and it was growing dark. The leaves on the ground rustled mournfully as I passed under two lime trees from which they had fallen, meaning to pass through the filbert walk, to reach a door that led through an orchard the nearest way to the house. As I did so I looked down it, and fancied that about the middle I saw the same figure that I had perceived before standing quite still. The leaves were thin on the filbert trees, and many had fallen. I now fancied it the dairy-maid, a young country girl, whom I was ordered never to speak to, but whom I *had* sometimes talked to when I could do it un-observed: she had occasionally put me upon my guard against the ill-humour of Mr Grimshaw, when he returned in one of his frantic fits. She seemed to pity me. I felt myself grateful for such little acts of kindness as it was in her power to shew me. Persuading myself now that she waited there to give me some intelligence, I stepped down the walk. The figure appeared stationary till I was within twenty paces, and I discerned it to be a woman; but when I was almost near enough to discover the features, the vision again seemed to

[1] Trees bearing hazel nuts.
[2] Amazement, wonder.

melt into air; and when I reached the spot where I thought it had stood, there was nothing!

A cold chill crept over me as I stood for a moment looking fearfully round. I listened in breathless terror. No sound but the faint rustling of the half-faded leaves broke the dead silence of the night, and it became almost entirely dark before, with trembling steps, I got back to my own room. I reached it, however, breathless, and sat down sighing loud and deep. My terror was not lessened when I heard the sigh repeated from a closet near the head of the bed, where I used to hang my clothes.

Starting up, I was going on the immediate impulse of fear to open the closet, but a low murmuring noise I heard in it deterred me. Faint dews hung upon my face: I became sick, and caught the post of the bed to save myself from falling. As I had nobody to listen to my terror, or by reasoning to remove it, I knew it would be useless to call for assistance, and I was a great way from the inhabited part of the house. I endeavoured, however, to argue with myself, and to enquire what I had to fear? Stories enough I had heard of ghosts and strange appearances; but it had also been impressed upon my mind, that these things never were seen but by the wicked. An internal consciousness of my own innocence, and at the same time a full sense of my own wretchedness, seemed somewhat to restore me. "What have I done," said I, "that ought to make me fear the dead? – Which way can misery reach me from among the living? and how can I be more unhappy than I am?"

By these arguments I acquired strength enough to open the door of my room, meaning to have gone down a narrow back stairs at the end of a long passage, that there joined another narrow stairs which led down to the cellars; and it was a way by which Rebecca, a woman of the village, who was sometimes employed in the house, used to come into my room, sometimes brought what I wanted; and I meant to call for a candle, which I supposed Mrs Pegham's having company for her to wait upon might have occasioned her to forget. I was slowly descending, when I thought I heard her coming up, and stopped: she soon appeared; but the moment she saw me she gave a loud shriek, let the candle fall, and I suppose, to save herself from falling, threw herself forward on the stairs. Hardly knowing what I said, I spoke to her, and, though we were in total darkness, tried to help her up. After a moment she was re-assured by the sound of my voice, and by being convinced it was I who spoke to her. I took her hand; and though my words trembled on my lips, I entreated her to let me know what had so alarmed her. – All the answer I could obtain was, "Oh! Madam, you don't know! Such a fright! but it serves me as I ought to be served. – I was told last year how 'twould be."

I found it vain to ask an explanation of all this, the woman still continuing to lament herself; I therefore desired she would try to rise and light the candle, for that I was extremely cold in my own room, and wished for a fire. At length I prevailed upon her to exert herself to go down, leaning on my arm; but as she went she continued to exclaim, "Cold! ah, well you may! Poor young thing! Who would be a great rich lady to live in this house? – Not I, I am sure." Of this and similar speeches I entreated an explanation, but in vain. Taken up entirely with herself, all I could obtain from the woman was, that when she saw me upon the stairs she had taken me for the spirit that walked in and about the house, and which the dairy-maid had declared she had seen standing against the pales of the great granary. I shuddered, and earnestly enquired what was meant. "Ah! poor young lady, you will know soon enough." was all the answer I could obtain from this person, who, as we approached the place where it was probable she might be heard by Mrs Pegham, lowered her voice, and seemed to subdue her fears by considering her interest. I could not prevail upon her to stay even while I waited for the dairy-maid: but she hastened away, and left me alone in the kitchen; for the servants now in the house, who were only two maids, and a sort of farming man, were all employed, as I supposed, in attending on the friends of the housekeeper: the kitchen was entirely deserted.

It was, however, comparatively cheerful; for there was a good fire, supper seemed to be preparing, and several dogs lay round the hearth. I thought it would have been a consolation, and in some sort a protection, if I could have prevailed on one of these to follow me to my room. There was an old water spaniel that I had sometimes fondled and fed, and which had often followed me in my solitary walks. I now, fancying I heard Mrs Pegham's voice, hastened to retire; for the terror of her insults was as great as almost any other, and I had been ordered by Mr Grimshaw never to be seen in the kitchen. I coaxed the spaniel to follow me, and taking up a candle, with which I intended to light my fire, I crept slowly back to my own room, dreading to look up the stairs, and somewhat re-assured by hearing the sound of my four-footed companion's steps after me. Hardly, however, had I reached the door of my room before the dog began to howl in a strange manner, and ran away with such speed, that any attempts to stop or overtake it would have been to no purpose. I cannot describe the terror with which I entered the room; but perceiving nothing, and feeling half-dead with fear and cold, I lit the fire, and, when it burnt up, sat down and ate what had been sent me for my supper, which Rebecca had left upon the stairs. I found myself restored to a little more courage, but on the apprehensions of the evening I dared not think. As soon, therefore, as I could, I hastened to my bed, having bolted the door of my chamber, and that of the closet, into which I dared not look.

I know not how, after such dread and apprehensions, the more terrible for not being ascertained, my spirits subsided into composure, so as to allow me to sleep: but I had certainly forgot myself for some time, when I started suddenly at some fancied noise, and through the curtains of my bed, that were of old thin linen, I thought I saw a figure standing before the fire, which burnt brightly. Involuntarily I reached toward the foot of the bed, and undrew the curtain. I saw very plainly a female figure, leaning with her head against the mantle piece, while her back was towards me. Immoveable with terror, I remained gazing at it some moments, till turning towards me it approached the foot of the bed, where I fell in an undescribable horror on beholding what appeared to be a corpse. It looked earnestly on me for some time; then I heard the same deep hollow sigh as had before reached my ears from the closet; and gliding towards that closet the spectre again melted away.

I cannot well describe the state of mind in which I remained the rest of the night; but the moment I saw day-light gleaming through the shutters I opened them, and sat there till it became broad day, when I crept more dead than alive to the kitchen, where my appearance at that unusual hour, and the horror marked on my countenance, were observed by the old servant who was most in Mrs Pegham's confidence, and who might well be called one of my keepers. She asked me fiercely and brutally what I did there, and why I looked so white? I told her that I had been very much terrified during the night by something that had appeared in my room: to which she gave me only a harsh answer, saying, I had better speak to Mrs Pegham, and hear what *she* would say, forsooth, to my indulging such vagaries. Contrary, however, to my expectation, Mrs Pegham sent for me to breakfast with her; and the woman having told her what I had said, she affected to laugh at my fears, and told me that she supposed I had taken such fancies into my head in consequence of some nonsensical stories I had heard of the house being haunted; "but such things are always said in these lone villages," added she, "of old fashioned houses like this. I would not advise you to take any notice of these nonsensical stories to Mr Grimshaw; for he will be very angry, and has often declared he should be tempted to send any body to the other world to keep company with ghosts, if they were such ideots as to talk of them in his house. I assure you he has turned three or four servants out of doors for it already."

Ah! thought I, how glad I should be, if he would turn *me* out of doors! And how willingly I would beg my way to London, if he would but let me leave this house of horrors!

Mrs Pegham, however, was more civil than usual to me during the rest of the day: she kept me to dine with her in the parlour; when, just as we were sitting down to table, a man's voice was heard in the hall. I turned pale with terror, concluding it to be Mr Grimshaw returned; when, to my great astonishment, I saw come into the room Mr Auberry, the young man who had lived for some time with my father, and who had shewn some partiality for me. He seemed in great confusion and distress of mind; and as he addressed himself to me, as the mistress of the house, I saw that he was struck with the change that had taken place in my appearance; while, as he turned to answer Mrs Pegham's rude enquiry of what his business was, and what was his name? I perceived his eyes lighten, and his cheeks glow with indignation. For my own part, I waited in breathless fear for the end of the dialogue between them, expecting nothing but to hear that my father or mother was dead, or that some great misfortune had happened to my family.

When with a trembling voice I made the enquiry, he assured me that they were all well; but, he added, imprudently enough, that my father had lately been much troubled in mind about me, from certain dreams he and my mother had been afflicted with, and that they neither of them were able to rest till somebody they could depend upon had seen me: therefore, as he was travelling into the north of England for orders, being shortly to be taken into partnership with my father, he had come about forty miles out of his way to convince them I was alive and well.

Mrs Pegham heard him with great impatience, and said, now that he had seen me, she supposed it was enough. She had no authority to invite any-body to the house, while Mr Grimshaw was abroad, so it was not in her power to ask him to dinner, but if he chose a glass of wine, or ale, or the like, he was welcome. I then ventured to speak, and told her that I hoped she would allow *me* to invite Mr Auberry to dinner, that I might have time to enquire after my friends, whom I had not heard of for so long a time. Auberry refused eating any thing, but said he hoped the housekeeper's permission was not necessary to speak to me, which he desired to do alone; but she positively refused, and told him, that if he came there only to set a young woman against her husband, and make unhappiness and discontent in a family, the sooner he was gone the better; that she should let no young fellows that came rambling about talk to Mr Grimshaw's wife, and she desired him to walk out, and not give her the trouble of having him turned out.

Auberry, convinced by my looks that my situation was dreadful, and feeling all the insolence of Mrs Pegham's conduct, persisted in saying, he would speak to me. Mrs Pegham hastened in a rage to the door to call for the farming men, and I took that opportunity to entreat of Auberry not to abandon me. "Oh! for God's sake," said I, "save me if you can! I am the most unhappy wretch breathing. You know not, nobody can know, all I endure."

Mrs Pegham by this time returned, and again insolently ordered Mr Auberry to leave the house. He again peremptorily refused. The woman, who seemed to have assumed all the qualities of a fury,[1] then beckoned to two men, who came in with pitchforks in their hands, and turned Mr Auberry by force out of doors; while I, driven to despair in proportion at this hope of deliverance seemed escaping from me, clung to him, till the woman, seizing me by the arm, tore me away; then dragging me toward my own room, while she loaded me with reproaches, and protested in the most virulent terms that she would inform Mr Grimshaw of all that had happened, and take care it never should be in my power to attempt to go away again, she locked the doors, barred the windows, and left me to myself!

I had a few hours before thought that nothing could be so dreadful as being shut up in that room; I now preferred it to the dread I felt of Grim-shaw's return, and wished for nothing but to die, rather than be exposed again to meet him.

Night came, and with it the recollection of those terrors I had undergone the night before; they were not less now. About midnight, the profound silence was broken by a rustling and a low moaning in the closet: it was as of

[1] Primeval being.

one confined there in pain and uneasiness, and striving to get out. If I had had a light, I do not know that I should have had courage to have opened the closet, though I had been endeavouring to obtain sufficient resolution, by repeating to myself the question – What have I to fear? and would not death be welcome? – As I had no light, I made that sort of excuse to myself for not attempting to assure myself of the cause of this extraordinary noise, to which I had not listened, in increased terror, above half an hour, before a pale dismal light gleamed through the room. I put back my curtain, and saw the same figure I had seen the night before. It glided from the closet-door, and placed itself again at the foot of the bed. I attempted in vain to shriek, to speak – fear quite overcame me; yet I could not withdraw my eyes from the figure, which, after remaining immoveable some time, waved its arm, and then passed to the door of the chamber, still motioning for me to follow. A strange impulse, which it seemed as if I could not resist, occasioned me to leave my bed, where I had thrown myself without being undressed. I stood then within a short distance of the object and to my astonishment I saw it pass through the door, which I knew to be shut; yet I still perceived it on the other side gliding slowly through the long passage that led to the back stairs. I involuntarily seized the lock. It opened – I followed the spectre along the passage – it descended the stairs; on the top of which I continued to stand half senseless with amaze, and doubting my senses. When the figure had reached the place where one staircase branched off toward the cellar, and the other toward the kitchen, it stopped and turned, then pointed with one hand down the staircase, while it seemed to beckon me with the other toward that which led to the kitchen: and then it became fainter and fainter, till, the semblance of the human form being lost, only a blueish and very feeble light remained which slowly went on, while, without any ascertained purpose, I followed it softly, my knees trembling, and my breath oppressed. It wavered through a great and almost empty space behind the kitchen to a large door made for the bringing in wood and turf, which was in winter piled up there to dry for the use of the kitchen. Through this door, which slowly opened at its approach, the mysterious light moved, and in a few paces I found myself standing in the midst of the wood-yard. The light was no where visible, but I saw a few stars above my head. I felt the air blow refreshing on my face. I breathed more freely and the idea that I might now leave my hideous prison for ever, and that Providence had interposed for my deliverance, suddenly occurred to me.

Having once seized this hope, I seemed to recover my strength. I looked round the place, in which I had never been above once before, for a door: I found one, and seized the latch eagerly, dreading lest it should be fastened. It was open: but it led to the orchard; and *that* was immediately under the windows of the room where I knew Mrs Pegham slept. I looked up and saw there was a light in her room, and I ran trembling to hide myself among the trees, though, as they were almost leafless, they did not afford me much shelter; but I had unfortunately disturbed a great house-dog, whose kennel was under her windows, and which I knew was very fierce. He came raving and barking towards me, while, entangling my feet in some boughs and loose wood that was scattered under them, I fell, and gave myself up for lost. The dog, however, no sooner approached me, than he ran howling away as if he had been beaten. This noise alarmed Mrs Pegham. Judge of my terror when I plainly perceived her open the casement and look out! After the other miracles I have seen, I will not say it was miraculous that she did not see me, for she did not; though, when I saw her shut the window, I expected nothing but that she was gone to call the servants to drag me to my former prison, where I was to suffer yet worse treatment than had been exercised upon me already. But after remaining some moments, and hearing no noise, and seeing no other light moving about the house, I took courage, and, creeping as much out of sight as I could, went round under the pales, and found the door that went into the lower garden (which I have described) a-jar. I hurried through it, shutting it as softly as I could after me, and bolting it. I thought now of nothing but my escape, for I believed I could get through the hedge by the yew arbour. I crossed towards it among some rows of French beans that were still high, and came into the walk. My heart beat almost to suffocation as I looked towards the seat, for I believed I should again see the spectre: but figure to yourself how much greater was my terror, when, being within a few paces of it, I saw (for the evening was clear, and the northern lights[1] were very strong and bright) a man, or what appeared to be such, leaning on the table! He perceived me at the same moment, started out, and seized me by the arm. I uttered an involuntary scream, and fell almost senseless to the ground. Terror, however, had not so entirely deprived me of recollection but that I knew, as soon as he spoke, the voice of Auberry.

"Eleanor! dear Eleanor! said he, "by what miracle are you here? This is beyond my hopes. Oh! try, try, to recover yourself, and hear what I have to say."

I clung to him as one drowning catches at an object that offers assistance; but I had only breath to say, "Oh! Auberry, do not leave me!" – "I will not," answered he; "I will not quit you but with my life; but cannot we escape from hence?"

I endeavoured then to recall all my recollection, and remembered that there was a place in the yew-hedge, not far from the spot where we stood, where I had remarked people had passed. I led towards it, and he helped me over a ditch that was on the other side. We were then on a wide marsh that spreads to a great distance, and I looked round with dread that there is no describing. I had never been out of the house before, and I was sure Mr Auberry could know nothing of the country. However, he bade me have courage, and led me, as quick as terror allowed me to walk, towards that side which he thought led to the road he came. At an alehouse on the side of that road he had left his horse, and the nights were now so long that we hoped to reach it before day should make my extraordinary appearance the subject of remark to such passengers as we might meet. The hope of escaping for ever

[1] Aurora borealis.

from my wretched imprisonment lent me strength. I walked with more ease than I expected, and we at last found ourselves on the banks of a river; and to pass farther seemed impossible, unless we could, pursuing its course, meet with a bridge. I still endeavoured to preserve my presence of mind; but weariness quite overcame me, and I was compelled to entreat my conductor to let me sit down on the ground for a few moments.

While I sat, I entreated him to tell me by what miracle he had thus been sent to my preservation. He related, that my father and mother being rendered very uneasy, not only by dreams that had tormented them on my account, but by reports about Mr Grimshaw's conduct to his first wife, they had desire that he would see me, and inform them in what situation I seemed to be, and whether I was well treated. "I accordingly," said he, "came to the next market-town; where, I am sorry to say, that from the answers I received to my enquiries, I had not much doubt but that all the reports we had heard in London were true. I learned that nobody ever saw you, and that the favourite housekeeper, not you, was the mistress of the house; and I besides found that Mr Grimshaw was universally execrated as a savage and a tyrant. As I came nearer to his house, I saw the people I spoke to answered me with mingled fear and detestation, and all I could gather of a certainty was, that I should not be suffered to see you, and that the only way that gave me any chance of it, was to enter the house unexpectedly while the master of it was absent, as he now was. I did so, and the event you know.

After I was compelled to quit the house, without having an opportunity of speaking to you alone, I was returning slowly to the little inn where I had left my horse, when I was overtaken by an odd, wild-looking woman, who turned, after she had passed me, and eyed me with an expression that raised my curiosity. She continued to look at me, and to mutter till she entered a poor cottage to the end of the village, whither I followed her; and putting half a crown into her hand (a sum which she seemed to consider as immense), I desired her to tell me if she knew any thing of the inhabitants of the manor house?

And now, dear Madam," said Auberry, "have you courage enough to hear what this woman related to me?"

I assured him I had, and he thus proceeded:

"She told me, then, that she should be ruined, if ever what she said came to the 'Squire's ears. It was well known in the country, that his first wife did not come fairly by her death, and that she was given out for dead long before she was so; because she was reduced by ill usage to such a state, that her wicked husband dared not let her be seen by the relations that he was afraid would enquire for her; and that instead of her, a parcel of stones was buried, and she lingered in a wretched place under ground, where at length she died; though even then it was believed her end was hastened by poison, or some such wicked means, which nobody could do more than guess at, because she had never been seen afterwards; but that it was well known that every year about the time she had thus lingered and died, her ghost appeared about the house, and that several people had seen it.

O think what I felt at hearing all this! and how great was my horror when I reflected that I was the wife of this wretch, and might again be in his power. I could with difficulty command myself to listen to what followed.

The woman told me," continued Mr Auberry, "that she had been hired in the house occasionally, and was just come from thence, having been frightened by the report of the servants – that this was the time the spirit walked, and that there was more than one bad story of wicked actions done by the 'Squire and his housekeeper; for it was said a brother of the young lady, his first wife, coming from beyond sea, and landing at Hull, crossed the country to visit his sister, whom he had never seen since her marriage, and that he was scarce in the house above one night before the horrid man picked some quarrel with him, and stabbed him; 'and moreover,' added the woman, 'they say his body was carried to a closet up stairs to hide it, till they could make away with it; and all the way from that closet across the room, and through the passage, folks say there is a drop of blood to be seen on the floor. And that is true enough, to my knowledge; for I've seen them myself. I have heard say that the 'Squire have had them floors planed ever so many times, but the blood always appears again; and moreover, that at last he had the boards turned, and some of the worst on 'em changed, but that still, do what he will, the blood-spots came exactly in the same place again, as red as if they had just sprung from the murdered gentleman.' I then remembered that there were pieces of old tapestry nailed down to the floor, quite from the door of that fatal closet to the end of the long passage, and that once I had dropped a little ring my mother had given me, and was trying to look under this tapestry cloth to find it, when Mrs Pegham, coming into the room, put herself in a great passion, and saying, she had no notion of having the furniture pulled and tore about in that manner, pushed me away, and nailed the carpet down closer than before.'"

This dreadful narrative seemed to renew the courage necessary for me to attempt making my escape. I begged Mr Auberry instantly to proceed, and again we walked on, I believe three miles at least, before we came to a bridge, where it crossed the river to a solitary farm. It was not yet day-light: therefore, after resting again about a quarter of an hour, I again proceeded, though so very weary, that nothing but the extreme dread I had of my tyrant could have induced me to undergo such suffering.

Soon after day-break we reached a market-town, and I now hoped to find shelter and repose in a small inn. We went under the gate-way, hoping at this early hour to pass unremarked, except by the people that belonged to it, to whom Mr Auberry thought he could account for my extraordinary appearance.

Ah! think what became of me when, standing at the stable door in the inn-yard, just ready to mount his horse, I saw Mr Grimshaw himself!

He uttered a furious oath, sprang forward, and caught me by the arm. I became instantly senseless, and only knew, by what I have heard since, that he loudly accused me of being an adultress; and as Mr Auberry did not deny that I was his (Grimshaw's) wife, nobody chose to listen to any thing he had to say, as reasons why I had left his house; but rather assisted, than tried to prevent, Mr Grimshaw, when he put me, senseless and fainting as I was, into the first carriage he could find, and conveyed me back to this den of wickedness and murder, his house. When I returned – (would I had never returned!) to my senses, I found myself in total darkness. Every thing that had passed seemed like a dream, and I tried to recollect distinctly the strange images confusedly impressed on my mind. As day dawned through my shutters, I found I was in the very same room from whence I had been liberated (if I had not really been dreaming) by supernatural means. Soon afterwards, however, I was too well convinced that the miseries of my fate were aggravated. My jailoress, and the inhuman wretch, her employer, soon appeared, and began, with the most barbarous insults, to insist on my telling them how I escaped from the room, where Mrs Pegham protested she had locked me in. I was desperate; and without trying to soften any part of what I had to relate, I told it all, and repeated all the horrors Mr Auberry had heard, in addition to those I had seen. I accused them of a double murder, and added, that I had nothing to desire of them, but that they would destroy me at once, as they had done the unfortunate young officer, and not let me linger like the miserable victim, whose fate I was convinced would sooner or later be mine.

Never was seen surely such malignant guilt, mingled with horror, as the countenance of Grimshaw exhibited; while that of his associate expressed the triumph of daring and confirmed cruelty over every other sensation. I was now confined for some time on bread and water in a sort of cellar, which I had reason to believe was the place where the poor young lady, my predecessor, had ended her miserable days; but I feared neither darkness nor confinement, nor want, equal to the presence of my cruel persecutor. Mrs Pegham found me tranquil, I complained not, I did not ask for liberty. Nothing moved me but the apprehension of seeing Mr Grimshaw, or the fear of what might have become of poor Auberry, who, I supposed, must have been murdered, or else, that he would have informed my friends of my situation, who would, I thought, have made some enquiry after me.

When this wretched imprisonment was found to make no impression upon me, I was dragged back to the fatal room stained with blood, and the scene of former murders; and there I was shewn a shirt-buckle and lock of hair, which Mrs Pegham told me insultingly was sent by my paramour, as his last gift, for that he had been tried I know not what crime, of associating with the rebels, and was to be executed. At another time I was informed that my father was a bankrupt, and my mother gone into an alms-house. Every device was used, during many months, to weaken and depress my mind, which gradually sunk under such treatment. I was at the same time exposed to hunger from having only disgusting food, and my clothes were often insufficient to save me from the rigours of winter, or the intolerable distress of squalid dirt, which was indeed the severest of my sufferings, except only when Mr Grimshaw himself approached me: then the only sensation I was conscious of was something like joy, that my appearance was so wretched, that I must be an object of abhorrence to him, instead of his finding any attraction in the frame or face which had been the cause of his hateful liking.

I was sometimes neglected, and without food for two days, and I have reason to believe Mrs Pegham and her master were at these times out; I tried once or twice to make my escape, but in vain. On her return, these attempts were always discovered, and then the cruel woman used to beat and drag me about the room, asking me why I did not get the ghost to come again and let me out? Of the ghost I was now no longer afraid. Rendered almost callous by unexampled hardships, I sometimes was nearly unconscious of what passed, and I believe I have, more than once, lain for days on my bed in a state of insensibility; then, as if my persecutors were afraid of losing their victim, they gave me more nourishing food, and relaxed in some degree their barbarity.

No interference, either natural or supernatural, now seemed likely to save me. When I ventured to look forward, nothing appeared but a course of the most deplorable sufferings terminating in the grave. If I looked backwards, the memory of former times overwhelmed me with vain and fruitless regret. I thought of the manner of my life in my father's house, where, though there was always a great disposition to sacrifice too much to the accumulation of wealth, I enjoyed the decencies of life; yet I had sometimes thought myself unhappy, and shed childish tears over imaginary miseries.' – 'How little,' said Mrs Blandford to Azemia, as she read this part of the narrative! 'how little, my sweet love, do we know in early youth the happiness we enjoy, merely from ignorance of evil! – How few are there, who, if they could see what this subsequent life promises, would wish for maturity, for middle life – for old age! – But go on, my dear Azemia, my reflections will only make us more melancholy than the narrative we are reading.' – Azemia proceeded.

'Winter now again approached, and to other distresses were added those of gloom and cold – I had been long since removed into the room of blood, because of that I seemed to have the greatest terror, and I had often heard the low murmuring, as of a wretch confined in pain, in the closet, and behind the wainscot of the room; but I dreaded the dead so much less than the living, that I considered this poor unquiet spirit as my friend; and such was the deep and steady despair of my mind, that I wished to converse with this spectre, and to escape, as the form it once inhabited had escaped from the unsupportable evil of being in the power of Grimshaw.

Such was the state of my mind, when late in the month of October I was one night awakened from disturbed sleep by some noise in my room. I listened; but then every thing was so still about the house, that I distinctly heard the clock, which was at a considerable distance from my room, strike twelve. After a few moments, the hollow undescribable noise that had startled me was repeated: it came from the fatal closet. I looked towards the door – a figure with a bleeding wound in its breast glided to the feet of the bed, and stood immoveable: it did not resemble that which I had seen before. I endeavoured, but in vain, to speak: the spectre pointed to the place from whence it had appeared. I again looked thither, and saw a shade insensibly form, as it were, from a thin vapour into the same figure of a woman that I had before seen, holding an infant in her arms. This too was soon visible at the foot of my bed: its stony and ghastly eyes were mournfully fixed upon me, who trembling with a sensation I cannot define, but which was not fear, at length, cried – "Tell me what you are! tell me, if I can do any thing for your repose?"

A low sepulchral voice answered, "I am Gertrude! The wretch destroyed me, with the baby you see here – the wretch murdered my brother in that closet – at this hour three years since, he murdered him. – I survived him twenty days and nights – so long you will see me – try to escape my fate!"

A dead cold pause ensued, I remained with my eyes fixed on these fearful shapes: they slowly, slowly melted into air!

Gradually the palpitations of my heart, the tremor of my spirits subsided. I slept; and when I awoke in the morning, I asked myself whether I had not dreamed all that seemed to have passed; but the circumstances that had before occurred left me no doubt as to the reality of what I had seen. I remembered that for twenty days the image of the murdered Gertrude was to present itself. Good God! if formerly I had been told that I should be haunted by a spectre, and fear it less than the sight of some existing beings around me, how should I have shrunk from a destiny which it would have appeared impossible to sustain!

I did, however, endure it; the next night, the next, and for many succeeding nights, the perturbed spirit of the murdered Gertrude, regularly at the hour of twelve, presented itself at the foot of my bed; but, instead of repeating all it had at first said, it only uttered in a moaning and hollow voice,

"Escape from a fate like mine!"

I now hardly ever slept before the shape appeared, expectation of it kept me awake. After it had faded away, I continued to attempt arguing myself into a resolution again to speak; and if I at any time obtained repose, it was broken and interrupted. I started at every noise of the wind, as it howled or sighed through the old casements of my room, and, at length, hardly obtained, in the four-and-twenty hours, one quarter of an hour's forgetfulness. Want of sleep disturbed my head and stomach. Of the food that was brought me every day, I scarce ate half an ounce in the course of it. I became emaciated, my eyes were sometimes heavy, sometimes wild, and I believe my was reason not unfrequently wandering. In these intervals I reproached the wretched Pegham; I told her of her crimes, and of her master's; I tore up with supernatural force the tapestry on the floor – pointed to the blood, and shriekingly proclaimed that I knew who had shed that blood, and to whom it belonged. Such conduct gave Mrs Pegham a good excuse to treat me as a lunatic; but in these fits of raving and desperation I spoke so much that she knew to be true. I asserted so much that was already suspected, that she dared not suffer even her most confidential servant to approach me; and began, no doubt, to hope that I should soon be out of the way of betraying the horrors of this den of infamy.

Gertrude every night at the same hour returned, and always repeated once in a Sepulchral and tremulous tone:

"Escape from a fate like mine!"

Eighteen of the twenty days on which I expected these nocturnal visits had now passed, when, without knowing why I again felt courage to speak to the apparition, I could only say:

How escape?

When the shade, waving its hand, pointed to the door I started instinctively and hastened to the door of my room; it slowly opened before me, though I heard Mrs Pegham carefully lock and bar it without[1] every night. The spectre glided before me. I followed. It led me down to a sort of vault adjoining to that where I had been confined. I saw the earth rise a little above the surface, as if there had there been a human body buried. The pale funereal light, emanating from the silvery and mist-like shade of my dis-embodied conduc-tress, shewed me this: then the form becoming more indistinct, seemed to creep, wavering before me, till I beheld myself, as I had done before, in the open air. I found the great gate of the wood-yard open. I passed it, and was at length out of the detested habitation; but so weak, and in such dread lest I should meet either of the wretches I had fled from, that when I had got about half way through the lane leading to the fields beyond the village, I could go no farther, but sat down on a small hillock, and tried to recover my breath and recollection. I knew nobody in the country likely to receive or protect me; yet suddenly I remembered the rector of the parish, whose house I had happened to remark the only time I had ever walked out, because it was somewhat superior to the surrounding cottages. The road was so flat and straight, that I thought I could hardly miss it, and I acquired courage to venture. How I obtained strength I know not. The night was wet and stormy, and at intervals very dark; but as the gusts of wind drove away the clouds, I saw the stars. I felt something like hope. I trusted in Providence, and at length I reached the asylum I sought; but when I was at length under the window in the orchard of the good clergyman I was so exhausted, that I despaired of making myself heard. What followed after I was received into his house is already known.'

It is hardly necessary to say, that the old-fashioned language of this narrative has been considerably modernised and cleared for the press.

It may be agreeable to some readers to hear that Eleanor was restored to her family; and after her first husband destroyed himself, (as he did in Lincoln jail to escape being hanged for murder, of which he was convicted with his associate), she was married to Mr Auberry, who having been, on her union with Grimshaw, dismissed by her father, because he suspected his attachment to her, was afterwards taken into his business. Eleanor always retained a dejected cast of mind, and her constitution was much injured; but

[1] Outside.

in the tenderness of the husband of her choice, and the affectionate regret of
her family, she endeavoured to lose the deep impression made on her mind by
these melancholy and supernatural adventures.

[Vol. I, pp, 151–254]

ODE, PANEGYRICAL AND LYRICAL

TO THE TUNE OF HOSIER'S GHOST

Ye, who places hold, or pensions,
    And as much as ye can get,
Come, and hear the praising mention
    I shall make of Mister Pitt.

All he does is grand and daring,
    All he says is right and fit;
Never let us then be sparing
    In the praise of Mister Pitt.

Who, like him, can prate down reason,
    Who so well on taxes hit?
Who detect a plot of treason
    Half so well as Mister Pitt?

He's the man to make these nations
    Own their millions of debit –
Well incurr'd, as prove orations
    Duly made by Mister Pitt.

That he's prov'd a great financier,
    'Tis as true as holy writ;
He's a *rate* and *duty fancier*,
    Heaven-born tax-man – Mister Pitt.

Opposition try to hurt him,
    Only in his place to fit;
Let *us* not, my friends, desert him,
    Stick ye close to Mr Pitt.

He the multitude is humbling,
    Britons that doth well befit;
Swinish crowds, who minds your grumbling?
    Bow the knee to Mister Pitt.

Tho' abroad our men are dying,
    Why should he his projects quit?
What are orphans, widows, crying,
    To our steady Mister Pitt?

His is fortitude of mind, Sir:
    That remark do not omit;
He by Heaven was design'd, Sir,
    To humble England – Glorious Pitt!

You ne'er see him love a wench, Sir,
    Driving curricle and tit;
He attends the Treasury-bench, Sir,
    Sober, honest, Mister Pitt.

What cares he for Fox's[1] raving,
    Or for Sherry's caustic wit?[2]
Still the *nation* he keeps shaving,
    Pretty close too – Mister Pitt!

Two thirds of that nation starving,
    Now of meat ne'er taste a bit;
For his friends he still is carving,
    This great statesman – Mister Pitt.

Mister Pitt has elocution
    Greater far than John De Witt;
Give up then our Constitution,
    As advises Mister Pitt.

He *out-herods* Opposition,
    Heedless he of every skit;
For the state a rare physician,
    To bleed and sweat, is Mister Pitt.

Britons once were *too* victorious,
    And they love it too much yet;
Humility is far more glorious,
    And 'tis taught by Mister Pitt.

Lo! fresh millions he will raise, Sir,
    Tho' we don't advance a whit;
Give him then imperial praise, Sir,
    Viva viva Mister Pitt!

Praise him, all ye Treasury Genii!
    That he's wrong, Oh! ne'er admit;
Fear not Fox's honest keen-eye,
    While ye stick to Mister Pitt.

---

[1] Charles James Fox (1749–1806), politician and parliamentarian.
[2] Richard Brinsley Sheridan (1751–1816), playwright, theatre owner and parliamentarian.

Laud him, Bishops, Deans, and Prebends,
  All by inspiration lit;
Praise him, blue and crimson ribands,
  Knights! bepraise your patron Pitt.

Stretch your throats, ye fat Contractors,
  He employs your pot and spit;
Laugh at impotent detractors,
  Envying you and Mister Pitt.

New-made Lords shall join the song, Sirs,
  Nor will Rose or Steele forget
To declaim, or right or wrong, Sirs,
  In the praise of Mister Pitt.

Oh! berhyme him, courtly writers!
  Nares and Gifford, men of wit;
Pye, and all ye ode-inditers,
  Strike your lyres to Mister Pitt!

Learn, each *Jacobin* Reviewer,
  Analytical or Crit.;[1]
Learn from *British* Critics, truer,
  To appreciate Mister Pitt.

So a chorus shall arise, Sir,
  That the welkin's brows shall hit;
Britons' joyous *grateful* cries, Sir,
  Shall be heard thro' earth and skies, Sir,
And the universe surprise, Sir,
  In honour of the heaven-born Pitt.

[Vol. II, pp. 12–17]

---

[1] See *above*, p. 157.

TRAVEL DIARIES

I

From *Dreams, Waking Thoughts and Incidents*, London, 1783. Beckford was forced to suppress the book because of family disapproval. All but a small number of the five hundred original copies printed by J. Johnson, the publisher, were destroyed. In an edited form, *Dreams* appeared as Volume I of *Sketches* in 1834.

LETTER I

June 19, 1780.

Shall I tell you my dreams? – To give an account of my time, is doing, I assure you, but little better. Never did there exist a more ideal being. A frequent mist hovers before my eyes, and, through its medium, I see objects so faint and hazy, that both their colours and forms are apt to delude me. This is a rare confession, say the wise, for a traveller to make; pretty accounts will such a one give of outlandish countries: his correspondents must reap great benefit, no doubt, from such purblind observations: – But stop, my good friends; patience a moment! – I really have not the vanity of pretending to make a single remark, during the whole of my journey: if ———[1] be contented with my visionary way of gazing, I am perfectly pleased; and shall write away as freely as Mr A, Mr B, Mr C, and a million others, whose letters are the admiration of the politest circles.

All through Kent did I dose as usual; now and then I opened my eyes to take in an idea or two of the green, woody country through which I was passing; then closed them again; transported myself back to my native hills; thought I led a choir of those I loved best through their shades; and was happy in the arms of illusion. The sun sat before I recovered my senses enough to discover plainly the variegated slopes near Canterbury, waving with slender birch-trees, and gilt with a profusion of broom. I thought myself still in my beloved solitude, but missed the companions of my slumbers. Where are they? – Behind yon blue hills, perhaps, or t'other side of that thick forest. My fancy was travelling after these deserters, till we reached the town; vile enough o'conscience, and fit only to be past in one's sleep. The moment after I got out of the carriage, brought me to the cathedral; an old haunt of mine. I had always venerated its lofty pillars, dim ailes, and mysterious arches. Last night they were more solemn than ever, and echoed no other sound than my steps. I strayed about the choir and chapels, till they grew so dark and dismal, that I was half inclined to be frightened; looked over my shoulder; thought of spectres that have an awkward trick of syllabling men's names in dreary places; and fancied a sepulchral voice exclaiming: 'Worship my toe at Ghent, my ribs at Florence; my skull at Bologna, Sienna, and Rome. Beware how you neglect this order; for my bones, as well as my spirit, have the miraculous property of being here, there, and every where.'[2] These injunctions, you may suppose, were received in a becoming manner, and noted all down in my pocket-book by inspiration (for I could not see) and hurrying into the open air, I was whirled away in the dark to Margate. Don't ask what were my dreams thither: – nothing but horrors, deep-vaulted

---

[1] Alexander Cozens whose approval Beckford is seeking.
[2] Ironic reference to Catholic habit of venerating remains of saints, sometimes of doubtful origin.

tombs, and pale, though lovely figures extended upon them; shrill blasts that sung in my ears, and filled me with sadness, and the recollection of happy hours, fleeted away, perhaps, for ever! I was not sorry, when the bustle of our coming-in dispelled these phantoms. The change, however, in point of scenery was not calculated to dissipate my gloom; for the first object in this world that presented itself, was a vast expanse of sea, just visible by the gleamings of the moon, bathed in watery clouds; a chill air ruffled the waves. I went to shiver a few melancholy moments on the shore. How often did I try to wish away the reality of my separation from those I love, and attempt to persuade myself it was but a dream!

This morning I found myself more chearfully disposed, by the queer Dutch faces with short pipes and ginger-bread complexions, that came smirking and scraping to get us on board their respective vessels; but, as I had a ship engaged for me before, their invitations were all in vain. The wind blows fair; and, should it continue of the same mind a few hours longer, we shall have no cause to complain of our passage. Adieu! Think of me sometimes. If you write immediately, I shall receive your letter at the Hague.

It is a bright sunny evening: the sea reflects a thousand glorious colours, and, in a minute or two, I shall be gliding on its surface.

LETTER II

Ostend, June 21.

T'other minute I was in Greece, gathering the bloom of Hymettus;[1] but now I am landed in Flanders, smoked with tobacco, and half poisoned with garlick. Were I to remain ten days at Ostend, I should scarcely have one delightful vision; 'tis so unclassic a place! Nothing but preposterous Flemish roofs disgust your eyes when you cast them upwards: swaggering Dutchmen and mungrel barbers are the first objects they meet with below. I should esteem myself in luck, were the woes of this sea-port confined only to two senses; but, alas; the apartment above my head proves a squalling brattery; and the sounds which proceed from it are so loud and frequent, that a person might think himself in limbo, without any extravagance. Am I not an object of pity, when I tell you, that I was tormented yesterday by a similar cause? But I know not how it is; your violent complainers are the least apt to excite compassion. I believe, notwithstanding, if another rising generation should lodge above me at the next inn, I shall grow as scurrilous as Dr Smollet,[2] and be dignified with the appellation of the Younger Smelfungus. Well, let those make out my diploma that will, I am determined to vent my spleen; and, like Lucifer, unable to enjoy comfort myself, teaze others with the detail of my vexations. You must know then, since I am resolved to grumble, that, tired

---

[1] Mountain overlooking Athens, famous for honey (and marble).
[2] Tobias Smollet, author of *Travels Through France and Italy*, 1766.

with my passage, I went to the Capuchin church, a large solemn building, in search of silence and solitude; but here again was I disappointed: half a dozen squeaking fiddles fugued and flourished away in the galleries, as many paralytic monks gabbled before the altars, whilst a whole posse of devotees, wrapped in long white hoods and flannels, were sweltering on either side. Such piety in warm weather was no very fragrant circumstance; so I sought the open air again as fast as I was able. The serenity of the evening, joined to the desire I had of casting another glance over the ocean, tempted me to the ramparts. There, at least, thought I to myself, I may range undisturbed, and talk with my old friends the breezes, and address my discourse to the waves, and be as romantic and whimsical as I please; but it happened, that I had scarcely begun my apostrophe,[1] before out flaunted a whole rank of officers, with ladies, and abbés, and puppy dogs, singing, and flirting, and making such a hubbub, that I had not one peaceful moment to observe the bright tints of the western horizon, or enjoy the series of antique ideas with which a calm sun-set never fails to inspire me. Finding therefore no quiet abroad, I returned to my inn, and should have gone immediately to bed, in hopes of relapsing again into the bosom of dreams and delusions, but the limbo, I mentioned before, grew so very outrageous, that I was obliged to postpone my rest till sugar-plumbs and nursery-eloquence had hushed it to repose. At length peace was restored, and about eleven o'clock I fell into a slumber, during which the most lovely Sicilian prospects filled the eye of my fancy. I anticipated all the classic scenes of that famous island, and forgot every sorrow in the meadows of Enna.[2] Next morning, awakened by the sun-beams, I arose quite refreshed with the agreeable impressions of my dream, and filled with presages of future happiness in the climes which had inspired them. No other ideas but such as Trinacria and Naples suggested, haunted me whilst travelling to Ghent. I neither heard the vile Flemish dialect which was talking around me, nor noticed the formal avenues and marshy country which we passed. When we stopped to change horses, I closed my eyes upon the whole scene, and was transported immediately to some Grecian solitude, where Theocritus[3] and his shepherds were filling the air with melody. To one so far gone in poetic antiquity, Ghent is not the most likely place to recall his attention; and, I know nothing more about it, than that it is a large, ill-paved, dismal-looking city, with a decent proportion of convents and chapels, stuffed with monuments, brazen gates, and glittering marbles. In the great church were two or three pictures by Rubens,[4] mechanically, excellent; but these realities were not designed in so graceful a manner as to divert my attention from the mere descriptions Pausanias[5] gives us of the works of Grecian artists, and I would at any time fall asleep in a Flemish cathedral, for a vision of a temple of Olympian Jupiter. But I think I hear, at this moment,

[1] Rhetorical address to an absent person.
[2] Town in Sicily.
[3] Born at Syracuse c. 270 BC; celebrated rustic life in Sicily in his verse.
[4] See *above*, p. 140 n. 1.
[5] A writer on Greek culture, second century AD.

some grave and respectable personage chiding me for such levities and saying
– 'Really, Sir, you had better stay at home, and dream in your great chair, than
give yourself the trouble of going post through Europe, in search of inspiring
places to fall asleep. If Flanders and Holland are to be dreamed over at this
rate, you had better take ship at once, and dose all the way to Italy.' – Upon my
word, I should not have much objection to that scheme and, if some cabalist
would but transport me in an instant to the summit of Ætna,[1] any body might
slop through the Low Countries that pleased. Being, however, so far advanced,
there was no retracting; and, as it is now three or four years since I have almost
abandoned the hopes of discovering a necromancer, I resolved to journey
along with quiet and content for my companion; These two comfortable
deities have, I believe, taken Flanders under their especial protection; every
step one advances discovering some new proof of their influence. The neatness of the houses and the universal cleanliness of the villages, shew plainly
that their inhabitants live in ease and good-humour. All is still and peaceful
in these fertile lowlands: the eye meets nothing but round unmeaning faces at
every door, and harmless stupidity smiling at every window. The beasts, as
placid as their masters graze on without any disturbance; and I don't recollect to have heard one grunting swine, or snarling mastiff, during my whole
progress. Before every town is a wealthy dunghill, not at all offensive,
because but seldom disturbed; and there they bask in the sun, and wallow at
their ease, till the hour of death and bacon arrives, when capacious paunches
await them. If I may judge from the healthy looks and reposed complexions
of the Flemings they have every reason to expect a peaceful tomb.

But it is high time to leave our swinish moralities behind us, and jog on
towards Antwerp. More rich pastures, more ample fields of grain, more
flourishing willows! – A boundless plain before this city, dotted with cows
and flowers, from whence its spires and quaint roofs are seen to advantage!
The pale colours of the sky, and a few gleams of watery sunshine, gave a true
Flemish cast to the scenery, and every thing appeared so consistent, that I had
not a shadow of pretense to think myself asleep. After crossing a broad,
noble river, edged on one side by beds of oziers, beautifully green, and on the
other by gates and turrets preposterously ugly, we came through several
streets of lofty houses to our inn. Its situation in the Place de Mer, a vast open
space, surrounded by buildings above buildings, and roof above roof, has
something striking and singular. A tall gilt crucifix of bronze, sculptured by
some famous artist, adds to its splendor; and the tops of some tufted trees,
seen above a line of magnificent hotels,[2] have no bad effect in the perspective.
It was almost dusk when we arrived, and, as I am very partial to seeing new
objects by this dubious, visionary light, I went immediately a rambling. Not
a sound disturbed my meditations: there were no groups of squabbling
children or talkative old women. The whole town seemed retired into their
inmost chambers; and I kept winding and turning about, from street to

[1] Volcano in Sicily.
[2] Town houses.

street, and from alley to alley, without meeting a single inhabitant. Now and then, indeed, one or two women in long cloaks and mantles glided about at a distance; but their dress was so shroud-like, and their whole appearance so ghostly, I was more than half afraid to accost them. As the night approached, the ranges of buildings grew more and more dim, and the silence which reigned amongst them more aweful. The canals, which in some places intersect the streets, were likewise in perfect solitude, and there was just light sufficient for me to observe on the still waters the reflexion of the structures above them. Except two or three tapers glimmering through the casements, no one circumstance indicated human existence. I might, without being thought very romantic, have imagined myself in the city of petrified people, which Arabian fabulists are so fond of describing. Were any one to ask my advice upon the subject of retirement, I should tell him: By all means repair to Antwerp. No village amongst the Alps, or hermitage upon Mount Lebanon, is less disturbed: you may pass your days in this great city, without being the least conscious of its sixty thousand inhabitants, unless you visit the churches. There, indeed, are to be heard a few devout whispers, and sometimes, to be sure, the bells make a little chiming; but, walk about, as I do, in the twilights of midsummer, and, be assured, your ears will be free from all molestation. You can have no idea how many strange amusing fancies played around me, whilst I wandered along; nor, how delighted I was with the novelty of my situation. But a few days ago, thought I, within myself, I was in the midst of all the tumult and uproar of London:[1] now, as if by some magic influence, I am transported to a city, equally remarkable for streets and edifices; but whose inhabitants seem cast into a profound repose. What a pity, that we cannot borrow some small share of this soporific disposition! It would temper that restless spirit, which throws us sometimes into such dreadful convulsions. However, let us not be too precipitate in desiring so dead a calm; the time may arrive, when, like Antwerp, we may sink into the arms of forgetfulness; when a fine verdure may carpet our exchange, and passengers traverse the Strand, without any danger of being smothered in crowds, or lost in the confusion of carriages. Reflecting, in this manner, upon the silence of the place, contrasted with the important bustle which formerly rendered it so famous, I insensibly drew near to the cathedral, and found myself, before I was aware, under its stupendous tower. It is difficult to conceive an object more solemn or imposing than this edifice, at the hour I first beheld it. Dark shades hindered my examining the lower galleries or windows; their elaborate carved work was invisible: nothing but huge masses of building met my sight, and the tower, shooting up four hundred and sixty-six feet into the air, received an additional importance from the gloom which prevailed below. The sky being perfectly clear, several stars twinkled through the mosaic of the spire, and added not a little to its enchanted effect. I longed to ascend it that instant, to stretch myself out upon its very summit, and calculate, from

[1] The Gordon Riots, during which a number of buildings were damaged or destroyed, took place in summer, 1780.

so sublime an elevation, the influence of the planets.[1] Whilst I was indulging my astrological reveries, a ponderous bell struck ten, and such a peal of chimes succeeded, as shook the whole edifice, notwithstanding its bulk, and drove me away in a hurry. No mob obstructed my passage, and I ran through a succession of streets, free and unmolested, as if I had been skimming along over the downs of Wiltshire. My servants, conversing before the hotel, were the only voices which the great Place de Mer echoed. This universal stillness was the more pleasing, when I looked back upon those scenes of horror and outcry, which filled London but a week or two ago, when danger was not confined to night only, and the environs of the capital, but haunted our streets at midday. Here, I could wander over an entire city; stray by the port, and venture through the most obscure alleys, without a single apprehension; without beholding a sky red and portentous with the light of fires, or hearing the confused and terrifying murmur of shouts and groans, mingled with the reports of artillery. I can assure you, I think myself very fortunate to have escaped the possibilty of another such week of desolation, and to be peaceably roosted at Antwerp. Were I not still fatigued with my heavy progress through sands and quagmires, I should descant a little longer upon the blessings of so quiet a metropolis: but it is growing late, and I must retire to enjoy it.

LETTER III

Antwerp, June 23.

My windows look full upon the Place de Mer, and the sun, beaming through their white curtains, awoke me from a dream of Arabian happiness. Imagination had procured herself a tent on the mountains of Sanaa, covered with coffee-trees in bloom. She was presenting me the essence of their flowers, and was just telling me, that you possessed a pavilion on a neighbouring hill, when the sunshine dispelled the vision; and, opening my eyes, I found myself pent in by Flemish spires and buildings; no hills, no verdure, no aromatic breezes, no hopes of being in your vicinity: all were vanished with the shadows of fancy, and I was left alone to deplore your absence. But I think it rather selfish to wish you were here; for what pleasure could pacing from one dull church to another, afford a person of your turn? I don't believe you would catch a taste for blubbering Magdalens and coarse Madonnas, by lolling in Rubens' chair; nor do I believe a view of the Ostades[2] and Snyders,[3] so liberally scattered in every collection, would greatly improve your pencil.[4]

[1] Like Caliph Vathek, see *above*, p. 31.
[2] Adrian Ostade (1610–85) and Isaac Ostrade (1621–49), Dutch painters of rustic life and also religious motifs.
[3] Frans Snyders (1579–1657), Flemish painter of still life and animal scenes.
[4] Referring to Alexander Cozens.

After breakfast this morning, I began my pilgrimage to all those illustrious cabinets. First, I went to Monsieur Van Lencren's, who possesses a suite of apartments, lined, from the base to the cornice, with the rarest productions of the Flemish School.

Heavens forbid I should enter into a detail if their niceties! I might as well count the dew-drops upon any of Van Huysem's[1] flower-pieces, or the pimples on their possessor's countenance; a very good sort of man, indeed; but, from whom I was not at all sorry to be delivered. My joy was, however, of short duration as a few minutes bought me into the court-yard of the Chanoin Knyfe's habitation; a snug abode, well furnished with easy chairs and orthodox couches. After viewing the rooms on the first floor, we mounted a gentle staircase, and entered an anti-chamber, which those who delight in the imitations of art, rather than of nature; in the likenesses of joint stools, and the portraits of tankards; would esteem most capitally adorned: but, it must be confessed, that, amongst these uninteresting performances, are dispersed a few striking Berghems,[2] and agreeable Polemburgs.[3] In the gallery adjoining, two or three Rosa de Tivolis[4] merit observation; and a large Teniers,[5] representing a St Anthony surrounded by a malicious fry of imps and leering devilesses, is well calculated to display the whimsical buffoonery of a Dutch imagination. I was observing this strange medley, when the Canon made his appearance; and a most repossessing figure he has, according to Flemish ideas. In my humble opinion, his Reverence looked a little muddled, or so; and to be sure the description I afterwards heard of his style of living, favours not a little my surmises. This worthy dignitary, what with his private fortune, and the good things of the church, enjoys a revenue of about five thousand pounds sterling, which he contrives to get rid of, in the joys of the table, and the encouragement of the pencil. His servants, perhaps, assist not a little in the expenditure of so comfortable an income; the Canon being upon a very social footing with them all. At four o'clock in the afternoon, a select party attend him in his coach to an ale-house, about a league from the city; where a table, well spread with jugs of beer and handsome cheeses, waits their arrival. After enjoying this rural fare, the same equipage conducts them back again, by all accounts, much faster than they came; which may be well conceived, as the coachman is one of the brightest wits of the entertainment. My compliments, alas! were not much relished, you may suppose, by this jovial personage. I said few favourable words of Polemburg, and offered up a small tribute of praise to the memory of Berghem; but, as I could not prevail upon Mynheer Knyfe to expand, I made one of my best bows, and left him to the enjoyment of his domestic felicity. In my way home, I looked into another cabinet, the greatest ornament of

---

[1] Justus Van Huysum (1659–1716), Dutch artist, famous for flower studies.
[2] See *above*, p. 143 n. 3.
[3] Nicolaes Berchem (1620–83), Dutch Italianate painter.
[4] Phillip Peter Roos (1657–1705), German painter who lived in Rome.
[5] David Teniers (1610–90), Flemish follower of Bruegel.

which was a most sublime thistle by Snyders, of the heroic size, and so
faithfully imitated, that I dare say no ass could see it unmoved. At length, it
was lawful to return home; and, as I positively refused visiting any more
cabinets in the afternoon, I sent for a harpsichord of Rucker,[1] and played
myself quite out of the Netherlands. It was late before I finished my musical
excursion, and I took advantage of this dusky moment to revisit the cathedral. A flight of starlings was fluttering about the pinnacles of the tower; their
faint chirpings were the only sounds that broke the stillness of the air. Not a
human form appeared at any of the windows around; no footsteps were
audible in the opening before the grand entrance; and, during the half hour I
spent in walking to and fro beneath the spire, one solitary Franciscan was the
only creature that accosted me. From him I learnt, that a grand service was
to be performed next day, in honour of Saint John the Baptist, and the best
music in Flanders would be called forth upon the occasion. As I had seen
cabinets enough to form some slight judgment of Flemish painting, I determined to stay one day longer at Antwerp, to hear a little how its inhabitants
were disposed to harmony. Having taken this resolution, I formed an acquaintance with Mynheer Vander Bosch, the first organist of the place, who
very obligingly permitted me to sit next to him in his gallery, during the
celebration of high mass. The service ended, I strayed about the aisles, and
examined the innumerable chapels which decorate them, whilst Mynheer
Vander Bosch thundered and lightened away upon a huge organ with fifty
stops. When the first flashes of execution were a little subsided, I took an
opportunity of surveying the celebrated descent from the cross, which has
ever been esteemed one of Ruben's *chef d'oeuvres*, and for which, they say,
old Lewis Baboon offered no less a sum than forty thousand florins.[2] The
principal figure, has, doubtless, a very meritorious paleness, and looks as
dead, as an artist could desire; the rest of the group have been so liberally
praised, that there is no occasion to add another tittle of commendation. A
swinging St Christopher,[3] fording a brook with a child on his shoulders,
cannot fail of attracting your attention. This colossal personage is painted on
the folding doors, which defend the capital performance just mentioned, from
vulgar eyes; and, here, Rubens, has selected a very proper subject to display the
gigantic coarseness of his pencil. Had this powerful artist confined his strength
to the representation of agonizing thieves, and sturdy Barabbasses, nobody
would have been readier than your humble servant, to offer incense at his
shrine; but, when I find him lost in the flounces of the Virgin's drapery, or
bewildered in the graces of St Catherine's smile,[4] pardon me, if I withhold my
adoration. After I had most dutifully observed all the Rubenses in the church,
I walked half over Antwerp in search of St John's relics,[5] which were moving

---

[1] Famous Antwerp firm of harpsichord makers established in 1580.
[2] See *above*, p. 140 n. 1.
[3] His christian duty was to help travellers cross a river.
[4] Catherine of Siena (?1347–80).
[5] John the Apostle (d. late 1st century), author of Fourth Gospel.

about in procession; but an heretical wind having extinguished all their tapers, and discomposed the canopy over the Bon Dieu, I cannot say much for the grandeur of the spectacle. If my eyes were not greatly regaled by the Saint's magnificence, my ears were greatly affected in the evening, by the music which sang forth his praises. The cathedral was crouded with devotees, and perfumed with incense. Several of its marble altars gleamed with the reflection of lamps, and, all together, the spectacle was new and imposing. I knelt very piously in one of the ailes, whilst a symphony, in the best style of Corelli,[1] performed with taste and feeling, transported me to Italian climates; and I was quite vexed, when a cessation dissolved the charm, to think that I had still so many tramontane regions to pass, before I could in effect reach that classic country, where my spirit had so long taken up its abode. Finding it was in vain to wish, or expect any preternatural interposition, and perceiving no conscious angel, or Loretto-vehicle, waiting in some dark consecrated corner to bear me away, I humbly returned to my hotel in the Place de Mer, and soothed myself with some terrestrial harmony; till, my eyes growing heavy, I fell fast asleep, and entered the empire of dreams, according to custom, by its ivory portal. What passed in those shadowy realms is too 'thin and unsubstantial' to be committed to paper. The very breath of waking mortals would dissipate all the train, and drive them eternally away; give me leave, therefore, to omit the relation of my visionary travels, and have the patience to pursue a sketch of my real ones, from Antwerp to the Hague.

Monday, June 26, we are again on the pavé, rattling and jumbling along, between clipped hedges and blighted avenues. The plagues of Egypt have been renewed, one might almost imagine, in this country, by the appearance of the oak-trees: not a leaf have the insects spared. After having had the displeasure of seeing no other objects, for several hours, but these blasted rows, the scene changed to vast tracts of level country, buried in sand, and smothered with heath; the particular character of which I had but too good an opportunity of intimately knowing, as a tortoise might have kept pace with us, without being once out of breath. Towards evening, we entered the dominions of the United Provinces, and had all the glory of canals, track-shuyts,[2] and windmills, before us. The minute neatness of the villages, their red roofs, and the lively green of the willows which shade them, corresponded with the ideas I had formed of Chinese prospects; a resemblance, which was not diminshed, upon viewing, on every side, the level scenery of enamelled meadows, with stripes of clear water across them, and innumerable barges gliding busily along. Nothing could be finer than the weather; it improved each moment, as if propitious to my exotic fancies; and, at sun-set, not one single cloud obscured the horizon. Several storks were parading by the water-side amongst flags and osiers; and, as far as the eye could reach, large herds of beautifully spotted cattle were enjoying the plenty of their pastures. I was perfectly in the environs of Canton, or Ning-Po, till we

[1] Arcangelo Corelli (1653–1713), Italian composer, violinist and collector of paintings.
[2] See *above*, p. 141 n. 2.

reached Meerdyke. You know the fumigations are always the current recipe in romance to break an enchantment: as soon, therefore, as I left my carriage, and entered my inn, the clouds of tobacco, which filled every one of its apartments, dispersed my Chinese imaginations, and reduced me in an instant to Holland. Why should I enlarge upon my adventures at Meerdyke? 'tis but a very scurvy topic. To tell you, that its inhabitants are the most uncouth bipeds in the universe, would be nothing very new, or entertaining; so, let me at once pass over the village, leave Rotterdam, and even Delft, that great parent of pottery, and transport you with a wave of my pen to the Hague.

As the evening was rather warm, I immediately walked out to enjoy the shade of the long avenue which leads to Scheveling.[1] It was fresh and pleasant enough, but I breathed none of those genuine, woody perfumes, which exhale from the depths of forests, and which allure my imagination at once to the haunts of Pan[2] and the good old Sylvanus.[3] However, I was far from displeased with my ramble; and, consoling myself with the hopes of shortly reposing in the sylvan labyrinths of Nemi, I proceeded to the village on the sea-coast, which terminates the perspective. Almost every cottage-door being open to catch the air, I had an opportunity of looking into their neat apartments. Tables, shelves, earthen-ware, all glisten with cleanliness: the country people were drinking tea after the fatigues of the day, and talking over its bargains and contrivances. I left them, to walk on the beach; and was so charmed with the vast azure expense of ocean which opened suddenly upon me, that I remained there a full half hour. More than two hundred vessels of different sizes were in sight, – the last sun-beams purpling their sails, and casting a path of innumerable brilliants athwart the waves. What would I not have given to follow this shining track! It might have conducted me, straight to those fortunate western climates, those happy isles, which you are so fond of painting, and I of dreaming about. But, unluckily, this passage was the only one my neighbours the Dutch were ignorant of. To be sure, they have islands rich in spices,[4] and blessed with the sun's particular attention, but which their government, I am apt to imagine, renders by no means fortunate. Abandoning therefore all hopes, at present, of this adventurous voyage, I returned towards the Hague; and, in my way home, looked into a country-house of the late Count Bentinck,[5] with parterres, and bosquets, by no means resembling (one should conjecture) the gardens of the Hesperides.[6] But, considering that the whole group of trees, terraces, and verdure were in a manner created out of hills of sand, the place may claim some portion of merit. The walks and alleys have all that stiffness and formality our ancestors admired; but the intermediate spaces, being dotted with clumps, and sprinkled

---

[1] Town on Dutch coast near the Hague.
[2] Greek god of shepherds.
[3] Roman spirit of woods.
[4] Dutch East Indies, now Indonesia.
[5] Christian Frederick Anthony, Count Bentinck de Veral (1734–68), resident of the Hague.
[6] Daughters of evening who guard the tree of the golden apple in Greek mythology.

with flowers, are imagined in Holland to be in the English stile. An English-man ought certainly to behold it with partial eyes; since every possible attempt has been made to twist it into the taste of his country. I need not say how liberally I bestowed my encomiums on Count B.'s tasteful intentions; nor, how happy I was, when I had duly serpentized over his garden, to find myself once more in the grand avenue. All the way home, I reflected upon the œconomical dispostition of the Dutch, who raise gardens from heaps of sand, and cities out of the bosom of the waters. I had still a further proof of this thrifty turn, since the first object I met, was an unwieldy fellow, (not able, or unwilling, perhaps, to afford hoses) airing his carcase in a one-dog chair! The poor animal puffed and panted; Mynheer smoked, and gaped around him with the most blessed indifference!

LETTER IV

June 30.

I dedicated the morning to the Prince of Orange's cabinet of paintings, and curiosities both natural and artificial. Amongst the pictures which amused me the most, is a St Anthony by Hell-fire Brughel,[1] who has shewn himself right worthy of the title; for a more diabolical variety of imps never entered the human imagination. Brughel has made his saint take refuge in a ditch filled with harpies, and creeping things innumerable, whose malice, one should think, would have lost Job himself the reputation of patience. Castles of steel and fiery turrets glare on every side, from whence issue a band of junior devils; these seem highly entertained with pinking poor St Anthony, and whispering, I warrant ye, filthy tales in his ear. Nothing can be more rueful than the patient's countenance; more forlorn than his beard; more pious than his eye, which forms a strong contrast to the pert winks and insidious glances of his persecutors; some of whom, I need not mention, are evidently of the female kind. But, really, I am quite ashamed of having detained you, in such bad company, so long; and, had I a moment to spare, you should be introduced to a better set in this gallery, where some of the most exquisite Berghems and Wouvermans[2] I ever beheld, would delight you for hours. I don't think you would look much at the Polemburgs; there are but two, and one of them is very far from capital: in short, I am in a great hurry, so pardon me. Carlo Cignani! if I don't do justice to your merit; and excuse me, Potter![3] if I pass your herds without leaving a tribute of admira-tion. Mynheer Van Something is as eager to precipitate my motions, as I was to get out of the damps and perplexities of Soorflect, yesterday evening; so, mounting a very indifferent stair-case, he led me into a suite of garret-like

[1] Pieter Breugel (c. 1525–69), follower of Hieronymous Bosch.
[2] Philips Wouvermans (1619–68), Dutch painter from Haarlem, pupil of Frans Hals.
[3] Paulus Potter (1624–54), Dutch animal painter.

apartments; which, considering the meaness of their exterior, I was rather surprized to find stored with some of the most valuable productions of the Indies. Gold cups enriched with gems, models of Chinese palaces in ivory, glittering armour of Hindostan, and japan caskets, filled every corner of this awkward treasury. What, of all its valuable baubles, pleased me the most, was a large coffer of some precious wood, containg enamelled flasks of oriental essences, enough to perfume a zennana;[1] and so fragrant, that I thought the Mogul himself a Dutchman, for lavishing them upon this in-elegant nation. If disagreeable fumes, as I mentioned before, dissolve en-chantments, such aromatic oils have doubtless the power of raising them; for, whilst I scented their fragrance, scarcely could any thing have persuaded me that I was not in the wardrobe of Hecuba,[2]

> where treasur'd odours breath'd a costly scent.

I saw, or seemed to see, the arched apartments, the procession of venerable matrons, the consecrated vestments, the very temple began to rise upon my sight; when a Dutch porpoise, approaching to make me a low bow, his complaisance was full as notorious as Satan's, when, according to Catholic legends, he took leave of Calvin, or Dr Faustus. No spell can resist a fumigation of this nature; away fled palace, Hecuba, matrons, temple, &c. I looked up, and lo! I was in a garret. As poetry is but too often connected with this lofty situation, you won't wonder much at my flight. Being a little recovered from it, I tottered down the stair-case, entered the cabinet of natural history, and was soon restored to my sober senses. A grave hippopo-tamos contributed a good deal to their re-establishment. The butterflies, I must needs confess, were very near leading me another dance; I thought of their native hills, and beloved flowers of Haynang and Nan-Hoa;[3] but the jargon which was prating all around me prevented the excursion, and I summoned a decent share of attention for that ample chamber, which has been appropriated to bottled snakes and pickled foetuses. After having enjoyed the same spectacle in the British Museum,[4] no very new or singular objects can be selected in this. One of the rarest articles it contains, is the representation in wax of a human head, most dextrously flayed indeed! Rapturous encomiums have been bestowed by amateurs on this perform-ance. A German professor could hardly believe it artificial; and prompted by the love of truth, set his teeth in this delicious morsel, to be convinced of its reality. My faith was less hazardously established, and I moved off, under the conviction, that art had never produced any thing more horridly natural. It was one o'clock before I got through the mineral kingdom, and another hour passed, before I could quit, with decorum, the regions of stuffed birds and marine productions. At length my departure was allowable, and I went to

---

[1] Women's quarters in Persian house.
[2] Wife of King Priam of Troy.
[3] Hills in the neighbourhood of Quang-Tong. [Beckford's note]
[4] Opened in 1759.

dine at Sir Joseph Yorke's,[1] with all nations and languages. The Hague is the place in the world for a motley assembly; and, in some humours, I think such the most agreeable. After coffee, I strayed to the great wood; which, considering that it almost touches the town with its boughs is wonderfully forest-like. Not a branch being ever permitted to be lopped, the oaks and beeches retain their natural luxuriances, and form some of the most picturesque groups conceivable. In some places, their straight boles rise sixty feet, without a bough; in others, they are bent fantastically over the alleys; which turn and wind about, just as a painter could desire. I followed them with eagerness and curiosity; sometimes deviating from my path amongst tufts of fern and herbage. In these cool retreats, I could not believe myself near canals and wind-mills: the Dutch formalities were all forgotten, whilst contemplating the broad masses of foliage above, and the wild flowers and grasses below. Several hares and rabbits passed me as I sat; and the birds were chirping their evening song. Their preservation does credit to the police of the country, which is so exact and well regulated, as to suffer no outrage within the precincts of this extensive wood, the depth and thickness of which, seemed calculated to favour half the sins of a capital.

Relying upon this comfortable security, I lingered unmolested amongst the beeches, till the ruddy gold of the setting sun ceased to glow on their foliage; then, taking the nearest path, I suffered myself, though not without regret, to be conducted out of this fresh sylvan scene, to the dusty, pompous parterres of the Greffier Fagel.[2] Every flower, that wealth can purchase, diffuses its perfume on one side; whilst every stench, a canal can exhale, poisons the air on the other. These sluggish puddles defy all the power of the United Provinces, and retain the freedom of stinking in spite of their endeavours: but, perhaps, I am too bold in my assertion; for I have no authority to mention any attempts to purify these noxious pools. Who knows but their odour is congenial to a Dutch constitution? One should be inclined to this supposition, by the numerous banquetting-rooms, and pleasure-houses, which hang directly above their surface, and seem calculated on purpose to enjoy them. If frogs were not excluded from the magistrature of their country (and I cannot but think it a little hard that they are) one should not wonder at this choice. Such burgomasters might erect their pavilions in such situations. But, after all, I am not greatly surprized at the fishiness of their scite, since very slight authority would persuade me there was a period when Holland was all water, and the ancestors of the present inhabitants fish. A certain oysterishness of eye, and flabbiness of complexion, are almost proofs sufficient of this aquatic descent; and, pray tell me, for what purpose are such galligaskins,[3] as the Dutch burthen themselves with, contrived, but to tuck up a flouncing tail, and cloak the deformity of their dolphin-like terminations? Having done penance, for some time, in the damp alleys which line the

[1] Joseph Yorke (1724–92), diplomat and envoy at the Hague.
[2] Hendrik Fagel (1706–90), Secretary of State.
[3] Wide hose or breeches, particularly loose.

borders of these lazy waters, I was led through corkscrew handwalks, to a vast flat, sparingly scattered over with vegetation. To puzzle myself in such a labyrinth there was no temptation; so taking advantage of the latenesss of the hour, and muttering a few complimentary promises of returning at the first opportunity, I escaped the ennui of this extensive scrubbery, and got home, with the determination of being wiser and less curious, if ever my stars should bring me again to the Hague. To-morrow I bid it adieu; and, if the horses but second my endeavours, shall be delivered in a few days from the complicated plagues of the United Provinces.

LETTER V

Haerlem, July 1st.

The sky was clear and blue when we left the Hague, and we travelled along a shady road for about an hour, then down sunk the carriage into a sand-bed; and I, availing myself of the peaceful rate we dragged at, fell into a profound repose. How long it lasted is not material; but when I awoke, we were rumbling through Leyden.[1] There is no need to write a syllable in honour of this illustrious city; its praises have already been sung and said by fifty professors, who have declaimed in its university, and smoked in its gardens; so let us get out of it as fast as we can, and breathe the cool air of the wood near Haerlem; where we arrived just as day declined. Hay was making in the fields, and perfumed the country far and wide, with its reviving fragrance. I promised myself a pleasant walk in the groves, took up Gesner,[2] and began to have pretty pastoral ideas; but when I approached the nymphs that were dispersed on the meads, and saw faces that would have dishonoured a flounder, and heard accents that would have confounded a hog, all my dislike to the walking fish of the Low Countries returned. I let fall the garlands I had wreathed for the shepherds; we jumped into the carriage, and were driven off to the town. Every avenue to it swarmed with people, whose bustle and agitation seemed to announce that something extraordinary was going forwards. Upon enquiry, I found it was the great fair-time at Haerlem; and, before we had advanced much further, our carriage was surrounded by idlers and gingerbread-eaters of all denominations. Passing the gate, we came to a cluster of little illuminated booths beneath a grove, glittering with toys and looking-glasses. It was not without difficulty that we reached our inn; and then, the plague was to procure chambers: at last we were accommodated, and the first moment I could call my own has been dedicated to you. You won't be surprized at the nonsense I have written, since I tell you the scene of riot and uproar from whence it bears date.

[1] Leiden University was one of the leading European institutions of the seventeenth and eighteenth centuries; its faculties of law and medicine were pre-eminent.
[2] Salomon Gessner, Swiss prose writer whose descriptions of rustic scenery were famous throughout Europe.

At this very moment, the confused murmur of voices and music stops all regular proceedings: old women and children tattling; apes, bears, and shew-boxes under the windows; the devil to pay in the inn; French rattling, English swearing, outrageous Italians, frisking minstrels; *tambours de basque*[1] at every corner; myself distracted; a confounded squabble of cooks and haranguing German couriers just arrived, their masters following open mouthed; nothing to eat, the steam of ham and flesh-pots all the while provoking their appetite; Mynheers very busy with the realities, and smoking as deliberately, as if in a solitary lust-huys[2] over the laziest canal in the Netherlands; squeaking chamber-maids in the galleries above, and prudish dames below, half inclined to receive the golden solicitations of certain beauties for admittance; but positively refusing them, the moment some creditable personage appears; eleven o'clock strikes; half the lights in the fair are extinguished; scruples grow less and less delicate; mammon prevails, darkness and complaisance succeed. Good night: may you sleep better than I shall!

LETTER VI

Utrecht, July 2d.

Well, thank heaven! Amsterdam is behind us: how I got thither signifies not one farthing; 'twas all along a canal, as usual. The weather was hot enough to broil an inhabitant of Bengal, and the odours, exhaling from every quarter, sufficiently powerful to regale the nose of a Hottentot.[3] Under these agreeable circumstances, we entered the great city. The Stadt-huys being the only cool place it contained, I repaired thither, as fast as the heat permitted, and walked in a lofty marble hall magnificently covered, till the dinner was ready at the inn. That dispatched, we set off for Utrecht. Both sides of the way are lined with the country houses and gardens of opulent citizens, as fine as gilt statues and clipped hedges can make them. Their number is quite astonishing: from Amsterdam to Utrecht, full thirty miles, we beheld no other objects than endless avenues, and stiff parterres, scrawled and flourished in patterns, like the embroidery of an old maid's work-bag. Notwithstanding this formal taste, I could not help admiring the neatness and arrangement of every inclosure, enlivened by a profusion of flowers, and decked with arbours, beneath which, a vast number of round, unmeaning faces were solacing themselves, after the heat of the day. Each lust-huys we passed, contained some comfortable party, dozing over their pipes, or angling in the muddy fishponds below. Scarce an avenue but swarmed with female josses; little squat pug-dogs waddling at their sides, the attributes, I suppose, of these fair divinities: — But let us leave them to loiter thus amiably

---

[1] Tambourines.
[2] Pleasure house, presumably floating boathouse.
[3] Native inhabitant of South Africa.

in their Ælysian groves,[1] and arrive at Utrecht; which, as nothing very remarkable claimed my attention, I hastily quitted, to visit a Moravian establishment at Siest, in its neighbourhood. The chapel, a large house late the habitation of Count Zinzendorf,[2] and a range of apartments filled with the holy fraternity, are totally wrapped in dark groves, overgrown with weeds, amongst which some damsels were straggling, under the immediate protection of their pious brethren. Transversing the woods, we found ourselves in a large court built round with brick edifices, the grass plats in a deplorable way, and one ragged goat, their only inhabitant, on a little expiatory scheme, perhaps, for the failings of the fraternity. I left this poor animal to ruminate in solitude, and followed my guide into a series of shops furnished with gewgaws and trinkets, said to be manufactured by the female part of the society. Much cannot be boasted of their handy-works: I expressed a wish to see some of these industrious fair ones; but, upon receiving no answer, found this was a subject of *which there was no discourse.* Consoling myself as well as I was able, I put myself under the guidance of another slovenly disciple, who shewed me the chapel, and harangued, very pathetically, upon celestial love. In my way thither, I caught a distant glimpse of some pretty sempstresses, warbling melodious hymns, as they sat needling and thimbling at their windows above. I had a great inclination to have approached this busy group, but a roll of the brother's eye corrected me. Reflecting upon my unworthiness, I retired from the consecrated buildings, and was driven back to Utrecht, not a little amused with my expedition. If you are as well disposed to be pleased as I was, I shall esteem myself very lucky, and not repent sending you so incorrect a narrative. I really have not time to look it over, and am growing so drowsy, that you will, I hope, pardon all its errors, when you consider that my pen writes in its sleep.

LETTER XXIII

November 8th.

This morning I awoke in the glow of sunshine; the air blew fresh and fragrant: never did I feel more elastic and enlivened. A brisker flow of spirits, than I had for many a day experienced, animated me with a desire of rambling about the shore of Baii, and creeping into caverns and subterraneous chambers. Off I set along Chaija, and up strange paths which impend over the grotto of Posilipo;[3] amongst the thickets, mentioned a letter or two ago: for, in my present lively humour, I disdained ordinary roads, and would

---

[1] In Greek mythology Elysium was the pleasant setting for souls favoured by the gods in after life.

[2] Nikolaus Ludwig Zinzendorf (1700–60), German religious leader.

[3] Beckford stayed at his cousin, Sir William Hamilton's villa at Posillipo in 1780 and 1782. See *above*, p. xii.

take paths and ways of my own. A society of kids did not understand what I meant, by intruding upon their precipices; and, scrambling away, scattered sand and fragments upon the good people, that were trudging along the pavement below. I went on from pine to pine, and thicket to thicket, upon the brink of rapid declivities. My conductor, a shrewd savage Sir William had recommended me, cheered our route with stories that had passed in the neighbourhood, and traditions about the grot over which we were travelling. I wish you had been of the party, and sat down by us on little smooth spots of sward, where I reclined; scarcely knowing which way caprice was leading me. My mind was full of the tales of the place, and glowed with a vehement desire of exploring the world beyond the grot. I longed to ascend the promontory of Misenus, and follow the same dusky route down which the Sybil conducted Æneas.[1] With these dispositions I proceeded; and, soon, the cliffs and copses opened to views of the Baian bay, with the little isles of Niscita and Lazaretto, lifting themselves out of the waters. Procita and Ischia appeared at a distance, invested with that purple bloom so inexpressibly beautiful, and peculiar to this fortunate climate. I hailed the prospect, and blessed the transparent air, that gave me life and vigour to run down the rocks, and hie, as fast as my savage, across the plain to Puzzoli. There we took bark, and rowed out into the blue ocean, by the remains of a sturdy mole:[2] many such, I imagine, adorned the bay in Roman ages, crowned by vast lengths of slender pillars; pavilions at their extremities, and taper cypresses spiring above their ballustrades: this character of villa, occurs very frequently in the paintings of Herculaneum.[3] We had soon crossed over the bay, and landing on a bushy coast, near some fragments of a temple, which they say was raised to Hercules, advanced into the country by narrow tracks, covered with moss, and strewed with shining pebbles; to the right and left, broad masses of luxuriant foliage, chesnut, bay, and ilex, that shelter the ruins of columbariums and sepulchral chambers, where the dead sleep snug, amidst rampant herbage. The region was still, save when a cock crew from the hamlets; which, as well as the tombs, are almost concealed by thickets. No parties of smart Englishmen, and connoisseurs were about. I had all the land to myself, and mounted its steeps, and penetrated into its recesses, with the importance of a discoverer. What a variety of narrow paths, between banks and shades, did I wildly follow! my savage laughing loud at my odd gestures, and useless activity. He wondered I did not scrape the ground for medals, and pocket little bits of plaster, like other plausible young travellers, that had gone before me. After ascending some time, I followed him into the *piscina mirabilis*, the wondrous reservoir which Nero[4] constructed to supply his fleet, when anchored in the neighbouring bay. 'Tis a grand labyrinth of solid vaults and pillars, as you well know; but you cannot conceive the

[1] Virgil, *Aeneid*, Book VI.
[2] Large stone breakwater.
[3] Ancient city near Pompei also destroyed by the eruption of Vesuvius AD 79.
[4] Roman Emperor AD 54–68.

partial gleams of sunshine which played on the arches, nor the variety of roots and ivies trailing from the cove. A noise of trickling waters prevailed, that had almost lulled me to sleep, as I rested myself on the celandine[1] which carpets the floor; but, curiosity urging me forwards, I gained the upper air; walked amongst woods a few minutes; and then, into grots and dismal excavations (prisons they call them) which began to weary me. After having gone up and down, in this manner, for some time, we at last reached an eminence, that looked over the Mare Morto, and Elysian fields trembling with poplars. The Dead lake, a faithful emblem of eternal tranquillity, looked deep and solemn. A few peasants were passing along its margin, their shadows moving on the water: all was serene and peaceful. The meridian sun played on the distant sea. I enjoyed the pearly atmosphere, and basked in the pure beams, like an inhabitant of Elysium. Turning from the lake, I espied a rock, at about a league distant, whose summit was clad with verdure; and, finding this to be the promontory of Misenus, I immediately set my face to that quarter. We passed several dirty villages, inhabited by an ill-favoured generation, infamous for depredations and murders. Their gardens, however, discover some marks of industry; the fields are separated by neat hedges of cane, and corn seemed to flourish in the inclosures. I walked on, with slowness and deliberation; musing at every step, and stopping, ever and anon, to rest myself by springs and tufted bay trees; when insensibly we began to leave the cultivated lands behind us, and to lose ourselves in shady wilds, which, to all appearance, no mortal had ever trodden. Here, were no paths; no inclosures; a primeval rudeness characterized the whole scene.

> Juvat arva videre,
> Non rastris, hominum non ulli obnoxia curæ.[2]

The idea of going almost out of the world, soothed the tone of mind, into which, a variety of affecting recollections had thrown me. I formed conjectures about the promontory to which we were tending, and, when I cast my eyes around the savage landscape, transported myself four thousand years into antiquity, and half persuaded myself, I was one of Æneas's companions. After forcing our way about a mile, through glades of shrubs and briars, we entered a verdant opening, at the base of the cliff which takes its name from Misenus.[3] The poets of the Augustan age, would have celebrated such a meadow with the warmest raptures: they would have discovered a nymph in every flower, and detected a dryad under every tree. Doubtless, imagination never formed a lovelier prospect. Here were clear streams and grassy hillocks; leafy shrubs, and cypresses spiring out of their bosom:

> Et circum irriguo surgebant lilia prato
> Candida purpureis mista papaveribus.[4]

---

[1] Yellow flower of poppy family.
[2] 'It is a delight to behold fields that owe nothing to the harrow, nor to any oversight of men.' Virgil, *Georgic* 2.438–9.
[3] Trumpeter, Virgil, *Aeneid*, Book VI.
[4] 'And round about in the water meadow grew white lilies mingled with crimson poppies.' Propertius, 1.20.37–8.

But, as it is not the lot of human animals to be contented, instead of reposing in the vale, I scaled the rock, and was three parts dissolved in attaining its summit; a flat spot, covered with herbage, where I lay contemplating the ocean, and fanned by its breezes. The sun darted upon my head: I wished to avoid its immediate influence; no tree was near; deep below, lay the pleasant valley; 'twas a long way to descend. Looking round and round, I spied something like a hut, under a crag, on the edge of a dark fissure. Might I avail myself of its covert? My conductor answered in the affirmative; and added, that it was inhabited by a good old woman, who never refused a cup of milk, or slice of bread, to refresh a weary traveller. Thirst and fatigue urged me speedily down an intervening slope of stunted mytle. Though oppressed with heat, I could not help deviating a few steps from the direct way, to notice the uncouth rocks which rose frowning on every quarter. Above the hut, their appearance was truly formidable: dark ivy crept among the crevices, and dwarf aloes with sharp spines, such as Lucifer himself might be supposed to have sown. Indeed, I knew not whether I was approaching some gate that leads to his abode, as I drew near a gulph (the fissure lately mentioned) and heard the hollow gusts which were imprisoned below. The savage, my guide, shuddered as he passed by, to apprize the old woman of my coming. I felt strangely, and stared around me; and but half liked my situation. To say truth, I wished myself away, and heartily regretted the green vale. In the midst of my doubts, forth tottered the old woman. 'You are welcome,' said she, in a feeble voice, but a better dialect, than I had heard in the neighbourhood. Her look was more humane, and she seemed of a superior race to the inhabitants of the surrounding valleys. My savage treated her with peculiar deference. She had just given him some bread, with which he retired to a respectful distance, bowing to the earth, I caught the mode, and was very obsequious, thinking myself on the point of experiencing a witch's influence, and gaining, perhaps, some insight into the volume of futurity. She smiled at my agitation, and kept beckoning me into the cottage. Now, thought I to myself, I am upon the verge of an adventure. O Quixote![1] O Sylvio di Rosalva! how would ye have strutted in such a situation! What fair Infantas would ye not have expected to behold, condemned to spinning-wheels, and solitude? I, alas, saw nothing but clay walls, a straw bed, some glazed earthen bowls, and a wooden crucifix. My shoes were loaded with sand: this, my old hostess perceived; and, immediately kindling a fire in an inner part of the hovel, brought out some warm water to refresh my feet, and set some milk and chestnuts before me. This patriarchal politeness was by no means indifferent, after my tiresome ramble. I sat down opposite to the door which fronted the unfathomable gulph; beyond, appeared the sea, of a deep cerulean, foaming with waves. The sky also, was darkening apace with storms. Sadness came over me like a cloud, and I looked up to the old woman for consolation. 'And you too are sorrowful, young stranger,' said she, 'that come from the gay world!

[1] M. de Cervantes Saavedra (1547–1616), author or *Don Quijote* (1604).

how must I feel, who pass year after year in these lonely mountains?' I answered, that the weather affected me, and my spirits were exhausted by the walk. All the while I spoke, she looked at me with such a melancholy earnestness, that I asked the cause; and began again to imagine myself in some fatal habitation,

> where more is meant than meets the ear.

Said she, 'Your features are wonderfully like those of an unfortunate young person, who, in this retirement. . . .' the tears began to fall as she pronounced these words: she seemed older than before, and bent to the ground with sorrow. My curiosity was fired. 'Tell me,' continued I, 'what you mean? who was this youth, for whom you are so interested? and why did he seclude himself in this wild region? Your kindness might no doubt alleviate, in some measure, the horrors of the place; but, may God defend me from passing the night near such a gulph! I would not trust myself in a despairing moment. . . .' 'It is,' said she, 'a place of horrors. I tremble to relate what has happened on this very spot; but your manner interests me; and, though I am little given to narrations, for once I will unlock my lips, concerning the secrets of yonder fatal chasm. I was born in a distant part of Italy, and have known better days. In my youth, fortune smiled upon my family; but in a few years they withered away; no matter, by what accident: I am not going, however, to talk much of myself. Have patience a few moments! A series of unfortunate events reduced me to indigence, and drove me to this desert, where, from rearing goats, and making their milk into cheese, by a different method than is common in the Neopolitan state, I have, for about thirty years, prolonged a sorrowful existence. My silent grief and constant retirement, had made me appear, to some, a saint; and, to others, a sorceress. The slight knowledge I have of plants, has been exaggerated; and, some years back, the hours I gave up to prayer, and the recollection of former friends, lost to me for ever! were cruelly intruded upon, by the idle and the ignorant. But soon I sunk into obscurity: my little recipes were disregarded; and you are the first stranger, who, for these twelve months past, has visited my abode. Ah, would to God its solitude had ever remained inviolate! It is now three and twenty years' – and she looked upon some characters cut on the planks of the cottage – 'since I was sitting by moon-light, under that cliff you view to the right, my eyes fixed on the ocean; my mind lost in the memory of my misfortunes; when I heard a step, and starting up, a figure stood before me. It was a young man, in a rich habit, with streaming hair, and looks, that bespoke the utmost terror. I knew not what to think of this sudden apparition. 'Mother,' said he, with faultering accents, 'let me rest under your roof; and deliver me not up to those, who thirst after my blood. Take this gold; take all, all! Surprize held me speechless; the purse fell to the ground; the youth stared wildly on every side: I heard many voices beyond the rocks; the wind bore them distinctly; but, presently, they died away. I took courage, and assured the youth, my cot should shelter him. 'O! thank you; thank you!' answered he, and pressed my and. He shared my scanty provision. Overcome with toil (for I had worked hard in the day) sleep closed my eyes for a short interval. When I awoke, the moon was set, but I heard my unhappy guest sobbing in darkness. I disturbed him not. Morning dawned, and he was fallen into a slumber. The tears bubbled out of his closed eye-lids, and coursed one another down his wan cheeks. I had been too wretched myself, not to respect the sorrows of another: neglecting therefore my accustomed occupations, I drove away the flies that buzzed around his temples. His breast heaved high with sighs, and he cried loudly in his sleep, for mercy. The beams of sun dispelling his dream, he started up like one that had heard the voice of an avenging angel, and hid his face with his hands. I poured some milk down his parched throat. 'Oh mother!' did he exclaim, 'I am a wretch unworthy of compassion; the cause of innumerable sufferings; a murderer! a parricide!' My blood curdled to hear a stripling utter such dreadful words, and behold such agonizing sighs swell in so young a bosom: for I marked the sting of conscience, urging him to disclose, what I am going to relate. It seems he was of high extraction, nursed in the pomps and luxuries of Naples, the pride and darling of his parents, adorned with a thousand lively talents, which the keenest sensibility conspired to improve. Unable to fix any bounds to whatever became the object of his desires, he passed his first years in roving from one extravagance to another; but, as yet, there was no crime in his caprices. At length, it pleased Heaven to visit his family, and make their idol the slave of an unworthy passion. He had a friend who from his birth had been devoted to his interest, and placed all his confidence in him. This friend loved to distraction a young creature, the most graceful of her sex (as I can witness); and she returned his affection. In the exultation of his heart, he shewed her to the wretch, whose tale I am about to tell. He sickened at her sight. She too, caught fire at his glances. They languished; they consumed away, they conversed, and his persuasive language finished, what his guilty glances had begun. Their flame was soon discovered; for he disdained to conceal a thought, however dishonourable. The parents warned the youth in the tenderest manner; but advice and prudent counsels were to him so loathsome, that, unable to contain his rage, and infatuated with love, he menaced the life of his friend, as the obstacle of his enjoyment. Coolness and moderation were opposed to violence and frenzy, and he found himself treated with a contemptuous gentleness. Stricken to the heart, he wandered about for some time, like one intranced. Meanwhile the nuptials were preparing, and the lovely girl he had perverted, found ways to let him know, she was about to be torn from his embraces. He raved; and, rousing his dire spirit, applied to a malignant dæmon, who sold the most inveterate poisons. These he presented, like a cup of pure iced water, to his friend; and, to his own affectionate father. They drank the draught, and soon began to pine. He marked the progress of their dissolution with a horrid firmness. He let the moment pass, beyond which all antidotes were vain. His friend expired; and the young criminal, though he beheld the dews of death hang on his parent's forehead, yet stretched not forth his hand. In a short space, the miserable father breathed his last, whilst his son was sitting aloof in the same chamber. The sight overcame him. He felt, for the first time, the pangs of remorse. His agitations passed not unnoticed. He was watched: suspicions beginning to unfold, he took alarm and, one evening, escaped; but not without previously informing the partner of his crimes, which way he intended to flee. Several pursued; but the inscrutable will of Providence blinded their search, and I was doomed to behold the effects of celestial vengeance. Such are the chief circumstances of the tale, I gathered from the youth. I swooned whilst he related it; and could take no sustenance. One whole day afterwards did I pray the Lord, that I might die, rather than be near an incarnate dæmon. With what indignation did I now survey that slender form, and those flowing tresses, which had interested me before, so much in his behalf! No sooner did he perceive the change in my countenance, than sullenly retiring to yonder rock, he sat careless of the sun and scorching winds; for it was now the summer solstice. Equally was he heedless of the unwholesome dews. When midnight came, my horrors were augumented; and I meditated, several times, to abandon my hovel, and fly to the next village; but a power, more than human, chained me to the spot, and fortified my mind. I slept, and it was late next morning, when some one called at the wicket of the little fold, where my goats are penned. I arose, and saw a peasant of my acquaintance, leading a female, strangely muffled up, and casting her eyes on the ground. My heart misgave me. I thought this was the very maid, who had been the cause of such unheard-of wickedness. Nor were my conjectures ill-founded. Regardless of the clown, who stood by in stupid astonishment, she fell to the earth, and bathed my hand with tears. Her large blue eyes gleamed between long eye-lashes, her bosom was more agitated than the waves, and whiter than their foam. Her trembling lips, with difficulty, enquired after the youth; and, as she spoke, a glow of conscious guilt lightened up her pale countenance. The full recollection of her lover's crimes shot through my memory. I was incensed, and would have spurned her away; but she clung to my garments, and seemed to implore my pity, with a look so full of misery, that, relenting, I led her in silence to the extremity of the cliff, where the youth was seated; his feet dangling above the sea. His eye was rolling wildly around, but it soon fixed upon the object, for whose sake he had doomed himself to perdition. I am not inclined to describe their extasies, nor the eagerness with which they sought each other's embraces. I turned indignantly my head; and, driving my goats to a recess amongst the rocks, sat revolving in my mind these strange events. I neglected procuring any provision for my unwelcome guests; and, about midnight, returned homewards by the light of the moon, which shone serenely in the heavens. Almost the first object of her beams discovered, was the guilty maid, sustaining the head of her lover; who had fainted, through weakness and want of nourishment. I fetched some dry bread; and, dipping it in milk, laid it before them. Having performed this duty, I set open the door of my hut; and, retiring to a neighbouring cavity, there stretched myself on a heap of leaves, and offered my prayers to Heaven. A thousand fears, till this moment unknown, thronged into my fancy. I mistook the shadow of leaves that chequered the entrance of the grot, for ugly reptiles, and repeatedly shook my garments. The flow of the distant surges, was deepened by my apprehensions into distant groans; in a word, I could not rest; but, issuing from the cavern, as hastily as my trembling knees would allow, paced along the edge of the precipice. An unaccountable impulse hurried my steps. Dark clouds were driving athwart the sky, and the setting moon was flushed with the deepest crimson. A wan gleam coloured the sea. Such was my terror and shivering, that, unable to advance to my hut, or retreat to the cavern, I was about to shield myself from the night in a sandy crevice, when a loud shriek pierced my ear. My fears had confused me: I was in fact hard by my hovel, and scarcely three paces from the brink of the cavern. It was from thence the cries proceeded. Advancing, in a cold shudder, to its edge, part of which was newly crumbled in, I discovered the form of the young man, suspended by one foot to a branch of juniper, that grew ten feet down. Thus dreadfully did he hang over the gulph, from the branch bent with his weight. His features were distorted, his eye-balls glared with agony, and his screams became so shrill and terrible, that I lost all power of assistance. Fixed I stood, with my eyes rivetted upon the criminal; who incessantly cried out, 'O God! O Father! save me, if there be yet mercy! Save me; or I sink into the abyss!' I am convinced he saw me not; for, not once, did he implore my help. My heart was dead within me. I called out upon the Lord. His voice grew faint; and, as I gazed intent upon him, he fell into utter darkness. I sunk to the earth in a trance; during which, a sound, like a rush of pennons,[1] assaulted my ear: methought, the evil spirit was bearing of his soul. I lifted up my eyes, but nothing stirred: the stillness that prevailed was awful. The moon looked stained with streaks of blood: her orb, hanging low over the waves, afforded a sickly light, by which I perceived some one, coming down that white cliff you see before you; and, soon, I heard the voice of the young woman, calling aloud on her guilty lover. She stopped. She repeated, again and again, her exclamation; but there was no reply. Alarmed and frantic, she hurried along the path; and now, I saw her on the promontory; and now, by yonder pine; devouring with her glances every crevice in the rock. At length, perceiving me, she flew to where I stood, by the fatal precipice; and, having noticed the fragments fresh crumbled in, pored importunately on my countenance. I continued pointing to the chasm. She trembled not; her tears could not flow; but she divined my meaning. 'He is lost!' said she; 'the earth has swallowed him! but, as I have shared with him the highest joy, so will I partake his torments. I will follow: dare not hinder me!' I shrunk back. Like the phantoms I have seen in dreams, she glanced beside me; and, clasping her hands high above her head, lifted a stedfast look on the hemisphere, and viewed the moon with an anxiousness that told me, she was bidding it farewell, for ever. Observing a silken handkerchief on the ground, with which she had, but an hour ago, bound her lover's temples, she snatched it up, and, imprinting it with burning kisses, thrust it into her bosom. Once more, expanding her arms

---

[1] Triangular streamer attached to head of lance.

in the last act of despair and miserable passion, she threw herself, with a furious leap, into the gulph. To its margin I crawled on my knees, and, shuddering, looked down into the gloom. There I remained in the most dreadful darkness; for now, the moon was sunk, the sky obscured with storms, and a tempestuous blast ranging the ocean. Showers poured thick upon me, and the lightning, in clear and frequent flashes, gave me terrifying glimpses of yonder accursed chasm.' – 'Stranger, dost thou believe in the great Being? in our Redeemer? in the tenets of our faith?' I answered with reverence, but said I was no catholic. 'Then,' continued the aged woman, 'I will not declare before an heretic, what were the sacred visions of that night of vengeance.' She paused: I was silent. After a short interval, with deep and frequent sighs, she resumed her narration. 'Day-light began to dawn, as if with difficulty; and it was late, before its radiance had tinged the watery and tempestuous clouds. I was still kneeling by the gulph, in prayer, when the cliffs began to brighten, and the beams of the morning sun to strike against me. Then did I rejoice. Then, no longer did I think myself of all human beings the most abject and miserable. How different did I feel myself from those, fresh plunged into the abodes of torment, and driven, for ever, from the morning! – Three days elapsed in total solitude: on the fourth, some grave and antient persons arrived from Naples, who questioned me, repeatedly, about the wretched lovers; and to whom I related their fate with every dreadful particular. Soon after I learned, that all discourse concerning them, was expressly stopped; and, that no prayers were offered up for their souls.' – With these words, as well as I recollect, the old woman ended her singular narration. My blood thrilled as I walked by the gulph to call my guide, who stood aloof under the cliffs. He seemed to think, from the paleness of my countenance, that I had heard some gloomy prediction; and shook his head, when I turned round to bid my old hostess, adieu! It was a melancholy evening, and I could hardly refrain from tears, as, winding through the defiles of the rocks, the sad scenes which had passed amongst them, recurred to my memory. Traversing a wild thicket, we soon regained the shore; where I rambled a few minutes, whilst the peasant went for the boat-men. The last streaks of light were quivering on the waters, when I stepped into the bark; and, wrapping myself up in an awning, slept, till we reached Puzzoli; some of whose inhabitants came forth with torches, to light us home. I was vexed to be roused from my visions; and had much rather have sunk into some deep cave of the Cimmerians,[1] than returned to Naples.

---

[1] Fabulous race whose land, according to Homer, was on the edge of the world.

LETTER XXIV

Naples, November 9th.

We made our excursion to Pompeii, passing through Portici, and over the last lava of Mount Vesuvius. I experienced a strange mixture of sensations, on surveying at once, the mischiefs of the late eruption, in the ruin of villages, farms, and vineyards; and, all around them, the most luxuriant and delightful scenery of nature. It was impossible to resist the impressions of melancholy from viewing the former, or not to admit that gaiety of spirits which was inspired by the sight of the latter. I say nothing of the museum at Portici, which we saw in our way, on account of the ample descriptions of its contents already given to the public; and, because, it should be described no otherwise, than by an exact catalogue, or by an exhibition of engravings. An hour and a half brought us from this celebrated repository to Pompeii. Nothing can be conceived more delightful than the climate and situation of this city. It stands upon a gently-rising hill, which commands the bay of Naples, with the islands of Caprea and Ischia, the rich coasts of Sorento, the tower of Castel a Mare; and, on the other side, Mount Vesuvius, with the lovely country intervening. It is judged to be about an Italian mile long, and three and an half in circuit. We entered the city at the little gate which lies towards Stabiæ. The first object upon entering, is a colonade round a square court, which seems to have formed a place of arms. Behind the colonade, is a series of little rooms, destined for soldiers barracks. The columns are of stone, plaistered with stucco, and coloured. On several of them we found names, scratched in Greek and Latin; probably, those of the soldiers who had been quartered there. Helmets, and armour for various parts of the body, were discovered, amongst the skeletons of some soldiers, whose hard fate had compelled them to wait on duty, at the perilous moment of the city's approaching destruction. Dolphins and tridents, sculptured in relief on most of these relics of armour, seem to shew they had been fabricated for naval service. Some of the sculptures on the arms, probably, belonging to officers, exhibit a greater variety of ornaments. The taking of Troy, wrought on one of the helmets, is beautifully executed; and much may be said in commendation of the work of several others.

We were next led to the remains of a temple and altar, near these barracks. From thence, to some rooms floored (as indeed were almost all that have been cleared from the rubbish) with tesselated, mosaic pavements; of various patterns, and most of them of very elegant execution. Many of these have been taken up, and now form the floors of the rooms in the museum at Portici; whose best ornaments of every kind, are furnished from the discoveries at Pompeii. From the rooms just mentioned, we descended into a subterraneous chamber, communicating with a bathing apartment. It appears to have served as a kind of office to the latter. It was, probably, here, that the

cloaths, used in bathing, were washed. A fire-place, a capacious caldron
bronze, and earthen vessels proper for that purpose, found here, have give
rise to the conjecture. Contiguous to this room, is a small circular one with
fire-place; which was the stove to the bath. I should not forget to tell yo
that the skeleton of the poor laundress (for so the antiquaries will have
who was very diligently washing the bathing cloaths, at the time of th
eruption, was found lying in an attitude of the most resigned death, not fa
from the washing caldron, in the office just mentioned.

We were now conducted to the temple, or rather chapel, of Isis.[1] The chi
remains are, a covered cloister; the great altar, on which was, probabl
exhibited the statue of the goddess; a little edifice to protect the sacred wel
the pediment of the chapel, with a symbolical vase in relief; ornaments
stucco on the front of the main-building, consisting of the lotus, the sistrun
representations of gods, Harpocrates, Anubis, and other objects of Egyptia
worship. The figures on one side of this temple, are Perseus[2] with th
Gorgon's head; on the other, Mars and Venus, with Cupids bearing the arm
of Mars. We next observe three altars of different sizes. On one of them,
said to have been found, the bones of a victim unconsumed; the last sacrific
having, probably, been stopt by the dreadful calamity which had occasione
it. From a niche in the temple, was taken a statue of marble; a woma
pressing her lips with her fore-finger. Within the area is a well, where th
priest threw the ashes of the sacrifices. We saw, in the Museum at Portic
some lovely arabesque paintings, cut from the walls of the cloister. Th
foilage, which ran round the whole sweep of the cloister itself, is in the fines
taste. A tablet of basalte, with Egyptian hieroglyphics, was transported fror
hence to Portici, together with the following inscription, taken from the fror
gate of the chapel:

N. POPIDIUS N. F. CELSINUS.
AEDEM ISIDIS TERRAE MOTU COLLAPSAM
A FUNDAMENTO P. SUA RESTITUIT.
HUNC DECURIONES OB LIBERALITATEM
CUM ESSET ANNORUM SEX ORDINI SUO
GRATIS ADLEGERUNT.[3]

Behind one of the altars we saw a small room, in which our guide informee
us a human skeleton was discovered, with some fishbones on a plate near it
and a number of other culinary utensils. We then passed on to anothe

[1] Egyptian goddess of the underworld.
[2] Perseus son of Zeus who cut off the Medusa's head.
[3]   'Numerius Popidius Celsinus, son of Numerius,
                   rebuilt from its foundations at his own expense
                   the temple of Isis, fallen down in an earthquake.'
                   Him the board of adminstrators/town council
            appointed to their committee free of charge on account of
                   his generosity when he was six year old.'

apartment, almost contiguous; where, nothing more remarkable had been found than an iron crow; an instrument with which, perhaps, the unfortunate wretch, whose skeleton I have mentioned above, had vainly endeavoured to extricate herself; this room being, probably, barricaded by the matter of the eruption, This temple, rebuilt, as the insciption imports, by N. Popidius, had been thrown down by a terrible earthquake, that likewise destroyed a great part of the city (sixteen years before the famous eruption of Vesuvius, described by Pliny,[1] which happened in the first year of Titus, AD 79) and buried, at once, both Herculaneum, and Pompeii. As I lingered alone in these environs sacred to Isis, some time after my companions had quitted them, I fell into one of those reveries, which my imagination is so fond of indulging; and, transporting myself seventeen hundred years back, fancied I was sailing with the elder Pliny, on the first day's eruption, from Misenum, towards Retina and Herculaneum; and, afterwards, toward the villa of his friend Pomponianus[2] at Stabiæ. The course of our galley seldom carried us out of sight of Pompeii; and, as often as I could divert my attention from the tremendous spectacle of the eruption, its enormous pillar of smoke standing conically in the air, and tempests of liquid fire, continually bursting out from the midst of it, then raining down the sides of the mountain, and flooding this beautiful coast with innumerable streams of red-hot lava, methought I turned my eyes upon this fair city, whose houses, villas, and gardens, with their long ranges of columned courts and porticos, were made visible through the universal cloud of ashes, by lightning from the mountain; and saw its distracted inhabitants, men, women, and children, running to and fro in despair. But in one spot, I mean the court and precincts of the temple, glared a continued light. It was the blaze of the altars; towards which I discerned a long-robed train of priests, moving in solemn procession, to supplicate by prayer and sacrifice, at this destructive moment, the intervention of Isis, who had taught the first fathers of mankind the culture of the earth, and other arts of civil life. Methought, I could distinguish in their hands, all those paintings and images sacred to this divinity, brought out, on this portentous occasion, from the subterraneous apartments, and mystic cells of the temple. There was every form of creeping thing, and abominable beast, every Egyptian pollution, which the true Prophet had seen in vision, among the secret idolatries of the temple at Jerusalem. The priests arrived at the altars; I saw them gathered round, and purifying the three, at once, with the sacred meal; then, all moving slowly about them, each with his right hand towards the fire: it was the office of some, to seize the firebrands of the altars, with which they sprinkled holy water on the numberless by-standers. Then, began the prayers, the hymns, and lustrations[3] of the sacrifice. The priests had laid the victims, with their throats downward, upon the altars; were ransacking the baskets of flour and salt, for the knives of slaughter, and proceeding in haste

[1] Pliny the Younger (AD 61–113) described the eruption of Vesuvius.
[2] Pomponius secundus, Roman dramatist, friend of Pliny who wrote his life.
[3] Purificatory rite.

to the accomplishment of their pious ceremonies; when one of our company, who thought me lost, returned with impatience, and, calling me off to some new object, put an end to my strange reverie. We were now summoned to pay some attention to the scene and corridor of a theatre, not far from the temple. Little more of its remains being yet cleared away, we hastened back to a small house and garden, in the neighbourhood of Isis. Sir W. Hamilton (in his account of Pompeii, communicated to the Society of Antiquaries)[1] when speaking of this house, having taken occasion to give a general idea of the private mansions of the ancient citizens, I shall take the liberty of transcribing the whole passage. 'A covered cloister, supported by columns, goes round the house, as was customary in many of the houses at Pompeii. The rooms in general are very small; and, in one, where an iron bedstead was found, the wall had not been pared away to make room for this bedstead; so that it was not six feet square, and yet this room was most elegantly painted, and had a tesselated, or mosaic floor. The weight of the matter erupted from Mount Vesuvius, has universally damaged the upper parts of the houses; the lower parts are mostly found as fresh as at the moment they were buried. The plan of most of the houses at Pompeii is a square court, with a fountain in the middle, and small rooms round, communicating with that court. By the construction and distribution of the houses, it seems, the inhabitants of Pompeii were fond of privacy. They had few windows towards the street, except where, from the nature of the plan, they could not avoid it; but, even in that case, the windows were placed too high for any one in the streets to overlook them. Their houses nearly resemble each other, both as to distribution of plan, and in the manner of finishing the apartments. The rooms are in general small, from ten to twelve feet, and from fourteen to eighteen feet; few communications between room and room; almost all without windows, except the apartments situated to the garden, which are thought to have been allotted to the women. Their cortiles, or courts, were often surrounded by porticos, even in very small houses. Not but there were covered galleries before the doors of their apartments, to afford shade and shelter. No timber was used in finishing their apartments, except in doors and windows. The floors were generally laid in mosaic work. One general taste prevailed, of painting the sides and ceilings of the rooms. Small figures, and medallions of low relief, were sometimes introduced. Their great variety consisted in the colours, and in the choice and delicacy of the ornaments, in which they displayed great harmony and taste. Their houses were some two, others three stories high.'

We now pursued our way through, what is with some probability thought to have been, the principal street. Its narrowness, however, surprised me. It is scarcely eleven feet wide, clear of the foot-ways raised on each side of it. The pavement is formed of a large sort of flattish-surfaced pebbles; not laid down with the greatest evenness, or regularity. The side-ways may be about a yard

---

[1] *Account of the Discoveries at Pompeii Communicated to the Society of Antiquaries of London* (1777).

wide, each paved, irregularly enough, with small stones. There are guard-stones, at equal intervals, to defend the foot-passengers from carriages and horses. I cannot say I found any thing either elegant or pleasant in the effect of this open street. But, as the houses in general present little more than a dead wall toward it, I do not imagine any views, beyond mere use and convenience, were consulted in the plan. It led us, however, through the principal gate, or entrance, to a sort of Villa Rustica, without the limits of the city; which amply recompensed our curiosity. The arcade, surrounding a square garden, or court-yard, offers itself first to the observer's notice. Into this, open a number of coved rooms, adorned with paintings of figures, and arabesque. These rooms, though small, have a rich and elegant appearance, their ornaments being very well executed, and retaining still their original freshness. On the top of the arcade runs a walk, or open terrace, leading to the larger apartments of the higher story. One of the rooms below, has a capacious bow-window, where several panes of glass, somewhat shattered, were found; but in sufficient preservation to shew, that the antients were not without knowledge of this species of manufacture. As Horace,[1] and most of the old Latin Poets, dwell much on the praises of antient conviviality, and appear to have valued themselves considerably on their connoisseurship in wine, it was with great pleasure I descended into the spacious cellars, sunk and vaulted beneath the arcade above-mentioned. Several earthen amphoræ were standing in rows against the walls; but the Massic and Falernian,[2] with which they were once stored, had probably long been totally absorbed by the earth and ashes, which were now the sole contents of these venerable jars. The antients are thought to have used oil instead of corks; and that the stoppers were of some matter that could make but little resistance, seems confirmed by the entrance of that, which now supplied the place of wine. The skeletons of several of the family, who had possessed this villa, were disco-vered in the cellar; together with brass and silver coins, and many such ornaments of dress as were of more durable materials. On re-ascending, we went to the hot and cold baths; thence, to the back of the villa, separated by a passage from the more elegant parts of the house: we were shewn some rooms which had been occupied by the farmer, and from whence several implements of agriculture had been carried, to enrich the collection at Portici. On the whole, the plan and construction of this villa are extremely curious, and its situation very happily chosen. I could not, however, help feeling some regret, in not having had the good fortune to be present at the first discovery. It must have been highly interesting to see all its antient relics (the greatest part of which are now removed) each in its proper place; or, at least, in the place they had possessed for so long a course of years. His Sicilian majesty has ordered a correct draught of this villa to be taken, which, it is hoped, will one day be published, with a complete account of all the discoveries at Pompeii.

[1] Quintus Horatius Flaccus (65–8 BC), Roman poet.
[2] Types of wine.

Our next walk was to see the Columbarium, a very solemn-looking edifice, where probably the families of higher rank only at Pompeii, deposited the urns of their deceased kindred. Several of these urns, with their ashes, and one, among the rest, of glass inclosed in another of earth, were dug out of the sepulchral vaults. A quantity of marble statues, of but ordinary execution, and colossal masks of terra cotta, constituted the chief ornaments of the Columbarium. It is situated without the gates, on the same side of the city with the villa, just described. There is something characteristically sad in its aspect. It threw my mind into a melancholy, but not disagreeable, tone. Under the mixed sentiments it inspired, I cast one lingering look back on the whole affecting scene of ruins, over which I had, for several hours, been rambling; and quitted it to return to Naples, not without great reluctance.

TRAVEL DIARIES

II

From The Journal of 1787. This extract is prepared from the Manuscript Beckford, d.5 fols 73–90, in the Beckford Papers, Bodleian Library, Oxford, with the kind permission of the Library. The last entry in this extract, dated 9th September, describes a visit to Cork Convent near Sintra. So that the reader may compare styles, the account of the same visit forms the first entry of the extract from the *Sketches,* Letter XXVIII which follows as the text after the *Journal.*

THE PORTUGUESE JOURNAL
1787

Friday, August 24th

Wind and sun cooling and broiling alternately, I remained at home all the morning reading a new history of Mexico translated from the Italian of the Abbade[1] Clavigero by Cullen, and full of very curious information.[2] The author stands up resolutely for the splendor and magnificence of Montezuma, the immense size of his palace and the admirable construction of his aviaries. Robertson[3] and M. de Pauw[4] are made very free with for treating the Americans with contempt, and Solis[5] accused, not without reason I believe, of a strong partiality for Cortes, who, according to this history, seems to have been guilty of the most wanton and unwarrantable acts of cruelty and oppression.

We were eight at dinner – Horne,[6] the Miss Sills[7] and their brother, Bezerra[8] and Aguila.[9] The wind, which in spite of all my curtains still finds a thousand ways of entering the lanthorn apartment, gave me an uncomfortable feel in my head very like the headache. I was prevailed on however to walk out, but grumbled all the way at finding every alley in the *quinta* thick strewn with fallen leaves. Had I but a large chimney like that in the great hall at Evian, I should have no objection to these signs of approaching winter, and I would soon make a cheerful blaze and warm myself with good humour. At Ramalhão,[10] there is not except in the kitchen, a single chimney; I shiver already at the idea of being fireless. Whilst we were straying about the thickets of bay and laurel, the Marquis[11] arrived and entered into close conversation with Bezerra. I am in hopes I have prejudiced him in his favor, and that he will do him essential service by explaining to the Queen[12] a law affair in which he is

---

[1] Abbade Xavier (born 1689) was an intimate friend of the Marialva family.

[2] C. Cullen, trans., *The History of Mexico by D. F. S. Clavigero* (1787).

[3] W. Robertson, *History of America*, 3 Vols (Dublin, 1777).

[4] C. Pauw, *de Récherches philosophiques sur les Américains*, 2 Vols (Berlin, 1768–9).

[5] A. Solis, *de Historia de la Conquista de Mexico* (Madrid, 1684).

[6] Thomas Horne (1772–92), long time resident of Lisbon who acted as Beckford's agent.

[7] Betty and Sophia Sill, relatives of Thomas Horne. Betty married Bezerra (see next note) and later became Viscondessa de Tagoahi.

[8] João Paulo Bezerra de Seixas (1756–1817), friend of Beckford who was a diplomat and later minister.

[9] Henrique de Aguilar e Menezes (Monsehnor), a prelate at the Patriarchate.

[10] Beckford's first Sintra residence.

[11] Dom Diogo, 5th Marquis (1739–1803).

[12] Queen Maria I (1734–1816) who reigned from 1777 until 1799 when she became demented.

deeply concerned. Monsignor Gomes Freire and his young cousin paid me a visit. They stayed but a short time, being on their way to Lisbon. In a few days they return, and I have invited them to come often to see me. Horne and his family went away at nine. The Marquis and I sat talking together upon the affairs of Portugal for two hours. The Archbishop[1] has suffered himself to be pressed into the Cabinet, and may perhaps consent ere long to be declared Prime Minister, though his natural laziness and monkish love of ease makes him heartily averse to so tempestuous a situation.

Saturday, August 25th

If I am sick of writing about the wind, how much more tired must I be of feeling it. I cannot put my nose out of my lanthorn[2] without having it ripped and reddened by a keen blast right worthy of the month of November. And yet the trees are in leaf, the flowers in blow, and the sun in splendor, and we are in the month of August, under the boasted sky of Portugal. Were there ever such contradictions? M. Verdeil[3] persuaded me to get on horseback and try whether the climate on the other side of the peaks of Sintra[4] would not prove more tolerable. He was in the right. I had no sooner turned the corner of the rock than we entered snug shady lanes, and rode unmolested by the wind almost the whole way to Colares. It was a clear transparent day like those I have enjoyed in Italy.

Lima, who came from Lisbon to ask me some further questions about my musicians, dined with us. In the evening came the Duke de Lafoes[5] and the Marquis. This is the identical personage so well known in every part of Europe by the name, style and title of Duke of Braganza. He is no business however [to be styled] with that illustrious dukedom which is merged with the crown. If he was called Duchess Dowager of Braganza I should think everyone would agree [that] the title was well bestowed. He is so like an old Lady of the Bedchamber, so fiddle-faddle, and so coquettish and so gossiping. He had put on rouge and patches and a solitaire, and though he has seen seventy years winters, contrived to turn on his heel and glide about with juvenile agility. I was much surprised at the ease of his motions, having been told he was almost crippled with the gout. After lisping French with a most refined accent, complaining of the wind and the roads and the state of our architecture etc., he departed – thank God! – to mark out a spot for the encampment of the Cavalry, who are to guard the Queen's sacred person during her residence amongst these mountains. The Marquis was in duty bound to accompany him, but soon returned. I made him write out an order

---

[1] Frei Inaçio de Caetano (1719–88), Titular Archbishop of Thessalonica, immensely influential cleric who was Confessor to the Queen of Portugal.

[2] Lantern.

[3] Dr Francois Verdeil (1747–1832), personal physician to Beckford, native of Lausanne.

[4] Sintra (spelt Cintra at this period) is a town near Lisbon which became a royal residence in the middle ages and was much favoured by the aristocracy as a country retreat.

[5] João Carlos de Bragança, 2nd Duke (1719–1806), 'Uncle of the Queen' who later married Henriqueta, Marialva's daughter.

to expedite Lima's[1] *aviso*.[2] We passed the evening in earnest conversation and agreed to go to Mafra the day after tomorrow. To avoid the importunities of the monks we shall lodge at the *Capitão-mor's*,[3] an old servant of the Marialva's and the companion of my friend's infancy.

Sunday, August 26th

No care being taken to fasten my windows, they rattled all night and kept me awake an hour or two. I cannot complain of the air of Sintra; it may be sharp, but it is very wholesome, and enables me to eat my breakfast with appetite. I walked in the *quinta*,[4] and visited my vases of flowers. Vegetation is so rapid in this climate that the oleanders, heliotropes, and geraniums, which in their way here from Lisbon were almost stripped naked, are again covered with leaves and blossoms. I went to dine at Horne's with D. José de Brito[5] and his homely spouse. Bezerra, who was also of the party, took a ramble with me in the evening up lofty crags and slopes of slippery greensward, from whence you look down upon the villa of Penha Verde and its groves. The rocks are covered with Latin inscriptions in honour of Pombal,[6] not inelegantly imagined. Upon our return to Horne's we found the Marquis waiting for me. He got into my carriage and we drove to his villa. Who should I find there but the Grand Prior[7] just arrived, wrapped up in an ample capote and execrating the cool breezes of Sintra. In these maledictions I heartily joined, and being fatigued with rock climbing, returned to Ramalhão and reposed till supper time on my sofas.

Monday, August 27th

We set off for Mafra[8] at nine in spite of the wind which blew full in our faces. The distance from the villa I inhabit to this stupendous convent is about fourteen English miles, and the road, which by good luck has been lately mended, conducted across a parched open country thinly scattered with windmills and villages. The look backwards on the woody hills and pointed rocks is pleasant enough, but when you look forwards nothing can be more bleak or barren than the prospect. Three relays of mules being stationed on the road, we advanced full speed, and in less than an hour and a quarter found ourselves under a strong wall which winds boldly across the hills and encloses the park of Mafra. We now caught a glimpse of the marble towers

---

[1] Jeronimo Francisco de Lima (1741–1822), composer of sacred music and of opera.

[2] Notice or formality needing completion.

[3] Commander-in-chief.

[4] Country villa.

[5] José de Brito Leal Heredia (1745–1805).

[6] Sebastião José de Carvalho e Melo (1699–1782), diplomat and autocratic ruler of Portugal in the reign of José I, Queen Maria's father.

[7] Manoel de Noronha e Menezes, Grand Prior of Aviz. Bastard brother of 4th Marquis of Marialva and uncle to Marialva.

[8] Mafra Convent, built between 1717–1770 on a monumental scale, and completed only seventeen years before Beckford's visit.

and dome of the convent, relieved by an expanse of ocean rising above the brow of heathy eminences, diversified here and there by the green heads of Italian pines and the tall spires of cypress. The roofs of the edifice were not yet visible and we continued for some time winding about the swells in the park before we discovered them. A detachment of lay brothers were waiting to open the gates of the royal enclosure, which is sadly blackened by a fire which about a month ago consumed a great part of its wood and verdure. Our approach spread a terrible alarm amongst the herds of deer; which were peacefully browsing on a rather greener slope; off they scudded and took refuge in a thicket of half-burnt pines.

After coasting the wall of the great garden, we turned suddenly and discovered one of the vast fronts of the convent, appearing like a street of palaces. I cannot pretend that the style of the building is such as a lover of pure Grecian architecture would approve; the windows and doors are fantastically shaped, but at least tolerably well proportioned. I was admiring their ample range as we drove rapidly along, when upon wheeling round the lofty square pavilion which flanks the edifice, the grand facade extending above eight hundred feet opened to my view. The middle is formed by the porticos of the church, richly adorned with columns, niches and bas-reliefs of marble. On each side two towers, somewhat resembling those of St Paul's in London, rise to the height of two hundred feet and join onto the enormous *corps de logis* of the palace terminated to the right and left by its stately pavilions. These towers are light and clustered with pillars remarkably elegant, but their shape borders too much on a gothic or what is still worse, a pagoda-ish style, and wants solemnity. They contain many bells of the largest dimensions and a famous chime which cost several hundred thousand crusados,[1] and which was set a-playing the moment our arrival was notified. The platform and flight of steps before the columned entrances of the church is strikingly grand and the dome which lifts itself up so proudly above the pediment of the portico merits great praise for its highness and elegance.

My eyes ranged along the vast extent of palace on each side till they were tired, and I was glad to turn them from the glare of marble and confusion of sculptured ornaments to the blue expanse of the distant ocean. A wide level space extends before the front of this colossal structure, at the extremity of which several white houses lie dispersed. Though these buildings are by no means inconsiderable, they appear when contrasted with the immense pile in their neighbourhood like the booths of workmen. For such I took them upon taking my first survey, and upon a nearer approach was quite surprised at their real dimensions. Few objects render the prospect from the platform of Mafra interesting. You look over the roofs of an indifferent village and the summits of sandy acclivities back by a boundless stretch of sea. On the left your view is terminated by the craggy mountains of Sintra; to the right a forest of pines in the Viscount of Ponte de Lima's[1] extensive garden affords the eye a refreshment.

---

[1] Currency of Portugal during this period.
[2] 14th Viscount and 1st Marquis of Ponte de Lima.

To screen ourselves from the sun, which darted powerfully on our heads, we entered the church, passing through its magnificent portico, which reminded me of the entrance to St Peter's, and is crowded by colossal statues of saints and martyrs carved with infinite delicacy out of blocks of the purest white marble. The first *coup d'oeil* of the church is very striking. The chief altar, supported by two majestic columns of reddish variegated marble, each a single block above thirty feet in height, immediately fixes the attention. Trevisani has painted the altar-piece in a masterly manner. It represents St Anthony[1] in the ecstasy of beholding the infant Jesus descending into his cell amidst an effulgence of glory. Tomorrow being the festival of St Augustine, whose followers are the actual possessors of this monastery, all the golden candelabras were displayed and tapers lighted. We knelt a few minutes in the midst of this bright illumination whilst the monks came forth bowing and cringing with their usual courtesy. Rising up, we visited the collateral chapels, each adorned with highly finished bas-relief and stately portals of black and yellow marble richly veined and so highly polished as to reflect objects like a mirror. Never did I behold such a profusion of beautiful marble as gleamed above, below and around me. The pavement, the roof, the dome, even the topmost lanthorn is encrusted with the same costly and durable materials. Roses of white marble and wreaths of palm branches most exquisitely sculptured enriched every part of the edifice. I never saw Corinthian capitals better modelled or executed with more precision and sharpness than the columns which support the dome. D. Pedro[2], who saw Mafra for the first time, and I having satisfied our curiosity by examining the various ornaments of the chapels, followed our conductors through a coved gallery into the sacristy, a magnificent vaulted hall panelled with a variety of marble and spread, as well as a chapel adjoining it, with the richest Persian carpets. We traversed several more halls and chapels adorned in the same style, till we were fatigued and bewildered like errant knights in the mazes of an enchanted palace. I began to think there was no end to these spacious apartments. The monk who preceded us, a good natured, slobbering grey beard, taking for granted I could not understand a syllable of his language, attempted to explain the objects which presented themselves by signs, and would hardly believe his ears when I asked him in good Portuguese when we should have done with chapels and sacristy. The old fellow seemed vastly delighted with the *meninos*,[3] as he called me and D. Pedro, and to give our young legs an opportunity of stretching themselves, trotted along with such expedition that the Marquis and M. Verdeil wished him in purgatory. To be sure, we advanced at a most rapid rate, striding from one end to the other of a dormitory six hundred feet in length in a minute or two. These vast corridors

---

[1] St Anthony of Padua (1195–1231), was born a Portuguese aristocrat. He was patron saint of Lisbon and adopted by Beckford as his own patron saint. His statue, by Joseph Theakston, later adorned Fonthill Abbey.

[2] Pedro de Marialva, 6th Marquis (1774–1823), son of Dom Diogo, 5th Marquis.

[3] Boys.

and the cells with which they communicate, three in number, are all arched in the most sumptuous and solid manner. Every cell, or rather chamber – for they are sufficiently lofty, spacious, and well-lighted to merit that appellation – is furnished with tables and cabinets of Brazil wood.

Just as we entered the library, the Abbot of the Convent, dressed in his ceremonial habit, with the episcopal cross dangling on his bosom, advanced to bid us welcome and invite us to dine with him tomorrow, St Augustine's[1] Day, in the refectory, which it seems is a mighty compliment, guests in general being entertained in private apartments. We thought proper, however, to decline the honours, being aware that to enjoy it we must sacrifice at least two hours of our time and be half parboiled[2] by the steam of huge roasted calves, turkeys and gruntlings, long fattening no doubt for this very occasion. The library is of a prodigious length, not much less than three hundred feet; the arched roof of a pleasing form, beautifully stuccoed, and the pavement of red and white marble. Much cannot be said in commendation of the cases in which the books are to be arranged. They are heavily designed and coarsely executed and are darkened to boot by a gallery running round like a shelf and projecting into the room in a very awkward manner. The collection of books, which consists of at least sixty thousand volumes is lodged at present in a suite of apartments which opens into the library. Several curious first editions of the Greek and Roman classics were handed to me by the Father Librarian. My nimble conductor would not allow me much time to examine them.

He set off full speed, and ascending a winding staircase, led us out upon the roofs of the convent and palace, which form a broad, smooth terrace guarded by a magnificent balustrade unencumbered by chimneys and commanding a bird's-eye-view of the courts and gardens. From this elevation the whole plan of the edifice may be traced at a glance. In the middle rises the dome like a beautiful temple from the spacious walks of a royal garden. It is infinitely superior in point of design to the rest of the edifice, and may certainly be reckoned amongst the lightest and best proportioned in Europe. D. Pedro and M. Verdeil proposed scaling a ladder which leads up to the lanthorn, but I begged to be excused accompanying of them, and amused myself during their absence with ranging about the extensive loggias, now and then venturing a look down on the court and parterres below; but oftener enjoying the prospect of the towers shining bright in the sunbeams, and the azure bloom of the distant sea. A fresh balsamic air wafted from the orchards of citron and orange fanned me as I rested a moment on the steps of the dome, and tempered the warmth of the glowing ether.

But I was soon driven from this peaceful situation by a confounded jingle of the bells; then followed a most complicated sonata, banged off on the chimes by a great proficient. The Marquis would have me approach to

---

[1] St Augustine of Hippo (354–430), church father and theologian, his feast day is 28 August, i.e. the next day from the date of this diary entry.
[2] Half-boiled.

examine the mechanism, and I was half stunned. I know very little indeed about chimes and clocks and am quite at a loss for amusement in a belfry. My friend, who inherits a mechanical turn from his father, investigated every wheel with the most minute attention. I, poor ignorant soul, who can only judge from exteriors in these matters, have little to observe upon the wondrous piece of mechanism I had been surveying, except that the brasswork is admirably polished, ornamented with sculpture, and like everything else at Mafra most highly finished.

Descending the stairs and escaping from our conductor, we repaired to the *Capitão-mor's*, whose jurisdiction extends over the park and district of Mafra. He has seven or eight thousand crowns a year, and his habitation wears every appearance of opulence. The floors are covered with neat mats, the doors hung with red damask curtains, and our beds quite new for the occasion and spread with satin coverlids richly embroidered and fringed. We had an excellent dinner prepared by the Marquis' cooks and confectioners, and a much better dessert than even the monks could have given us. The *Capitão-mor* waited behind our chairs, taking the dishes from his servants and placing them on the table. Whilst coffee was serving up, we heard the sound of a carriage, and behold the Grand Prior entered the room, to our great joy and surprise; for I had tried in vain last night to persuade him to be of our party.

We left him with M. Verdeil to take some refreshment, and hurried to Vespers in the great church of the Convent. Advancing between the range of illuminated chapels, we fell down before the High Altar with a devout and dignified composure. Two shabby-looking Englishmen confounded amongst the rabble at the entrance of the choir watched all my motions and followed me with their eyes till I was seated between the Marquis and D. Pedro in the royal tribune. We had not been long in our places before the monks entered in procession, preceding their Abbot, who ascended his throne, having a row of sacristans at his feet and canons on his right hand in their cloth-of-gold embroidered vestments. The service was chanted with a most imposing solemnity to the awful sound of organs, for there are no fewer than six in the church, all of an enormous size.

When it was ended we joined the *Prior-mor*[1] and M. Verdeil who were just come in, and being once more seized hold of by the nimble lay brother, were conducted up a magnificent staircase into the Palace. The suite extends seven or eight hundred feet, and the almost endless succession of lofty doors seen in perspective strikes with astonishment; but we were soon weary of being merely astonished and agreed to pronounce these apartments, the dullest and most comfortless I ever beheld. There is no variety in their shape and little in the dimensions: a naked sameness universally prevails; not a niche, not a cornice, not a carved moulding breaks the tedious uniformity of dead-white walls. I was glad to return to the Convent and refresh my eyes with the sight of marble pillars and my feet by treading on Persian carpets. We were

[1] I.e. the Grand Prior of Aviz.

followed wherever we moved into every cell, chapel, hall, passage or sacristry by a strange medley of inquisitive monks, sacristans, lay brothers, *corregedors*,[1] village curates and country beaux with long rapiers and pigtails. If I happened to ask a question half-a-dozen poked their necks out to answer it, like turkey poults when addressed in their native hobble-gobble dialect. The Marquis was quite sick at being trotted after in this tumultuous manner and tried several times to leave the crowd behind him, by making sudden turns; but sticking close to our heels, it baffled all his endeavours and increased to such degree that we seemed to have swept the whole Convent and village of its inhabitants and to draw them after us like the rolling Giaour in my story of *Vathek*.[2] At length perceiving a large door open into the garden, we bolted out and striking into a labyrinth of myrtle and laurels, got rid of our pursuers. The garden, which is about a mile and a half in circumference, contains, besides a wild thicket of pine and bay trees, several orchards of lemon and orange, and two or three parterres, more filled with weeds than flowers. I was much disgusted at finding this beautiful enclosure so wretchedly neglected and its luxuriant plants withering away for want of being properly watered. You may suppose that after adding a walk in the principal alleys of the gardens to our other peregrinations, we began to find ourselves somewhat fatigued and were not sorry to repose ourselves in the Abbot's apartment till we were summoned once more to our tribune to hear Matins performed.

It was growing dark, and the innumerable tapers burning before the altars and in every part of the church, to diffuse a mysterious light. The organs joined again in full accord, the long series of monks and novices entered with slow, solemn steps played and the Abbot resumed his throne with the same pomp as at Vespers. The Marquis began muttering his orisons, the Grand Prior to recite his breviary, and I to fall into a profound reverie which lasted as long as the service – that is to say about three hours. Verdeil, ready to expire with ennui, could not help leaving the tribune and the cloud of incense which filled the choir, to breathe a freer air in the body of the church and its adjoining chapels. My orthodox companions seemed as much scandalised by these heretical fidgeting as edified by the pious air and strict silence I happened to have the patience to maintain.

It was almost nine when the monks, after chanting a hymn in praise of their venerable father, St Augustine, quitted the choir. We followed their procession through lofty chapels and arched cloisters which by glimmering light appeared to have neither roof nor termination, till it entered an octagon[3] forty feet in diameter with fountains in the four principal angles, and the monks, after dispersing to wash their hands at the several fountains, again resumed their order and passed two and two under a portal thirty foot high into a vast hall communicating with their refectory by another portal of the same lofty dimensions. Here the procession made a pause, for this chamber is

[1] Local officials.
[2] See *above*, p. 40 n. 1.
[3] Later Beckforxd had an octagon constructed at the centre of Fonthill Abbey.

consecrated to the remembrance of the departed, and styled the Hall De Profundis.[1] Before every repast the monks, standing around it in solemn ranks, silently resolve in their minds, the precariousness of our frail existence, and offer up their prayers for the salvation of their predecessors. I could not help being struck with awe when I beheld by the glow of flaming lamps so many venerable figures in their black and white habits bending their eyes on the pavement and absorbed in the most interesting and gloomy of meditations. The moment allotted to this solemn supplication being past, everyone took his place at the long tables in the refectory, which are made of Brazil wood covered with the whitest linen. Each monk had his glass carafe of water and wine, his plate of apples and salad set before him. Neither fish nor flesh were served up, the vigil of St Augustine's Day being observed as a fast with the utmost strictness. To enjoy at a glance this singular and majestic spectacle, we retreated to a vestibule preceding the octagon, and from thence looked through the portals down the long row of lamps into the refectory, which owing to its vast length of full two hundred feet seemed ending in a point. After remaining a few minutes enjoying this perspective, four monks advanced with torches to light us out of the Convent and bid us good night with many bows and genuflexions.

Our supper at the *Capitão-mor's* was very cheerful. D. Pedro, in high spirits, delighted with what he had seen, gave way to a childish vivacity. We sat up late notwithstanding our fatigue, talking over the variety of objects which had passed before our eyes in so short a space of time, the crowd of grotesque figures which had stuck to our heels so long and so closely, and the awkward activity of the lay brother.

Tuesday, August 28th

I was half asleep, half awake when the sonorous bells of the Convent struck my ears. The Marquis' and D. Pedro's voices in earnest conversation with the *Capitão-mor* in the adjoining chamber completely roused me. We swallowed our coffee in haste. The Grand Prior reluctantly left his pillow and accompanied us to high Mass. The monks once more exerted their efforts to prevail on us to dine with them; but we remained inflexible, and to avoid their importunities hastened away as soon as mass was ended to the Viscount Ponte de Lima's garden. The deep shades screened us from the meridian sun. The Marquis and I, seating ourselves on the edge of a basin of clear water, entered into serious conversation about my stay in Portugal. He entreated me not to think of abandoning him, and begged me to be assured that the Queen, who had warmly espoused my interests, was very desirous of my marrying and forming an establishment in Portugal. 'I myself,' continued my friend with the utmost earnestness, 'will answer for your forming the first alliance in the Kingdom, and connecting yourself by such a match with all the crowned heads in Europe. A formal renunciation of the Protestant religion is not at all necessary; we can procure a dispensation from Rome. The Queen,

[1] From the depths.

when she finds you married to perhaps the most distinguished lady of her Court, will employ all her power and influence to procure your re-establishment at home by soliciting your King[1] to give you the peerage we know you were promised[2] and which the vile plots of your enemies alone prevented your receiving three years ago.' I was not more surprised than pleased at all idea of abjuration being laid aside and struck, I must confess, with the apparent liberality of the proposition. I dared not enquire what person he meant to bestow on me in marriage lest I should have heard the name of D. Henriqueta de Menezes, his daughter.[3] Such a declaration would have thrown me into the utmost embarrassment. I continued therefore soothing him by professions of my regard and grateful thanks for the Queen's favourable opinion, enlarging at the same time upon the difficulties of bringing my relations to approve a foreign alliance however splendid, and the deep-rooted affection I bore to Fonthill, the happy scene of my childhood and place of my nativity. How could I persuade myself to make such long and frequent absences as he would undoubtedly expect from this beloved spot. What hopes could I have that the lady would imbibe a similar attachment, and consent to pass several years away from her parents and her country. Sea voyages, I observed, were so repugnant to my constitution that I never could safely undertake them, and to be often performing the journey from hence to England by land would be exposing myself and the lady to endless harassment. These arguments, though vigorously supported, had little effect in cooling the ardour of his projects. He seemed to flatter himself every difficulty in England might be surmounted by employing Pinto[4] in the negotiation, and that once married to the person he had in his eye, her superior merit would win me entirely over to Portugal.

I was happy when the return of D. Pedro and his uncle, who had been walking to the end of a long avenue of pines, broke the thread of a conversation that pressed too hard upon me. We returned to the *Capitão-mor* all together and found dinner ready. At four we set off for Sintra. Both D. Pedro and myself were sorry to leave Mafra, and should have had no objection to another race along the cloisters and dormitories with the lay brother. The evening was bright and clear and the azure tints of the distant sea inexpressibly lovely. We drove so rapidly over the rough paved roads that the Marquis and I could hardly hear a word we said to each other. D. Pedro had mounted his horse. M.Verdeil, who preceded us in the *carrinho*,[5] seemed to outstrip the winds. His mule, one of the most fiery and gigantic of her species, excited by repeated floggings and shouts of a hulking Portuguese postilion perched up behind the carriage, galloped at an ungovernable rate, and about

---

[1] King George III who reigned from 1760–1820.

[2] See *above*, p. xiv and p. 157 n. 1. A patent for 'Lord Beckford of Fonthill' had been made out in 1784.

[3] Henriqueta de Lorenza Menezes (1772–1810), daughter of Diogo who later became Duchess of Lafões.

[4] Luis Pinto de Sousa Coutinho (1735–1804), 1st Viscount Balsemão, Ambassador in London 1774–88.

[5] Small carriage.

a league from the rocks of Sintra thought proper to seek out its driver at the foot of a lofty bank nearly perpendicular. There did they still lay sprawling when we passed by. Verdeil hobbled up to us and pointed to the *carrinho* in the ditch below. Except a slight contusion in the knee, he escaped without any hurt. I exclaimed immediately his escape was miraculous and that perhaps St Anthony had some hand in it. My friend, who has always the horrors of heresy before his eyes, whispered me that the Devil had saved him this time, but might not be so moderately disposed another. It was not quite half past five when we reached Sintra. The Marchioness, the Abbade and the children were waiting our arrival in the pavilion.

Feeling a good deal fatigued, I returned home soon after it fell dark, and was agreeably surprised to find the metamorphosis of my lanthorn room into a magnificent tent completed. The drapery falling in ample folds over the large sofas and glasses produces a great effect and forms the snuggest recesses imaginable. Four tripod stands of burnished gold, supporting lustres of brilliant glass half concealed by chintz curtains, add greatly to the richness of the scenery. The mat smoothly lain down and woven of the finest straw assumes by candlelight the softest and most agreeable colour, quite in harmony with the other objects. It looked so cool and glistening that I could not refrain from stretching myself upon it.

There did I lie supine, contemplating the serene summer sky and the moon rising slowly from behind the brow of a shrubby hill. The curtains blown aside by a gentle wind discovered the summits of the woods in the garden, and beyond a wide expanse of country terminated by plains of sea and hazy promontories.

Wednesday, August 29th

I trifled away the whole morning in my tent amusing myself with the different views reflected in the glasses. Aguilar dined with us. The Abbade came in at the dessert in full cry with a rare story of the miraculous conversion of an old consumptive Englishwoman, who finding herself on the eve of departure had called out for a priest to whom she might make confession and abjure her errors. Happening to lodge at the Sintra Inn[1] kept by a most flaming Irish Catholic, her pious desires were speedily complied with, and Acciaioli,[2] Mascarenhas,[3] and two or three priests and monsignors summoned to further the good work. To work they went, baptism was administered, all sins remitted, and the feeble old creature despatched to Paradise in the very nick of time, without having a moment to conceive a sinful thought or merit the least singeing from the flames of purgatory. 'Great,' said the Abbade, 'are the rejoicing of the faithful upon this occasion. This evening the aged innocent is

---

[1] Hotel Lawrence, Sintra was the favourite residence of itinerant Englishmen. On his visit in 1809 Lord Byron stayed there.
[2] Octaviano Acciaioli (b. 1731) of Italian extraction.
[3] Luiz Manoel de Menezes Mascarenhas, a prelate at the Patriarchate.

to be buried in triumph. Your friend, the Count of S. Lourenço[1], the Viscount de Asseca and several more of the principal nobility are already assembled to grace the festival. Supposing you were to come with me and join the procession?' 'With all my heart,' said I, 'though I have no great taste for funerals, so gay a one as this you talk of may form an exception.'

Off we set, driving as fast as the mules would carry us, lest we should come too late for the entertainment. A great mob was assembled before the Inn door. At one of its windows stood the Grand Prior, looking as if he wished himself a thousand leagues away, and reciting his breviary. I went upstairs and was immediately caught in the embraces of my friend, and surrounded by the old Count of S Lourenço and other believers, overflowing with congratulations, turning up the whites of their eyes, and praising God for delivering this strayed sheep from the jaws of eternal perdition. Mascarenhas one of the soundest limbs of the Patriarchal, a most capital devotee and seraphic doctor, was introduced to me. Acciaoli skipped about the room, rubbing his hands for joy, with a cunning leer on his broad jovial countenance, and snapping his fingers at Satan as much as to say, 'I don't care a damn for you. We have got one at least safe out of your clutches and clear at this very moment of the smoke of your cauldron.' There was such a bustle in the interior apartments, where the wretched corpse was laid, such chanting and praying, for not a tongue was idle, that my head swam round and I took refuge by the Grand Prior. He by no means relished the party and kept shrugging up his shoulders and saying that to be sure it was very wonderful indeed, and that Acciaoli had been very active, very alert, and deserved great commendation, but that so much fuss might have been spared.

By some hints that dropped, I won't say from whom, I discovered the innocent, now on the high road to eternal felicity, by no means to have suffered the cup of joy to pass by her untasted in this existence, and to have long lived on a very easy footing with a stout English bachelor. However, she had taken a sudden tack upon finding herself driving apace down the steep of a galloping consumption, and had been fairly towed into port by the joint efforts of the Irish hostess and the Monsignors Acciaoli and Mascarenhas. All her peccadilloes, according to their firm persuasion, were remitted, and as she expired with the cross of baptism still wet on her forehead, the Devil and all his imps could not prevent her marching straight to the gates of Paradise and gaining immediate admittance. 'Blessed soul!' said the Marquis, 'how much is thy fate to be envied! No ante-chambering in Purgatory; immediate access will be granted thee to the Supreme Presence, and in this world thy body will have the honour of being borne to its grave by persons of the first distinction, followed by men of the most exalted piety, the favourites of the most illustrious saints, by you my dear friend, by my uncle, Mascarenhas and Acciaoli.'

---

[1] João Jose Alberto de Noronha (1725–1804), 6th Count of S. Lourenço.

The arrival of a band of priests and sacristans with tapers lighted and cross erected called us to the scene of action. The procession was marshalled in due form, the corpse dressed in virgin white, laying snug in a sort of rose-coloured bandbox with six handles, strewed with flowers, brought forth. My friend, who abhors the sight of a dead body, reddened up to his ears and would have given a good sum to have made an honourable retreat. But no retreat could now be made, consistent with piety. He was obliged to conquer his disgust and take a handle of the bier. Another was placed in the murderous grip of the Count de São Vicente;[1] a third fell to the share of the poor old snuffling Count of S. Lourenço; a fourth to the Viscount de Asseca, a mighty simple looking young gentleman; the fifth and sixth were allotted to the *Capitão-mor* of Sintra and the village Judge, a gaunt fellow with a hang-dog countenance. No sooner did the Grand Prior catch a sight of the ghastly visage of the dead body as it was conveying downstairs in the manner I have recited, than he made an attempt to move on and precede instead of following the procession. But Acciaoli who acted as Master of the Ceremonies would not let him off so easily. He allotted him the post of honour immediately at the head of the corpse, and placed himself on his left hand, giving the right to Mascarenhas.[2]

All the bells of Sintra struck up a loud peal, and to their merry jinglings we hurried along up to the knees in dust, a rabble of children frolicking on each side, and their old grandmothers hobbling after, telling their beads, and grinning from ear to ear at this triumph over the Prince of Darkness.[3] Thank heaven the way to the Church was not long, or the dust would have choked us. The Grand Prior kept his mouth close not to admit a particle of it, but Acciaoli and his colleague were too full of their notable exploit not to chatter incessantly. Poor old S Lourenço, who is fat, squat and pursy,[4] gasping for breath, with eyes as red and as watery as those of a stewed carp, stopped several times to rest on his journey. My friend whom disgust rendered heartily fatigued with his burden, and whose piety had much ado to keep his stomach from turning, was very glad likewise to make a pause or two. Happily, as I said before, the distance from the inn to the church was short. We found all the altars blazing with lights, the grave gaping for its immaculate inhabitant, and a band of priests and friars waiting to receive us in procession. The moment it entered, the very same hymn which is chanted at the obsequies of babes and sucklings was bellowed, incense diffused in clouds, and joy and gladness shining in the eyes of the whole congregation. A murmur of applause and congratulation went round anew, Acciaoli and Mascarenhas receiving with much affability and meekness the compliments of the occasion. Old S. Lourenço waddling up to the Grand Prior, hugged

---

[1] Manoel Carlos da Cunha e Tavora (1730–95), 6th Count, brother-in-law of Marialva.

[2] The manuscript shows that Beckford changed the story to distance himself somewhat from an over-enthusiastic participation in a Catholic ceremony.

[3] Satan.

[4] Short-winded.

him in his arms, and strewing him all over with snuff, set him violently a-sneezing.

São Vicente, as soon as the innocent was safely deposited, sneaked away, being never rightly at ease in the presence of his brother-in-law Marialva. As for Marialva, exaltation and triumph carried him beyond all bounds of decorum. He scoffed bitterly at Satan and heritics, represented in glowing colours the actual felicity of the convert, and just as we went out of church cried out loud enough for all those who were near, had they understood French, to have heard him: *Elle se fou[t] de nous touts à présent.*[1] Our pious toil being ended, we walked to the heights of Penha Verde to breathe fresh air untainted by dust. Then returning soberly to Ramalhão, drank tea and concluded the evening with much rapturous discourse on the happiness of the sheep now in the arms of the Shepherd.

Thursday, August 30th

The holy party who had so notably distinguished themselves yesterday honoured me with their company at dinner. Old S. Lourenço has a prodigious memory and a warm imagination, heightened by a slight touch of madness. He seems passingly well acquainted with the general politics of Europe, and this [n]ever beyond the limits of Portugal, giving so circumstantial and plausible detail of the part he acted at the Congress at Aix-la-Chapelle that I was complementing his dupe. Notwithstanding the high favour he enjoyed with the Infant D. Pedro,[2] Pombal cast him into a dungeon with the other victims of the Averio conspiracy[3] and for eighteen years was his active mind reduced to prey upon itself for sustenance. Upon the Queen's accession, he was released, and found his intimate friend D. Pedro sharing the throne. But thinking himself coldly received and neglected, he threw the key of Chamberlain which was sent him into a place of less dignity than convenience and retired to the Convent of the Necessidades.[4] No means, I have been assured, were left untried by the King to soothe and flatter him; but they all proved fruitless. Since this period, though he has quitted the convent after a short residence, he has never appeared at Court and has refused all employment. Devotion seems at present to gain ground upon him and take up his whole attentions. Except when the chord of imprisonment and Pombal is touched upon, he is calm and reasonable. I found him extremely so today, full of the most instructive and amusing anecdotes.

After dinner I sat down to the pianoforte and played almost without interruption. Mascarenhas, who is passionately fond of music, never quitted his chair by the side of my instrument. I cannot help flattering myself that my compositions resembled those of my dear Lady Hamilton, those pastoral

[1] She is beside herself with all of us present.

[2] D. Pedro III (1717–86), uncle of the Queen and also her consort.

[3] In 1758, the Marquis of Pombal imprisoned and executed a number of leading nobles who were alleged to have been involved in a plot to murder the King, José I, the Queen's father.

[4] To the west of Lisbon. Given to the Order of S. Philip Neri, 1747.

movements full of childish bewitching melody I have heard her so frequently compose during the autumn I passed at Caserta.[1] The reflection of her being for ever lost to me, and the thought too that my lovely Margaret[2] was fled to the same dark cold regions from whence there is no return, and had left me desolate and abandoned, steeped my mind in profound melancholy. I yielded up my soul to its influence, and scarce moving my fingers over the keys, drew forth modulations so plaintive and pathetic that every person in the apartment was affected. My friend sighed bitterly, the Grand Prior hung his head, Mascarenhas seemed beside himself, Acciaioli had no spirits for joking, and D. Pedro, leaning over my chair, breathed short with frequent sobbings. He begins to be conscious of existence since he has laid aside his reserve in my company. When first I knew him, no boy I ever beheld was so dull or inanimate. The full moon, rising like a globe of fire from behind the wild hillocks which skirt the garden, cast a yellow gleam on the verandas level with the saloon. I hastened out to inhale the perfumed evening air and view the wide extended landscape by this serene and mellow light. D. Pedro followed me, and as we sat fondly leaning on each other, admiring the beauty of the scene, gave me a lesson of Portuguese. I shall soon acquire the genuine accent.

Friday, August 31st

We are no longer vexed with howling winds. The flowers on the edge of the verandas blow in peace without having their seed scattered prematurely. I take great delight in the saloon I have so comfortably curtained, and lay listlessly on the smooth mat reading Tibullus[3] and composing tales. This is the first time since my arrival in this land that I begin to enjoy myself. An agreeable variety prevails in the apartment I am so fond of: half its curtains admit no light and display the richest folds, the other half are transparent and cast a mild glow on the mat and sofas, where I lay and read. The glasses multiply this profusion of drapery, and like a child I am not yet tired of running from corner to corner to view the different groups of objects reflected in them, and fancying myself admitted by enchantment into a series of magic saloons.

Nobody interrupted my day-dreams this morning. M. Verdeil and I dined alone. In the evening he drew me reluctantly from my mat to take some exercise, and rumble over rough pavement to Mr Horne's, where we drank tea. There is a sad bustle of preparation in Sintra for Her Majesty's arrival. Houses are taken by force from their proprietors to accommodate her train, and a row of sheds intended for kitchens and stables starting up on the flat space before the Dutch Consul's new building.[4] I am in high luck to have got

---

[1] Lady Catherine Hamilton, wife of Sir William Hamilton, Beckford's cousin. See *above*, pp. xii and xiii.

[2] Lady Margaret Gordon whom Beckford had married in 1783 and who died three years later. See *above*, pp. xiii and xiv.

[3] Albus Tibullus (c. 60–19 BC), Roman elegaic poet.

[4] The Palace of Setéais, later to be bought by Marialva.

roosted at Ramalhão out of the way of racket and defended from the dust and stir of a constant thoroughfare by lofty walls and woody *quintas*. I went from Horne's to Mrs Gildemeester's[1] in hopes of unkenneling and giving chase to Goody Fussock, but she was not there. The party was more than usually dull. I gaped and ennuied myself sadly and could not get away so soon as I wished, Verdeil having been allured into a party of *volterete* with [the] Miss Sills[2] and a scrubby female companion of Mrs Staits.[3] We supped at my friend's. D. Pedro and I took a run in the garden by our beloved moonlight. One of the little ones, D. Joaquina,[4] in attempting to follow us, fell down on the flat stones before the pavilion and set up a rueful squall, not without reason, for she had given herself a severe thump. The Marchioness and José Antonio, an ingenious young surgeon in great favour with the Marialvas, came forth to her assistance, and administered poultices with due solemnity.

Saturday, September 1st

Miss Cotter, one of the toads in waiting on the Consuless Mme Gildemeester, plucked up resolution to dine with me today, though her patroness declare I shall spoil her by civilities, and to be sure I never was more attentive in my life than I have been to this neglected nymph, and she repays my attentions with the warmest encomiums. She came with Horne and his family. Bezerra and Aguilar escorted them on horseback. The Marquis, Grand Prior and Abbade were likewise at dinner. I was in a very musical humour and felt loath to quit my pianoforte upon the Marquis calling me out on the veranda to consult with him on a fête he is persuading me to give the Queen. I have no great wish to have this honour. It will cost me a great sum and a vast deal of trouble into the bargain. Besides, I am at a loss how to decorate the garden and terraces. We are too much at the mercy of the wind here to trust to external illuminations. One moment he proposed a masked ball, and another a French play. He knows not what he would be at, nor I neither.

Sunday September 2nd

Packet[5] sailed with letters dated the 2nd. Soon after we had breakfast, Lima and six musicians arrived in one of the royal lumbering coaches with eight mules, which the Marquis lent me for the occasion. D. José de Sousa[6] came also from Lisbon to pass a day or two with me. I was delighted to see him, and vexed to have engaged myself to dine at the Marquis'. Whilst I was there

---

[1] Mrs Gildermeester was wife of Daniel Gildermeester the Elder (1727–93), wealthy Dutch consul and owner of Setéais Palace.

[2] Betty and Sophia Sills. Betty married Bezerra and later became Viscondessa de Tagoahi.

[3] Also spelt Steets, a member of English community. Voltrete is a card game.

[4] Joaquina de Marialva (1782–1846), third child of Marialva who became Marchioness of Louriçal.

[5] Ship bearing mail from England to Portugal.

[6] José Maria de Sousa Botelho Mourão, e Vasconcelos (1758–1825), friend of Bezerra and owner of estates in the north of Portugal. Beckford calls him D. José.

early in the evening a packet of English letters was brought me. I tore them open in haste and find my mother, sister and relations all scared out of their senses by accounts sent them from Portugal of my going to abjure the Protestant religion and accept titles and employments at the expense of my honour, future and liberty. Mr Wildman[1] too appears by these furious epistles to be also the prey of bugbears. He thinks, as men would throw a cucumber, that I shall throw myself away.

The Marquis looked blank upon my explaining the cause of my agitation. The Marchioness[2] and D. Henriqueta were dressed out to go to Sintra and sit dully in their carriage in the midst of the street, staring at the people assembled at a wretched fair. The Marquis and I followed them in my chaise. D. Pedro and his uncle brought up the rear. It was horribly dusty. The roads are bedevilled with loose sand strewn thick all over them.

Whilst the ladies stopped to look about them, my friend and I went to the Palace and took a survey of the preparations going on in the Royal Apartments. The Alhambra itself cannot well be more morisco[3] in point of architecture than this confused pile which seems to grow out of the summit of a rocky eminence and is broken into a variety of picturesque recesses and projections. 'Tis a thousand pities that they have whitened its venerable walls, stopped up a range of bold arcades and sliced out the great hall into three or four mean apartments that look like the dressing rooms belonging to a theatre. From the windows, which are all of an oriental fantastic style, crinkled and crankled, and supported by twisted pillars of smooth marble, the more striking views of the cliffs of Sintra are commanded. Several irregular courts and loggias are formed by the angles of square towers enlivened by fountains of marble and gilt bronze. The flat summit of one of the loftiest terraces is laid out in a neat parterre, which, like an embroidered carpet, is spread before the entrance of a huge square tower, almost entirely occupied by a hall encrusted with bright tiles and crowned by a dome most singularly shaped and glittering with mosaic ornaments – red, blue and gold. Amidst the scrolls of arabesque foliage appear the arms of the chief Portuguese nobility gaudily emblazoned. The achievements of the unfortunate House of Tavora[4] are blotted out and the panels which they occupied left bare. We had climbed up to this terrace and tower by one of those steep corkscrew staircases, of which there are numbers in the Palace. Almost every apartment has its vaulted passage and staircase winding up to it in a secret and suspicious manner. The Marquis made me observe a small chamber whose mosaic pavement was fretted and worn away in several places by the steps of Alfonso the Sixth,[5] who was confined to its narrow space a longevity

---

[1] Thomas Wildman of Lincoln's Inn, Beckford's solicitor.
[2] Margarida, 5th Marchioness wife of D. Diogo.
[3] Moorish.
[4] Noble family involved in the Aveiro conspiracy, see *above*, p. 238 n. 3.
[5] Afonso VI, King of Portugal from 1656–67, brother of Catherine of Bragança, imprisoned after his abdication.

of twenty years. I followed the Marquis into the rooms preparing for the Queen and the Infantas. They are awkward and ill-proportioned, with low narrow doors and wooden ceilings which a swarm of signpost painters were employed in daubing. Instead of hanging these antique saloons with rich arras and tapestry, representing the battles and adventures of knights and worthies, Her Majesty's upholsterers are hard at work covering the stout wall with light silks and satins of the softest colours. No furniture as yet has been put up in the palace, neither beds, glasses nor tables.

After my friend had given some orders with which the Queen had charged him, we rejoined the Marchioness, bought toys for the children, and drove out of the bustle and dust of the fair. The Marchioness, Acciaoli and Mascarenhas drank tea with me at Ramalhão, D. Henriqueta having been prudently dropped by the way. The old Abbade cried out 'A miracle, a miracle!' when he saw me handing the Marchioness into my apartments. She seldom consents to move anywhere, not even to the houses of her nearest relation[s], and according to Portuguese etiquette her visit to me might be looked upon as a prodigy. The night was serene and delightful, the folding doors which communicate with the veranda thrown wide open, and the harmonious notes of French horns and oboes issuing from thickets of citron and orange; not a breath of wind disturbed the clear flame of the lights in the lustres, and they cast a soft gleam on the shrubs shooting up above the terraces. In the course of the evening D. Pedro and I danced several minuets. We are growing much attached to each other. The scenery of my apartment, the musick I select, the prints and books which lie scattered about it, have led his imagination into a new world of ideas, and if I am not mistaken he will long remember the period of my stay in Portugal.

Monday, September 3rd

Verdeil went to my friend's in the morning and enlarged copiously on the innumerable difficulties which would attend my marriage and establishment in this kingdom. All his eloquence however could not convince the Marquis, who still flatters himself, by the assistance of Pinto's negotiations, to surmount all obstacles in England, obtain my peerage, and give my hand to D. Henriqueta with the full approbation of all my relations. Whilst the Marquis was exhausting Verdeil's attention by calling it continually to the contemplation of fairy castles, I remained indolently reclined on my sofas conversing with D. José[1] and Bezerra.

Verdeil brought the Marquis to dine with us, and in the evening arrived Horne and his family, Acciaoli, Mrs Steets, her fat confidante, husband and lover. The last mentioned pair, in defiance of common prejudices, are upon the most peaceful amicable footing, and never give each other the least disturbance. Both are equally dull and equally insipid; both portion out their attentions to the lady in a sober phlegmatic manner, and I should almost imagine from the style of their appearance and conversation keep a balance

---

[1] D. José de Brito, see *above*, p. 227 n. 5.

of debit and credit with commercial regularity. Notwithstanding the wildness of the lady's glances and the slenderness of her waist, she found little favour in my eyes this evening. If the belonging to such a husband excited my pity, the selection of so dull a lover roused my disgust. I felt out of humour, and kept parading up and down the long suite of apartments with the Marquis, paying my company little or no attention. Verdeil, who had invited them in the morning, contrived likewise they should stay supper. Just before it was brought in, I walked two or three minuets. The violins and French horns played so enchantingly that I was inspired with musical ideas, called for Lima and sung the *Serene tornate pupille vezzose* of Sacchini[1] in its native key, with so clear a voice that I half believe Mrs Staits suspects me of bordering on a soprano, and blesses God for the deep tones of her spouse and his coadjutor.

Tuesday, September 4th

I am ashamed to say that I passed my whole morning without reading a sentence, writing a line, or entering into any conversation, lulled by the plaintive harmony of the wind instruments, softened by distance. These notes steal into my soul and swell my heart with tender and melancholy recollections. It was in vain I attempted several times to retire out of the sound and compose myself. I was as often drawn back as I attempted to snatch myself away. Did I consult the health of my mind, I ought to dismiss these musicians. The harmony they produce awakens a thousand enervating and voluptuous ideas in my bosom. Extended on my mat, I look wistfully round me in search of an object to share my affection. I find a silent melancholy void. I stretch out my arms in vain. I form confused and dangerous projects, and as they successively rise and wither in my imagination, am depressed or elated. The general result of these conflicts is a deep and chilling dejection which renders me incapable of any exertion, and forces me to consume my time and trifle away my precious youthful hours.

D. José took leave of me after dinner. He is going to his estate in the province of Tras-os-Montes,[2] and has been pressing [me] in the kindest manner to make an excursion that way, offering to be my conductor. Verdeil wishes much I would accept this proposition, and promises me great amusement. Really t'would be no bad scheme. I should take the Convents of Batalha and Alcobaça[3] in my way, pass a few days at Coimbra, and after meeting D. José at Oporto, ramble into the interior of the green shady province of Minho under his auspices. M. Verdeil forced me out after D. José had left us. We went as usual to Horne's and supped with the Marquis.

Wednesday, September 5th

The Marquis, Grand Prior and D. Pedro dined with me. The Grand Prior

---

[1] Antonio Maria G. Sacchini (1734–86), Neapolitan composer. The words may be translated 'Become serious again, o pretty eyes'.

[2] In the north-east of Portugal.

[3] Visited by Beckford in 1794. See *below*, p. 273 ff.

every wit as indolent, as lounging and as fond of musick as myself. Not one of Boileau's[1] *chanoines*[2] ever sunk into a sofa more voluptuously. It was with difficulty either of us could be persuaded to stir after dinner. D. Pedro made me dance a minuet with him, and after having been once set going I consented to walk in the alleys of the *quinta*. The Marquis is fallen a little lame and hobbles. D. Pedro and I, having the full use of our limbs, coursed each other like greyhounds.

Thursday, September 6th

Music has once more taken full possession of me. I bow under its influence, and imbibe thirstily those enervating sounds that impair the force of my understanding. My voice is returned with all its powers and I execute the most difficult passages with facility. Bezerra who dined with us today could scarce draw from me one reasonable idea. The Marquis and the Grand Prior came in the evening. Their presence roused me at intervals from my musical delirium. M. Verdeil began describing Fonthill, and I seconded him with an energy that alarmed my friend and convinced him it would be no easy matter to allure me from England.

Friday, September 7th

Whilst I was walking amongst the orange trees in the *quinta* after breakfast, the Grand Prior made his appearance on the veranda, and I hastened up to him. I plainly perceived that the fondness with which I had spoken of Fonthill last night had made a strong impression on him, and that he feared I should be soon persuaded to leave Portugal. I waived this topic of conversation, which I saw cast a gloom over his good-natured countenance, and summoning Lima to the pianoforte, sung one of his best compositions – *Ah! non turbi quae fiero sembiante.*[3] The Marquis joined us at dinner and at six drove me out towards Colares in the *carrinho*. The weather proved misty and uncomfortable. We stopped in our way home at Horne's and drank tea. The woody scene discovered from his veranda had assumed this evening a dingy hue and the cliffs were lost in clouds. It was pitch dark when we returned to Ramalhão. I threw myself on my sofa shuddering at the gloomy aspect of the night. A whistling wind inspired me with sadness; but after all I believe it was the absence of D. Pedro that rendered me so disconsolate.

Saturday, September 8th

I sent M. Verdeil to my friend's and they had a long conversation upon the usual topics. The Marquis still continues indulging himself in the hopes of levelling all obstacles by the Archbishop's assistance, who I have indeed every reason to believe is strongly prepossessed in my favour. But what talents have

[1] Nicolas Boileau-Despréaux (1636–1711), French poet and critic.
[2] Enjoyer of an easy life.
[3] 'Ah do not trouble that proud mien.'

I for Court intrigue? None. I am too indolent, too listless, to give myself any trouble. Bezerra passed the morning with me in expatiating upon the friendship with which I had inspired Marialva, and the effects which might, if I please, result from it. Whilst we were seated on the sofa, in earnest consultation, the Marquis entered and was soon followed by D. Pedro and the Grand Prior. D. Pedro looked confused, as if he had been too often thinking of me since we last parted. Lima sat down to the pianoforte and I sung till dinner. Never in my life did I sing with more expression. There is a scene in one of Lima's operas in which the ghost of Polydorus calls upon Aeneas, just arrived on the Thracian shore, to revenge his death on Polynestor.[1] The music is melancholy and pathetic to a striking degree, and I gave the bitter cry of *Vendica i torti miei*,[2] which often recurs in the air, its full energy. I was so possessed by these affecting sounds that I could hardly eat. Lima was enchanted with the attention I paid his compositions. The evening turning out mild and pleasant, we rambled about the *quinta* till dark. The waters, flowing in rills round the roots of the lemon trees, formed a rippling murmur. Not a leaf rustled, the most profound calm reigned amongst the thickets. D. Pedro and I, who become every day more and more attached to each other, run hand in hand along the alleys, bounding like deer and leaping up to catch at the *azareiro*[3] blossoms which dangled over our heads. No child of thirteen ever felt a stronger impulse to race and gambol than I do. My limbs are as supple and elastic as those of a stripling, and it gives me no pain to turn and twist them into the most playful attitudes.

Sunday, September 9th

The Prior of the Cork Convent is appointed by the Marialvas, so we all set forth this morning – the Marquis, Grand Prior, D. Pedro, and the old Abbade – to dine with him and be present at his installation. He is a sturdy, clownish-looking fellow, very jovial and open-hearted. After Mass, D. Pedro and M. Verdeil posted themselves on a mossy stone and began sketching something which they imagined to be a view of the Convent with the rocks and thickets which surround it. Though the sun broiled them unmercifully and lighted up the verdure of the citron and laurel shrubberies with his liveliest rays, the vast plains of land and ocean which are discovered from these eminences were lost in clouds. The effect was singular and I sat on the shelving acclivity of the mountain to enjoy it. The hanging shrubberies of arbutus, bay and myrtle, and the bushy pines which bend over the crags reminded me of the scenery of Mount Edgecumbe. Between the crevices of the rude rocks which lie tumbled about in the wildest confusion, you find luxuriant tufts of herbage which on the least pressure exhale a fresh aromatic perfume. I delight in exploring these nooks and corners. The Marquis was too lame to accompany my

[1] Polymestor, King of Thracian Chersonese, murdered Polydorus, youngest son of Priam and Hecuba.

[2] 'Avenge my wrongs'.

[3] Portuguese laurel.

rambles, and sat with the monks and Luis de Miranda,[1] the Colonel of the Cascais regiment, at the entrace of the cells, so I remained, till dinner was announced, in total solitude. We had a greasy repast and abundance of high-flavoured cabbage stewed in the essence of ham and partridge, four sucking pigs, as many larded turkeys, and two pyramids of rice, as yellow as saffron could tinge them. Three of the principal monks were of our party. The Grand Prior made wry faces at the copper forks and spoons which were set before us. We could hardly persuade him to make use of them. For my part I am always glad of an excuse to eat in the oriental style with my fingers. for never mortal handled a knife so awkwardly. Our dessert both in point of fruit and sweetmeats was truly luxurious. Pomona[2] herself need not have been ashamed of carrying in her lap such peaches and nectarines as rolled by dozens about the table.

The Abbade seemed animated after dinner by the spirit of contradiction, and would not allow the Marquis or Luis de Miranda to know more of King John the Fifth[3] and his Court than of that of Pharaoh King of Egypt. D. Pedro and I ran out of the sound of the dispute in which the monks began to join, and climbed up amongst the mossy rocks to a little platform overgrown with lavender. There we sat, lulled by the murmur of distant waves rushing over a broken shore. The clouds came slowly sailing over the hills. My companion pounded the cones of the pine and gave me the kernels which have an agreeable almond taste. The evening was far advanced before we abandoned our peaceful retired situation, and joined the Marquis who had not yet been able to appease the Abbade. The vociferous old man made so many appeals to the Father Guardian of the Convent in defence of his opinions that I thought we should never have got away. At length we departed, and after wandering about in clouds and darkness for two hours, reached Sintra exactly at ten. The Marchioness and the children had been much alarmed at our long absence, and rated the Abbade severely for having occasioned it.

---

[1] Luis José Xavier de Miranda Henriques (1726–93), 3rd Count of Sandomil, friend of Prince of Brazil.

[2] Roman goddess of fruit.

[3] João V of Portugal (1706–50), whose reign was marked by acts of public munificence including the bulding of Mafra Convent and the University Library at Coimbra.

TRAVEL DIARIES

III

From *Italy, with Sketches of Spain and Portugal,*
1834. This extract is from *The Travel Diaries of
William Beckford of Fonthill,* by Guy Chapman, 2
Vols, London, 1928. Chapman's edition was based
on the second edition of 1834. The extract is from
Volume 2.

ITALY WITH SKETCHES OF SPAIN
AND PORTUGAL
1787

LETTER XXVIII

Sept. 19th, 1787

Never did I behold so fine a day, or a sky of such lovely azure. The M——[1] were with me by half-past six, and we rode over wild hills, which command a great extent of apparently desert country; for the villages, if there are any, are concealed in ravines and hollows.

Intending to explore the Cintra mountains from one extremity to the other of the range, we placed relays at different stations. Our first object was the Convent of Nossa Senhora da Penha,[2] the little romantic pile of white buildings I had seen glittering from afar when I first sailed by the coast of Lisbon. From this pyramidical elevation the view is boundless: you look immediately down upon an immense expanse of sea, the vast, unlimited Atlantic. A long series of detached clouds of a dazzling whiteness, suspended low over the waves, had a magic effect, and in pagan times might have appeared, without any great stretch of fancy, the cars of marine divinities just risen from the bosom of their element.

There was nothing very interesting in the objects immediately around us. The Moorish remains in the neighbourhood of the convent are scarcely worth notice, and indeed seem never to have made part of any considerable edifice. They were probably built up with the dilapidations of a Roman temple, whose constructors had perhaps in their turn availed themselves of the fragments of a Punic or Tyrian fane raised on this high place, and blackened with the smoke of some horrible sacrifice.

Amidst the crevices of the mouldering walls, and particularly in the vault of a cistern, which seems to have served both as a resevoir and a bath, I noticed some capillaries and polypodiums of infinite delicacy; and on a little flat space before the convent a numerous tribe of pinks, gentians, and other alpine plants, fanned and invigorated by the pure mountain air. These refreshing breezes, impregnated with the perfume of innumerable aromatic herbs and flowers, seemed to infuse new life into my veins, and, with it, an

---

[1] The Marialvas.
[2] The monastery was on the heights of Sintra and is described by Byron in *Childe Harold*, Stanza XX. The words mean, 'Our Lady of the Rocks'.

almost irrestible impulse to fall down and worship in this vast temple of Nature the source and cause of existence.

As we had a very extensive ride in contemplation, I could not remain half so long as I wished on this aërial and secluded summit. Descending by a tolerably easy road, which wound amongst the rocks in many an irregular curve, we followed for several miles a narrow tract over the brow of savage and desolate eminences, to the Cork convent,[1] which answered exactly, at the first glance we caught of it, the picture one represents to one's self of the settlement of Robinson Crusoe.[2] Before the entrance, formed of two ledges of ponderous rock, extends a smooth level of greensward, browsed by cattle whose tinkling bells filled me with recollections of early days passed amongst wild and alpine scenery. The Hermitage, its cells, chapel, and refectory, are all scooped out of the native marble, and lined with the bark of the cork-tree. Several of the passages about it are not only roofed, but floored with the same material, extremely soft and pleasant to the feet. The shrubberies and garden plants, dispersed amongst the mossy rocks which lie about in the wildest confusion, are delightful, and I took great pleasure in exploring their nooks and corners, following the course of a transparent, gurgling rill, which is conducted through a rustic water-shoot, between bushes of lavender and rosemary of the tenderest green.

The Prior of this romantic retirement is appointed by the Marialvas, and this very day his installation takes place, so we were pressed to dine with him upon the occasion, and could not refuse; but as it was still very early, we galloped on, intending to visit a famous cliff, the Pedra d'Alvidrar, which composes one of the most striking features of that renowned promontory the Rock of Lisbon.

Our road led us through the skirts of the woods which surround the delightful village of Collares,[3] to another range of barren eminences extending along the sea-shore. I advanced to the very margin of the cliff, which is of great height, and nearly perpendicular. A rabble of boys followed at the heels of our horses, and five stout lads, detached from this posse, descended with the most perfect unconcern the dreadful precipice. One in particular walked down with his arms expanded, like a being of a superior order. The coast is truly picturesque, and consists of bold projections, intermixed with pyramidical rocks suceeding each other in theatrical perspective, the most distant crowned by a lofty tower, which serves as a lighthouse.

No words can convey an adequate idea of the bloom of the atmosphere, and the silvery light reflected from the sea. From the edge of the abyss, where I had remained several minutes like one spell-bound, we descended a winding path, about half a mile, to the beach. Here we found ourselves nearly shut in by shattered cliffs and grottos, a fantastic amphitheatre, the best calculated that can possibly be imagined to invite the sports of sea nymphs. Such coves,

---

[1] Capuchan monastery founded by the Franciscans in the range behind Sintra.
[2] Defoe's book appeared in 1719.
[3] Colares is near Sintra; Beckford enjoyed riding in the valley.

such deep and broken recesses, such a play of outline I never beheld, nor did I ever hear so powerful a roar of rushing waters upon any other coast. No wonder the warm and susceptible imagination of the ancients, inflamed by the scenery of the place, led them to believe they distinguished the conchs of tritons sounding in these retired caverns; nay, some grave Lusitanians[1] positively declared they had not only heard, but seen them, and despatched a messenger to the Emperor Tiberius[2] to announce the event, and congratulate him upon so evident and auspicious a manifestation of divinity.

The tide was beginning to ebb, and allowed us, not without some risk however, to pass into a cavern of surprising loftiness, the sides of which were incrusted with beautiful limpets, and a variety of small shells grouped together. Against some rude and porous fragments, not far from the aperture through which we had crept, the waves swell with violence, rush into the air, form instantaneous canopies of foam, then fall down in a thousand trickling rills of silver, The flickering gleams of light thrown upon irregular arches admitting into darker and more retired grottos, the mysterious, watery gloom, the echoing murmurs and almost musical sounds, occasioned by the conflict of winds and waters, the strong odour of an atmosphere composed of saline particles, produced altogether such a bewildering effect upon the senses, that I can easily conceive a mind, poetically given, might be thrown into that kind of tone which inclines to the belief of supernatural appearances. I am not surprised, therefore, at the credulity of the ancients, and only wonder my own imagination did not deceive me in a similar manner.

If solitude could have induced the Nereids[3] to have vouchsafed me an apparition, it was not wanting, for all my company had seperated upon different pursuits, and had left me entirely to myself. During the full half-hour I remained shut out from the breathing world, one solitary corvo marino[4] was the only living creature I caught sight of, perched upon an insulated rock, about fifty paces from the opening of the cavern.

I was so stunned with the complicated sounds and murmurs which filled my ears, that it was some moments before I could distinguish the voices of Verdeil and Don Pedro, who were just returned from a hunt after seaweeds and madrapores, calling me loudly to mount on horseback, and make the best of our way to rejoin the Marquis and his attendants, all gone to mass at the Cork convent. Happily, the little detached clouds we had seen from the high point of Nossa Senhora da Penha, instead of melting into the blue sky, had been gathering together, and skreened us from the sun. We had therefore a delightful ride, and upon alighting from our palfreys found the old abade just arrived with Luis de Miranda, the colonel of the Cascais regiment, surrounded by a whole synod of monks, as picturesque as bald pates and venerable beards could make them.

[1] Roman names for Portuguese.
[2] Roman Emperor AD 14–37.
[3] Sea-maidens in Homeric legend.
[4] A type of raven found near the shore.

As soon as the Marquis came forth from his devotions, dinner was served up exactly in the style one might have expected at Mequinez or Morocco – pillaus[1] of different kinds, delicious quails, and pyramids of rice tinged with saffron. Our dessert, in point of fruits and sweetmeats, was most luxurious, nor would Pomona[2] herself been ashamed of carrying in her lap such peaches and nectarines as rolled in profusion about the table.

The abade seemed animated after dinner by the spirit of contradiction and would not allow the Marquis or Luis de Miranda to know more about the court of John the Fifth,[3] than of that of Pharaoh, king of Egypt.

To avoid being stunned by the clamours of the dispute, in which two or three monks with stentorian voices began to take part most vehemently, Don Pedro, Verdeil, and I climbed up amongst the hanging shrubberies of arbutus, bay, and myrtle, to a little platform carpeted with delicate herbage, exhaling a fresh, aromatic perfume upon the slightest pressure. There we sat, lulled by the murmur of distant waves, breaking over the craggy shore we had visited in the morning. The clouds came slowly sailing over the hills. My companions pounded the cones of the pines, and gave me the kernels, which have an agreeable almond taste.

The evening was far advanced before we abandoned our peaceful, sequestered situation, and joined the Marquis, who had not been yet able to appease the abade. The vociferous old man made so many appeals to the father-guardian of the convent in defence of his opinions, that I thought we never should have got away. At length we departed, and after wandering about in the clouds and darkness for two hours, reached Cintra exactly at ten. The Marchioness and the children had been much alarmed at our long absence, and rated the abade severely for having occasioned it.

LETTER XXIX

September 22nd, 1787

When I got up, the mists were stealing off the hills, and the distant sea discovering itself in all its azure bloom. Though I had been led to expect many visiters of importance from Lisbon, the morning was so inviting, that I could not resist riding out after breakfast, even at the risk of not being present at their arrival.

I took the road to Collares, and found the air delightfully soft and fragrant. Some rain which had lately fallen, had refreshed the whole face of the country, and tinged the steeps beyond Penha Verde[4] with purple and green; for the numerous tribe of heaths had started into blossom, and the little

---

[1] Oriental seasoned rice with meat.
[2] See *above*, p. 246 n. 2.
[3] See *above*, p. 246 n. 3.
[4] Sintra peak, literally 'green rock'.

irregular lawns, overhung by crooked cork-trees, which occur so frequently by the way-side, are now covered with large white lilies streaked with pink.

Penha Verde itself is a lovely spot. The villa, with its low, flat roofs, and a loggia projecting at one end, exactly resembles the edifices in Gaspar Poussin's[1] landscapes. Before one of the fronts is a square parterre with a fountain in the middle, and niches in the walls with antique busts. Above these walls a variety of trees and shrubs rise to a great elevation, and compose a mass of the richest foliage. The pines, which, by their bright green colour, have given the epithet of verdant to this rocky point (Penha Verde), are as picturesque as those I used to admire so warmly in the Negroni garden at Rome, and full as ancient, perhaps more so: tradition assures us they were planted by the far-famed Don John de Castro,[2] whose heart reposes in a small marble chapel beneath their shade.

How often must that heroic heart, whilst it still beat in one of the best and most magnanimous of human bosoms, have yearned after this calm retirement! Here, at least, did it promise itself that rest so cruelly denied him by the blind perversities of his ungrateful countrymen: for his had been an arduous contest, a long and agonizing struggle, not only in the field under a burning sun, and in the face of peril and death, but in sustaining the glory and good fame of Portugal against court intrigues, and the vile cabals of envious, domestic enemies.

These scenes, though still enchanting, have most probably undergone great changes since his days. The deep forests we read of have disappeared, and with them many a spring they fostered. Architectural fountains, gaudy terraces, and regular stripes of orange-gardens, have usurped the place of those wild orchards and gushing rivulets he may be supposed to have often visited in his dreams, when removed some thousand leagues from his native country. All these are changed; but mankind are the same as in his time, equally insensible to the warning voice of genuine patriotism, equally disposed to crouch under the rod of corrupt tyranny. And thus, by the neglect of wise and virtuous men, and a mean subserviency to knavish fools, eras which might become of gold, are transmuted by an accursed alchymy into iron rusted with blood.

Impressed with all the recollections this most interesting spot could not fail to inspire, I could hardly tear myself away from it. Again and again did I follow the mossy steps, which wind up amongst shady rocks to the little platform, terminated by the sepulchral chapel –

>——denis quam pinus opacat
>Frondibus et nulla lucos agitante procella
>Stridula coniferis modulatur carmina ramis.[1]

---

[1] Nicolas Poussin (1584–1665). His neo-classical landscapes and those of Claude Lorraine were taken as ideal representations of classical life and legend.

[2] João de Castro (1500–48), Vice-roy of India who retired to Sintra where he built a *quinta* or country villa.

[3] ——'which a pine shades with its close branches, and, tho' no storm stirs the groves, it tunes whistling songs in its cone-bearing boughs.' Claudian, *de Raptu Proserpinae* ll. 203–5.

You must not wonder then, that I was haunted the whole way home by these mysterious whisperings, nor that, in such a tone of mind, I saw with no great pleasure a procession of two-wheeled chaises, the lord knows how many out-riders, and a caravan of bouras,[1] marching up to the gate of my villa. I had, indeed, been prepared to expect a very considerable influx of visiters; but this was a deluge.

Do not let me send you a catalogue of the company, lest you should be as much annoyed with the detail, as I was with such a formidable arrival *en masse*. Let it suffice to name two of the principal characters, the old pious Conde de San Lorenzo,[2] and the prior of San Juliaô, one of the archbishop's prime favourites, and a person of great worship. Mortier's Dutch bible happening to lie upon the table, they began tumbling over the leaves in an egregiously awkward manner. I, who abhor seeing books thumbed, and prints demonstrated by the close application of a greasy fore-finger, snapped at the old Conde, and cast an evil look at the prior, who was leaning his whole priestly weight on the volume, and creasing its corners.

My musicians were in full song, and Pedro Grua, a capital violoncello, exerted his abilities in his best style; but San Lorenzo was too pathetically engaged in deploring the massacre of the Innocents[3] to pay him any attention, and his reverend companion had entered into a long-winded dissertation upon parables, miracles, and martyrdom, from which I prayed in vain the Lord to deliver me. Verdeil, scenting from afar the saintly flavour of the discourse, stole off.

I cannot say much in praise of the prior's erudition, even in holy matters, for he postitively affirmed that it was Henry the Eighth himself, who knocked St Thomas à Becket's brains out, and that by the beast in the Apocalypse, Luther was positively indicated. I hate wrangles, and had it not been for the soiling of my prints, should never have contradicted his reverence; but as I was a little out of humour, I lowered him somewhat in the Conde's opinion, by stating the real period of St Thomas's murder, and by tolerably specious arguments, shoving the beast's horns off Luther, and clapping them tight upon – whom do you think? Œcolampadius![4] So grand a name, which very probably they had never heard pronounced in their lives, carried all before it, (adding another instance of the triumph of sound over sense,) and settled our bickerings.

We sat down, I beleive, full thirty to dinner, and had hardly got through the dessert, when Berti[5] came in to tell me that Madame Ariaga,[6] and a bevy of the palace damsels, were prancing about the quinta on palfreys and bouras. I hastened to join them. There was Donna Maria do Carmo, and

[1] Donkeys.
[2] See *above*, p. 236 n.
[3] Massacre of young males by King Herod (Matthew 11:16).
[4] An early Reformer, Bishop of Basle, friend of Zwingli.
[5] Beckford's manservant.
[6] Widow of Miguel de Arriaga, a colleague of Pombal.

Donna Maria de Penha, with her hair flowing about her shoulders, and her large beautiful eyes looking as wild and roving as those of an antelope. I called for my horse, and galloped through alleys and citron bushes, brushing off leaves, fruit, and blossoms. Every breeze wafted to us the sound of French horns and oboes. The ladies seemed to enjoy the freedom and novelty of this scamper prodigiously, and to regret the short time it was doomed to last; for at seven they are obliged to return to strict attendance on the Queen, and had some strange fairy-tale metamorphosis into a pumpkin or a cucumber been the penalty of disobedience, they could not have shown more alarm or anxiety when the fatal hour of seven drew near. Luckily, they had not far to go, for her Majesty and the Royal Family were all assembled at the Marialva villa, to partake of a splendid merenda[1] and see fireworks.

As soon as it fell dark Verdeil and I set forth to catch a glimpse of the royal party. The Grand Prior and Don Pedro conducted us mysteriously into a snug boudoir which looks into the great pavilion, whose gay, fantastic scenery appeared to infinite advantage by the light of innumerable tapers reflected on all sides from lustres of glittering crystal. The little Infanta Donna Carlotta[2] was perched on a sofa in conversation with the Marchioness and Donna Henriquetta, who, in the true oriental fashion, had placed themselves cross-legged on the floor. A troop of maids of honour, commanded by the Countess of Lumieres, sat in the same posture at a little distance. Donna Rosa, the favourite dwarf negress, dressed out in a flaming scarlet riding-habit, not so frolicsome as the last time I had the pleasure of seeing her in this fairy bower, was more sentimental, and leaned against the door, ogling and flirting with a handsome Moor belonging to the Marquis.

Presently the Queen, followed by her sister and daughter-in-law, the Princess of Brazil, came forth from her merenda, and seated herself in front of the latticed-window, behind which I was placed. Her manner struck me as being peculiarly dignified and conciliating. She looks born to command; but at the same time to make that high authority as much beloved as respected. Justice and clemency, the motto so glaringly misapplied on the banner of the abhorred Inquisition, might be transferred with the strictest truth to this good princess. During the fatal contest betwixt England and its colonies, the wise neutrality she persevered in maintaining was of the most vital benefit to her dominions, and hitherto, the native commerce of Portugal has attained under her mild auspices an unprecedented degree of prosperity.

Nothing could exceed the profound respect, the courtly decorum her presence appeared to inspire. The Conde de Sampayo and the Viscount Ponte de Lima knelt by the august personages with not much less veneration, I should be tempted to imagine, than Moslems before the tomb of their prophet, or Tartars in the presence of the Dalai Lama. Marialva alone, who

---

[1] Picnic or meal taken outside.

[2] Carlota Joaquina (1775–1830), daughter of Charles V of Spain, later consort to João V of Portugal. She lived, separated from the King, at Ramalhão after their return from Brazil in 1821.

took his station opposite her Majesty, seemed to preserve his ease and cheerfulness. The Prince of Brazil[1] and Don Joaô[2] looked not a little ennuied; for they kept stalking about with their hands in their pockets, their mouths in a perpetual yawn, and their eyes wandering from object to object, with a stare of royal vacancy.

A most rigorous etiquette confining the Infants of Portugal within their palaces, they are seldom known to mix even incognito with the crowd; so that their flattering smiles or confidential yawns are not lavished upon common observers. This sort of embalming princes alive, after all, is no bad policy; it keeps them sacred; it concentrates their royal essence, too apt, alas! to evaporate by exposure. What is so liberally paid for by the willing tribute of the people as a rarity of exquisite relish, should not be suffered to turn mundungus.[3] However the individual may dislike this severe regimen, state pageants might have the goodness to recollect for what purpose they are bedecked and beworshipped.

The Conde de Sampayo, lord in waiting, handed the tea to the Queen, and fell down on both knees to present it. This ceremony over, for everything is ceremony at this stately court, the fireworks were announced, and the royal sufferers, followed by their sufferees, adjourned to a neighbouring apartment. The Marchioness, her daughters, and the Countess of Lumieres, mounted up to the boudoir where I was sitting, and took possession of the windows. Seven or eight wheels, and as many tourbillons[4] began whirling and whizzing, whilst a profusion of admirable line-rockets darted along in various directions, to the infinite delight of the Countess of Lumieres, who, though hardly sixteen, has been married four years. Her youthful cheerfulness, light hair, and fair complexion, put me so much in mind of my Margaret, that I could not help looking at her with a melancholy tenderness: her being with child increased the resemblance, and as she sat in the recess of the window, discovered at intervals by the blue light of rockets bursting high in the air, I felt my blood thrill as if I beheld a phantom, and my eyes were filled with tears.

The last firework being played off, the Queen and the Infantas departed. The Marchioness and the other ladies descended into the pavilion, where we partook of a magnificent and truly royal collation. Donna Maria and her little sister, animated by the dazzling illumination, tripped about in their light muslin dresses, with all the sportiveness of fairy beings, such as might be supposed to have dropped down from the floating clouds, which Pillement[5] has so well represented on the ceiling.

---

[1] José, Prince of Brazil (1761–88), heir to the throne died in mysterious circumstances in 1788.

[2] Dom João, his brother, Prince Regent from 1791; King in 1816.

[3] Evil smelling.

[4] Firework with spiral flight.

[5] Jean-Baptiste Pillement (?1728–1808), who painted the frescoes at various palaces and quintas in Sintra, including Setéais and Ramalhão.

LETTER XXX

November 8th, 1787

Verdeil and I rattled over cracked pavements this morning in my rough travelling-coach, for the sake of exercise. The pretext for our excursion was to see a remarkable chapel, inlaid with jasper and lapis-lazuli, in the church of St Roch;[1] but when we arrived, three or four masses were celebrating, and not a creature sufficiently disengaged to draw the curtain which veils the altar, so we went out as wise as we came in.

Not having yet seen the cathedral, or See-church,[2] as it is called at Lisbon, we directed our course to that quarter. It is a buiding of no striking dimensions, narrow and gloomy, without being awful. The earthquake[3] crumbled its glories to dust, if ever it had any, and so dreadfully shattered the chapels, with which it is clustered, that very slight traces of their having made part of a mosque are discernible.

Though I had not been led to expect great things, even from descriptions in travels and topographical works, which, like peerage-books and pedigrees, are tenderly inclined to make something of what is next to nothing at all: I hunted away, as became a diligent traveller, after altar-pieces and tombs, but can boast of no discoveries. To be sure, we had not much time to look about us: the priests and sacristans, who fastened upon us, insisted upon our revisiting the corner of a bye staircase, where are to be kissed and worshipped the traces of St Anthony's fingers. The saint, it seems, being closely pursued by the father of lies and parent of evil, alias Old Scratch, (I really could not clearly learn upon what occasion,) indented the sign of the cross into a wall of the hardest marble, and stopped his proceedings. A very pleasing little picture hangs up near the miraculous cross, and records the tradition.

All this was admirable; but nothing in comparison with some stories about certain holy crows. 'The very birds are in being,' said a sacristan. 'What!' answered I, 'the individual[4] crows who attended St Vincent?' – 'Not exactly,' was the reply, (in a whisper, intended for my private ear); 'but their immediate descendants.' – 'Mighty well; this very evening, please God, I will pay my respects to them, and in good company, so adieu for the present.'

Our next point was the Theatine[5] convent. We looked into the library,

---

[1] Church of S. Roque in Lisbon.
[2] Sé Cathedral in Lisbon.
[3] On 1 November, 1755 a severe earthquake, followed by fire and flooding, caused immense damage to Lisbon.
[4] At the time I wrote this, half Lisbon believed in the individuality of the holy crows, and the other half prudently concealed their scepticism. [Beckford's note]
[5] Convento dos Clerigos Regulares de S. Caetano in Lisbon.

which lies in the same confusion in which it was left by the earthquake; half the books out of their shelves, tumbled one over the other in dusty heaps. A shrewd, active monk, who, I am told has written a history of the House of Braganza,[1] not yet printed, guided our steps through this chaos of literature; and after searching half-an-hour for some curious voyages he wished to display to us, led us into his cell, and pressed our attention to a cabinet of medals he had been at some pains and expense in collecting.

Not feeling any particular vocation for numismatic researches, I left Verdeil with the monk, puzzling out some very questionable inscriptions, and went to beat up for recruits to accompany me in the evening to the holy crows. First, I found the Abade Xavier, and secondly, the famous missionary preacher from Boa Morte, and then the Grand Prior, and lastly, the Marquis of Marialva; Don Pedro begged not to be left out, so we formed a coach full, and I drove my whole cargo home to dinner. Verdeil was already returned with his reverend medallist, and had also collected the governor of Goa, Don Frederic de Sousa Cagliariz,[2] his constant attendant a bullying Savoyard, or Piedmontese Count, by name Lucatelli; and a pale, limber, odd-looking young man. Senhor Manuel Maria,[3] the queerest, but, perhaps, the most original of God's poetical creatures. He happened to be in one those eccentric, lively moods, which, like sunshine in the depth of winter, come on when least expected. A thousand quaint conceits, a thousand flashes of wild merriment, a thousand sartirical darts shot from him, and we were all convulsed with laughter; but when he began reciting some of his compositions, in which great depth of thought is blended with the most pathetic touches, I felt myself thrilled and agitated. Indeed, this strange and versatile character may be said to possess the true wand of enchantment, which, at the will of its master, either animates or petrifies.

Perceiving how much I was attracted towards him, he said to me, 'I did not expect an Englishman would have condescended to pay a young, obscure, modern versifier, any attention. You think we have no bard but Camões, and that Camões has written nothing worth notice, but the Lusiad.[4] Here is a sonnet worth half the Lusiad.

CXCII

A fermosura desta fresca serra,
E a sombra dos verdes castanheiros,
O manso caminhar destes ribeiros,
Donde toda a tristeza se desterra;
O rouco som do mar, a estranha terra,
O esconder do Sol pellos outeiros,
O recolher dos gados derradeiros,
Das nuvens pello ar a branda guerra:
Em fim tudo o que a rara natureza

[1] The Bragança dynasty began in 1640 when the Duke became King João IV of Portugal.
[2] Federico Guilherme de Sousa (1737–90), Vice-roy of India 1779–86.
[3] Manuel Maria du Bocage (1765–1805), satiric poet.
[4] Luíz Vaz de Camões (?1524–80), epic poet, whose Os Lusíadas is an account of the seafaring and crusading exploits of the Portuguese explorers.

Com tanta variedade nos ofrece,
Me està (se não te vejo) magoando:
Sem ti tudo me enoja, e me aborrece,
Sem ti perpetuamente estou passando
Nas mòres alegrias, mòr tristeza!'[1]

Not an image of rural beauty has escaped our divine poet; and how feelingly are they applied from the landscape to the heart! What a fascinating languor, like the last beams of an evening sun, is thrown over the whole composition! If I am anything, this sonnet has made me what I am; but what am I, compared to Monteiro?[2] Judge,' continued he, putting into my hand some manuscript verses of this author, to whom the Portuguese are vehemently partial. Though they were striking and sonorous, I must confess the sonnet of Camões, and many of Senhor Manuel Maria's own verses, pleased me infinitely more, but in fact, I was not sufficiently initiated into the force and idiom of the Portuguese language to be a competent judge; and it was only in fancying me one, that this powerful genius discovered any want of penetration.

Our dinner was lively and convivial. At the dessert the Abadè produced an immense tray of dried fruits and sweetmeats, which one of his hundred and fifty *protégés* had sent him from, I forget what exotic region. These good things he kept handing to us, and almost cramming down our throats, as if we had been turkeys and he a poulterer, whose livelihood depended upon our fattening. 'There,' said he, 'did you ever behold such admirable productions? Our Queen has thousands and thousands of miles with fruit-groves over your head, and rocks of gold and diamonds beneath your feet. The riches and fertility of her possesions have no bounds, but the sea, and the sea itself might belong to us if we pleased; for we have such means of ship-building, masts two hundred feet high, incorruptible timbers, courageous seamen. Don Frederic can tell you what some of our heroes achieved not long ago against

---

[1]
> The mountain cool, the chestnut's verdant shade.
> The loit'ring walk along the river side,
> Where never woe her sad abode hath made,
> Nor sorrow linger'd on the silv'ry tide —
> The sea hoarse sound — the earth with verdure gay
> The gilded pomp of Phoebus' parting rays —
> The flocks that tread at eve their homeward way —
> The soft mist yielding to the sunny blaze —
> Not all the varied charms and beauties rare
> That nature boasts — when thou, my sole delight!
> Art absent from me, to my aching sight
> Can comfort give, but as a prospect drear
> And cold before me stand — I onward go,
> And as the joys increase, increase my woe.

A Sonnet of L. de Camõens translated by John Adamson. J. Adamson, *Memoirs of the Life and Writings of Luis de Camõens*, 2 vols (London, 1820), 1:255.

[2] Domingos Monteiro de Albuquerque e Amaral (1744–1830), minor poet of sarcastic and indecent verse.

the gentiles at Goa. Your João Bulles[1] are not half so smart, half so valorous.'

Thus he went on, bouncing and roaring us deaf. For patriotic rodomontades and flourishes, no nation excels the Portuguese, and no Portuguese the Abadè!

At length, however, all this tasting and praising having been gone through with, we set forth on the wings of holiness, to pay our devoirs to the holy crows. A certain sum having been allotted time immemorial for the maintenance of two birds of this species, we found them very comfortably established in a recess of a cloister adjoining the cathedral, well fed and certainly most devoutly venerated.

The origin of this singular custom dates as high as the days of St Vincent,[2] who was martyrized near the Cape, which bears his name, and whose mangled body was conveyed to Lisbon in a boat, attended by crows. These disinterested birds, after seeing it decently interred, pursued his murderers with dreadful screams and tore their eyes out. The boat and the crows are painted or sculptured in every corner of the cathedral, and upon several tablets appear emblazoned an endless record of their penetration in the discovery of criminals.

It was growing late when we arrived, and their feathered sanctities were gone quietly to roost; but the sacristans in waiting, the moment they saw us approach, officiously roused them. O, how plump and sleek, and glossy they are! My admiration of their size, their plumage, and their deep-toned croakings carried me, I fear, beyond the bounds of saintly decorum. I was just stretching out my hand to stroke their feathers, when the missionary checked me with a solemn forbidding look. The rest of the company, aware of the proper ceremonial, kept a respectful distance, whilst the sacristan, and a toothless priest, almost bent double with age, communicated a long string of miraculous anecdotes concerning the present holy crows, their immediate predecessors, and other holy crows in the old time before them.

To all these super-marvellous narrations, the missionary appeared to listen with implicit faith, and never opened his lips during the time we remained in the cloister, except to enforce our veneration, and exclaim with pious composure, '*honorado corvo*.'[3] I really believe we should have stayed till midnight, had not a page arrived from her Majesty to summon the Marquis of M—— and his almoner away.

My curiosity being fully satisfied upon the subject of the holy crows, I was easily persuaded by the Grand Prior to move off, and drive through the principal streets to see the illuminations in honour of the Infanta, consort to Don Gabriel of Spain,[4] who had produced a prince. A great many idlers being abroad upon the same errand, we proceeded with difficulty, and were

---

[1] Meaning 'John Bulls', i.e. Englishmen.
[2] St Vincent of Saragossa (d. 304), persecuted by various Roman emperors.
[3] Holy crow.
[4] Gabriel, younger son of Charles I of Spain.

very near having the wheels of our carriage dislocated in attempting to pass an old fashioned, preposterous coach, belonging to one of the dignitaries of the patriarchal cathedral. I cannot launch forth in praise of the illuminations; but some rockets which were let off in the Terreiro do Paço,[1] surprised me by the vast height to which they rose, and the unusual number of clear blue stars into which they burst. The Portuguese excel in fireworks; the late poor, drivelling, saintly king having expended large sums in bringing this art to perfection.

From the Terreiro do Paço we drove to the great square, in which the palace of the Inquisition is situated.[2] There we found a vast mob, to whom three or four Capuchin preachers were holding forth upon the glories and illuminations of a better world. I should have listened not uninterested to their harangues, which appeared, from the specimen I caught of them, to be full of fire and frenzy, had not the Grand Prior, in perpetual awe of the rheumatism, complained of the night, so we drove home. Every apartment of the house was filled with the thick vapour of wax-torches, which had been set most loyally a blazing. I fumed and fretted and threw open the windows. Away went the Grand Prior, and in came the Policarpio,[3] the famous tenor singer, who entertained us with several bravura airs of glib and surprising volubility, before supper and during it, in a style equally professional, with many private anecdotes of the *haute noblesse*,[4] his principal employers, not infinitely to their advantage.

I longed, in return, to have enlarged a little upon the adventures of the holy crows, but prudently repressed my inclination. It would ill-become a person so well treated as I had been by the crowfanciers, to handle such subjects with any degree of levity.

LETTER XXXI

Oct. 19th, 1787

My health improves every day. The clear exhilarating weather we now enjoy calls forth the liveliest sense of existence. I ride, walk, and climb, as long as I please, without fatiguing myself. The valley of Collares affords me a source of perpetual amusement. I have discovered a variety of paths which lead through chestnut copses and orchards to irregular green spots, where self-sown bays and citron-bushes hang wild over the rocky margin of a little river, and drop their fruit and blossoms into the stream. You may ride for miles along the bank of this delightful water, catching endless perspectives of

---

[1] Now the Praça do Comércio in the centre of Lisbon.
[2] Rossio Square, officially Praça D. Pedro IV.
[3] Polycarpio José Antonio da Silva (1745–1803), tenor at the Royal Chapel, teacher and composer.
[4] Higher aristocracy.

flowery thickets, between the stems of poplar and walnut. The scenery is truly elysian, and exactly such as poets assign for the resort of happy spirits.

The mossy fragments of rock, grotesque pollards, and rustic bridges you meet with at every step, recall Savoy and Switzerland to the imagination; but the exotic cast of the vegetation, the vivid green of the citron, the golden fruitage of the orange, the blossoming myrtle, and the rich fragrance of a turf, embroidered with the brightest-coloured and most aromatic flowers, allow me without a violent stretch of fancy to believe myself in the garden of the Hesperides,[1] and to expect the dragon under every tree. I by no means like the thoughts of abandoning these smiling regions, and have been twenty times on the point this very day of revoking the orders I have given for my journey. Whatever objections I may have had to Portugal seem to vanish, since I have determined to leave it; for such is the perversity of human nature, that objects appear the most estimable precisely at the moment when we are going to lose them.

There was this morning a mild radiance in the sunbeams, and a balsamic serenity in the air, which infused that voluptuous listlessness, that desire of remaining imparadised in one delightful spot, which, in classical fictions, was supposed to render those who had tasted the lotus forgetful of country, of friends, and of every tie.[2] My feelings were not dissimilar, I loathed the idea of moving away.

Though I had entered these beautiful orchards soon after sunrise, the clocks of some distant conventual churches had chimed hour after hour before I could prevail upon myself to quit the spreading odoriferous bay-trees under which I had been lying. If shades so cool and fragrant invited to repose, I must observe that never were paths better calculated to tempt the laziest of beings to a walk, than those which opened on all sides, and are formed of a smooth dry sand, bound firmly together, composing a surface as hard as gravel.

These level paths wind about amongst a labyrinth of light and elegant fruit-trees; almond, plum, and cherry, something like the groves of Tonga-taboo, as represented on Cook's voyages;[3] and to increase the resemblance, neat cane fences and low open sheds, thatched with reeds, appear at intervals, breaking the horizontal lines of the perspective.

I had now lingered and loitered away pretty nearly the whole morning, and though, as far as scenery could authorize and climate inspire, I might fancy myself an inhabitant of elysium, I could not pretend to be sufficiently ethereal to exist without nourishment. In plain English, I was extremely hungry. The pears, quinces, and oranges which dangled above my head, although fair to the eye, were neither so juicy nor gratifying to the palate, as might have been expected from their promising appearance.

Being considerably

[1] See *above*, p. 202 n. 6.
[2] Lotus eaters were a fabulous people in Greek mythology.
[3] Captain James Cook (1728–79), *A Voyage to the Pacific Ocean* . . . (1776–80).

More than a mile immersed within the wood,[1]

and not recollecting by which clue of a path I could not get out of it, I remained at least half-an-hour deliberating which way to turn myself. The sheds and enclosures I have mentioned were put together with care and even nicety, it is true, but seemed to have no other inhabitants than flocks of bantams, strutting about and destroying the eggs and hopes of many an insect family. These glistening fowls, like their brethren described in Anson's[2] voyages, as animating the profound solitudes of the island of Tinian, appeared to have no master.

At length, just as I was beginning to wish myself very heartliy in a less romantic region, I heard the loud, though not unmusical, tones of a powerful female voice, echoing through the arched green avenues; presently, a stout ruddy young peasant, very picturesquely attired in brown and scarlet, came hoydening along, driving a mule before her, laden with two enormous panniers of grapes. To ask for a share of this luxuriant load, and to compliment the fair driver, was instantaneous on my part, but to no purpose. I was answered by a sly wink, 'We all belong to Senhor José Dias, whose corral, or farm-yard, is half a league distant. There, Senhor, if you follow that road, and don't puzzle yourself by straying to the right or left, you will soon reach it, and the bailiff, I dare say, will be proud to give you as many grapes as you please. Good morning, happy days to you! I must mind my business.'

Seating herself between the tantalizing panniers, she was gone in an instant, and I had the good luck to arrive straight at the wicket of a rude, dry wall, winding up and down several bushy slopes in a wild irregular manner. If the outside of this enclosure was rough and unpromising, the interior presented a most cheering scene of rural opulence. Droves of cows and goats milking; ovens, out of which huge cakes of savoury bread had just been taken; ranges of beehives, and long pillared sheds, entirely tapestried with purple and yellow muscadine grapes, half candied, which were hung up to dry. A very good-natured, classical-looking magister pecorum,[3] followed by two well-disciplined, though savage-eyed dogs, whom the least glance of their master prevented from barking, gave me a hearty welcome, and with a genuine hospitality not only allowed me the free range of his domain, but set whatever it produced in the greatest perfection before me. A contest took place between two or three curly-haired, chubby-faced children, who should be first to bring me walnuts fresh from the shell, bowls of milk, and cream-cheeses, made after the best of fashions, that of the province of Alemtejo.[4]

I found myself so abstracted from the world in this retirement, so perfectly transported back some centuries into primitive patriarchal times, that I don't recollect having ever enjoyed a few hours of more delightful calm. 'Here,' did

---

[1] Dryden. [Beckford's note]
[2] George, Baron (1697–1762), who travelled around the world in 1740–44 and published an account of his journey in 1748.
[3] Leader of the pack.
[4] A province to the S.E. of Lisbon, bordering on Spain.

I say to myself, 'am I out of the way of courts and ceremonies, and common-place visitations, or salutations, or gossip,' But, alas! how vain is all one thinks or says to one's self nineteen times out of twenty.

Whilst I was blessing my stars for this truce to the irksome bustle of the life I had led ever since her Majesty's arrival at Cintra, a loud hallooing, the cracking of whips, and the tramping of horses, made me start up from the snug corner in which I had established myself, and dispelled all my soothing visions. Luis de Miranda,[1] the colonel of the Cascais regiment, an intimate confidant and favourite of the Prince of Brazil, broke in upon me with a thousand (as he thought) obliging reproaches, for having deserted Ramalhão the very morning he had come on purpose to dine with me, and to propose a ride after dinner to a particular point of the Cintra mountains, which commands, he assured me, such a prospect as I had not yet been blessed with in Portugal. 'It is not even now,' said he, 'too late. I have brought your horses along with me, whom I found fretting and stamping under a great tree at the entrance of these foolish lanes. Come, get into your stirrups for God's sake, and I will answer for your thinking yourself well repaid by the scene I shall disclose to you.'

As I was doomed to be disturbed and talked out of the elysium in which I had been lapped for these last seven or eight hours, it was no matter in what position, whether on foot or horseback; I therefore complied, and away we galloped. The horses were remarkably sure-footed, or else, I think, we must have rolled down the precipices; for our road,

If road it could be call'd where road was none,

led us by zigzags and short cuts over steeps and acclivities about three or four leagues, till reaching a heathy desert, where a solitary cross staring out of a few weather-beaten bushes, marked the highest point of this wild eminence, one of the most expansive prospects of sea, and plain, and distant mountains, I ever beheld, burst suddenly upon me, rendered still more vast, aërial, and indefinite, by the visionary, magic vapour of the evening sun.

After enjoying a moment or two the general effect, I began tracing out the principal objects in the view, as far, that is to say, as they could be traced, through the medium of the intense glowing haze. I followed the course of the Tagus, from its entrance till it was lost in the low estuaries beyond Lisbon. Cascais appeared with its long reaches of wall and bomb-proof casemates like a Moorish town,[2] and by the help of a glass I distinguished a tall palm lifting itself above a cluster of white buildings.

'Well,' said I, to my conductor, 'this prospect has certainly charms worth seeing; but not sufficient to make me forget that it is high time to get home and refresh ourselves.' 'Not so fast,' was the answer, 'we have still a great deal more to see.'

---

[1] See *above*, p. 246 n. 1.

[2] The Moors occupied Lisbon until 1147 when they were expelled by Afonso Henriques (1109–85), first King of Portugal.

Having acquired, I can hardly tell why or wherefore, a sheep-like habit of following wherever he led, I spurred after him down a rough declivity, thick strewn with rolling stones and pebbles. At the bottom of this descent, a dreary sun-burnt plain extended itself far and wide. Whilst we dismounted and halted a few minutes to give our horses breath. I could not help observing, that the view we were now contemplating but ill-rewarded the risk of breaking our necks in riding down such rapid declivities. He smiled, and asked me whether I saw nothing at all interesting in the prospect. 'Yes,' said I, 'a sort of caravan I perceive, about a quarter of a mile off, is by no means uninteresting; that confused group of people in scarlet, with gleaming arms and sumpter-mules,[1] and those striped awnings stretched from ruined walls, present exactly that kind of scenery I should expect to meet with in the neighbourhood of Grand Cairo.' 'Come then,' said he, 'it is time to clear up this mystery, and tell you for what purpose we have taken such a long and fatiguing ride. The caravan which strikes you as being so very picturesque, is composed of the attendants of the Prince of Brazil, who has been passing the whole day upon a shooting-party, and is just at this moment taking a little repose beneath yonder awnings. It was by his desire I brought you here, for I have his commands to express his wishes of having half-an-hour's conversation with you, unobserved, and in perfect incognito. Walk on as if you were collecting plants or taking sketches, I will apprize his royal highness, and you will meet as it were by chance, and without any form. No one shall be near enough to hear a word you say to each other, for I will take my station at the distance of at least one hundred paces, and keep off all spies and intruders.'

I did as I was directed. A little door in the ruined wall, against which an awning was fixed, opened, and there appeared a young man of rather a prepossessing figure, fairer and ruddier than most of his countrymen, who advanced towards me with a very pleasant engaging countenance, moved his hat in a dignified graceful manner, and after insisting upon my being covered, began addressing himself to me with great precipitation, in a most fluent lingua-franca, half Italian and half Portuguese. This jargon is very prevalent at the Ajuda[2] palace, where Italian singers are in much higher request and fashion than persons of deeper tone and intellect.

The first question his royal highness honoured me with was, whether I had visited his cabinet of instruments. Upon my answering in the affirmative, and that the apparatus appeared to me extremely perfect, and in admirable order, he observed, 'The arrangement is certainly good, for one of my particular friends, a very learned man, had made it; but notwithstanding the high price I have paid, your Ramsdens and Dollonds have treated themselves more

[1] Pack-mules.
[2] The royal chapel of the Ajuda, though somewhat fallen from the unequalled splendour it boasted during the sing-song days of the late king, Don Joseph, still displayed some of the finest specimens of vocal manufacture which Italy could furnish. It possessed, at the same time, Carlo Reina, Ferracuti, Totti, Fedelino, Ripa, Gelati, Venanzio, Biagino, and Marini – all these *virtuosi*, with names ending in vowels, were either *contraltos* of the softest note, or *sopranos* of the highest squeakery. [Beckford's note]

generously than me. I believe,' continued his royal highness, 'according to what the Duke d'Alafoens has repeatedly assured me, I am conversing with a person who had no weak, blind prejudices, in favour of his country, and who sees things as they are, not as they have been, or as they ought to be. That commercial greediness the English display in every transaction has cost us dear in more than one particular.'

He then ran over the ground Pombal[1] had so often trodden bare, both in his state papers and in various publications which had been promulgated during his administration, and I soon perceived of what school his royal highness was a disciple.

'We deserve all this,' continued he, 'and worse, for our tame acquiescence in every measure your cabinet dictates; but no wonder, oppresses and debased as we are, by ponderous, useless institutions. When there are so many drones in a hive, it is in vain to look for honey. Were you not surprised, were you not shocked, at finding us so many centuries behind the rest of Europe?'

I bowed, and smiled. This spark of approbation induced, I believe, his royal highness to blaze forth into a flaming encomium upon certain reforms and purifications which were carrying on in Brabant, under the auspices of his most sacred apostolic Majesty Joseph the Second. 'I have the happiness,' continued the Prince, 'to correspond not unfrequently with this enlightened sovereign. The Duke d'Alafoens, who has likewise the advantage of communicating with him, never fails to give me the detail of these salutary proceedings. When shall we have sufficient manliness to imitate them!'

Though I bowed and smiled again, I could not resist taking the liberty of observing that such very rapid and vigorous measures as those his imperial Majesty had resorted to, were more to be admired than imitated; that people who had been so long in darkness, if too suddenly broken in upon by a stream of effulgence, were more likely to be blinded than enlightened; and that blows given at random by persons whose eyes were closed were dangerous, and might fall heaviest perhaps in directions very opposite to those for which they were intended. This was rather bold, and did not seem to please the novice in boldness.

After a short pause, which allowed him, at least, an opportunity of taking breath, he looked steadily at me, and perceiving my countenance arrayed in the best expression of admiration I could throw into it, resumed the thread of his philosophical discourse, and even condescended to detail some very singular and, as they struck me, most perilous projects. Continuing to talk on with an increased impetus (like those whose steps are accelerated by running down hill) he dropped some vague hints of measures that filled me not only with surprise, but with a sensation approaching to horror. I bowed, but I could not smile. My imagination, which had caught the alarm at the extraordinary nature of the topics he was discoursing upon, conjured up a train of appalling images, and I asked myself more than once whether I was not under the influence of a distempered dream.

[1] See *above*, p. 227 n. 6.

Being too much engaged in listening to himself to notice my confusion, he worked as hard as a pioneer in clearing away the rubbish of ages, entered minutely and not unlearnedly into the ancient jurisprudence and maxims of his country, its relations with foreign powers, and the rank from whence it had fallen in modern times, to be attributed in a great measure, he observed, to a blind and mistaken reliance upon the selfish politics of our predominant island. Although he did not spare my country, he certainly appeared not over partial to his own. He painted its military defects and priest-ridden policy in vivid colours. In short, this part of our discourse was a '*deploratio Lusitanicæ Gentis,*'[1] full as vehement as that which the celebrated Damien a Goes, to show his fine Latin and fine humanity, poured forth some centuries ago over the poor wretched Laplanders.

Not approving in any degree the tendency of all this display, I most heartily prayed it might end. Above an hour had passed since it began, and flattered as I was by the protraction of so condescending a conference, I could not help thinking that these fountains of honour are fountains of talk and not of mercy; they flow over, if once set a going, without pity or moderation. Persons in supreme stations, whom no one ventures to contradict, run on at a furious rate. You frequently flatter yourself they are exhausted; but you flatter yourself in vain. Sometimes indeed, by way of variety, they contradict themselves, and then the debate is carried on between self and self, to the desperation of their subject auditors, who, without being guilty of a word in reply, are involved in the same penalty as the most captious disputant. This was my case. I scarcely uttered a syllable after my first unsuccessful essay; but thousands of words were nevertheless lavished upon me, and innumerable questions proposed and answered by the questioner with equal rapidity.

In return for the honour of being admitted to this monological dialogue, I kept bowing and nodding; and towards the close of the conference, contrived to smile again pretty decently. His royal highness, I learned afterwards, was satisfied with my looks and gestures, and even bestowed a brevet[2] upon me of a great deal more erudition than I possessed or pretended to.

The sun set, the dews fell, the Prince retired, Louis de Miranda followed him, and I remounted my horse with an indigestion of sounding phrases, and the most confirmed belief that '*the church was in danger.*'

Tired and exhausted, I threw myself on the sofa the moment I reached Ramalhão; but the agitation of my spirits would not allow me any respose. I swallowed some tea with avidity, and driving to the palace, evocated the archbishop confessor, who had been locked up about half-an-hour in his interior cabinet.[3] To him I related all that had passed at this unsought, unexpected interview. The consequences in time developed themselves.[4]

---

[1] A lament on the Portuguese.
[2] A document conferring a privilege from a sovereign.
[3] Small room or bureau.
[4] See *above*, p. 256 n. 1.

LETTER XXXII

Nov. 9th, 1787

M—— and his principal almoner, a renowned missionary, and one of the most eloquent preachers in her Majesty's dominions, were at my door by ten, waiting to take me with them to the convent of Boa Morte.[1] This is a true Golgotha, a place of many skulls, for its inhabitants, though they live, move, and have a sort of being, are little better than skeletons. The priest who officiated appeared so emaciated and cadaverous, that I could hardly have supposed he would have had strength sufficient to elevate the chalice. It did not, however, fall from his hands, and having finished his mass, a second phantom tottered forth and began another. From the pictures and images of more than ordinary ghastliness which cover the chapels and cloisters, and from the deep contrition apparent in the tears, gestures, and ejaculations of the faithful who resort to them, I fancy no convent in Lisbon can be compared with this austerity and devotion.

M—— shook all over with piety, and so did his companion, whose knees are become horny with frequent kneelings, and who, if one is to believe Verdeil. will end his days in a hermitage, or go mad, or perhaps both. He pretends, too, that it is this grey-beard that had added new fuel to the flame of M——'s devotion, and that by mutually encouraging each other, they will soon produce fruits worthy of Bedlam,[2] if not of Paradise. To be sure, this father may boast a conspicuously devout turn, and a most resolute manner of thumping himself; but he must not be too vain. In Lisbon there are at least fifty or sixty thousand good souls, who, without having travelled so far, thump full as sonorously as he. This morning, at Boa Morte, one shrivelled sinner remained the whole time the masses lasted with outstretched arms, in the shape and with all the inflexible stiffness of an old-fashioned branched candlestick. Another contrite personage was so affected at the moment of consecration, that he flattened his nose on the pavement, and licked the dirt and dust with which it was thickly encrusted.

I must confess that, notwithstanding this very superior display of sanctity, I was not sorry to escape from the dingy cloisters of the convent, and breathe the pure air, and look up at the blue exhilerating sky. The weather being delightful, we drove to several distant parts of the town, to which I was yet a stranger. Returning back by the Bairro Alto,[3] we looked into a new house, just finished building at an enormous expense, by João Ferreira,[4] who, from an humble retailer of leather, has risen, by the archbishop's favour, to the

---

[1] S. Jesus da Boa Morte, an austere Capuchin monastery founded in 1736; references to M—— are to Dom Diogo, 5th Marquis of Marialva.

[2] Mental institution.

[3] A district of Lisbon, meaning 'high quarter'.

[4] João Ferreira (d. 1788), a wealthy Lisbon merchant who lived in the Bairro Alto.

possession of some of the most lucrative contracts in Portugal. Uglier-shaped apartments than those the poor shoe-man had contrived for himself I never beheld. The hangings are of satin of the deepest blue, and the fiercest and most sulphureous yellow. Every ceiling is daubed over with allegorical paintings, most indifferently executed, and loaded with gilt ornaments, in the style of those splendid sign-posts which some years past were the glory of High-Holborn and St Giles's.

We were soon tired of all this finery, and as it was growing late, made the best of our way to Belem. Whilst M—— was writing letters, I walked out with Don Pedro on the verandas of the palace, which are washed by the Tagus, and flanked with turrets. The views are enchanting, and the day being warm and serene, I enjoyed them in all their beauty. Several large vessels passed by as we were leaning over the balustrades, and almost touched us with their streamers. Even frigates and ships of the first rate approach within a quarter of a mile of the palace.

There was a greater crowd of attendants than usual round our table at dinner to-day, and the huge massy dishes were brought up by a long train of gentlemen and chaplains, several of them decorated with the orders of Avis[1] and Christ. This attendance had quite a feudal air, and transported the imagination to the days of chivalry, when great chieftains were waited upon like kings, by noble vassals.

The Portuguese had need have the stomachs of ostriches to digest the loads of savoury viands with which they cram themselves. Their vegetables, their rice, their poultry, are all stewed in the essence of ham, and so strongly seasoned with pepper and spices, that a spoonful of peas, or a quarter of an onion, is sufficient to set one's mouth in a flame. With such a diet, and the continual swallowing of sweetmeats, I am not surprised at their complaining so often of head-aches and vapours.

Several of the old Marquis of M——'s confidants and buffoons crept forth to have a peep at the stranger, and hear the famous missionary descant upon martyrdom and miracles. The scenery of Boa Morte being fresh in his thoughts, his descriptions were gloomy and appalling: Don Pedro, his sisters, and his cousin, the young Conde d'Atalaya,[2] gathered round him with all the trembling eagerness of children who hunger and thirst after hobgoblin stories. You may be sure he sent them not empty away. A blacker dose of legendary superstition was never administered. The Marchionesss seemed to swallow these terrific narrations with nearly as much avidity as her children, and the old Abade, dropping his chin in a woful manner, produced an enormous rosary, and kept thumbing his beads and mumbling orisons.

M—— had luckily been summoned to the palace by a special mandate from his royal mistress. Had he been of the party, I fear Verdeil's prophecy would have been accomplished, for never did mortal hold forth with so much scaring energy as this enthusiastic preacher. The most terrible denunciations

---

[1] Dynastic house of Portugal which began in 1495 with the accession of King Manuel I.
[2] Now Marquis of Tancos. [Beckford's note]

of divine wrath which ever were thundered forth by ancient or modern writers of sermons and homilies recurred to his memory, and he dealt them about him with a vengeance. The last half hour of the discourse we were all in total darkness, — nobody had thought of calling for lights: the children were huddled together, scarce venturing to move or breathe. It was a most singular scene.

Full of the ghastly images the good father had conjured up in my imagination, I returned home alone in my carriage, shivering and shuddering. My friends were out, and nothing could be more dreary than the appearance of my fireless apartments.

TRAVEL DIARIES

IV

From *Recollections of an Excursion to the Monasteries of Alcobaça and Batalha*, 1835. This extract is from *The Travel Diaries of William Beckford of Fonthill* by Guy Chapman, 2 Vols, London, 1928. Chapman's edition was based on the only edition in Beckford's lifetime, that of 1835. The extract is from Volume 2.

ADVERTISEMENT

The other day, in examining some papers, I met with very slight notes of this Excursion. Flattering myself that, perhaps, they might not be totally unworthy of expansion, I invoked the powers of memory – and behold, up rose the whole series of recollections I am now submitting to that indulgent Public, which has shown more favour to my former sketches than they merited.

London, June 1835

ALCOBAÇA AND
BATALHA

FIRST DAY

The Prince Regent of Portugal,[1] for reasons with which I was never entirely acquainted, took it into his royal head, one fair morning, to desire I would pay a visit to the monasteries of Alcobaça and Batalha,[2] and to name my intimate and particular friends, the Grand Prior of Aviz, and the Prior of St Vincent's, as my conductors and companions.[3] Nothing could be more gracious, and, in many respects, more agreeable, still, just at this moment, having what I thought much pleasanter engagements nearer home, I cannot pretend that I felt so much enchanted as I ought to have been.

Upon communicating the supreme command to the two prelates, they discovered not the smallest token of surprise; it seemed they were fully prepared for it. The Grand Prior observed that the weather was dreadfully hot, and the roads execrable: the other prelate appeared more animated, and quite ready for the expedition. I thought I detected in one corner of his lively, intelligent eye, a sparkle of hope that, when returned from his little cruise of observation, the remarks it was likely enough to inspire might lead to more intimate conferences at Queluz,[4] and bring him into more frequent collision with royalty.

As my right reverend companions had arranged not to renounce one atom of their habitual comforts and conveniences, and to take with them their confidential acolytes and secretaries, as well as some of their favourite quadrupeds, we had in the train of the latter-mentioned animals a rare rabble of grooms, ferradors,[5] and mule-drivers. To these, my usual followers being added, we formed altogether a caravan which, camels and dromedaries excepted, would have cut no despicable figure even on the route of Mecca or Mesched-Ali!

The rallying point, the general rendezvous for the whole of this heterogeneous assemblage, was my quinta of San José, commanding in full prospect

---

[1] See *above*, p. 256 n. 2.

[2] Alcobaça was founded in the twelfth century by the Cistercian Order; Batalha was built after the Portuguese victory (over the Spanish) at Aljubarrota in 1385.

[3] There is some doubt as to whether the Prior of St Vincent accompanied the travellers or met them at Tojal. See *Alexander, Intro*, xx.

[4] Royal palace near Lisbon, finished in 1760.

[5] Horse-drivers.

the entrance of the Tagus, crowded with vessels arriving from every country under the heavens, messengers of joy to some, of sorrow to others, but all with expanded sails equally brightening in the beams of the cheerful sun, and scudding along over the blue sparkling waves with equal celerity.

'Here I am, my dear friend,' said the Grand Prior to me as I handed him out of his brother the old Marquis of Marialva's[1] most sleepifying dormeuse, which had been lent to him expressly for this *trying* occasion. 'Behold me at last,' (at last indeed, this being the third put-off I had experienced,) 'ever delighted with your company, but not so much so with the expedition we are going to undertake.'

'I hope it will not turn out so unpleasant after all,' was my answer: 'for my own part, I quite long to see Alcobaça.'

'So do not I,' rejoined the Grand Prior:, 'but let that pass. Is Ehrhart[2] come? is Franchi[3] ready? Has the first secured the medicine-chest he was in such an agony about the other day, and the second the piano-forte he swore he would break to pieces unless it would get into better tune?'

'All safe – all waiting – and dinner, too, my dear Lord Prior; and after that, let us get off. No easy matter, by the bye, even yet, some of the party being such adepts at dawdling.'

Why the Grand Prior should have dreaded the journey so much I really could not imagine, every pains having been taken to make it so easy and smooth. It was settled he should loll in his dormeuse or in my chaise just as he best pleased, and look at nothing calculated to excite the fatigue of reflection; topographical inquiries were to be waived completely, and no questions asked about who endowed such a church or raised such a palace. We were to proceed, or rather creep along, by short and facile stages; stopping to dine, and sup, and repose, as delectably as in the most commodious of homes. Everything that could be thought of, or even dreamed of, for our convenience or relaxation, was to be carried in our train, and nothing left behind but Care and Sorrow; two spectres, who, had they dared to mount on our shoulders, would have been driven off with a high hand by the Prior of St Vincent's, than whom a more delightful companion never existed since the days of those polished and gifted canons and cardinals who formed such a galaxy of talent and facetiousness round Leo the Tenth.[4]

We were absolutely roused form our repast, over which the Prior of St Vincent's gay animated conversation was throwing its usual brilliance, by a racket and hubbub on the sea-shore that was perfectly distracting. The space between my villa and the sea was entirely blocked up, half the population of Belém having poured forth to witness our departure. The lubberly drivers of

---

[1] The Old Marquis was the Fourth Marquis (1713–99), father of Dom Diogo, Beckford's friend.

[2] Dr Ehrhart, Beckford's physician who had replaced Dr Verdeil.

[3] Gregorio Franchi (1770–1828), student at Patriarchal Seminary who was Beckford's lover and later confidant. See *above*, p. xv.

[4] Pope Leo X (1475–1521), Pope from 1513, one of the Medici family.

the baggage-carts were fighting and squabbling amongst themselves for precedence. One of the most lumbering of these ill-constructed vehicles, laden with a large heavy marquee, had its hind wheels already well buffeted by the waves. At length it moved off; and then burst forth such vociferation and such deafening shouts of 'Long live the Prince!' and 'Long live the Marialvas, and all their friends into the bargain!' – the Englishman of course included – as I expected, would have fixed a headache for life upon the unhappy Grand Prior.

Amongst other noises which gave him no small annoyance, might be reckoned the outrageous snortings and neighings of both his favourite high-pampered chaise-horses, out of compliment to one of my delicate English mares, who was trying to get through the crowd with a most engaging air of sentimental retiring modesty.

Half laughing and half angry lest some unfortunate kick or plunge might deprive me of her agreeable services, I refrained not from crying out to the Grand Prior, 'For pity's sake, let us dawdle and doodle no longer, but drive through this mob if it be possible. You see what a disturbance the glorious fuss which has been making about this journey has occasioned; you see the result of a surfeit of superfluities: really, if we had been setting forth to explore the kingdom of Prester John, or the identical spot where Don Sebastian[1] left his bones, (if true it be that the shores of Africa, and not some pet dungeon of King Philip's, received them,) we could scarcely have gotten together a grander array of incumbrances. At this rate, we shall have occasion to put our tent in requisition this very night, unless we defer our journey again, and sleep under my roof at San José.'

'No, no,' said the Prior of St Vincent's, 'we shall sleep at my convent's pleasant quinta of Tojal. I shall set off with my people immediately to prepare for your reception.'

The deed followed the word: his attendant muleteers cracked their whips in the most imposing style – his ferradors pushed on – the crowd divided – a passage was cleared; the Grand Prior, ordering his dormeuse to follow, got into my enormous travelling chaise, and by the efforts of six stout mules we soon reached Bemfica.

Beyond this village, a shady lane overhung by elms brought us to Nossa Senhora de Luz; a large pile of buildings in the majestic style which prevailed during the Spanish domination in Portugal[2] but much shattered by the earthquake. From hence we passed on to Lumiares, through intricate paved roads bordered by aloes, sprouting up to the height of ten or twelve feet, in shape and colour not unlike gigantic asparagus.

Lumiares contains a quinta belonging to the Marquess of Anjeja,[3] upon which immense sums have been lavished for the wise purpose of pebbling

[1] King of Portugal (1554–78), who lead a disastrous crusade against the Moors and died with the flower of Portuguese aristocracy at the battle of Alcacer Quibir in 1578.

[2] From 1580–1640 Portugal was occupied by Spain.

[3] Pedro José de Noronha (1716–88), 3rd Marquis, one-time prime minister.

alleys in quaint mosaic patterns, red, black, and blue; building colossal reservoirs for gold and silver fish, painting their smooth plastered sides with diverse flaming colours, and cutting a steep hill into a succession of stiff terraces, under the sole pretext, one should think of establishing flights of awkward narrow marble steps to communicate one with the other, for they did not appear to lead to any other part of the garden.

The road from Lumiares to Loures is conducted along a valley, between sloping acclivities variegated by fields of grain, and wild shrubby pastures. The soft air of the evening was delightful; and the lowing of herds descending from the hills to slake their thirst after a sultry day, at springs and fountains, full of pastoral charm.

It grew dark when we passed the village of Tojal, and crossing a bridge over the river Trancaz, entered the woody domain of the monks of St Vincent. Lights glimmering at the extremity of an avenue of orange-trees directed us to the house, a low picturesque building, half villa, half hermitage. Our reception was so truly exhilarating, so perfectly all in point of comfort and luxury that the heart of man or even churchman could desire, that we willingly promised to pass the whole of tomorrow in this cheerful residence, and defer our further progress till the day following.

SIXTH DAY

8th June

I rose early, slipped out of my pompous apartment, strayed about endless corridors – not a soul stirring. Looked into a gloomy hall, much encumbered with gilded ornaments, and grim with the ill-sculptured effigies of kings; and another immense chamber, with white walls covered with pictures in black lacquered frames, most hideously unharmonious.

One portrait, the full size of life, by a very ancient Portugese artist named Vasquez,[1] attracted my minute attention. It represented no less interesting a personage than St Thomas à Becket, and looked the character in perfection, – lofty in stature and expression of countenance; pale, but resolute, like one devoted to death in his great cause; the very being Dr Lingard has portrayed in his admirable History.

From this chamber I wandered down several flights of stairs to a cloister of the earliest Norman architecture, having in the centre a fountain of very primitive form, spouting forth clear water abundantly into a marble basin. Twisting and straggling over this uncouth mass of sculpture are several orange-trees, gnarled and crabbed, but covered with fruit and flowers, their branches grotesque and fantastic, exactly such as a Japanese would delight in, and copy on his caskets and screens; their age most venerable, for the traditions of the convent assured me that they were the very first imported

---

[1] Possibly Nuno Gonçalves (active 1450–67), who painted the monks at Alcobaça.

from China into Portugal. There was some comfort in these objects; every other in the place looked dingy and dismal, and steeped in a green and yellow melancholy.

On the damp, stained and mossy walls, I noticed vast numbers of sepulchral inscriptions (some nearly effaced) to the memory of the knights slain at the battle of Aljubarota.[1] I gave myself no trouble to make them out, but continuing my solitary ramble, visited the refectory, a square of seventy or eighty feet, begloomed by dark-coloured painted windows, and disgraced by tables covered with not the cleanest or least unctuous linen in the world.

I had proceeded thus far, when three venerable fathers, of most grave and solemn aspect, made their appearance; to whom having bowed as lowly as Abraham did to his angelic visitors, I received as many profound obeisances in return, and a summons to breakfast. This I readily obeyed: it wanted three-quarters of eight, and I was as hungry as a stripling novice. The Prior of Aviz having supped too amply the night before, did not appear; but he of St Vincent's, all kindness and good digestion, did the honours with cordial grace, and made tea as skilfully as the most complete old dowager in Christendom. My Lord of Alcobaça was absent, – engaged, as I was told, and readily believed, upon conventual affairs of urgent importance.

The repast finished, and not soon, our whole morning was taken up with seeing sights, though not exactly the sights I most wished to see. Some MSS. of the fourteenth century, containing, I have been assured, traditional records of Pedro the Just and the Severe,[2] were what I wished for; but they either could not or would not be found; and instead of being allowed to make this interesting research, or having it made for me, we were conducted to a most gorgeous and glistening sacristy, worthy of Versailles itself, adorned with furbelows of gilt bronze, flaunting over panels of jasper and porphyry: copes and vestments, some almost as ancient as the reign of Alfonzo Henriquez[3] and others embroidered at Rome with gold and pearl, by no means barbaric, were displayed before us in endless succession.

One of the sacristans or treasurers who happened to have a spice of antiquarianism, guessing the bent of my wishes, produced, from a press or ambery elaborately carved, the identical candlesticks of rock-crystal, and a cross of the same material, studded with the most delicately-tinted sapphires, which were taken by the victorious John the First from the King of Castile's portable chapel, after the had-fought conflict of Aljubarota; and several golden reliquaries, as minutely chased and sculptured as any I ever saw at St Denis,[4] though wrought by St Eloy's[5] holy hands: one in particular, the

---

[1] João I of Portugal defeated Juan I of Castile at the battle of Aljubarrota in 1385 thus consolidating Portuguese independence. See *below*, p. 281.
[2] Pedro I of Portugal (1320–67), known for his impartial administration of justice to rich and poor alike.
[3] King Afonso I (?1109–85), who in 1143 declared himself King of Portugal, marking the birth of the nation.
[4] Cloister at St Dénis in Paris, burial place of kings of France.
[5] Bishop of Noyon (c. 588–660).

model of a cathedral in the style of the Sainte Chapelle at Paris, struck me as being admirable. Ten times at least did I examine and almost worship this highly wrought precious specimen of early art, and as many times did my excellent friend the Prior of St Vincent's, who had come in search of me, express a wish that I should not absolutely wear out my eyes or his patience.

'It is growing insufferably warm,' said he, 'and the hour of siesta is arrived; and I cannot help thinking that perhaps it would not be unpleasant for you to retire to your shady chamber: for my part, I can hardly keep my eyes open any longer. But I see this proposal does not suit you – you English are strangely given to locomotion, and I know full well that of all English you are not the least nimble. Here,' continued he, calling a young monk, who was sitting by in a nook of the sacristy peeling walnuts, 'suspend that important occupation, and be pleased to accompany this fidalgo[1] to any part of your domain he likes to ramble to.'

'Right willingly,' answered this sprout of holiness: 'whither shall we go?'

'Through the village, into the open country, if you have no objection,' answered I; 'to any point, in short, where I may enjoy rural scenery, trees, and rocks, and running waters.'

'Trees, and rocks, and running waters!' re-echoed the monk with a vacant stare. 'Had you not better visit our rabbit-warren – the finest in this world? Though, to be sure, the rabbits, poor things! are all asleep at this time of day, and it would be cruel to disturb even them.'

This was a broad hint, but I would not take it. The monk, finding I was bent on he could not imagine what pursuit, and that there was no diverting me from it, tucked up his upper garments, shadowed his sleek round face with an enormous straw hat, offered me another of equal size quite new and glossy, and, with staves in our hands, we set forth like the disciples journeying to Emmaus in some of Poelemburg's smooth landscapes.[2]

We passed through quadrangles after quadrangles, and courts after courts, till, opening a sly door in an obscure corner, which had proved a convenient sally-port, no doubt, for many an agreeable excursion, we found ourselves in a winding alley, bordered by sheds and cottages, with irregular steps leading up to rustic porches and many a vine-bower and many a trellised walk. No human being was to be heard or seen; no poultry were parading about; and except a beautiful white macaw perched on a broken wall, and nestling his bill under his feathers, not a single member of the feathered creation was visible. There was a holy calm in this mid-day silence – a sacredness, as if all nature had been fearful to disturb the slumbers of universal Pan.[3]

I kept, however, straggling on – impiously, it would have been thought in Pagan times – between long stretches of garden-walls overhung by fig-trees, the air so profoundly tranquil that I actually heard a fruit drop from a bough. Sometimes I was enticed down a mysterious lane by the prospect of a crag

[1] Nobleman.
[2] See *above*, p. 199 n. 2.
[3] Greek god of flocks and shepherds.

and a Moorish castle which offered itself to view at its termination, and sometimes under ruined arches which crossed my path in the most pictur esque manner. So I still continued my devious course with a pertinacity that annoyed my lazy conductor – past utterance, it seems; for during our whole excursion we scarcely exchanged a syllable.

At length, he could bear with romanceishness no longer; an irresistible somnolency came over him; and, stretching himself out on the bare ground, in the deep shadow of some tall cypress, he gave way to repose most delectably. I was now abandoned entirely to myself, unsubdued by the quiet of the place, and as active as ever. Some tokens of animation, however, in other beings besides myself would not have been displeasing – the dead silence which prevailed began to oppress me.

At length, a faint musical murmur stole upon my ear: I advanced towards the spot whence it seemed to come – a retired garden-house at the end of a pleasant avenue, which, to add to its pleasantness, had been lately watered. Drawing nearer and nearer, my heart beating quickly all the while, I disting uished the thrilling cadences of a delightful Brasileira (sinha che vem da Bahia)[1] – well known sounds. I looked up to a latticed window just thrown open by a lovely arm – a well known arm: – 'Gracious heavens! Donna Francisca, is it you? What brought you here? What inspired you to exchange Queluz and the Ajuda[2] for this obscure retirement?'

'Ascent these steps, and I will tell you: but your stay must not exceed ten minutes – not a second more.'

'Brief indeed,' answered I: 'I see there is no time to lose.'

Up I sprung – and who should receive me? Not the fascinating songstress – not the lady of the lovely arm, but her sedate though very indulgent mother.

'I know whom you are looking for,' said the matron; 'but it is in vain. You have heard, but are not to see, Francisca, who is no longer the giddy girl you used to dance with; her heart is turned, – nay, do not look so wild, – turned, I tell you, but turned to God. A most holy man, a saint, the very mirror of piety for his years, – he is not yet forty, only think! – operated this blessed change. You know how light-hearted, and almost indiscreetly so, my poor dear heart's comfort was. You recollect hearing, and you were terribly angry, I remember, that the English Padre told the Inviada it was shameful how very rapturously my poor dear girl rattled here castanets, and threw back her head, and put forward every other part of her dear little person, at the Factory[3] ball – Shame ON HIM, scandalous old crabbed heretic! Well, it so happened that my Lord High Almoner came to court upon state affairs, accompanied by the precious man I have been talking of, – the most exem plary monk in that noble convent, and its right hand. One day at Queluz he saw my daughter dancing divinely, as you know she did; he heard her sing - you know how she warbles – she still warbles; HE said (and he has such an

---

[1] Brazilian song entitled 'the young lady from Bahia'.
[2] Royal palaces.
[3] English merchant community in Portugal.

eye,) that under the veil of all this levity were lurking the seeds of grace. 'I will develope them.' exclaimed this saint upon earth, in a transport of holy fervour. So he set about it, - and a miraculous metamorphosis did he perform: my gay, my dissipated child, became an example of serious piety; no flirting, no racketing,[1] nothing but pious discourse with this best of discoursers. Two months passed away in this exemplary manner. When the time came for my Lord High Almoner to return, our holy friend was in duty bound to accompany him. What was to be done? Francisca had forgotten everything and everybody else in this sinful world; she existed but for this devout personage; she lived but in his holy smiles when he approved her conduct, and almost died under his reproof when any transient little fault of hers occasioned his enjoining her severe penances: and I shudder to think how severe they sometimes were; for, would you believe it? he had made her submit to flagellation – and, more than once, to goadings with sharp points. In due course, the hour of departure arrived. 'We must all die,' said Francisca; 'my hour is come.' She looked all she said: she pined and languished, and, I am convinced, would have kept her word, if I had not said, 'Dearest child, there is but one remedy: it is the will of God we should go to Alcobaça; and to Alcobaça we will go, let all your uncles, cousins, and adorers say what they choose to the contrary.' So we took this house and this garden – a nice little garden – only look at these pretty yellow carnations! - and we are very happy in our little way, entirely given up to devotion, under the guidance of our incomparable spiritual director, who allows us to want for nothing, even in this world. See what fruit! what fine sweetmeats! what a relishing Melgaço ham! look at these baskets!'

She was just lifting up the rich damask covers thrown over them, when a most vigorous 'Hem! hem!! hem!!!' in the rustic street snapped short the thread of her eloquence, by calling her to the balcony with the utmost precipitation – 'Jesu Maria José! – he comes! he comes!' Had she seen a ghost instead of a very substantial friar, she could not have started with greater abruptness; her scared looks showed me the door so intelligibly that I was off in a twinkling; it would have been most indiscreet – nay, sacrilegious, to remain a moment longer.

It was now half-past one, and the world of Alcobaça was alive again – the peasant had resumed her distaff, the monk his breviary, the ox his labour, and the sound of the nora, or water-wheel, was heard in the land. The important hour of dinner at the convent I knew was approaching: I wished to scale the crag above the village, and visit the Moorish castle, which looked most invitingly picturesque, with its varied outline of wall and tower; but I saw a possé of monks and novices advancing from the convent, bowing and beckoning me to return.

So I returned, – and 'twas well I did, as it turned out. Fourteen or fifteen sleek well-fed mules, laden with paniers of neat wicker-work, partially covered with scarlet cloth, were standing about the grand platform before the

---

[1] Debauched social living.

convent; and the reverend father, one of the prime dignitaries of the chapter, who was waiting at the entrance of the apartment assigned to me, pointing to them, put me in mind that last night I had expressed a vehement wish to visit Batalha; adding most graciously, that the wishes of a person so strongly recommended to them as I had been by the good and great Marquis of Ponte de Lima were laws.

'This very night, if it so please you,' said his reverence, 'we sleep at Batalha. The convent is poor and destitute, unworthy – nay, incapable of accommodating such guests as my lords the Grand Priors, and yourself; but I hope we have provided against the chill of a meagre reception. These mules will carry with them whatever may be required for your comfort. To-morrow, I hope, you will return to us; and the following day, should you inflict upon us the misfortune of losing your delightful society, myself and two of my comrades will have the honour of accompanying you as far back as one of our farms called Pedraneira, on your return to Lisbon.'

There was nothing on my part to object to in this arrangement; I fancied too I could discern in it a lurking wish to be quit of our most delightful society, and the turmoil and half-partial restraint it occasioned. Putting on the sweetest smiles of grateful acquiescence, to hear was to obey; everything relating to movements being confirmed by the terzetto of Grand Priors during our repast – copious and splendid as usual.

The carriages drew up very soon after it was ended; my riding horses were brought out, all our respective attendants mustered, and, preceded by a long string of sumpter-mules and baggage-carts, with all their bells in full jingle and all their drivers in full cry, off we set in most formidable array, taking the route of Aljubarota.

Our road, not half so rough as I expected, led us up most picturesquely-shaped steep acclivities, shaded by chesnuts, with here and there a branching pine, for about a league. We then found ourselves on a sort of table-land; and, a mile or two further, in the midst of a straggling village. There was no temptation to leave the snug corner of our comfortable chaises; so we contented ourselves with surveying at our perfect ease the prospect of the famous plain, which formed the termination of a long perspective of antiquated houses.

Here, on this very plain, was fought in 1385, the fierce battle which placed the diadem of Portugal on the brow of the glorious and intrepid bastard. It was down that ravine the Castilian cavalry poured along in utter confusion, so hotly pursued that three thousand were slain. On yonder mound stood the King of Castile's tent and temporary chapel, which he abandoned, with all its rich and jewelled furniture, to the conquerors, and scampered off in such alarm that he scarcely knew whether he had preserved his head on his shoulders, till safe within the walls of Santarem, where he tore his hair and plucked off his beard by handfuls, and raved and ranted like a maniac. – The details of this frantic pluckage are to be found in a letter from the Constable Nuno Alvarez Pereira to the Abbot of Alcobaça.

I tried to inspire my right reverend fellow-travellers with patriotic enthusiasm, and to engage them to cast a retrospective glance upon the days of Lusitanian glory. Times present, and a few flasks of most exquisite wine, the produce of a neighbouring vineyard, engrossed their whole attention. 'Muito bom - primoroso – excellente,'[1] were the only words that escaped their most grateful lips.

The Juiz de Fora [2] of the village, a dabbler in history – for he told us he had read the Chronicles, and who stood courteously and obsequiously on the step of our carriage door, handing us the precious beverage – made some attempts to edge in a word about the battle, and particularly about a certain valiant English knight, whose name he did not even pretend to remember, but who might have been a relation of mine for aught he knew to the contrary. Well, this valiant knight, who had vanquished all the chivalry of France and England, had the honour of being vanquished in his turn by the flower of warriors, the renowned Magriço: a great honour too, for Magriço had excellent taste in the choice of his antagonists, and would only fight with the bravest of the brave. 'Even so,' continued the worthy magistrate, bowing to the earth, 'as our great Camões testifies.' – No answer to all this flourish except 'Ten thousand thanks for your excellent wine: drive on.' And drive on we did with redoubled briskness.

The highest exhilaration prevailed throughout our whole caravan. All my English servants were in raptures, ready to turn Catholics. My famous French cook, in the glow of the moment, unpatriotically declared Clos de Vougeot, puddle compared to Aljubarota, – divine, perfumed ethereal Aljubarota! Dr Ehrhart protested no country under the sun equalled Portugal for curiosities in mineralogy, theology, and wineology – which ology he was convinced was the best of them all. Franchi mounted one of my swiftest coursers – he had never ventured to mount before – and galloped away like the King of Castile on his flight to Santarem. The Grand Prior and all his ecclesiastical cortege fell fast asleep; and it would have been most irreverend not to have followed so respectable an example. I can therefore describe nothing of the remainder of our route.

The sun had sunk and the moon risen, when a tremendous jolt and a loud scream awakened the whole party. Poor Franchi lay sprawling upon the ground; whilst my Arabian, his glossy sides streaming with blood, was darting along like one of the steeds in the Apocalypse; happily his cast-off rider escaped with a slight contusion.

My eyes being fairly open, I beheld a quiet solitary vale, bordered by shrubby hills; a few huts, and but a few, peeping out of the dense masses of foliage; and high above their almost level surface, the great church, with its rich cluster of abbatial buildings, buttresses, and pinnacles, and fretted spires, towering in all their pride, and marking the ground with deep shadows that appeared interminable, so far and so wide were they stretched along. Lights glimmered here and there in various parts of the edifice; but a strong

---

[1] 'Very good – exquisite – excellent'.
[2] Magistrate.

glare of torches pointed out its principal entrance, where stood the whole community waiting to receive us.

Whilst our sumpter-mules were unlading, and ham and pies and sausages were rolling out of plethoric hampers, I thought these poor monks looked on rather enviously. My more fortunate companions – no wretched cadets of the mortification family, but the true elder sons of fat mother church – could hardly conceal their sneers of conscious superiority. A contrast so strongly marked amused me not a little.

The space before the entrance being narrow, there was some difficulty in threading our way through a labyrinth of panniers, and coffers, and baggage, –and mules, as obstinate as their drunken drivers, which is saying a great deal, – and all our grooms, lackeys, and attendants, half asleep, half muddled.

The Batalha Prior and his assistants looked quite astounded when they saw a gauze-curtained bed, and the Grand Prior's fringed pillow, and the Prior of St Vincent's superb coverlid, and basins, and ewers, and other utensils of glittering silver, being carried in. Poor souls! they hardly knew what to do, to say, or be at – one running to the right, another to the left – one tucking up his flowing garments to run faster, and another rebuking him for such a deviation from monastic decorum.

At length, order being somewhat re-established, and some fine painted wax tapers, which were just unpacked, lighted, we were ushered into a large plain chamber, and the heads of the order presented by the humble Prior of Batalha to their superior mightinesses of San Vicente and Aviz. Then followed a good deal of gossiping chat, endless compliments, still longer litanies, and an enormous supper.

One of the monks who partook of it, though almost bent double with age, played his part in excellent style. Animated by ample potations of the very best Aljubarota that ever grew, and which we had taken the provident care to bring with us, he exclaimed lustily. 'Well, this is as it should be – rare doings! such as have not been witnessed at Batalha since a certain progress that great King, John the Fifth, made hither more than half a century ago. I remember every circumstance attending it as clearly as though it had only taken place last week. But only think of the atrocious impudence of the gout! His blessed Majesty had hardly set down to a banquet ten times finer than this, before that accursed malady, patronized by all the devils in hell, thrust its fangs into his toe. I was at that period in the commencement of my noviciate, a handsome lad enough, and had the much-envied honour of laying a cloth of gold cushion under the august feet of our glorious sovereign. No sooner had the extremities of his royal person come in contact with the stiff embroidery, than he roared out as a mere mortal would have done, and looked as black as a thunder-storm; but soon recovering his most happy benign temper, gave me a rouleau[1] of fine, bright, golden coin, and a tap on the head, – ay, on this once comely, now poor old shrivelled head. Oh, he was a gracious, open-hearted, glorious monarch, – the very King of Diamonds

---

[1] Roll.

and Lord of Hearts! Oh, he is in Heaven, in Heaven above! as sure – ay, as sure as I drink your health, most esteemed stranger.'

So saying, he drained a huge silver goblet to the last drop, and falling back in his chair, was carried out, chair and all, weeping, puling, and worse than drivelling, with such maudlin tenderness that he actually marked his track with a flow of liquid sorrows.

As soon as an act of oblivion had been passed over this little sentimental mishap by effacing every trace of it, we all rose up and retired to rest; but little rest, however, was in store for me; the heat of my mid-day ramble, and perhaps some baneful effect from our moon-lit journey, the rays of our cold satellite having fallen whilst I was asleep too directly on my head, had disordered me; I felt disturbed and feverish, a strange jumble of ideas and recollections fermented in my brain – springing in part from the indignant feelings which Donna Francisca's fervour for her monk, and coldness for me, had inspired. I had no wish to sleep, and yet my pleasant retired chamber, with clean white walls, chequered with the reflection of waving boughs, and the sound of a rivulet softened by distance, invited it soothingly. Seating myself in the deep recess of a capacious window which was wide open, I suffered the balsamic air and serene moonlight to quiet my agitated spirits. One lonely nightingale had taken possession of a bay-tree just beneath me, and was pouring forth its ecstatic notes at distant intervals.

In one of those long pauses, when silence itself, enhanced by contrast, seemed to become still deeper, a far different sound than the last I had been listening to caught my ear, – the sound of a loud but melancholy voice echoing through the arched avenues of a vast garden, pronouncing distinctly these appalling words – 'Judgment! judgment! tremble at the anger of an offended God! Woe to Portugal! woe! woe!'

My hair stood on end – I felt as if a spirit were about to pass before me; but instead of some fearful shape – some horrid shadow, such as appeared in vision to Eliphaz, there issued forth from a dark thicket, a tall, majestic, deadly-pale old man: he neither looked about nor above him; he moved slowly on, his eye fixed as stone, sighing profoundly; and at the distance of some fifty paces from the spot where I was stationed, renewed his doleful cry, his fatal proclamation: – 'Woe! woe!' resounded through the still atmosphere, repeated by the echoes of vaults and arches; and the sounds died away, and the spectre-like form that seemed to emit them retired, I know not how nor whither. Shall I confess that my blood ran cold – that all idle, all wanton thoughts left my bosom, and that I passed an hour or two at my window fixed and immovable?

Just as day dawned, I crept to bed and fell into a profound sleep, uninterrupted, I thank Heaven, by dreams.

SEVENTH DAY

9th June

A delightful morning sun was shining in all its splendour, when I awoke, and ran to the balcony, to look at the garden and wild hills, and to ask myself ten times over, whether the form I had seen, and the voice I had heard, were real or imaginary. I had scarcely dressed, and was preparing to sally forth, when a distinct tap at my door, gentle but imperative, startled me.

The door opened, and the Prior of Batalha stood before me. 'You were disturbed, I fear,' said he, 'in the dead of the night, by a wailful voice, loudly proclaiming severe impending judgments. I heard it also, and I shuddered, as I always do when I hear it. Do not, however, imagine that it proceeds from another world. The being who uttered these dire sounds is still upon the earth, a member of our convent – an exemplary, a most holy man – a scion of one of our greatest families, and a near relative of the Duke of Aveiro, of whose dreadful, agonizing fate you must have heard.[1] He was then in the pride of youth and comeliness, gay as sunshine, volatile as you now appear to be. He had accompanied the devoted duke to a sumptuous ball given by your nation to our high nobility: – at the very moment when splendour, triumph, and merriment were at their highest pitch, the executioners of Pombal's[2] decrees, soldiers and ruffians, pounced down upon their prey; he too was of the number arrested – he too was thrown in to a deep, cold dungeon: his life was spared, and, in the course of years and events, the slender, lovely youth, now become a wasted, care-worn man, emerged to sorrow and loneliness.

'The blood of his dearest relatives seemed sprinkled upon every object that met his eyes; he never passed Belém[3] without fancying he beheld, as in a sort of frightful dream, the scaffold, the wheels on which those he best loved had expired in torture. The current of his young, hot blood was frozen; he felt benumbed and paralysed; the world, the court, had no charms for him; there was for him no longer warmth in the sun, or smiles on the human countenance: a stranger to love or fear, or any interest on this side the grave, he gave up his entire soul to prayer; and, to follow that sacred occupation with greater intenseness, renounced every prospect of worldly comfort or greatness, and embraced our order.

'Full eight-and-twenty years has he remained within these walls, so deeply impressed with the conviction of the Duke of Averio's innocence, the atrocious falsehood of that pretended conspiracy, and the consequent unjust

[1] See *above*, p. 238 n. 3.
[2] See *above*, p. 227 n. 6.
[3] Those accused of being conspirators and their families were incarcerated by Pombal in the Tower of Belém, near Lisbon.

tyrannical expulsion of the order of St Ignatius,[1] that he believes – and the belief of so pure and so devout a man is always venerable – that the horrors now perpetrating in France are the direct consequence of that event, and certain of being brought home to Portugal; which kingdom he declares is foredoomed to desolation, and its royal house to punishments worse than death.

'He seldom speaks; he loathes conversation, he spurns news of any kind, he shrinks from strangers; he is constant at his duty in the choir – most severe in his fasts, vigils, and devout observances; he pays me canonical obedience – nothing more: he is a living grave, a walking sepulchre. I dread to see or hear him; for every time he crosses my path, beyond the immediate precincts of our basilica, he makes a dead pause, and repeats the same terrible words you heard last night, with an astounding earnestness, as if commissioned by God himself to deliver them. And, do you know, my lord stranger, there are moments of my existence, when I firmly believe he speaks the words of prophetic truth: and who, indeed, can reflect upon the unheard-of crimes committing in France – the massacres, the desecrations, the frantic blasphemies, and not believe them? Yes, the arm of an avenging God is stretched out – and the weight of impending judgment is most terrible.

'But what am I saying? – why should I fill your youthful bosom with such apprehensions? I came here to pray your forgiveness for last night's annoyance; which would not have taken place, had not the bustle of our preparations to receive your illustrious and revered companions, the Lord Priors, in the best manner our humble means afford, impeded such precautions as might have induced our reverend brother to forego, for once, his dreary nocturnal walk. I have tried by persuasion to prevent it several times before. To have absolutely forbidden it, would have been harsh – nay, cruel – he gasps so piteously for air: besides, it might have been impious to do so. I have taken opinions in chapter upon this matter, which unanimously strengthen my conviction that the spirit of the Most High moves within him; nor dare we impede its utterance.'

I listened with profound seriousness to this remarkable communication; – the Prior read in my countenance that I did so, and was well pleased. Leading the way, he conducted me to a large shady apartment, in which the splash of a neighbouring fountain was distinctly heard. In the centre of this lofty and curiously-groined vaulted hall, resting on a smooth Indian mat, an ample table was spread out with viands and fruits, and liquors cooled in snow. The two Prelates, with the monks deputed from Alcobaça to attend them, were sitting round it. They received me with looks that bespoke the utmost kindness, and at the same time suppressed curiosity; but not a word was breathed of the occurrence of last night, – with which, however, I have not the smallest doubt they were perfectly well acquainted.

I cannot say our repast was lively or convivial; a mysterious gloom seemed

---

[1] St Ignatius de Loyola (1491–1556), founder of the Jesuit Order expelled from Portugal by Pombal in 1759.

brooding over us, and to penetrate the very atmosphere – and yet that atmosphere was all loveliness. A sky of intense azure, tempered by fleecy clouds, discovered itself between the tracery of innumerable arches; the summer airs (*aure estive*) fanned us as we sat; the fountain bubbled on; the perfume of orange and citron flowers was wafted to us from an orchard not far off: but, in spite of all these soft appliances, we remained silent and abstracted.

A sacristan, who came to announce that high mass was on the point of celebration, interrupted our reveries. We all rose up – a solemn grace was said, and the Prior of Batalha taking me most benignantly by the hand, the prelates and their attendants followed. We advanced in procession through courts and cloisters and porches, all constructed with admirable skill, of a beautiful grey stone, approaching in fineness of texture and apparent durability to marble. Young boys of dusky complexions, in long white tunics and with shaven heads, were busily employed dispelling every particle of dust. A stork and a flamingo seemed to keep most amicable company with them, following them wherever they went, and reminding me strongly of Egypt and the rites of Isis.

We passed the refectory, a plain solid building, with a pierced parapet of the purest Gothic design and most precise execution, and traversing a garden-court divided into compartments, where grew the orange trees whose fragrance we had enjoyed, shading the fountain by whose murmurs we had been lulled, passed through a sculptured gateway into an irregular open space before the grand western façade of the great church – grand indeed – the portal full fifty feet in height, surmounted by a window of perforated marble of nearly the same lofty dimensions, deep as a cavern, and enriched with canopies and imagery in a style that would have done honour to William of Wykeham,[1] some of whose disciples or co-disciples in the train of the founder's consort, Philippa of Lancaster,[2] had probably designed it.

As soon as we drew near, the valves of a huge oaken door were thrown open, and we entered the nave, which reminded me of Winchester in form of arches and mouldings, and of Amiens in loftiness. There is a greater plainness in the walls, less panelling, and fewer intersections in the vaulted roof; but the utmost richness of hue, at this time of day at least, was not wanting. No tapestry, however rich – no painting, however vivid, could equal the gorgeousness of tint, the splendour of the golden and ruby light which streamed forth from the long series of stained windows: it played flickering about in all directions, on pavement and on roof, casting over every object myriads of glowing mellow shadows ever in undulating motion, like the reflection of branches swayed to and fro by the breeze. We all partook of these gorgeous tints – the white monastic garments of my conductors seemed

---

[1] William of Wykeham (1324–1404), patron of English Gothic art.
[2] Daughter of the Duke of Lancaster who married King João I of Portugal in 1387, the year after the Treaty of Windsor had been signed binding England and Portugal in perpetual alliance.

as it were embroidered with the brightest flowers of paradise, and our whole procession kept advancing invested with celestial colours.

Mass began as soon as the high prelatic powers had taken their stations. It was celebrated with no particular pomp, no glittering splendour; but the countenance and gestures of the officiating priests were characterised by a profound religious awe. The voices of the monks, clear but deep-toned, rose pealing through vast and echoing spaces. The chant was grave and simple – its austerity mitigated in some parts by the treble of very young choristers. These sweet and innocent sounds found their way to my heart – they recalled to my memory our own beautiful cathedral service, and – I wept! My companions, too, appeared unusually affected; their thoughts still dwelling, no doubt, on that prophetic voice which never failed to impress its hearers with a sensation of mysterious dread.

It was in this tone of mind, so well calculated to nourish solemn and melancholy impressions, that we visited the mausoleum where lie extended on their cold sepulchres the effigies of John the First, and the generous-hearted, noble-minded Philippa; linked hand in hand in death as fondly they were in life. – This tomb is placed in the centre of the chapel. . . .

TWELFTH DAY[1]

14th June

The morning was the very essence of summer – and summer in Portugal, consequently tremendously hot. Such heat was oppressive enough, but the Grand Prior thought early rising still more abominable, and notwithstanding the Prior of St Vincent's exhortations to set forth whilst any degree of coolness lingered in the atmosphere, there was no persuading him to move before half-past eight.

Being myself pretty well seasoned to meridian excursions, and bronzed all over like a native Portuguese, I set the sun at defiance, mounted my Arabian, and steering my course as directly as was possible without the aid of a compass, traversed the wide expanse of country between Cadafaiz and Queluz; – and a sad dreary expanse it was, exhibiting only now and then a straggling flock, looking pretty and pastoral – a neglected quinta of orange-trees with its decaying garden-house, the abode of crime or innocence, whichever you like best to fancy – or a half-ruined windmill, with its tattered vans, revolving lackadaisically in the languid and feeble breeze.

Exactly at the hour named, I arrived, not a little ennuied and wearied, at the palace of Queluz. The chaises belonging to the Priors of Aviz and St Vincent's were waiting before the royal entrance, for both prelates were still closeted with the Prince Regent. Blessing heaven that I had nothing to do with the business, whatever it might be, that was in agitation, I gladly took

[1] Boyd Alexander doubts if there ever was a twelfth day. See Introduction, p. xix ff.

refuge from the intolerable sunshine in the apartments allotted to the lord in waiting; – shabby enough they were, bare as many an English country church, and not much less dingy.

The beings who were wandering about this limbo, or intermediate state, belonged chiefly to that species of living furniture which encumber royal palaces – walking chairs, animated screens, commodes and conveniences, to be used by sovereigns in any manner they like best; men who had little to feed on besides hope, and whose rueful physiognomies showed plainly enough the wasting effects of that empty diet, – weather-beaten equerries, superannuated véadors,[1] and wizened pages. The whole party were yawning over dusty card-tables.

Making them many lower bows, which were returned with equal courtesy, I passed forward into an interior apartment, where the Marquis of Anjeja[2] and his son the Conde de Villaverde were waiting for me, and immediately dinner was served up. Our repast was not particularly distinguished by good cheer or lively conversation.

As soon as it was over, and the motley tribe of attendants who had crowded tumultuously round our table sent about their no business at all, the Marquis observed to me in a very subdued and rather melancholy tone, that the Prince had been greatly disturbed of late by strange apprehensions and stranger dreams; that his temper was much ruffled, and that something, he could not tell what, bore heavily on his mind. He would have entered, I believe, into further details of still greater importance, had not a page called him away to the royal presence.

'I shall return in half an hour,' said he 'and finish what I had to say to you.' This half hour exceeded three quarters, and two quarters added to that; but they passed rapidly, for both the young Conde and myself, oppressed by a warm atmosphere, and lulled by the drone of humblebees, and the monotonous buzzing of courtiers and lacqueys, in the adjoining apartments, had fallen fast asleep.

When I awoke from this happy state of forgetfulness, one of my servants, who had followed me from Cadafaiz with a change of dress, took me into a room which a principal attendant of the palace had given up to him, and out of which I issued completely renovated, and met the Marquis hastily bearing to me the interesting intelligence, that in the course of the evening, or as soon after nightfall as possible, the Prince Regent would give me an audience. 'In the intervening time,' he added, 'if you wish to see the curious birds and flowers last sent from the Brazils, the gardens, though accessible of late to very few persons, shall be open to you. Villaverde would most gladly accompany you, but even he has not been in the habit of straying about them for some time past. As to myself, the Prince has a long series of deputations and petitions to receive, and it is my duty to remain near his royal person on these

---

[1] A Véador is something less than a Camarista, or chamberlain, and something more than a groom of the bedchamber. [Beckford's note]

[2] José de Noronha (1741–1811), 4th Marquis and Pedro (1771–1804), 5th Marquis.

occasions: so pardon my not offering myself as your guide. At the extremity of the avenue you see from these windows, stands a pavilion well worthy your attention, and I rather wish you might principally employ it in examining the paintings and china, till the moment arrives when the Prince will be at leisure to receive you.'

I bowed, the Marquis and his son bowed also, and I entered the grand avenue, wondering what in the name of mystery all these precautions could mean. The enigma was not long in meeting with some explanation. A gardener, who had left my service only last year, and was now established prime guardian of carnations and anemones in this regal paradise, advanced towards me with looks of the greatest surprise, and touching the extremities of my garments with his exuberant lips – for he was neither more nor less than a negro – stammered out, 'Most excellent sir, by what chance do I see you here, where so few are permitted to enter?' – 'By the chance of having the Prince's permission.' 'Ah, sir,' continued he, 'it is the Princess who reigns here almost exclusively.' 'Well,' answered I, 'her indignation I hope, will not visit me too severely: here I am, and here I shall continue.'

With a low salam in the style of a regular Bostangi,[1] the poor African, not a little confounded, humbly retired, and left me at full liberty to enter the pavilion, whose richly gilded trellised doors stood wide open. Many entertaining objects, arabesque paintings by Costa[2] full of fire and fancy, and mandarin josses[3] of the most supreme and ridiculous ugliness, kept me so well amused that half an hour glided away pretty smoothly.

The evening was now drawing towards its final close, and the groves, pavilions, and aviaries sinking apace into shadow: a few wandering lights sparkled amongst the more distant thickets – fire-flies perhaps – perhaps meteors; but they did not disturb the reveries in which I was wholly absorbed.

'So then' thought I within myself, 'the Infanta Donna Carlotta is become the predominant power in these lovely gardens, once so profusely adorned and fondly cherished by the late kind-hearted and saintly king. She is now Princess of Brazil and Princess Regent; and what besides, Heaven preserve me from repeating!'

Reports, I well knew, not greatly to the good fame of this exalted personage, had been flying about, numerous as butterflies; some dark-coloured, like the wings of the death-head moth, and some brilliant and gay, like those of the fritillaria.[4]

This night I began to perceive, from a bustle of preparation already visible in the distance, that a mysterious kind of fête was going forwards; and whatever may have been the leading cause, the effect promised at least to be highly pleasing. Cascades and fountains were in full play; a thousand sportive

---

[1] A Turkish palace guard.
[2] Possibly Lorenzo Costa (?1459–1535), Italian painter of school of Ferrara.
[3] Idols.
[4] A spotted butterfly.

jets d'eau were sprinkling the rich masses of bay and citron, and drawing forth all their odours, as well-taught water is certain to do upon all such occasions. Amongst the thickets, some of which received a tender light from tapers placed low on the ground under frosted glasses, the Infanta's nymph-like attendants, all thinly clad after the example of her royal and nimble self, were glancing to and fro, visible one instant, invisible the next, laughing and talking all the while with very musical silvertoned voices. I fancied now and then I heard gruffer sounds; but perhaps I was mistaken. Be that as it pleases Lucifer, just as I was advancing to explore a dusky labyrinth, out came, all of a sudden, my very dear friend Don Pedro, the young Marquis of Marialva.[1]

'What! at length returned from Alcobaça,' said he, lifting me a foot off the ground in a transport of jubilation; 'where is my uncle?'

'Safe enough,' answered I, perhaps indiscreetly: 'he had his audience five or six hours ago, and is gone home snug to his cushions and *calda da galinha*.[2] I am waiting for my turn.'

'Which will not come so soon as you imagine,' replied Don Pedro, 'for the Prince is retired to his mother's apartments, and how long he may be detained there no one can tell. But in the mean while come with me. The Princess, who has learnt you are here, and who has heard that you run like a greyhound, wishes to be convinced herself of the truth of a report she thinks so extraordinary.'

'Nothing so easy,' said I, taking him by the hand; and we sprang forwards, not to the course immediately, but to an amphitheatre of verdure concealed in the deepest recess of the odoriferous thickets, where, seated in the oriental fashion on a rich velvet carpet spread on the grass, I beheld the Alcina[3] of the place, surrounded by thirty or forty young women, every one far superior in loveliness of feature and fascination of smile to their august mistress.

'How did you leave the fat waddling monks of Alcobaça,' said her royal highness. 'I hope you did not run races with them; – but that would indeed have been impossible. There,' continued she, 'down that avenue, if you like, when I clap my hands together, start; your friend Pedro and two of my donzellas[4] shall run with you – take care you are not beaten.'

The avenue allotted for this amusing contest was formed of catalpas and orange trees, and as completely smooth and level as any courser, biped or quadruped, upon whom all the best in the universe were depending, could possibly desire. The signal given, my youthful friend, all ardour, all agility, and two Indian-looking girls of fourteen or fifteen, the very originals, one would have thought, of those graceful creatures we often see represented in Hindoo paintings, darted forth with amazing swiftness. Although I had given them ten paces in advance, exerting myself in right earnest, I soon left them

---

[1] From this mild night, I have been told repeatedly, may be traced the marked predilection of the future empress-queen for this graceful young nobleman – a predilection about which much has been said and more conjectured. [Beckford's note]

[2] Chicken stew.

[3] Princess.

[4] Lady attendants.

behind, and reached the goal – a marble statue, rendered faintly visible by lamps gleaming through transparent vases. I thought I heard a murmur of approbation; but it was so kept down, under the terror of disturbing the queen, as to be hardly distinguishable.

'Muy bien, muy bien,'[1] said the Princess in her native Castilian, when we returned to the margin of the velvet carpet upon which she was still sitting reclined, and made our profound obeisances. 'I see the Englishman can run – report has not deceived me. Now,' continued her royal highness, 'let me see whether we can dance a bolero; they say he can, and like one of us: if that be true – and I hope it is, for I abhor unsuccessful enterprises – Antonita shall be his partner, – and she is by far the best dancer that followed me from Spain.'

This command had been no sooner issued, than a low, soft-flowing choir of female voices, without the smallest dissonance, without the slightest break, – smooth, well-tuned, and perfectly melodious, – filled my ear with such enchantment, that I glided along in a delirium of romantic delight.

My partner, an Andalusian, as full of fire and animation as the brightest beauties of Cadiz and Seville, though not quite so young as I could have wished her to be, was rattling her castanets at a most intrepid rate, and raising her voice to a higher pitch than was seemly in these regions, when a universal 'Hush, hush, hush!' arrested our movements, suspended the harmonious notes of the choir, and announced the arrival of the Marquis of Anjeja.

After a thousand kind and courteous compliments he was pleased to pay me, he begged another thousand pardons of the Princess for having ventured to interrupt her recreations: 'But, madam,' continued he, 'the Prince Regent has been waiting several minutes for the Englishman, and I leave you to judge whether he has a minute to lose.'

Her Royal Highness looked rather blank at this intelligence, and, compassionating my disappointment, held out her hand, which I kissed with fervour, and three or four of her attendants as many silken handkerchiefs, which I found very convenient in removing those dews which not only the night, but such violent exercise as I had lately taken, occasioned. Panting, and almost breathless, I quitted the enchanted circle with great reluctance.

What a contrast the dark, dull antechambers of the palace presented to that lively and graceful scene! It was in the long state gallery where the Prince habitually receives the homage of the court upon birthdays and festivals – a pompous, richly gilded apartment, set round with colossal vases of porcelain, as tall and as formal as grenadiers, – that his Royal Highness was graciously pleased to grant me audience.

He was standing alone in this vast room, thoughtful, it appeared to me, and abstracted. He seemed, however, to brighten upon my approach; and although he was certainly the reverse of handsome, there was an expression of shrewdness, and at the same time benignity, in his very uncommon

---

[1] 'Very good, very good'.

countenance, singularly pleasing: it struck me that he had a decided look, particularly about the mouth, of his father's maternal ancestors. John the Fifth having married the Archduchess, daughter of the Emperor Charles the Sixth,[1] he had therefore an hereditary claim to those wide-spreading, domineering lips, which so remarkably characterised the House of Austria, before it merged into that of Lorraine.

'Welcome back from Alcobaça!' said his Royal Highness to me, with the most condescending kindness: 'I hope your journey was pleasant – how did you find the roads?'

'Not half so bad as I expected, especially upon our return from the great convent, the reverend fathers having summoned all their numerous dependents to mend them with astonishing expedition: the Lord Abbot took care of that.'

'He takes excellent care of himself, at least,' observed the Prince, – 'nobody better. Is it not true that he is become most gloriously corpulent, and fallen passionately in love with the fine French cookery you gave him an opportunity of enjoying?'

I perceived by this sally that the Grand Prior had been a faithful narrator of our late proceedings, as was proved more and more by the following queries.

'You had a stage-play too, had you not? The fathers at Mafra have often regaled me with performance of a similar nature; and many a hearty laugh have I had at them, and with them, before now. I dare say you must have thought them half out of their senses; their poet particularly, who, I hear, is one of the most ridiculous buffoons, the most impudent blockhead (*tolerão*) in the kingdom. I shall send for him one of these days myself; they say he is highly diverting, and I want something to cheer my spirits. Every despatch from France brings us such frightful intelligence, that I am lost in amazement and horror; the ship of the state in every country in Europe is labouring under a heavy torment, – God alone can tell upon what shore we shall be all drifted!'

With these prophetic words, most solemnly and energetically pronounced, the Prince thought fit to dismiss me, honouring me again with those affable expressions of regard which his excellent heart never failed to dictate. Let me observe, whilst the recollections of the interviews I have had with this beneficent sovereign remain fresh in my memory, that not one of his subjects spoke their native language – that beautiful harmonious language, with greater purity and eloquence than himself. When in his graver moods, there was a promptitude, a facility in his diction, most remarkable: every word he uttered was to the purpose, and came with the fullest force. When he chose to relax, – which he certainly was apt enough to do more than now and then, – a quaint national turn of humour added a zest to his pleasantries, that, upon my entering heart and soul into the idiom of the language, has often afforded me capital entertainment. No one knew how to win popular affection, after its own fashion, more happily than this well-intentioned, single-minded prince. Had it not been for the baneful influence of his despotic

---

[1] Charles VI (1685–1740), Holy Roman Emperor.

consort, – her restless intrigues of all hues, political as well as private – her wanton freaks of favouritism and atrocious acts of cruelty, – his reign would have gone down to the latest times in the annals of his kingdoms surrounded with a halo of gratitude.

Upon my reaching the great portal of this silent gallery, and fumbling to open its valves – for this extremity of the apartment was but very feebly illuminated, – the Marquis, who had been giving some orders to somebody of whom I only caught a glimpse, spared me the trouble of further rattlings at locks or door-knobs, and we entered together another shadowy world – another immense saloon. Here, by the wan light of one solitary lustre, containing but half its complement of yellowish wax tapers drooping with dismal snuffs, I discovered some fifteen or twenty unhappy aspirants to court benefits still loitering and lingering about. The sovereign of Portugal was at this period as completely despotic as the most decided amateur of unlimited monarchy could possibly desire: they who entered these palace regions came with as many hopes of success and fears of the contrary as if they were resorting to a table of hazard. The sovereign, in their eyes, was Chance personified; his decrees for or against you, modestly styled *avisos*, were pieces of advice to the judicial obeyers of his commands, which, if once obtained, were never slighted.

Most of the victims of this system, at this time in this great hall assembled, appeared visibly suffering under the sickness of hope deferred. 'Five hours have I been walking up and down, to and fro, to no purpose,' said an old General, my very particular acquaintance. 'Is there no chance yet of delivering my memorial into his royal highness's own hand?' whispered another veteran, decorated with scars as well as orders; 'None,' answered the Marquis: 'the Prince is retired for the night, and you had better follow his example.'

Had there been more light, we should have been fastened upon by a greater number of petitioners; but, thanks to the pervading gloom, we slipped along half-undiscovered.

Our next movements were directed through an ante-chamber of large size and much simplicity, for its walls were quite plain, and the roof as unornamented as that of a barn. A few expiring lamps gave me an opportunity of perceiving another assemblage of the votaries of royal favour in some of its shapes, less dignified than the company we had just quitted, but who had been equally eager, and who now were equally exhausted, – country magistrates, sea captains, provincial noblesse, and I know not who besides; some of them, if truth may be spoken, looking more like the *bad* than the *beau* idéal of bandits and bravoes; but what they were in reality, thank God, I am perfectly ignorant. Anjeja paid them no attention as we passed on through their opening ranks,: his looks, though not his voice, told me plainly enough,

Non ragionam di lor,
Ma guarda e passa.[1]

[1] 'Lets not talk of them but look and pass on'.

These looks seemed to tell me at the same time that he wished to converse with me in private.

I was tired of close conferences in close apartments; I longed for the refreshing sea-breezes of my quinta on the banks of the Tagus; the very name of which (San José de Riba-mar) was music to my ears at this moment. A page announced that my carriages, just arrived from Cadafaiz, were in waiting. This was tantalizing indeed: I would have taken leave of my most obliging Marquis without any very deep regret after all, but he would not let me off so soon as I eagerly desired; he absolutely insisted upon taking me into an interior apartment I had never visited before, where we sat down, – for here, at least, were plenty of chairs and sofas, – and he addressed me with considerable emotion in the following manner:

'You see, his royal highness is more gloomy than he used to be.'

'Upon the whole,' answered I, 'his spirits are less depressed than I was led to imagine: my friends the Priors seem to have regaled him with many a good story about convents, for he laughed several times at my Lord Almoner's charities of all kinds beginning so comfortably at home.'

'Ah!' replied Anjeja, 'you little think, notwithstanding this apparent levity, what an accumulated weight of sorrows press him down: he is the most affectionate of sons, the most devoted, and being such, feels for his mother's sufferings with the acutest poignancy. Those sufferings are frightfully severe, more heart-rending than any words of mine can express. This very evening he knelt by the Queen's couch above two hours, whilst, in a paroxysm of mental agony, she kept crying out for mercy, imagining that, in the midst of a raging flame which enveloped the whole chamber, she beheld her father's image a calcined mass of cinder – a statue in form like that in the Terreiro do Paço,[1] but in colour black and horrible, – erected on a pedestal of molten iron, which a crowd of ghastly phantoms – she named them, I shall not – were in the act of dragging down. This vision haunts her by night and by day; and should she continue to describe it in all its horrible details again and again to my royal master, I fear his brain will catch fire too.' There is a remedy – my relation, her confessor, knows it well – there is a medicine, and of the highest and most salutary kind – such might be administered – restitutions might be made – infernal acts revoked, and justice rendered. But hitherto the powers of evil – certain demons in the shape of some of Pombal's ancient counsellors, and others equally culpable, though not so old in iniquity, have impeded measures which would conciliate the disaffected, and although they might excite the gibes and murmurs of the disciples of new doctrines, would attach all us, the ancient nobles of the realm, to the House of Braganza[2] more closely than ever. May I ask, has the Princes ever touched upon this subject to you? I think Marialva told me he had, and once in his presence.'

I answered, 'If he did, it was ambiguously, and with so much slightness that it passed like a fleeting cloud.'

---

[1] In central Lisbon, now Praça do Comercio.
[2] See *above*, p. 258 n. 1.

After a long pause, during which Anjeja appeared lost in thought, he said to me with the greatest earnestness, 'If, at the next audience the Prince may give you, he should pour forth his sorrows for his mother's malady into your bosom – which I have reason to conjecture he shortly may, for I know that he feels himself towards you affectionately well inclined' (*sumamente affeiçoado*), 'remember the kind regard you entertain for our family.' (he meant the Noronhas in general, from which great house all the Marialvas are paternally descended,) 'remember to let it suggest such observations as may further a great and interesting cause. I wish also you would dwell particularly on what the late Archbishop,[1] your devoted friend, may probably have said to you upon this subject. Whatever that may have been, give it the turn we wish, and do not let it lose any charm in the narration.'

I could hardly repress a smile at this urgent request to launch forth beyond the exact limits of truth, if not of probability; for I perfectly recollected the good Archbishop's opinions were everything but favourable to the reversal of those attainders. However, I preserved a decorous gravity. I said nothing; but I contrived that my looks should express a disposition to second his wishes the first opportunity of doing so that might present itself.

At this moment, the most terrible, the most agonizing shrieks – shrieks such as I hardly conceived possible – shrieks more piercing than those which rung through the Castle of Berkeley, when Edward the Second was put to the most cruel and torturing death[2] – inflicted upon me a sensation of horror such as I never felt before. The Queen herself, whose apartment was only two rooms off from the chamber in which we were sitting, uttered those dreadful sounds: 'Ai Jesous! Ai Jesous!' did she exclaim again and again in the bitterness of agony.

I believe I turned pale; for Anjeja said to me, 'I see how deeply you are affected: think what the sufferings must be that prompt such cries; think what a son must feel, and such a son as our royal master.'

I undoubtedly thought all this, and a great deal more: not only the tears in my eyes, but the faltering of my voice, expressed the intensity of my feelings. The Marquis, far from displeased at the effect produced upon me, embraced me with redoubled kindness. Notwithstanding my entreaties for him to remain in his apartment, he was determined, after I had taken leave, to conduct me to the outward door of the palace; nor did he cease gazing, I was afterwards told, upon the carriage which bore me away, till the sound of the wheels grew fainter and fainter, and even the torches which were borne before it became invisible.

[1] See *above*, p. 226 n. 1.
[2] In 1327.

SELECT BIBLIOGRAPHY

I PRIMARY SOURCES: WORKS OF WILLIAM BECKFORD

1. Manuscripts
Beckford Papers. Bodleian Library, Oxford.

2. Published Works
A Dialogue in the Shades & Rare Doings at Roxburghe Hall (1819).*
Azemia, A Descriptive or Sentimental Novel (1797).
Biographical Memoirs of Extraordinary Painters (1780).
Dreams, Waking Thoughts and Incidents (1783).†
Italy, with Sketches of Spain and Portugal (1834).
Modern Novel Writing or the Elegant Enthusiast (1796).
Popular Tales of the Germans (1791).*
Recollections of an Excursion to the Monasteries of Alcobaça and Batalha (1835).
The Story of Al Raoui (1799).*
Vathek, An Arabian Tale (1786).

*Not represented in this collection
†Printed but not released

3. Modern Editions Consulted or Used*
Biographical Memoirs of Extraordinary Painters, ed. R. Gemmett (Cranbury, New Jersey, 1971).
Biographical Memoirs of Extraordinary Painters, intro. P. Ward (New York, 1977).
Dreams, Waking Thoughts and Incidents, ed. R. Gemmett (Cranbury, New Jersey, 1969).
Excursion à Alcobaça et Batalha ed. A. Parreau, preface, G. Chapman (Lisbon, 1956).
Life at Fonthill, 1807–22, ed. Boyd Alexander (London, 1957).
Recollections of an Excursion to the Monasteries of Alcobaça and Batalha, ed. Boyd Alexander (Sussex, 1956).
Suites des Contes Arabes, ed. Didier Girard (Paris, 1992).
The Episodes of Vathek, trans. Sir Frank T. Marzials (London, 1912).
The Journal of William Beckford in Portugal and Spain (1787–1788), ed. Boyd Alexander (London, 1954).

The Transient Gleam. A Bouquet of Beckford's Poesy, ed. D. Varma (Cheshire, 1991).

The Travel Diaries of William Beckford of Fonthill, ed. G. Chapman, 2 Vols (London, 1928).

The Vision & Liber Veritatis, ed. G. Chapman (London, 1930).

Vathek, ed. R. Lonsdale (Oxford, 1983)

Vathek, Conte Arabe, foreword, E. Bressy, preface, S. Mallarmé (Paris, 1984).

Vathek, Conte Arabe, ed. M. Lévy (Paris, 1981).

William Beckford's Vathek, A Critical Edition, K. W. Graham, 2 Vols, Unpublished PhD Thesis (London, 1971).

*See half-title to each extract for details of edition that has been used in this collection.

II SELECTED BOOKS AND AUTHORS REFERRED TO BY BECKFORD*

Arabian Nights Entertainments . . . (trans. from the Arabian), by M. Galland, 4 Vols (London, 1783).

Ariosto, L., *Orlando Furioso*.

Bailly, J. S., *Histoire de l'Astronomie Moderne depuis la fondation de l'ecole d'Alexandre*, 3 Vols (Paris, 1779–82).

Bocage, M. M. de, *Sonnets*.

Boiardo, M. M., *Orlando Innamorato*.

Brucker, J., *Historia Critica Philosophiae A Mundi*, 2nd Edn, 6 Vols (Leipzig, 1767).

Camoens, L. de, *The Lusiads*.

Cardonne, D., *A Miscellany of Eastern Learning*, 2 Vols, (1771).

Catullus, *Poems*.

Chardin, J., *Astrologie Judiciaire, Voyages . . . en Perse . . .* (Amsterdam, 1711).

Claudian, *De Raptu Proserpinae*.

Cook, Captain James, *A Voyage to the Pacific Ocean*, 1776–80, 3 Vols (London, 1784).

Cook, John, *Voyages and Travels Through the Russian Empire, Tartary and Part of the Kingdom of Persia*, 2 Vols (Edinburgh, 1770).

Cullen, C., trans, *The History of Mexico by D. F. S. Clavigero*, (1787).

Dante, A., *The Divine Comedy*.

Descamps, J. B., *La vie des peintres flamands, allemands et hollandois* . . . 4 Vols (Paris, 1753–64).

Dow, A., *Tales Translated from the Persian of Inatulla of Delhi*, 2 Vols (1768).

Ghiga, A., *The Present State of the Ottoman Empire . . . Translated from the French manuscript of Elias Habesci* (1784).

Gibbon, Edward, *The History of the Decline and Fall of the Roman Empire*, 6 Vols (London, 1774–8).

Gray, Thomas, *The Progress of Poesy*, (1757).

Harmer, T., *Observations on Divers Passages of Scripture*, 2nd Edn, 4 Vols (1776).

Hasselquist, F., *Voyages and Travels in the Levant* (Stockholm, 1766).

Jones, Sir William, 'A Persian Song of Hafiz' and 'A Turkish Ode of Mesihi', from *Poems Consisting Chiefly of Translations from the Asiatic Languages* (Oxford, 1772).

——, *Poeseos Asiaticae Commentariorum Libri Sex* (1774).

——, trans. *The Moallakat, Or Seven Arabian Poems Which Were Suspended on the Temple at Mecca* (1783).

Lucian, *On Funerals.*

Marsden, W., *The History of Sumatra*, (London, 1783).

Milton, *Paradise Lost.*

Molainville, B. d'Herbelot de, *Bibliotheque Orientale* . . . (Paris, 1697).

Montagu, Lady Mary Wortley, *Letters . . . Written during her Travels in Europe, Asia and Africa*, 4 Vols (London, 1763).

Ockley, S., *The History of the Saracens*, 3rd Edn, 2 Vols (Cambridge, 1757).

Olearius, A., *Voyages faits en Moscovie, Tartarie et Perse* . . . 2 Vols (Leiden, 1718).

Ovid, *Amores.*

——, *Metamorphoses.*

Pauw, J. C. de, *Recherches Philosophiques sur les Americains*, 2 Vols (Berlin, 1768–9).

Phaedrus, *Fables.*

Pitts, J., *A True and Faithful Account of the Religion and Manners of the Mohammetans* (Exeter, 1704).

Pliny, *Natural History.*

Plutarch, *Lives.*

Pococke, R., *A Description of the East and Some Other Countries*, 2 Vols (London 1743–45).

Propertius, *Elegies.*

Richardson, J., *A Dictionary, Persian, Arabic and English*, 2 Vols (Oxford, 1777–80).

——, *A Dissertation on the Languages, Literature and Manners of the Eastern Nations* (Oxford, 1777).

Robertson, W., *History of America*, 3 Vols (Dublin, 1777).

Sale, G., *The Koran, Commonly Called the Alcoran of Mohammed, Translated into English* . . . (1734), 2nd ed., 4 Vols (1764).

Sherley, Sir Anthony, *His Relation of His Travels into Persia* . . . (London, 1613).

Solis, A. de, *Historia de la Conquista de Mexico* (Madrid, 1684).

Thales, *Fragments.*

Thevenot, J. de, *Travels . . . into the Levant*, in three Parts, trans. A. Lovell (1687).

Virgil, *Aeneid.*

——, *Georgic.*

White, J., *Sermons Preached before the University of Oxford* . . ., 2nd Edn (1785).

*Note: A specific edition has been cited where it is likely that Beckford or Henley used it.

III SECONDARY SOURCES

1. Eighteenth-Century and Pre-Eighteenth-Century Sources

Addison, J. & Steele, R., *The Spectator*, 8 Vols (London, 1726).

——, *The Tatler; The Lucubrations of Isaac Bickerstaff*, 5 Vols (London, 1720).

Beckford, Peter, *Thoughts on Hunting* (London, 1781).

Boswell, J., *An Account of Corsica* (Glasgow, 1768).

Brydone, P., *Tour Through Sicily and Malta* (London, 1778).

Coxe, W., *Sketches of the Natural, Civil and Political State of Switzerland*, 3 Vols (London, 1789).

Defoe, Daniel, *A Grand Tour Through the Whole Island of Great Britain* (London, 1724–6).

Gilpin, William, *Observations on the Mountains and Lakes of Cumberland and Westmoreland*, 3 Vols (London, 1786).

Hamilton, A., *Histoire de Fleur d'Epine*, 2 Vols (Paris, 1749).

——, *Mémoires du Comte de Gramont* (Paris, 1713).

Hawkesworth, John, *Almoran and Hamet*, 2 Vols (London, 1761).

Johnson, Dr S., *Lives of the Poets*, 2 Vols (Oxford, 1952).

——, *Rasselas, Prince of Abysinnia* (London, 1759).

Middleton, C., *Letter from Rome* (London, 1729).

Montaigne, Michel de, *Oeuvres Completes*, ed. du Seuil (Paris, 1969).

Montesquieu, C. de S., *Lettres Persanes* (Paris, 1721).

Piozzi, H., *Observations and Reflections made in the Course of a Journey through France, Italy and Germany* (London, 1789).

Purchas, S., *Purchas his Pilgrimage* (London, 1614).

Smollet, T. G., *Travels Through France and Italy* (London, 1766).

Voltaire, F-M Arouet, *Histoire d'un Bon Bramin* (1761).

——, *Histoire Orientale, Zadig ou la Destinée* (Paris, 1749).

——, *Mahomet* (Bruxelles, 1742).

Walpole, Horace, *Castle of Otranto* (London, 1764).

——, *Three Princes of Serendip* (1754).

Young, A., *A Six Weeks Tour Through the Southern Counties of England and Wales* (London, 1768).

2. Nineteenth Century and Modern Sources

Acton, H., *Three Extraordinary Ambassadors* (London, 1983).

Adamson, J., *Memoirs of the Life and Writing of Luis de Camoens*, 2 Vols (London, 1820).

Alexander, B., *England's Wealthiest Son* (London, 1962).

——, Unpublished manuscripts, *MS. Eng. lett. c. 687–95 etc.* Bodleian Library, Oxford.

Brito, C de, '*A Musica Em Portugal No Tempo de William Beckford*', *William Beckford & Portugal*, Catalogue of an Exhibition at Queluz (Lisbon, 1987).

Brockman, H. A. N., *The Caliph of Fonthill* (London, 1956).

Butt, J. & Carnall, G., eds, *The Oxford History of English Literature: The Mid-Eighteenth Century*, 13 Vols (Oxford, 1979).

Cary, H. F., trans. *The Vision; or Hell, Purgatory and Paradise by Dante Alighieri* (1814). 2nd ed., 3 Vols (London, 1819).

Chapman, G., *Beckford* (London, 1952).

Chapman, G. & Hodgkin, J., *A Bibliography of William Beckford of Fonthill* (London, 1930).

Conant, M., *The Oriental Tale in England in the Eighteenth Century* (New York, 1966).

Drabble, M., ed. *Companion to English Literature* (London, 1985).

Fothergill, B., *Beckford of Fonthill* (London, 1979).

Gemmett, R. J., *William Beckford* (Boston, 1977).

Girard, D., 'Beckford's Juvenilia?' *Beckford Tower Trust Newsletter*, (Bath, Spring, 1992).

Gosse, E., *Gray* (London, 1930).

Graham, K. W., 'Beckford's Adaptation of the Oriental Tale in *Vathek*', *Enlightenment Essays*, 5 No. 1 (1974): 24–33.

——, '*Vathek* in English and French', *Studies in Bibliography*, 28 (1975): 153–66.

——. ed. *Vathek and The Escape from Time: Bicentenary Revaluations* (New York, 1990).

Hibbert, C., *The Grand Tour* (London, 1987).

Jack, M., 'How Wealthy was England's Wealthiest Son?' *Beckford Tower Trust Newsletter* (Bath, Spring, 1987).

——, *William Beckford: An English Fidalgo* (New York, 1994).

Langford, P., *A Polite and Commercial People, England 1727–83* (Oxford, 1989).

Lansdown, H. V., *Recollections of the late William Beckford of Fonthill, Wilts and Lansdown* (Bath, 1893).

Lees-Milne, J., *William Beckford* (Wiltshire, 1976).

Macaulay, R., *They Went to Portugal* (London, 1985).

Mahmoud, F. M., ed. *William Beckford of Fonthill, 1760–1844. Bicentenary Essays* (Cairo, 1960).

Marques, A. H. de Oliveira, *Historia de Portugal*, 3 Vols (Lisbon, 1984).

Melville, L. *The Life and Letters of William Beckford of Fonthill* (London, 1910).

Oliver, J. W., *The Life of William Beckford* (London, 1932).

Parreaux, A., *William Beckford. Auteur de Vathek* (Paris, 1960).

Pires, M. L. B., *William Beckford e Portugal* (Lisbon, 1987).

Price, M., ed. *The Oxford Anthology of English Literature* (Oxford, 1973).

Redding, C., *Memoirs of William Beckford of Fonthill*, 2 Vols (London, 1859).

Redding, C., 'Recollections of the Author of Vathek' *New Monthly Magazine,* LXXI (June, 1844): 151–2.
Sage, V., ed., *The Gothick Novel* (London, 1990).
Sitwell, S., *Beckford and Beckfordism* (London, 1930).
Thacker, C., *The History of Gardens* (London, 1985).
Willey, B., *The Eighteenth-Century Background*, (London, 1962).

INDEX

Only Beckford's works are referred to under his entry